also by peter clement

Lethal Practice
Death Rounds
The Procedure

mutant

peter clement

ballantine books

new york

www.ballantinebooks.com

LIBRARY OF CONGRESS CATALOGING-IN-PUBLICATION DATA
Clement, Peter, M.D.
Mutant / Peter Clement.—1st ed.
p.   cm.
ISBN 0-345-44337-3
I. Title.

PS3553.L3938 M88 2001
813'.54—dc21
2001025364

Text design by Holly Johnson

Manufactured in the United States of America

First Edition: July 2001

10 9 8 7 6 5 4 3 2 1

To James, Sean, and Vyta,
for being there to launch each new day

Too early may be too late when the geni has been
released, you've lost control of it and don't know
how to get it back into the lamp.

Terge Traavik
"Too Early May Be Too Late"
Research report to the Directorate
for Nature Management,
Norway, 1999

mutant

prologue

Friday, October 28, 1998, 1:00 A.M.
Kailua, Oahu Island, Hawaii

His screams woke her and brought her running to where he slept. "Mommeeee!"

Not bothering with the lights, she covered the twenty feet of corridor separating their bedrooms with a half dozen strides. "I'm here, Tommy," she reassured, rushing to his bed. By the time she swept him into her arms, he was choking. "I'm here, darling," she repeated, ready to tell him that he'd just had a bad dream. Even when she felt him burning up, the front of him wet through her nightgown, she figured that his cold must have gotten worse and he'd vomited from coughing. She'd always taken pride in disciplining her awareness of what *could* happen, not letting it cloud her objectivity or make her imagine the worst whenever he got sick. But his continued hacking and struggling to breathe began to fill her with alarm. She snapped on the light and saw bloody foam pouring from his nose and mouth as he sputtered and gagged.

Panic jolted through her with the force of an executioner's current. "Oh, my God, no!" she uttered, as if she could protest the sight, order it away, blink it gone.

Then her instincts took over. Turning him facedown so the blood could run clear of his airway, she tore downstairs with him, leaving a trail of crimson on the rug. In an instant she decided that driving him to the hospital herself would be fastest, grabbing keys and a cellular phone off the kitchen table as she passed it. She dashed out of the house repeating, "Mommy's got you. Mommy's got you. Spit out and breathe in." He gasped for a breath between fits of sobbing, and through her palm, supporting his chest, she felt tiny vibrations—the purring of a lung filled with fluid.

The knowledge increased her terror while her mind scrolled through what he might have, the possibilities all grim. "Oh, my poor baby. That's a good baby. It'll be all right!" she continued, sprinting breathlessly across the lawn toward the garage. She knew that the words were lies, yet hoped the sound of her voice would reassure him. But, practiced as she was at mouthing such comforts to others, she felt so filled with dread that she gagged on the words midphrase. She knew her son to be on the brink of respiratory arrest, and they were a half hour too far from where she could save his life. The isolation and distance from the city that she'd so fervently sought when choosing her piece of paradise on the beach became his death sentence. "What's killing him?" she whispered with all the intensity of a prayer, as if God could provide the diagnosis. In His silence she racked her own mind for the answer, but her thoughts tumbled in free fall. Yesterday he'd seemed to have only a cold. Had her obsession with not overreacting led her to miss something that could have alerted her?

By the time she yanked open the car door, got herself into the driver's seat, and, keeping him facedown, placed him across her lap, he started to emit shrill little cries with each expiration. She jammed the key into the ignition, squealed out of the driveway in reverse, and rocketed up the road.

One hand on the wheel, the other on her phone, she punched the automatic dial button.

After two rings came the reply. "Emergency, Honolulu General—"

"This is Dr. Sandra Arness. I'm on the Pali Highway heading toward you from Kailua. It's my son. He's a precode in acute respiratory distress—from sepsis and what must be pneumonia. For God's sake, have 911 dispatch an ambulance to meet me, and make sure they're carrying resus equipment for a three-year-old—" She broke into a sob, unable to bear the thought of having to resuscitate him herself.

"Right away, Dr. Arness!" the receptionist crisply replied. "And I'll alert our team."

The boy, emitting ever weaker sounds as he struggled to breathe, raised his head from where it lay across her thighs. "Kiss it, Mommy. Kiss it and make it all better," he whimpered in a faint wheeze that she could barely hear.

"Oh, Tommy, be brave. Mommy will help you soon."

"Help now, Mommy."

She held back her own tears, determined to stay in control and not frighten him further. Yet her helplessness had her in agony. As if to torment her further, they shot past the darkened remnants of the sole place on this side of the island that might once have saved him. Their local hospital had been shut down last year as a cost-cutting measure.

Whenever she could take her hand off the wheel, she stroked his head. That was always his favorite thing—let me at least give him that, she prayed. But this part of the road snaked back and forth up a series of switchbacks as it crossed the Koolau Range separating Kailua from Honolulu. She needed both hands on the wheel to fight the car through yet another turn, and at the loss of her touch, he immediately became restless.

Emerging from the long tunnel that marks the halfway point, she saw the flashing red of the ambulance through a break in the trees as it approached on the highway far below. Behind it, in the distance, the golden lights of Honolulu cascaded down the dark hills to the shores of Waikiki—she'd once described them as a spray of fairy dust in a magic kingdom to a wide-eyed Tommy as he'd stared in wonder at the sight. Memories of his squealing with delight seared through her.

"I see the ambulance, Tommy, and the twinkling city. Mommy will help you breathe now—" She broke off, feeling him start to shake in her lap. He was seizing.

"Oh, God, no! No! No!"

The ambulance still looked to be several minutes away. Tommy's life was down to a matter of seconds. Already doing a hundred, she floored the accelerator. There were fewer turns here, but hurtling downhill she nearly lost control several times, her tires slithering in the roadside grass and gravel. When she'd halved the distance between her and the oncoming flashers, she skidded to a stop, straddling a break in the median. Pulling Tommy to her, she struggled out of the car and stood in the light of its high beams with his jerking body in her arms. She could see him turning blue. More bloody froth seeped out between his clenched teeth. He seemed to be grunting, but she knew it to be the force of each convulsion pushing what little air he had left out of his lungs.

She knelt on the asphalt with him in her lap and tried to pry his jaw open with her fingers. It wouldn't budge. She covered his lips with her mouth and attempted to blow air through them, but they were locked in their grimace. She even tried to deliver a breath to his lungs through his nasal passage, yet no matter how hard she strained, the air went nowhere. His tongue must have fallen into the back of his throat, blocking the way. The sound of the siren grew louder, like the wail of an approaching banshee.

"Tommy! Tommy!" she began screaming over the noise, out of options and feeling the pulse in his neck drop to practically nothing.

The rhythmic jerking slowed, his arms and legs still flopping as if someone were shaking him, but only once every two seconds. The vehicle roared up just as she felt him go limp.

An instant later the paramedics lifted him onto a stretcher and into the back of the ambulance. In a daze she crouched over his precious face and forced herself to practice her profession—opening his airway with a pediatric laryngoscope, suctioning away the bloody foam, sliding a tube the size of his little finger into his small trachea. They then went careening back down the mountain toward the lights, one of the paramedics riding in the back to help her.

But despite her bagging oxygen directly into his trachea, despite a young healthy heart that valiantly fluttered to come alive again, despite all his other organs being perfectly ready to spring back into action, his lungs were finished. The infection had destroyed so much of their delicate lacy tissue and membranous sacs that his blood could find no air, leaving the rest of him to suffocate cell by cell.

When they unloaded him at the ambulance entrance, she already knew that he was dead. Absently, as she ran alongside the stretcher, she noticed the breeze stir his locks of hair and heard the sound of palms rustling overhead. She glanced up, only to see the blue-black sky scattered with silver—a sight that had always welcomed her when she came off duty and headed home. Now, its beauty seemed coldly indifferent, as if God mocked her for ever having marveled at it.

Less than a week later, Dr. Julie Carr, Director of Research at the Honolulu Virology Institute, felt her pulse quicken as she stared at the mainly black-and-white image on the screen of her electron microscope. A green ovoid creature covered with thousands of spines caught her attention amid a slew of similarly shaped but gray, uncolored forms. They all resembled things that might float about in the darkness of an undersea abyss, but in fact they were viruses.

Always the consummate teacher, she called over a first-year medical student who was doing an elective in Hospital Sciences, gestured toward the screen, and declared, "It took me four days to identify the green one."

"Four days?" replied the young man with surprise. Usually they could peg a virus within forty-eight hours.

"That's right. Are you familiar with the Tommy Arness case?"

"Isn't that the doctor's son who supposedly had only a cold but died suddenly? I don't know the details—only what I've overheard from the technicians."

"At first I performed all the standard tests for the usual suspects in an acute respiratory infection. Have you read about ELISA yet?"

"No, Dr. Carr," he answered sheepishly. "But I'll get to it—"

"Just as police keep fingerprint records of known criminals," she went on, not at all interested in his excuses, "virologists have antibody 'fingerprints' of the usual troublemakers we deal with day to day. We've tagged each one of these antibodies with an enzyme molecule that produces a specific color change if that antibody finds its match, thereby making a reagent that can give us visual confirmation whether a particular virus is present in sera or tissue samples. The procedure we follow while using these substances is the enzyme-linked immunosorbent assay—ELISA for short. When I added the reagent for influenza to the specially prepared specimens I'd taken from Tommy Arness's bodily fluids and lung tissue, it lit them up as red as glowing hot embers."

"So what killed him was influenza?"

"I didn't buy that. The influenza bug which attacks the mucosal lining of the nose, throat, and lungs in humans is capable of causing a bloody exudate, but I've never encountered a strain producing the degree of hemorrhage and destruction I witnessed at Tommy Arness's autopsy. His lungs had turned to a bloody pulp."

"My God!" exclaimed her student.

"Was this some new virulence in an old bug? I wondered. But in the manner of most physicians encountering something they've never seen before, I initially succumbed to doubts about my own database and attributed the strangeness of it to gaps in my knowledge. 'Probably someone's already reported this, and I'm simply not up-to-date,' I told myself."

Her young protégé grinned, obviously delighted at this admission of a shared failing by his teacher.

"That is certainly not a habit that I'm suggesting you can afford to emulate," she added sternly, wincing at the thought of all the unread journals stacked in her office. In an era of cutbacks, even chiefs must assume extra duties, and keeping up with the literature is usually the first casualty. "I just want to be sure you understand the logic behind my thinking this problem through, mistakes and all, so you'll learn the process of attacking a clinical puzzle."

His smile vanished. "Of course, Dr. Carr. I never meant any disrespect—"

"Then I had another thought. Perhaps what the boy's mother figured to be a cold had in fact been the flu. Such a scenario would explain the presence of the influenza and leave open the possibility that something else caused the catastrophic meltdown in his lung—an esoteric organism which came along at the same time but for which I hadn't the means to test."

The young man's eyes widened. "An esoteric organism?"

"But almost immediately I discarded the idea, sharing the well-founded skepticism of most doctors toward invoking coincidence and diagnosing more than one disease to explain symptoms we don't understand."

His puzzlement folded into his brow. "So what did you do?"

"The hardest thing for a doctor to do: admitted I was stymied and called for help. I contacted the Centers for Disease Control and Prevention in Atlanta. After the CDC reviewed the boy's clinical findings and autopsy results, the people in the viral infection group couriered me the ELISA reagents for all the uncommon microbes they could think of which might cause such a rapid destruction of the respiratory system. Also, to save the time of confirmatory tests for the moment, they included electron micrographs of each bug—as grisly a set of mug shots as I've ever seen. Most have never been reported before in the U.S."

She paused, as all good storytellers do, to let her listener's curiosity intensify. She smiled inwardly as she observed him lean ever so slightly toward her from his stool, his head cocked in anticipation. "The third reagent in the CDC's kit nailed the culprit, glowing a bright green the second a few drops of the stuff hit the sample well," she continued, lowering her voice to draw him in further. "The label on the test solution's bottle gave the bug a name; H5N1, aka an influenza strain that normally infects and kills only birds, particularly domestic fowl, such as chickens. It's been the scourge of farms in Asia for the better part of the decade. A year ago, however, it gave the world a scare when, in Taiwan, it jumped the species barrier and infected a young girl, killing her in a matter of hours, her lungs filled with blood. The media christened it *bird flu*, and the moniker stuck, especially after authorities there carried out the slaughter of a million chickens in an attempt to contain the lethal organism. The story carried around the globe."

"I remember reading it!" said her pupil. "Fortunately there were no more cases."

"Until now," stated Julie as she strode to the wall phone in her laboratory. Punching in the number for the CDC and working her way through innumerable layers of receptionists, she regarded the flush of excitement on her student's face. Who knows, she mused, perhaps my melodramatic teaching methods ignited enough enthusiasm in the future doctor that he'll at least do his reading.

"Confirmation by more elaborate and lengthy testing procedures I'll leave to you," she informed the virologist who took her call. The computer-enhanced green specimen on the screen, taken from the lung tissue she'd treated with the ELISA reagent for H5N1, provided proof enough for her that the bird flu had jumped the species barrier once more. "We'll have our hands more than full here trying to contain it."

Immediately the local public health authorities feared that the virus might have been transported to Hawaii by a human carrier from another outbreak in Asia. But according to the CDC, there'd been no recurrences reported there or anywhere else on the planet since the initial case in Taiwan. "That means the source is probably here," Julie advised a hastily assembled meeting of her own staff and a half dozen epidemiologists from Honolulu's medical faculty. "We'll have to visit every poultry coop in the Kailua district and draw off blood samples from anything that clucks, quacks, or chirps."

There were no arguments from anyone at the table, and within hours they mobilized a platoon of technicians and off-duty health care workers to do the job. The subsequent testing revealed that the source of the microbe had been a flock of infected chickens in a small farm next door to where Sandra Arness and Tommy lived. Tommy, they learned later, had sometimes walked over to feed and handle the chicks with his baby-sitter.

The slaughter of poultry on the island of Oahu began.

1

winter

1

Thirteen Months Later
New York City Hospital

Dr. Richard Steele found today's shift his worst ever in ER. Of course, Mondays were always bad compared to the rest of his week. More people arrived in emergency with heart attacks and every other kind of medical crisis on that day—a fact he knew well as a twenty-year veteran and longtime chief of the department. But this Monday's marathon seemed particularly hard, and all afternoon he felt a step behind.

One of the nurses slammed down the phone and sprinted toward the resuscitation room. "There's a precode coming—a fifteen-year-old asthmatic!" she yelled over her shoulder the way a quarterback calls a play. Everyone within earshot leaped up to help her get ready, instantly understanding what would be demanded of them. Past an overflow of stretcher patients crammed into the corridor, they scrambled after her, briskly navigating the jumble of IV poles, bags, and lines that hung like webs from the ceiling.

As he watched them go, Steele knew that not only the protocols for running a respiratory arrest would be flashing automatically into their minds. The patient's age would pump their adrenaline levels higher than usual. The prospect of losing someone so young always exacerbated the fear of failure in ER. It would be his job to make sure that the extra anxiety didn't affect his team's performance. At one time he accepted this added burden as simply another part of his role.

These days he found himself dreading it. While his abilities as a resuscitator were as sharp as ever, his people skills had become nonexistent. "Put the MI who's still in resus near the head of the line!" he called after them, making himself heard above the noise of a department already loud from overcrowding.

He grabbed the nearest receiver and punched in the numbers for the cardiac care unit. In no time two nurses raced back from the resuscitation room pushing a gurney that bore a frightened-looking elderly woman attached to an armada of portable monitors, intravenous tubes, and a tank of oxygen. By then he'd at least managed to bully the covering cardiologist into giving the woman a bed upstairs, where they could treat her heart attack properly. Years of cost-cutting had made such fights into another of his "routine" duties, but this time the argument left him feeling drained and sweaty.

A low rumble of protest broke out from those who were also waiting for beds when the nurses wheeled the woman past their convoy of stretchers and parked her at the front. "Christ, it's warm in here," he complained in an overloud voice to no one in particular, continuing to scribble his clinical notes in her chart. "Would someone call maintenance again and tell them to turn down the goddamned heat? It's too bloody hot to work!"

One of the nearby clerks, already wearing a sweater, gave him a curious glance. The cardiac lady, despite being so sick, skewered her face into an expression of disapproval, pulled her covers up around her neck, and muttered loudly enough for everyone in the nursing station to hear, "I'm lucky to make it out of this zoo before I freeze to death."

The ambulance attendants rushed in with a tall adolescent who had blue lips, a gray face, and such respiratory distress that beneath his open shirt the muscles between his ribs sucked inward each time he attempted to breathe. Even though they'd given him oxygen, he kept pulling off the mask, frantically rolling his eyes and straining his head in every direction, the way a man trapped in an airless chamber might cast about trying to find a final puff of breath.

As Steele followed the stretcher between the rows of patients lining the way, he huddled with his resident. "What's your immediate course of action here?" he demanded.

"Albuterol, by aerosol, to dilate his bronchi?" she replied timidly.

"No! At least not first off. This guy's bronchi are clamped so tight that he can't inhale air, let alone medication. What are you going to do about that?"

"Give him IV steroids?" she said hopefully.

"Again, later. Right now you're going to intubate him before he arrests on you."

She flushed from the neck of her clinical jacket to the tips of her earlobes. "I'm sorry, Dr. Steele, I knew that. It's just that you're making me nervous—"

"Knowledge at the ready, Doctor, is the best and only antidote around here for being nervous," he snapped. With a wave at the boy, he added, "And your apologizing for not having that knowledge isn't exactly going to cut it with him!"

Her eyes welled up with tears.

Shit, he thought, what an asshole I've become! He hadn't always been so impatient and sarcastic when he taught. The woman on the verge of weeping in front of him appeared young enough to be his daughter, and so far during her rotation she'd proved herself no better or worse than the thousand other novice doctors whom he'd guided through the shoals of ER over the years. With a pang of loss he remembered the heady days when he'd actually adored taking them under his wing and building their confidence. Teacher of the Year, they'd repeatedly voted him before he lost all capacity for the joy of it. Now the phrase made him wince: If any resident had said it of him over the past eighteen months it could only have been in sarcasm. He knew that the sole reason they still put up with him were the skills he could impart. A rotation under his temperamental watch had become known as a trial by fire—a passage to be endured and survived, and then joked about over beer—one of the horror stories that all training programs generate. But causing his charges to cry was a new low, even for him. And if he didn't make it right with her, she could report him for it. Shit, she probably should, he thought, disgusted with himself. "So how do we do a crash induction?" he asked her a tad more gently.

"Administer IV midazolam for short-acting sedation, give an antifasciculation dose of pancuronium, then paralyze him with succinylcholine . . ."

The answers poured out of her now that he'd adopted a less frightening tone. As they hurried into the resuscitation room, he gladly let her talk. The brisk pace left him out of breath. Damn cigarettes, he thought, wondering if he'd ever regain the courage to quit.

The nurses converged around the teenager, plying him with pressure cuffs, stethoscopes, IV lines, and monitor leads.

"BP ninety over fifty. Pulse fifty-five."

"O-two sat—eighty-seven."

"Respirations labored at fifty; minimal air entry at the bases!"

As they measured his agony by the numbers and the resident ordered the meds she'd rattled off before, Steele moved to the head of the bed.

The boy's eyes were blue rims around pupils wide with terror. He attempted to talk, but issued little more than a barely audible squeak.

"It's okay, son," the physician said gently, easily offering the professional comfort he so readily gave to frightened patients but withheld from others around him. With a pang of guilt, he thought of his own child, who was nearly the same age, to whom he'd repeatedly uttered those same words, but never with the conviction that he offered daily to strangers. "We're going to sedate you and have you breathing right in no time. Just nod yes or shake your head no to my questions. Is your asthma usually this bad?"

The youth shook his head. No.

"Do you use your pumps regularly, the steroids as well as the bronchodilators?" If he'd been properly taught how to administer his medication and manage his problem, Steele knew, he'd understand the distinction. If not, he'd been poorly trained, and poor control would be his norm.

The youth nodded. Yes!

Various screens lit up around them, and beeping sounds filled the tiled echo chamber. Oxygen hissed out the side vents of the patient's large green mask, which the nurses had substituted for the one he'd arrived with. Quick terse orders bounced around the room.

". . . get his bloods . . ."

". . . do an arterial gas . . ."

". . . a portable chest film . . ."

Through the din Steele thought he heard a small wheezing sound emanating from the boy's throat each time he breathed in as well as out. His own pulse rocketing, he announced, "He's also got stridor!" That meant an obstructed upper airway as well as bronchospasm, and a big jump up in the league of trouble they were dealing with. Upper airway obstruction sometimes required a tracheotomy—the act of cutting a hole through the front of the windpipe. Even in the most skilled hands, as an emergency procedure it could be a tricky maneuver. "Were you stung?" Steele demanded, his mind leaping to the most common causes of such a severe reaction.

No.

"Do you have food allergies?"

The boy vigorously nodded.

"To nuts?" The most common culprit.

More head bobbing.

"You ate something with nuts?"

The boy immediately protested, shaking his head back and forth.

The trouble with nut allergies, Steele knew, is that people can ingest the allergen unknowingly when it's ground up and used as flour in baked goods or added in minute pieces to salads or dips. He also knew that it didn't matter anyway at this point how the nuts got into his patient. Having recognized the possibility of their ingestion, he quickly added a third enemy to the list of what they might be battling—anaphylactic shock, or the vascular collapse unique to an extreme allergic response. A glance at one of the monitors confirmed the teenager's pressure dropping like a stone. "Give him a half milligram bolus of epi," he ordered, adrenaline being the drug of choice.

"I've got it!" somebody said.

"Ready for the intubation," declared the resident at his shoulder, a laryngoscope in her gloved hands and an array of endotracheal tubes in different sizes spread out on a tray beside her.

Steele found himself giving her full credit for being willing to step up and attempt the job despite his abysmal treatment of her. Feeling even more ashamed of himself, he told her quietly, "Good for you, Doctor."

In no time the medication she'd ordered took hold, and with a few twitches, the boy fell paralyzed from head to toe. The resident easily scissored his slack jaw open with her fingers. "Oh, my God, look at this!" she exclaimed while sliding the illuminated blade down the side of a tongue swollen as big as a Polish sausage.

Steele watched intently from behind, ready to move in at the slightest sign of a problem.

"And the pharyngeal walls are edematous as well," she reported, pushing the tip of the light through the swells of pink mucous membranes that kept bulging around her instrument and obscuring her view.

"Pulse fifty. Pressure sixty-five over forty," intoned the nurse who'd taken charge of recording the boy's vitals.

Everyone in the room knew that the slowing heart rate resulted from apnea, or his not breathing, and that it compounded the shock of his allergic reaction. They stood in silence now, waiting for the resident to get the airway, knowing that if she didn't succeed fast, they'd be treating a cardiac arrest as well as his respiratory problems.

"Can you see the cords?" asked Steele in the cool tone he saved for the tightest situations.

"Not yet," she replied, her voice shooting an octave higher. She nevertheless persisted, steadfastly continuing to dab into the swollen orifice with a suction catheter, drawing off pooling secretions of saliva while cautiously advancing the light.

The nurses exchanged uneasy, knowing glances, and Steele got ready to take over.

"Wait, I think I see them," she announced excitedly.

Steele bent down and confirmed the sighting just in time to see her lay aside the suction device and deftly slip the tip of an endotracheal tube through the V of the patient's vocal cords. "Now repeat the bolus of epi IV, give him the bronchodilators by aerosol mask, and run in the IV Solu-Medrol over twenty minutes," she commanded with authority while beaming a triumphant smile at Steele.

He nodded his approval, then watched as she expertly fixed the airway in place, hooked up a ventilation bag, and pumped it hard.

He left the room knowing that in the years to come he'd be the deserving butt of her jokes as she regaled friends with tales about the day she'd stood up to an ogre in ER at New York City Hospital. As he passed a mirror over the sink, sunken sockets ringed by baggy dark circles returned his gaze, making him appear a decade older than his forty-five years. "God, I've let myself go," he muttered angrily as he returned to the nursing station. "And why is it still so hot in here? Christ, I'm sweating like a pig."

As he wrote a note on the boy's chart, he had to pause and rub his left wrist. It had been hurting him lately, and being a southpaw, he'd attributed the pain to one of the repetitive movement injuries that plagued people who worked on computers or had to write a lot. That's all I need, he thought, acutely aware that an ER doctor who couldn't quickly record the hundreds of written notes and orders wouldn't be able to work emergency at all.

"Excuse me, Dr. Steele, but the boy's mother, a Mrs. Armstrong, is here," interrupted one of the nurses.

He stepped into the corridor to greet her. A thin, straight-haired blond woman who appeared to be in her early thirties stared at him with frightened blue eyes as he approached. She and her son had practically identical features, Steele noticed, and their resemblance stirred thoughts of another mother and son who'd been the image of each other. "Your boy's all right," he announced before he'd even reached her, and instantly he saw the fear leave her face.

"Thank God," he heard her whisper as she let out a long breath and dropped her shoulders a notch.

As they headed toward resus, threading their way through the stretchers, he prepared her for what she'd see. "He's intubated and sedated, but the worst is over. He should recover quite speedily and be back breathing on his own by tonight. But he had a close call, and from now on should carry a syringe of adrenaline at all times. He must have inadvertently eaten some nuts."

"No, Doctor," she protested, stopping in her tracks. "It couldn't have been that. He's meticulous about avoiding them. His friends called me at work and told me what happened. They were having veggie burgers at a local health food store. Besides, the owners know him there, and are as careful with his food as we are."

"Soya!" exclaimed Steele.

"Pardon?"

"It's a major ingredient in so-called vegetarian substitutes for meat and is soaring up the list of food allergies over the last couple of years, especially for people allergic to nuts. No one has definite proof, but suspicions run high in the scientific community that the rise stems from the genetic manipulation of the soya plant itself, in particular the insertion of DNA from a species of Brazilian nut tree to increase its hardiness. To make matters worse, people like your son who are at risk can't avoid this modified version because it isn't labeled as such. I'm afraid there's no alternative but to eliminate all soya-containing products from his diet. . . ."

As Steele explained the heightened vigilance that would be the lot of her son and virtually everyone involved in his care from now on, the pain in his wrist increased to the point where he found it difficult not to wince. Back at the nursing station it further hampered him while he attempted to complete his clinical notes. Already the head nurse stood at the door, summoning him for yet another ambulance case. "It's a man bleeding from both ends who's shocky, probably from an ulcer. We've started O_2, IVs, and bloods, but it's not enough. . . ."

Her words suddenly droned into the background. He tried to listen more carefully, but the sound of her voice remained tinny and far away. He felt dizzy, then nauseated. The pain in his wrist crept up his arm.

His respirations quickened, and a weight settled on his chest. Despite it all being exactly as he'd heard patients describe it over the years, he still tried to deny it. He got to his feet, determined to walk it off. The darkness came over him like a wave, and he didn't even feel the crack of his skull hitting the linoleum floor. His last thoughts as his heart sputtered to a standstill and he slipped toward death were for Luana, his greatest love, and loss, in life.

2

He felt no rising above his body, no hurtling toward a light, no encountering heavenly figures. Just white explosions inside his skull that, even in his clinically dead state with no pulse or respirations, his brain correctly interpreted as countershocks. And, of course, some idiot was pounding on his chest. Next would come the hose down his throat as they intubated him, he thought, and was right about that as well. What struck him most was how little he cared which way things went. The voices around him, far away yet familiar, all seemed so needlessly frantic.

"... get a blood gas ..."

"... give him epi ..."

"... stand clear ..."

Why were they bothering?

Another white explosion seared through his head.

Then they left him alone.

Either they'd given up or he was successfully resuscitated. As he drifted off, he still didn't mind which it was.

The next time he awoke, he felt far more a part of this world. He hurt everywhere, but especially in his head and chest. Even before he opened his eyes, his thinking became less scrambled and the doctor in him reflexively took inventory. The general aches, he knew, were from the kick the countershocks had delivered to every single muscle in his body, convulsing each of them through the equivalent of a full

workout in a fraction of a second. The pain in his chest he attributed
to the combined effect of the electrical discharges and external cardiac massage. A tentative exploration of his head with his fingers
found bandages over what at the very least had to be a hematoma, or
goose egg, if not an outright laceration.

The movement of his arms set off a cacophony of alarm bells and
beeps, and only then did he feel the tug of the various intravenous
lines that ran into his arms. He finally got his eyelids working enough
to open them and, seeing an achingly familiar face, tried to speak.
But his throat seized around the endotracheal tube that was still in his
airway, and he convulsed in a paroxysm of choking.

"Daddy?" he heard his son cry, the voice rising in pitch the way it
always did when he was frightened, even at the age of thirteen. Just
how frightened Steele could tell from the teenager's use of *Daddy*.
The boy hadn't called him that in years, not since declaring it "too
babyish" when he'd turned ten. For an instant the physician was
transported back to the happy time when they'd still been pals and
had had no idea of the trial that lay ahead for them.

"I'm okay, Chet." Steele automatically tried to reassure the young
man who shared his mother's features, but the noise that came out of
him sounded like a moan sent through a pipe.

A nurse whisked into the curtained cubicle, issuing comforting
phrases in his stead while scanning the many blinking readouts and
fluorescent green squiggles on the screens amassed around him. The
numbers must have met with her approval, because she saw no need
to adjust any of their myriad dials and switches. She did, however, re-
duce the rate of the two IV solutions flowing into his arms. One
would be nitroglycerin, the other heparin, Steele knew, recognizing
that he now lay in the cardiac care unit.

"The angioplasty went well," the nurse continued to tell his son.
"That's the passage of a catheter with a balloon on its end into the ar-
teries of your father's heart. We use this device after a heart attack,
when possible, to immediately dilate the obstruction and reestablish a
normal blood flow before much injury is done to the cardiac muscle
itself. Your father needs rest, and time, but his outlook is good."

How good? Steele immediately wanted to know, quickly discovering that he had a will to live after all, now that he'd visited death's door. And which artery had been obstructed? How much of the heart wall damaged? Most important: What remained of its strength to pump? The thought of being subjected to the limits of permanent heart failure, if he even survived, filled him with sudden panic despair. A single number—the ejection fraction, or force in each heartbeat—would tell him his fate.

But the nurse spoke only to Chet and ignored Steele entirely, as if his being intubated and unable to speak rendered him not even there. He made more moaning noises into his airway and frowned ferociously to indicate his displeasure, but earned a mere pat on the head and a shot of Valium.

As he drifted off, he noticed Chet's expression switch from alarm to the angry belligerence that had become all too common whenever the two of them were in the same room.

The nurse noticed the shift in the boy as well. "What's the matter?" she asked. "Did you not understand? I just told you that he had a good prognosis."

"That's what *he* used to say all the time about my mother," his son answered accusingly just before Steele felt the sedation take full effect and catapult him into darkness.

That same evening a dozen reporters—and representatives from twice as many environmental groups—packed the boardroom at Agrenomics International, a research facility located north of White Plains, New York.

"And so to conclude, let us enter the millennium as partners," said Bob Morgan, the chief executive officer. "I offer you this new facility as evidence of our profound desire to use genetic technology in a responsible and beneficial way." He threw his arms wide as if to embrace those seated on each side of the table in a group hug. He heard a few groans but ignored them. Instead he gestured to a row of technicians standing behind him in lab coats with the Agrenomics insignia above their breast pockets. "After you've pried up the floor-boards and stormed our Frankenstein lab—" He paused for the laughter. None came. Shrugging with a good-natured show of humility, he continued. "—I assure you the snacks we'll be serving later will be better than my jokes."

This time there were a few polite chuckles as people pushed back their chairs, gathering up their notepads or tape recorders, and shouldered their cameras.

Morgan, a man of medium build possessing a high clear brow and thriving waves of curly brown hair, had just begun to heave a sigh of relief over his having ducked a rough ride from his "guests" when the person in the room whom he most feared piped up, "Will our cookies and milk be genetically modified, Mr. Morgan?"

This got a loud round of laughter as Morgan bristled.

The handsome woman asking the question had close-cut auburn hair verging on gold, appeared to be in her late thirties, and, he knew, had done more to popularize genetics in books and on TV than anyone in her field. He would even have found the trace of an Irish lilt in her voice a delight to listen to, if it weren't for his foreboding sense that she intended to rip him apart with her razor-sharp mind. He chose his words of reply carefully, all too aware that she had a nation-wide following and that on matters of science, he couldn't match her. "Really, Dr. Sullivan, we simply hired the best caterer we could find. I know I'm going to have some—"

"That's hardly the point, Mr. Morgan. I'm sure we'd all like to 'have some.' I simply want to know if it's genetically modified or not. Can you tell me that?"

"I couldn't say, Dr. Sullivan, but I don't see the point of you making an issue of the food we're serving at a reception—"

"But this is exactly the point, Mr. Morgan. Not you or anyone else can tell whether the food we're eating in America is genetically modified, because it's not labeled."

By now all the reporters in the room had their cameras and microphones pointed at the two of them.

Silently cursing her and feeling the sweat break out on his brow under the glare of the lights, as calmly as possible he slowly gave the answer he'd always resorted to in such confrontations. "There is no scientific evidence that eating genetically modified foods has ever harmed anyone."

His adversary rolled her eyes and shook her head as if she were about to say *Pleeease!* Instead she flashed a disarmingly beautiful smile and said to the camera, "No evidence of harm is not evidence of no harm."

He wanted to throttle her.

Sullivan gave him no time to reply. "And what will the guides on your tour be telling us about the infectious strands of naked DNA which you use to make vectors?" She turned to the people with the microphones and cameras. "Vectors are the carriers of genetic engineering," she explained, "used to transport the genes from one species and incorporate them into the genetic structure of another."

"*Infectious* is an awfully strong word, Doctor. There have been no proven dangers of naked DNA to date—"

"No, but there have been some alarming studies that raise very troubling questions," interrupted Sullivan, reaching into her briefcase and pulling out a stack of printouts about an inch thick. Laying them on the table and fanning them out like a deck of cards, Sullivan turned again to the reporters who'd been lapping up the spat, their lips pulled back from their teeth the way sharks grin just before they attack. "Here is a collation of recent research which proposes questions you should be putting to the technicians and scientists whom you will meet in this facility. And keep in mind that genetic engineers make a key assumption as they put a gene from one species into the DNA of another—that once it's inserted into another species this particular gene will act in the way it always has in its natural host. Some recent work shows that this is not so. How a gene behaves depends on its context amongst other genes, and we are mixing genes that have never been together since the beginnings of life." She then pulled a few individual articles from the pack, handing them to those nearest to her. "These cover the five most contentious issues to date. One outlines the impact of feeding genetically modified potatoes to lab rats—a subsequent weight loss and increased immune response. The scientist who published the report ended up being fired by the laboratory he worked for. Incredibly, despite even his critics calling for subsequent studies, no follow-up work has been done to date." She held up a second article. "This offers evidence that when an organism is genetically modified by the DNA of another species, the viruses, bacteria, and parasites in that organism are modified as well. The findings raise the possibility that these hitchhiker bugs, now carrying the DNA of synthetic vectors designed to jump the species barrier, may acquire new virulence, even the capacity to invade new species. The consequence could be diseases peculiar to one species of plant or animal becoming prone to leap the existing barriers which normally keep those diseases from occurring in other species, such as man. When this jump has previously occurred in nature, the results are usually catastrophic. I remind you, the Spanish flu epidemic in 1918 that killed twenty-one million people may have arisen from a virus normally found in swine, and the origin of AIDS in man is a simian, or monkey virus which vaulted the species barrier, probably in the 1930s, killing fifteen million so far. More recently the 'bird flu' strain of influenza has appeared in humans—"

"Really, Dr. Sullivan, you're being outrageous!" interrupted Morgan, his face flushed with anger. "You presume to hijack our attempt to show responsible behavior in our pursuit of bringing the benefits of genetics to humankind in a safe—"

"Oh, don't you be telling me about the benefits of genetics, *Mr.* Morgan," she protested in her full Irish brogue, flashing her thousand-watt smile once more at her audience and finessing her emphasis on the *Mr.* with a playful wink.

Laughter filled the room.

You bitch! he silently cursed, fuming at her snide way of reminding everyone that he couldn't claim to be a doctor of anything.

"Dr. Sullivan," called out one of the reporters. "You alleged that these naked DNA vectors are infectious. Could you elaborate on that, please?"

"Of course. It's the third issue I'm coming to," she continued, ignoring Morgan, who blustered helplessly at his end of the table, "and in my mind the most contentious of all—the ongoing effects of naked DNA vectors *after* they've been used in the process of gene insertion which I alluded to earlier."

"Now wait a minute," the flustered CEO managed to spit out. "I insist all of you remember that you are here as our guests, and as such should respect *our* agenda!"

No one in the room paid him the slightest attention, least of all Kathleen Sullivan. His employees, still all in a row behind him, looked nervously at him and at one another, appearing uncertain of what to do.

"When genetic engineers make a vector," she continued, "they first combine the gene they wish to transfer with strands of DNA from viruses or bacteria adept at invading the targeted host, or intended recipient of the transfer." She spoke quickly, obviously aware that her stay could be cut short. "They construct these carriers, or vectors, not only to assure invasion of the host organism and insertion of the gene into its DNA, but also to include bits of what we call promoter DNA, a segment which maximizes expression of the gene in its new host, thereby guaranteeing the appearance of whatever trait it carries." She collected another group of papers from the table and began to deal them out. "This one suggests how naked strands of these man-made DNA vectors can subsequently escape intact from the host into the environment as the result of cell death, excretion, or secretion." She passed out another article. "We all once thought that these discarded entities were inert unless they were within a living cell or virus and that they would quickly break down once exposed to the elements. Here is recent evidence to the contrary, showing that they can exist much longer in soil than previously expected." She proffered a third batch of documents. "Other research indicates that they in themselves have the capacity to infect species other than their intended host and incorporate their DNA into the genes of accidental targets. Outlined in these pages is a single study which demonstrates that vectors have found their way from the gut of laboratory mice into their liver, spleen, and reproductive organs. I think you'll find it a particularly disturbing read, and the obvious question—could the same thing happen in humans—has never been looked at."

Those men and women who hadn't had copies handed to them moved forward and picked some off the table for themselves. They frowned as they leafed through the pages and listened to her ongoing explanation of the information before them.

"You see, these vectors are soluble and capable, theoretically, of penetrating the skin. They can also be ingested and taken up through the gut. For brief periods of time it's even remotely possible they could exist long enough in the air we breathe to be inhaled."

"That does it!" screamed Morgan. "Such unfounded fear-mongering from someone as reputable as yourself, Dr. Sullivan, is an abomination. I'm sure the members of the press will not engage in such speculative, unsubstantiated sensationalism. Why, it's the equivalent of crying 'Fire!' in a crowded theater—"

"Read this evidence, Mr. Morgan, before you accuse *me* of crying 'Fire,' " she retorted, and flung a fistful of her handouts at him, her green eyes flashing. He stood speechless as she quickly returned her attention to the press. "The fourth matter I want to stress," she continued, "is that although I'm stating *theoretical* risks—dangers which research suggests *might* be present in current practices involving genetically modified organisms—the authors of all the articles which I've given you stipulate that these theoretical risks demand far more controls and much more use of caution than are currently in use." As she spoke, she gathered up her belongings and appeared to be making ready to leave, all the while eyeing Morgan as if trying to gauge how many seconds she had before he threw her out.

I bet she'd actually like that, thought the CEO as he glumly eyed her back. Helplessly he imagined the news images that would flash across the nation if he were so stupid as to order security to evict her and provide the "guests" with a photo-op of his guards manhandling the woman. Better to wait her out, he decided, seeing that she appeared about to leave anyway, but he seethed with frustration at not being able to shut her up.

Pulling on her coat, Sullivan turned her back to him and stated, "These scientists are issuing an appeal for further research into the questions which their work raises, to promote a logical and rational discussion of the problem, and I wholeheartedly support their call." She slung her purse over her shoulder, then added, "To anyone with half a brain I think it's self-evident that such a process is the very antithesis of yelling 'Fire!' "

"The hell it is!" Morgan said, his rage once again getting the better of his resolve not to do battle with her in front of the media. "I know the kind of so-called scientist who writes these diatribes. They'd cripple progress by fears that are only speculation, not proved. People like you and them would have us in the Stone Age—"

"Can it, Morgan!" cut in one of the ladies with a microphone.

He gasped, horrified that the carefully planned briefing had slipped so badly out of his control.

"Dr. Sullivan," the woman continued. "I'm from *Environment Watch* on public radio. Though what you say is alarming, a lot of these papers seem to focus on gene transfers among microbes in everything from yeast buds to plants and the occasional lab rat. Just as Mr. Morgan said, you haven't offered us a single shred of direct evidence that any of this stuff is harmful to humans. So my question to you is, based on existing data, why the flap?"

"The lack of data is the flap. Until we get it, I don't like the idea of unknowingly eating a plateful of vectors that might slither up alongside my DNA and modify me."

"Yuck!" said the man opposite her with a shudder, screwing up his face as if he had a bad taste in his mouth.

A few others reacted with forced chuckles as they squirmed in their seats and looked uneasy.

"But if naked DNA vectors are such a danger to people," persisted the woman from *Environment Watch*, "why isn't there research going on using human subjects to answer some of the questions you raise?"

"Good question," replied Sullivan, heading for the door. "I certainly can't understand why not."

"Do you think it's because your claims are groundless?" persisted the reporter.

"Hey! I don't have claims so much as questions," retorted Sullivan as she headed for the door. "That's what makes this whole business scary—*so many* unanswered questions, yet people like Mr. Morgan here insist it's safe to barge ahead without safeguards or checking for those answers."

She paused with her hand on the door handle and turned back to the cameras and microphones. "I'd love to talk further, but far be it from me to stay where I'm not wanted. Instead, I leave you with a thought. As sooner or later you're bound to ingest something containing a strand of naked DNA from a viral, bacterial, or parasitic vector, which would serve you better? Research, controls, and precautions, or Mr. Morgan's reassurances?"

A murmur of approval went through the room.

"You said there were five important issues. I think you only gave us four," called out another woman holding up a tape recorder.

"If any of you want further information you can reach me at my university office in downtown Manhattan. I'm in the book." On issuing the invitation, she left.

Morgan immediately launched into a desperate attempt at damage control. "If Dr. Sullivan hadn't been so determined to give us such a grandstand performance with her preformed point of view, she might have learned just what safeguards a state-of-the-art facility such as this can and does offer to redress groundless fears. . . ."

But all the time he thought, I'll kill her. I'll fucking kill her!

Outside in the corridor, Kathleen Sullivan exhaled long and hard as she scurried toward the front door. She winced with embarrassment at how she'd played to the press and staged her exit. What a prima donna performance, she thought, rolling her eyes to the ceiling, but it had been necessary. Throwing Morgan on the defensive and keeping him off guard long enough so that she could leave on her own had been crucial to her plan.

Striding up to the guards at the main door, she hoped they weren't expecting anyone to finish the visit so early. Briskly signing off her name from the visitors list and walking out, she clearly took them by surprise—they never even thought to escort her to the front gate. This she'd also counted on.

The grounds outside were spacious, covered with landscaped lawns, massive evergreen shrubs, and occasional tall pines. A flagstone walk wound its way through these various living ornaments and gave the place the overall effect of a well-tended park, inviting one of the reporters to comment as they'd been going in, "Biotechnology corporations always spend a fortune on looking *green*." Her own eyes had been peeled for a spot where she could step into the bushes undetected under the cover of darkness.

She found the place and made her move. In seconds she lay facedown in the dirt deep within the branches of an eight-foot-high, twenty-foot-wide sprawl of ornamental spruce.

She stayed motionless, wanting to make sure there were no approaching footsteps from the guards at the front gate who might have seen her duck out of sight. As she waited, her excitement mounted at finally being in a position to obtain solid evidence to back up her assertions that naked DNA vectors were dangerous.

Because as sensational as she'd made it all sound, she'd given the press nothing about current practices in genetically modifying organisms they couldn't already find on the Internet, if they knew where to look and could decipher scientific papers. And while her evidence *suggested* possible ways the vectors could do environmental harm or be hazardous to human health, Morgan had been right about one thing—his insistence that no one had yet implicated them with direct proof. She knew all too well that for people like the *Mr.* Bob Morgans of the world—"Gurus in finance, willing zeros in science," she muttered through chattering teeth—nothing short of a smoking gun would stop them. And that's what she'd come to get.

Neither the layer of thermal underwear she wore under her pantsuit nor her black ensemble of a full-length coat, ski hat, and gloves—chosen for warmth as well as camouflage—were keeping out the cold. But the prospect of what lay ahead—taking cuttings from plants immediately around the Agrenomics lab, the DNA of which she could subsequently check for evidence of man-made genetic vectors—had her mind on fire. If she succeeded and the vectors were there, she'd have demonstrated that once they escaped from the lab they were as "infectious" as she and other scientists feared. Such a finding would blow the lid off the whole issue, force a recognition of accidental contamination for the hazard it is, and make mandatory the kind of safety regulations that she'd always argued for. Though many in her profession had discussed doing this kind of analysis, official requests for such testing had always been turned down. And as far as she knew, no one had succeeded in doing it surreptitiously. She'd be the first.

When boots failed to sound on the stone path, she figured it was safe, and immediately went to work. Rolling on her back and pulling a pair of manicure scissors out of her purse, she snipped sprigs of blue needles from the branches over her head. She then took tiny cuttings from the stems and roots near the ground. The latter might provide evidence that vectors were taken up from contaminated soil. On the other hand, if she found traces of foreign DNA only in the needles, the implication would suggest a mechanism of airborne infection through the vector's direct contact with foliage. She put the two types of specimens in separate stoppered tubes already labeled MIDRANGE. She'd smuggled a dozen of the small sterile containers past the guard who had inspected her purse on the way into the building by hiding them in a box of tampons and then making sure she got into the line where a man did the checking.

Her overall objective included getting similar foliage and root samples from shrubs and grasses at different distances from the building. Since conventional wisdom in the industry held that naked DNA vectors were harmless, most places took none of the special isolation precautions with them that they routinely used with viruses, bacteria, and parasites. Instead technicians handled and prepared the vectors without the benefit of venting hoods and allowed their release into the regular heat and air-conditioning ducts. The most likely reservoirs of contamination on the grounds would therefore be nearest the outlets that expelled this. Knowing all this, she determined especially to get foliage and root samples from around the base of the building.

Though the shadows kept her invisible where she hid, she'd spotted security cameras at the gate and above the front door. Enough ambient light from the sodium lamps in the parking lot spilled out onto the lawns in her immediate vicinity that anyone would easily see her on the open grass. She decided to wait until there were fewer people around before moving on to the rest of the grounds.

"That damn Sullivan woman—she's going to be a problem, I can tell," exclaimed Morgan, pacing behind his desk as he talked into his phone. "We held this session in order to disarm the media and hopefully avoid too close a scrutiny from yahoo environmentalists, but what we get is her putting us under a fucking microscope. Next she'll have picketers dressed as giant corncobs at the front gate."

"Relax," said the voice at the other end. "From what you told me, she merely recycled the usual old charges. She's got no idea what we're really up to. When are you expecting the new vectors to arrive so you can start production?"

"Not until after New Year's."

"And the work with the first batch?"

"It's going well. We resumed right after the dog and pony show with the reporters finished. Seed from our first crop should be ready for shipment next week, and testing with the liquid format is on schedule."

"When will you start delivering the liquid?"

"If the results are good, mid-January. By end of February, a tank car of the stuff will be parked near every target in the half dozen southern states where we intend to start. By early April, we'll have done the same for the more temperate regions."

"Apart from the group conducting the animal trials, none of your regular technicians suspect what they're doing?"

"Nope. They think they're making the usual modifications under stricter controls is all. 'As part of our bowing to the tree huggers,' I tell them. By the way, I got ordered to inform you that our client is getting impatient."

"He called you at the plant?"

"No. His messenger told me when she brought the samples we're working with now. Man, she's a looker. Ever seen her?"

"No! And I don't intend to see her or any of them—they could blow my cover."

"What's your reply to our client, then? I'm due to travel back to that accursed sanctuary of his again. Christ, I hate going there."

From the very beginning both men had agreed they would always assume their conversations were monitored. They'd gotten into the habit of never mentioning names, places, and many other specifics, particularly when referring to the man who employed them, for the sake of their own safety as well as his.

"Tell him nothing. Better yet, tell him everything is going fine, but that for security's sake, the less he knows of the details, the better."

Morgan frowned. "*You* can tell him that if you like. Every time we meet, it's the details that he demands. Plus he's perpetually reminding me about all the money he's paying us and who works for whom. Believe me, he doesn't have to add that it's exceedingly unhealthy to deny him what he wants. I swear, he probably pays off those bandits he surrounds himself with in human flesh."

A heavy sigh came from the receiver, followed by, "He's an asshole. Perhaps you should remind him of his many previous failed attempts to 'strike at the heart of America,' as he puts it. Point out that his fucking bombing campaign against U.S. embassies led to his own labs and personnel being blown up, leaving us nowhere to work and barely enough vector to finish the first clinical trials. And that rigmarole we're going through in France to get the second vector is insane!" His voice kept rising as his tone grew angrier.

Morgan remained silent, barely controlling his own fury at once more being stuck with having to mollify the madman he'd be meeting in a few days halfway around the world.

"Have a nice trip," said the voice before leaving Morgan listening to a dead line.

In New York City the man who'd been talking with Bob Morgan reclined in his high-backed chair and stretched the tension out of his neck and legs. As he stared at the Manhattan skyline, the nearby World Trade Towers reflected so many of the surrounding lights that they resembled a pair of obelisks made of stars. "Another of your bungled schemes," he muttered, eyeing the twin structures.

He absently pressed his hands together in front of his mouth and tapped his lower lip with his index finger. Anyone who saw him might have thought he was about to pray. Instead he murmured a parting thought to the client—one which he would never dare say to his face. "Thanks to me, asshole, by this time next year, you will have brought the United States to its knees."

The time crawled by. She hadn't even dared lift her head for a peek through the spruce branches when she heard the chatter of her group leaving. Someone might glimpse the whiteness of her face in the shadows. Minutes later, the growl of the chartered bus that had brought them filled the night as it drove away. Morgan must have assumed I called a cab, she thought idly.

She listened as the remaining staff departed in smaller groups. More noises came from the vicinity of the parking lot—doors slamming, car motors roaring to life, and tires crunching on gravel. Soon those sounds also faded into the night.

Only the soothing rush of the wind through the branches around her remained. From time to time a few cars passed on the road in front. A train rumbled by in the distance. She once made out the faint cries of a distant owl. Otherwise, the countryside surrounding the isolated facility had fallen quiet.

Time to move, she told herself, stretching her legs and rolling the kinks out of her neck. Groaning as her limbs protested, she crawled out from cover and, crouching low, headed for the shadows along the perimeter of the spacious grounds. Once there she began collecting the specimens she wanted, getting on her hands and knees and using a penlight she'd brought. She first checked for an area of grass that hadn't gone dormant yet. Luckily for her, it had been mild through most of November, and a lot of the lawn remained green.

In the midst of cutting the roots out of a tiny divot with her scissors, she heard several vehicles approaching in the distance. Thinking they'd simply drive on by as had the previous bits of traffic, she paid them no heed.

Suddenly the beams of their headlights cut a swath through the darkness where she'd been working, and, glancing up, she saw two minivans swing into the parking area under the yellow glare of the lot's sodium lamps. "What the hell!" she muttered, snapping off her penlight and throwing herself once more on the ground.

Not daring to lift her head—again for fear someone might see the white of her face—she listened intently as the two motors cut off, doors clicked or slid open, and the sound of men's voices accompanied by the crunch of their shoes carried across the crisp night air. Oh, God, she thought, there's a lot of them.

She desperately wanted to risk a look. But could she get away with it? Though it was darker here than near the front, she lay on open ground. If any of these new arrivals took a glance in her direction and came close enough, they'd see her easily. Even her breath, rising like a white plume in the frosty temperatures, might give her away.

Covering her face with her gloved hands, she peeked through her fingers and saw about a dozen figures walking across the lot toward the front gate. Six were dressed in civilian clothes, while the others wore peaked caps and the gray uniforms often adopted by private security firms. These men, she saw with alarm, carried sidearms in holsters. "Jesus Christ," she exclaimed softly, having expected to encounter nothing more out here than the pair of aging watchmen she'd seen when she first entered the front gate.

She had to find better cover. Jamming the sample she'd just cut into one of her tubes and securing it in her purse, she got to her hands and knees. Damned if I'm going to forgo my samples from near the base of the walls, she thought, and, crouched low as before, sprinted toward the rear of the building, where it seemed darkest. She took a bead on the vents she could see silhouetted against the night sky as she ran. Grabbing at branches and shrubs on the way, she resigned herself to the fact that whatever vegetation she broke off on the run would have to serve as the remainder of her midrange specimens.

Rounding the corner and huddling against the back wall, she peered out again toward the gate. Two of the uniformed men had taken up position there. Two more seemed to be starting on a tour around the inside of the fence. The final pair were accompanying the men in casual dress as they walked toward the front entrance.

Sullivan ducked down amid the shrubbery lining the foundation of the building. Hunched over her penlight, she hurriedly stuffed the vegetation she'd picked up on the fly into appropriately labeled tubes and then hastily turned her attention to the greenery around her, grasping boughs of cedar between her fingers and sliding the fronds into containers marked SHORT-RANGE. As she worked, she kept taking hasty glances over her shoulder to where the two guards patrolling the perimeter would appear once they got this far. Seeing nothing, she listened for their voices, but only the steady sigh of the wind through a grove of pine trees off to her right filled her ears.

Where have they gone? she wondered, turning her attention to the roots and storing the last of her samples back in her purse. Still on her hands and knees, she crept to the corner of the building and again looked around it.

The darkness here made it easy to see the front and side of the property where the ambient light penetrated even farther in from the parking lot than she'd initially realized. Apart from where shrubs and trees obscured her view, she could readily make out most of the fence in that section, and the guards were nowhere to be seen. Had they doubled back? It became vital that she learn where they were before she made a run for it. She'd already decided it best to try and get over the fence to the rear of the building where the shadows were deepest.

The distant sound of men laughing behind her sent Sullivan diving for cover again, this time pressed against the building's foundation, between it and the low row of evergreens where she'd just been taking cuttings. Once more, she covered her face with gloved hands and peeked out between her fingers. They *had* doubled back, following the fence around in the other direction. To her horror, she saw the two guards make a ninety-degree left turn and start directly toward where she lay.

Christ! Have they seen me? she thought in panic. Instantly she imagined the headlines if she were caught. CELEBRITY GENETICIST BUSTED FOR TRESPASSING!

Then she remembered that these men were armed. They wouldn't kill me in cold blood, she reassured herself. But guards with guns might pull them if they were startled by someone in the shadows. "Oh, boy," she whispered under her breath, wondering for a second if it wouldn't be better to call out and surrender before anything disastrous happened by accident. A second later, she changed her mind. No, goddamn it. That would let Agrenomics and Morgan, the smug bastard, off the hook. Let his guards find me if they can. I'm staying put! Besides, they're not likely to shoot if they trip over me first.

Besides, she'd arranged for a diversionary action in the parking lot to kick in at eight P.M., in case she hadn't made it back by then to the car waiting for her at a rendezvous point. She took a quick glance at the luminous dial on her watch. It read 7:57. Just hold tight, she told herself, hoping that with a little luck she could still get out of there undetected with her samples intact.

She began to make out snippets of the men's conversation as they drew closer.

". . . when do the weekly pickups start? . . ."

". . . apparently early in the new year . . ."

". . . always the same day? . . ."

They were already walking along the rear wall, still about twenty yards from where she lay. Silhouetted by the ambient light behind them, they were otherwise in complete darkness. She figured that in twenty seconds they'd be stepping on her head. She'd barely started to slither backwards when suddenly they stopped and began inspecting something on the building. By now they were close enough that she could hear every word.

". . . they're going to show us how to work these hoses. Morgan doesn't want the train guys handling the stuff."

"Are you sure it'll be safe?"

"With what we'll be wearing it will be."

One of them struck a match, and a gold portrait of his face flared out of the darkness. His skin was deeply pockmarked, its tiny craters cast in flickering round shadows. Like a moonscape, she thought, transfixed by the sight of him. The space between his dark eyes furrowed as he cupped his hands around the flame and drew two quick puffs on the cigarette jutting at an angle from his lips. Then the apparition vanished.

They'd barely resumed their inspection of whatever they were looking at when a burst of static sounded. The one with the cigarette grabbed a walkie-talkie from his belt. "What's up?" he asked.

Through sputters of interference came the reply. "We've got a pair of kids just pulled into the parking lot and started necking. It's probably nothing, but you better be nearby, in case."

"Roger. We're on our way."

The pair took off at a run the way they'd come, turning the corner and passing out of sight seconds later.

Sullivan grinned broadly, knowing that the "kids" were Lisa, her seventeen-year-old daughter, with Abe, the girl's latest beau. She quickly got to her feet, but before running toward the back fence, she stepped along the wall to see what the two men had been looking at. Using her penlight, she could see a huge control panel fitted with dials and levers. Emanating from its center, a heavy-duty hose about six inches in diameter with metal rings on the end hung suspended in an overhead harness. The whole apparatus looked as if it could be pulled away from the back of the building.

It must be removable so that the hose can reach whatever it connects with, thought Sullivan.

Puzzled, but anxious to get out of there, she snapped off her light and started feeling her way in the dark toward the back fence. She hadn't gone a few yards when she tripped over something hard and went down heavily on her hands and knees. The stinging in her palms and throb in her patellae brought tears to her eyes, but she managed to stifle her urge to cry out. She'd landed in what felt like gravel and, feeling around for her light, found herself on wooden ties between a set of rails.

She got to her feet and, limping at first, followed the tracks to the fence. Though a locked steel gate blocked the exit, there was enough clearance between it and the roadbed to let her easily slip under.

Her eyes well used to the dark by now, she could see that the tracks curved left before she lost sight of them in the blackness. Straight ahead she could make out what looked like massive greenhouses, a half dozen of them, each at least a hundred yards long. Curious, she started toward them, but came up to yet another chain-link fence, this one twenty feet high with a big curl of razor wire along the top—the kind they erect around prisons.

"Well, well, Mr. Morgan," she muttered, standing there and peering in at the darkened glass structures, "what does your garden grow?" As if reluctant to answer, the wind whistled evasively through the diamond-shaped wires blocking her way.

As she hurried across the neighboring fields back to the highway, she grew increasingly curious about what she'd seen and overheard. Why would a pure research facility such as Agrenomics need to make bulk shipments by train once a week? A place like that usually exported the innovative ideas and techniques required to create new lines of genetically modified organisms, not the products themselves.

And why so many greenhouses? Of course, they'd need somewhere they could transplant their modified plants after getting them started in the lab, in order to grow them big enough to obtain their sample seed. But they had *acres* of land under glass back there. To mass-produce new seed lines in a greenhouse, not at a farm, seemed strange.

And why were they hiring men with guns to protect whatever they were doing? She knew that the ongoing crusade by her and others for tighter regulations made companies like Agrenomics nervous. *And they have cause to be worried,* she thought with satisfaction, hugging her purse to her with its hard-won specimens as she crossed a particularly uneven patch of ground covered with a bristly stubble of wild grasses.

Yet somehow, naively perhaps, she hadn't expected guns.

3

His endotracheal tube came out the next morning.

He got the answers to his questions a few hours later.

That's when the chief of cardiology dropped by to inform him personally that Steele had obstructed the left anterior descending branch of his coronary artery, the supplier of blood to the entire front of his heart.

This came as no surprise. He knew it to be the site most commonly associated with ischemia, or loss of circulation, in a large enough area of cardiac muscle to induce ventricular fibrillation—the state where the chambers stop pumping and the entire organ becomes a quivering useless mass.

"But the balloon restored your perfusion quickly enough that it minimized the permanent damage, Richard, and your all-important ejection fraction remains near normal. You certainly picked the best spot possible to arrest," the old man assured him.

Yeah, right, thought Steele. How clever of me.

"Such a good outcome is the result of our getting to you so fast, made possible of course by Dr. Betty Clarke's being so on the ball."

"Betty who?"

"Your resident, man! The one who resuscitated you and saved your life in the first place."

Steele spent the rest of the day hurtling between memories and dreams, and they were all of Luana.

Just like at home, he thought. Except here he couldn't get up and brace himself with a cigarette or knock back one of the increasingly large nightcaps he'd resorted to ever since her death. Instead, he had to lie inside the curtains of that cubicle, enduring his grief without the usual diversions, until the sense of confinement left him feeling suffocated and his heart doing sprint trials, setting off all the alarms again.

The nurses ran in and once more sedated him past remembering, but this time he ended up in a nightmare. Dreaming that he was spread out and shackled, he became a specimen on a slide, squirming under the glare of some unknown inquisitor who tried to dissect him with questions.

Will you stop running now?

I can't.

Don't you realize you nearly died?

Of course.

You could still be out of time, yet you care so little for Chet?

He woke up screaming and pulling on his IV lines while struggling to get out of bed.

When they brought out the restraining belts and threatened to tie him down, he determined simply to stay awake. Sitting there alone, unable to escape his thoughts, for the first time in his life he felt that there might never again be a tomorrow for him. "Physician, heal thyself," he muttered nervously, wanting to take stock, yet having lost faith long ago in the powers of introspection. After all, as a doctor he grasped from the beginning what had happened to him since Luana died. *Prolonged grief reaction* read the official diagnosis, except naming it and reading about it had never once stopped him from being in its grip for the last eighteen months. Even when he understood, with counseling, that it wasn't so much the grief, but rather *"a sustained, panic-ridden obsession to escape the process altogether"* that was at the root of his problem, he simply refined his avoidance techniques. Working extra shifts in ER had been his greatest diversion. Then, while trying to kid himself that he'd covered up the problem and that no one would notice, he declared himself cured and dropped out of therapy.

Of course, the doctor in him continued to understand. He'd launched on a fool's strategy, he knew—*"serving only to prolong the patient's agony, leaving him trapped forever in the very grief he runs from"* the textbooks had assured him. But like a junkie fleeing before the fearful horrors of withdrawal, he couldn't stop. As a result, he robbed his work of the joy it had once held for him, turning it instead into a mind-numbing ordeal that left him exhausted and barely able to feel anything at day's end—at least nothing he couldn't dispatch with a tumblerful of scotch or a dozen cigarettes. When a nurse took him aside one morning and advised him to get some help, warning him that they all could smell the liquor on his breath when he came to work in the morning, he switched to vodka, a less detectable beverage.

Not that he'd ever gotten outright drunk. Nor did his drinking ever compromise a patient's safety, thank God. But through it all, he committed an equally unforgivable betrayal, at least by his own judgment. He ran from Chet at a time when the boy needed him most.

"Physician, heal thyself," he repeated through clenched teeth, a familiar bitter loathing settling in his heart, which no cardiologist could heal.

Steele woke that evening to see Chet sitting in a chair that hadn't been there earlier. The boy balanced a book on one knee while using the other to support the three-ring binder he wrote in.

Doing his homework, thought Steele. Keeping his eyes half closed, he continued to study his son who so resembled Luana. All the nights he'd looked into the boy's room at home and seen him concentrating on the ritual task flashed through his mind, stretching back to Chet's first days of school, and becoming a yardstick of times past. To it, collages of other memories from the boy's childhood tethered themselves and swirled around in circles, until the spin of images compressed all he'd lost with Luana and could still lose with Chet into a single dizzying panoramic sweep. It caused him to break out in a sweat. Shouldn't I have gone through this when I was dying? he wondered, trying to chase the past from his head. But the presence of his son made that impossible.

Though Chet had gone through a few early growth spurts, he still seemed little in some ways—his curly black hair, so like hers, was no less resistant to a brush now than it had been when she'd been there to groom it for him. He also had the same complexion as his mother—one that appeared to change with the light—delicate as porcelain in winter while robust with the sun's gold during summer. But the similarities of their eyes always struck him the most. The curves of their brows and the rich brown of their pupils had been such a close match that at times he could swear he saw her looking at him through Chet.

"Hi, son," he said quietly.

The boy started. For an instant his face actually showed a flash of pleasure at the sound of his father's voice. The look quickly vanished, replaced by the scowl of resentment that had become his more natural expression. "Hi, Dad," he replied, the words given out like quick nervous chirps.

"I'm happy to see you here," continued Steele.

Silence.

"What time is it?" In the clockless world of CCU—the cardiac care unit—it could have been three A.M., for all Steele knew.

"About seven."

"Where's Martha?"

"Downstairs, having a bite in the cafeteria."

Martha McDonald was their live-in housekeeper. She'd been helping to take care of Chet in one way or another ever since his birth. When Luana died, neither Chet nor Steele would have survived without her.

"Have you eaten?"

"Not yet. I'll get something after she's finished."

"It's late for your supper, isn't it?"

The boy shrugged and returned to his books.

What is he feeling? Steele wondered. *Afraid that I'm going to die on him just like his mother? Of course, he is. Christ, I almost left* him an orphan. And like father, like son, he's still just as torn up inside about her death as I am. After all, he's a child. How could he feel otherwise? Wake up, *Daddy*!

As he focused on what to say that would comfort Chet's present fears, an old unwelcome puzzle rolled through his head. What if *I* had coped better before, during, and after Luana's death? Might Chet find it less painful by now? Had I sentenced my own son to a prolonged grief as well?

"You know, Chet, my heart is probably going to be all right," he said hesitantly, not at all certain he'd be able to reassure him about anything anymore.

The boy didn't look up, but his pen paused in midstroke.

He's interested, thought Steele, hoping that this time he'd say the right words. "In fact, I'll be coming home in about ten days."

"Mom came home, too," he answered glumly, still staring at the page of his notebook.

Steele swallowed once or twice as he tried to think up a reply. After a few seconds he settled on what he thought would most directly address Chet's anxiety. "My heart attack isn't like Mom's cancer. I *can* get completely better. And who knows, if you and Martha nag me enough about diet and exercise, I might end up healthier than ever."

Chet winced as if he'd been poked in a still-fresh bruise. Flushing with anger, he threw down his books and leaped from the chair. "You lied to me about Mom. You told me she'd be okay, too. Why should I believe you now? And what makes you think I even care if you're going to be all right or not?"

Steele found the hurt in his son's glare so penetrating that for an instant he thought he saw Luana reproaching him from the grave. "Chet, come here, please," he commanded quietly.

The boy looked uneasy, but his expression softened, and he stepped tentatively forward.

When he got close enough, Steele took him by the hand and said, "How about giving your daddy a hug."

Chet hesitated and then leaned over, his hands awkward as he slipped them around his father's shoulders.

Steele gently wrapped his son in his arms and held him. He felt Chet initially stiffen and then relax. "I love you, Chet," he whispered. "I swear I'm going to get out of here, and I promise you I'll be your daddy again."

Chet said nothing; neither did he relax his hold.

Perhaps it's a start, Steele thought.

Having spent a lifetime sentencing others to the consequences of illness, he didn't take well to being sentenced himself.

"No ER work for at least six months," declared the same chief of cardiology who'd previously been so enthused about the success of the angioplasty, "and then we'll see."

"Sitting on my can for six months?" Steele protested incredulously. "That'll kill me! How about three?"

"You know the rules governing the return to normal activity as well as I do, Doctor."

"Those are guidelines, dammit! Meant to *guide* doctors in their clinical decision making, not bind them."

"And they've done exactly that, Richard. Guided *me*, the doctor, in making my decision about *you*, the patient. And that still makes them rules as far as you're concerned."

"But you yourself said that I had 'such a good outcome.' Doesn't that give me an edge?"

"Of course, your smoking days are over," continued the older man, overruling Steele's objections by ignoring them totally. "The nurses will provide you with printed matter on diet, exercise, and a schedule regarding the resumption of regular physical exertion. As for sex, nothing for three months; then you can gently begin relations again."

I'll let my hand know, Steele nearly quipped, growing increasingly peeved at the lecture.

"How's Chet doing?" he asked Martha on the eve of his going home. She'd brought in the clothing he'd need. Chet himself had stopped visiting him as soon as he'd transferred from CCU to a regular room—nearly a week ago.

"How do you think?" replied the lithe sexagenarian. "He's mad at you for making him afraid that you'll die, and he's mad at you for still making him care if you do. And, of course, those feelings are all mixed up with the usual need of a thirteen-year-old to have his old man around so he can defy the hell out of him."

Steele found himself grinning at the feisty white-haired woman who'd never failed to be blunt with him when it came to harsh truths or his needing a kick in the ass. Nor had the fact that he didn't have the sense or courage to listen lately deter her any. In an odd way he took her harrassing him as a comforting vote of confidence—her way of saying that she still believed he could stop being such a jerk and get on with his life.

A widow, Martha had no children, and when Luana had become ill she offered to expand her housekeeping by moving in to help care for her. Just weeks before her death six months later, Luana, her bright eyes glittering from the depths of hollow sockets, informed Steele that Martha would be staying on permanently. Steele, barely able to care for himself at that point, gratefully surrendered to the arrangement.

Cringing at the memory of his wife's features on that dreadful morning, he forcefully sustained a happy face. "Gee, Martha. Don't start going easy on me now," he replied with a weak chuckle.

"Now that's something I haven't seen in a while," she told him, pointing to his smile as her own flint-gray eyes softened. "It's a pathetic little bitty thing, but better than nothing. Make sure you don't forget to bring it home with you."

The sound of the phone brought him out of a deep sleep.

"I told you she'd be trouble!" he heard Morgan declare excitedly at the other end of the line.

"Who?"

"Sullivan! I think she's been poking around the place."

"What are you talking about?"

"A couple of kids parked in the lot the night of the press conference, apparently to smooch. One of the guards took down the plate number when he shooed them off. He passed it on a few days later to a friend who's a cop and asked him to trace it when he could, just to be on the safe side. It turned out to be Sullivan's car. The head of security called me just now after he got the match. I figure those kids were waiting for her, maybe creating a diversion with the guards to let her get away. Why else would they be in our neck of the woods?"

"Are you sure she left the building that afternoon?"

"Absolutely. I called the day shift, and the guards at the door told me that they signed her out. But no one at the gate remembers a solitary woman leaving early. She may have hid out on the grounds in the dark."

"Is there any way she could have sneaked back into the building?"

"No. Of that we're sure. The electronics in there make it safer than a bank vault. But she could have been outside on her own for hours."

The second man gave no reply, thinking over this last piece of information for nearly a minute.

Morgan broke the silence. "She's on to us after all, isn't she!" he declared, his voice cracking with anxiety.

"No, not necessarily."

"Then what the fuck was she doing here?"

"Probably collecting twigs and leaves."

"What!"

"It's how she would check out a lab in your business, hoping to find what vectors you're using and if they're infecting the DNA of every living thing in the vicinity."

"Then we're okay," he said, his voice immediately dropping an octave. "With our new filters, she'll find no traces of what we're making, right?"

"Right," he answered, getting out of bed and growing uneasy over how readily Morgan grew rattled whenever they encountered a problem. The man would need a lot steadier nerve for what lay ahead. "And more than that, she could be doing us a big favor," he reassured, figuring the more secure he made Morgan feel, the better.

"How do you mean?"

"Think about it. You could confront her with the fact that you know she snooped around the place illegally, then challenge the great Dr. Kathleen Sullivan to release the results she obtained from the samples she took. She'd have to pronounce us clean as a whistle. A seal of approval like that from someone with her credibility would guarantee we won't be under any additional scrutiny for the time being. What better conditions could we have for preparing the attack?"

"But what if her finding nothing fails to make her back off?"

"Then our client will arrange that she disappears."

Three Weeks Later

Sullivan recognized most of the reporters sitting around the long conference table from their visit to Agrenomics together. The woman representing *Environment Watch*, who'd challenged her on the lack of research findings relating directly to humans, rose to her feet. "So what were your test results, Dr. Sullivan?" she demanded.

"Good afternoon, ladies and gentlemen, and welcome to my laboratory," Sullivan replied, pointedly ignoring the question. "Before we get down to business let me introduce the newest member of our team, Azrhan Doumani, our chief resident, who is with us on scholarship from the University of Kuwait and doing his graduate thesis on the effects of naked DNA. I figured that since he did the testing you want to discuss, he should be here."

The young man sitting beside her at the head of the table smiled nervously and nodded, his dark features in brilliant contrast to his lab coat.

"And to his right is a special guest I invited to join us today whom some of you may already know, CEO of the Blue Planet Society, environmentalist Steve Patton, a longtime friend and colleague."

A distinguished-looking gray-haired man in a dark suit seated beside Doumani rose to his feet. His lean physique and tanned features lent him the healthy aura of an outdoorsman at odds with the sallow complexions and doughy body shapes that predominated among those reporting the nature beat. "Glad to be here," he acknowledged, grinning broadly.

"And I won't be puttin' up with any rudeness to these two gentlemen from you lot," Sullivan added, punctuating her lilting admonishment with a pointed finger and the flash of her own well-known smile.

Everyone laughed except the grim spokesperson for *Environment Watch*. "Really, Dr. Sullivan," she began, raising her voice over the chuckling of her colleagues, "we didn't come here to hear you act cute—"

"*You* requested this interview, not me!" retorted Sullivan, her eyes all at once shooting flares of emerald fire at the woman. "Any point in my asking who tipped you off about my extracurricular activity at Agrenomics?"

Silence.

"Ah, yes, never reveal a source. Well, as long as you're here, we might as well talk."

"So you admit you surreptitiously took samples from the grounds of the laboratory?" inquired a man seated opposite her.

"Of course."

Her reply set off a flurry of questions.

"Why?"

"What did you take?"

"How did you test them?"

She surveyed their expectant faces for a few seconds and then replied, "I'll begin by reminding you what I explained three weeks ago back at Agrenomics—that genetic engineers create vectors of naked DNA to jump genes from one species to another, and how afraid I am that these agents, once they are released into the environment, will infect other organisms, including humans. I figured one way of demonstrating their infectiousness would be to demonstrate traces of them in the plant life growing near the outlet vents at a facility using genetic vectors."

More questions erupted.

"What did you find?"

"You've confirmed your suspicions?"

"Are we in danger?"

"First let me outline what I did," she shouted above the noise, "and then I'll conclude with my results." She immediately held up a green binder with a handwritten title in black ink which read, *DNA Fingerprinting for Veggies*.

Everyone at the table burst into laughter, including the austere woman from *Environment Watch*.

"Some wag in our lab did the label, but it's not far off," Sullivan continued when the room grew quiet again. "What forensic scientists can do to bloodstained gloves in L.A., we can do to pine needles, roots from Kentucky bluegrass, and bits of soil. Except I'm looking for man-made strands of naked DNA vectors that have set up shop in the chromosomes of an unintended host."

The absolute silence of the listeners in the room confirmed to Sullivan that she had their attention. "Mr. Doumani will now explain the process in detail."

A very astonished Azrhan Doumani, who obviously didn't expect to be called on so soon, hesitantly got to his feet, swallowed a few times, and stated, "When Dr. Sullivan came back with her samples, we first treated each of the specimens to a shot of liquid nitrogen, freezing them into a brittle solid that we can easily grind to a fine mash using a mortar and pestle."

"We also go for the dry ice effect," Sullivan interjected with a wink to her nervous colleague. "White vapors billowing out of beakers and rolling over the lab bench—it makes for great visuals whenever the media's around."

The quip brought a few chuckles, but more important to Sullivan, she saw her young protégé's shoulders relax a notch.

"We then reach into the geneticist's toolbox," he continued, his manner less stiff than before, "take out a concoction of chemical washes called C-Tab, add them to our ground-up powder through a complex series of steps, and, after a spin in the centrifuge, end up with a solution of pure chromosomes—the gene strands of the organism—floating above all the debris. We siphon this off, again reach into our bag of tricks, this time to pull out what geneticists use to cut and paste DNA—restriction enzymes. We add them to our solution, where they break the chromosomes into genes and the genes into even smaller strands of DNA suitable for testing. Each enzyme attacks a specific site on the chain, and in this case, we treated our samples with the enzymes that would break off among other things pieces of DNA from a cauliflower mosaic virus, or CaMV. This is the most common invasive organism used in genetic engineering. Our idea was to look for DNA fragments from it, reasoning that by demonstrating their presence we'd have confirmation of a vector's having infected the vegetation we were testing."

He paused, taking a sip of water, and Sullivan used the moment to gauge the audience's interest. Several chairs squeaked, there were a few coughs, but tape recorders continued to roll and pens remained poised in midair, ready to write. Good, he's still got them, she thought, breathing a sigh of relief, because unless they understood the test process, they wouldn't grasp the real story hidden behind it all.

Doumani continued. "Searching for and identifying these fragments amongst all the rest involves a few more of the standard procedural tools of our trade—separating out the various pieces of DNA on an electrophoretic gel, locating them by using a hideous carcinogen called ethidium bromide, which turns them pink, then literally giving them a scrub with a wash called GENE CLEAN—until we're finally ready to lift a genetic fingerprint from them. Now, whether we're after a drop of blood at a crime scene or a vector in plants, the identification technique involves the most basic tool a geneticist uses—stock DNA preparations called primers. When we add a specific set of them to strands of DNA, they line up and lock on to the portions of the strands where the nucleic acid sequences are exactly complementary to their own. In other words, for our purposes here, we can use these primers as probes, to find whether a particular type of DNA is present in the chain we're studying, provided we know what to test for. In this case, since we could only make an educated stab at what they used in the vectors, we also were guessing about what primers to employ, again settling on those for the cauliflower mosaic virus." He paused again.

No one made a sound.

Still so far so good, thought Sullivan.

"We heated each tiny specimen of DNA we were testing to near boiling," resumed Doumani, "ninety-four degrees centigrade exactly, to break the DNA's double helix structure into single strands. Afterward, we lowered the temperature to fifty-five degrees centigrade and added the primers, letting this mix stand for sixty seconds. . . ."

Sounds of a dozen chairs scraping and people noisily clearing their throats quickly filled the room as his audience expressed their disinterest in the technical detail. Continuing to talk, Azrhan gave desperate little glances toward his supervisor that begged for a rescue.

"Just like making soup," broke in Sullivan. "In fact I could cook up a batch of the stuff in my kitchen if the oven timer weren't broken." There were a few isolated chuckles, but the restlessness persisted. "In the lab it's even easier, because we have a machine the size of a double microwave to do all this finicky business for us, so let's give that part a pass."

"Thank God!" someone muttered gratefully.

"Because what comes now is the secret ingredient," she continued, lowering her voice and drawing them to her, "an enzyme called Taq polymerase."

"Taq what?" exclaimed a man taking notes two seats away.

"Taq polymerase," she said lightly, as if to imply everyone should be familiar with the term. "Marine biologists first discovered this reagent decades ago, in the bacteria which thrive midst the scalding waters of thermal vents at the ocean floor. The substance's job is to set in motion the process that replicates DNA in these microbes, the same role all polymerases play in plants and animals throughout the planet. But a man named Karry Mullis realized that, unlike the others, this polymerase could function at the high temperatures we need to uncoil and mark specific segments of DNA with primers, as Azrhan so eloquently described. In 1993 Mullis received the Nobel

Prize for using this observation to develop the polymerase chain reaction, or PCR—the technique used today to multiply a specific portion of a DNA strand starting from just a few molecules. Since that discovery, mankind's study of DNA became infinitely easier, our unlocking the human genome is proceeding faster than anyone expected, and our ability to free the innocent or convict the guilty from evidence based on a microscopic drop of blood or semen has changed justice forever." She paused to let what she'd said sink in so she wouldn't overwhelm them with what came next.

"Dr. Sullivan, cut to the chase. What did you find?" demanded the woman from *Environment Watch*, her tone a splash of acid against the eardrum.

To Sullivan's surprise, Azrhan, who had sunk into his seat when she first started talking, now leaped to his feet and, taking a deep breath as if to steel himself, took over the press conference again. "Our machine nudged the temperature up to seventy-five degrees centigrade, added the Taq polymerase, and stirred in a good supply of nucleotides—the basic building blocks of DNA. Normally this would start the reaction we were after, if the cauliflower mosaic virus was present. For those of you who are interested, Taq polymerase moves up and down the DNA strand to be replicated and, using it as a template, brings in the appropriate nucleotides, stringing them together in the right order. The result is a new strand of DNA complementary to the original. But as Mullis discovered, it can only set up on the strand to be copied at the points where that strand has a primer on it." His voice confident, his delivery assured, and his eyes sparkling with enthusiasm for the work he obviously loved, he recaptured everyone's attention. "In other words, since our primers were specific to cauliflower mosaic virus, if replication occurred at all, we'd have our proof that a naked DNA vector successfully infiltrated the flora on the grounds at Agrenomics. Furthermore, passing these copied bits and pieces of CaMV genes through an electrophoretic gel would sort them out according to molecular weight, thereby offering up that intruder's genetic fingerprint." He abruptly retook his seat, leaving everyone leaning forward expectantly in their chairs. Instead of saying anything, he looked at his mentor, as if waiting for her to speak.

"Can we finally know what you found once you studied all this DNA you made?" a man at the end of the table called out, his voice brimming with exasperation.

"Nothing," said Sullivan.

At first there was dead quiet.

"Pardon?" the man finally managed to say, his tone incredulous.

"I said we found nothing," repeated Sullivan. "No replication occurred."

A chorus of disbelief erupted.

"What!"

"You wasted our time for this?"

"Jesus Christ!"

Above the din the familiar shrill voice of *Environment Watch* called out, "Does this mean your concerns over naked DNA vectors are bogus?"

"Not at all!" shouted Sullivan to make herself heard. "It could simply mean that we don't know what vectors Agrenomics is using. Or it could even be that they've installed proper filters."

"Are you saying they take your claims seriously?"

"Ask them that."

"How do we know you wouldn't come up just as empty around other research centers which use naked DNA vectors, filters or no filters—that the stuff just isn't infectious?"

"We don't. I'm suggesting we check the grounds of every such plant worldwide, to find out. And for the tests to be reliable, the companies must be pressured to disclose what vectors they're using so we'd know which primers to use."

The initial outburst subsided to a sullen grumbling as the rest of the reporters, most of them ignoring the two women's conversation, angrily shoved back their chairs, stuffed notepads into briefcases, and packed up tape recorders. More than once Sullivan heard the word *hoax*.

"Wait a minute. Listen, all of you!" said Steve Patton, jumping up from his chair. "Don't you realize the real story here is the testing method we just walked you through—that there exists an easy and cheap way to screen whether naked DNA has infected the environment?"

"Sit on it, mister," snarled the man at the end of the table. "I don't like being manipulated." He stormed out the door.

"The fact no one is running such tests is really what you should be in an uproar about," Patton shouted after him. "The fact that not one corporation worldwide provides independent geneticists with the access they need to company grounds or discloses the vectors we should be testing for—that's the true outrage. And I'm here to announce that the Blue Planet Society would finance any such study."

The reporter never looked back.

Patton turned to Sullivan and shrugged.

Sullivan eyed those who were still packing up their equipment. "Won't you grasp the opportunity here? You could report *how* these simple standard procedures can be used to establish essential screening, then maybe pressure will build to make it happen. If it does, possibly someone somewhere will find the hard evidence we need to wake everyone up to the fact that the risks are real. And if we're truly lucky, that will happen before some lab accidentally causes a catastrophe with permanent consequences, such as resurrecting a new equivalent of the Spanish flu."

A few paused to listen, but most left, still fuming. The woman from *Environment Watch* said nothing more, but rather stood where she was and regarded Sullivan with a steady, thoughtful gaze. After a few seconds, she nodded and joined the others.

"It's so unfair," consoled Azrhan later as he took a cup of tea with Sullivan and Patton in his mentor's office. "They were the ones who insisted on coming here." He appeared much more relaxed now that he'd proved himself in his first encounter with the press.

Sullivan sighed wearily. "I'd so hoped that we could convince them to get on board with us—issue a call for mandatory screening and a disclosure of vectors." She gave a sarcastic laugh. "As it is, we'll get pasted for crying wolf, or if we're lucky, they'll consider it 'no news' and run nothing." She absently fingered the printouts that documented their negative findings. "If I didn't know better, I'd think that somehow Bob Morgan discovered what I did and was so confident I'd 'come up empty,' as that shrew from *Environment Watch* put it, he leaked the fact that I was running the tests to the media—all to discredit me."

"That's ridiculous," scoffed Patton with a laugh.

"Is it? Who else would know? Surely no one here spilled the beans. And he's such a creep—I can just imagine him gloating over *me* having to say that I could find no evidence of environmental contamination around his plant."

Patton smiled behind his hand, his round wire-rimmed glasses and curly gray hair making him look owlishly wise in a way she found irksome.

Azrhan, on the other hand, stared at her, his eyes widening in earnest amazement. "You really think he'd do that?" he said.

"You bet I do. And for him to be that certain I'd find nothing, it means for sure they're using a vector he knows we'll never guess the primers for, or they really do have effective filters."

Azrhan nodded and continued to sip his tea in silence, letting his gaze slip out the window to where the winter dusk was settling over downtown Manhattan. Sullivan absently followed his line of sight, and saw he was watching the Twin Towers reflect the final seconds of the setting sun and turn themselves into pillars of fire.

"Concentrate on the press, Kathleen," said Patton with a chuckle. "You'll accomplish more if you succeed in getting our message out with them than by obsessing about Agrenomics." He got up from the easy chair opposite her desk. "And I wouldn't write off that 'shrew' from *Environment Watch*. She seemed to be listening to you at the end."

"You're going?" said Sullivan, feeling a twinge of disappointment. She'd hoped to have dinner with him.

"Sorry, but I'm meeting a potential donor to the Blue Planet Society for drinks. But let's talk later. I'll be at home."

"Sure," she said, trying to quell the pangs of jealousy that shot through her. Most of his "potential donors" were wealthy socialites, women who adored being in his company and were willing to offer him much more than cash. Easy Sullivan, she cautioned herself, you knew what he was when you allowed yourself to climb into his bed. "Hope you score big, for the sake of the environment," she added with a smile, the rude tease a throwback to the time when they'd been just friends and she'd reveled in ribbing him about his wicked ways.

He gave her a merry grin and bent over to kiss her good-bye. She turned her face, offering him her cheek instead of her lips.

As he vanished out the door, she returned her attention to Azrhan. He discreetly continued to stare out the window. Finding the silence embarrassing, she said, "There's still one thing I can't figure."

"What's that, Dr. Sullivan?" If he sensed anything between her and Patton, he showed no sign of it.

"Why should the people at Agrenomics be such nervous Nellies about people getting onto the grounds?"

"What do you mean?"

"If Morgan's feeling so secure that the likes of me with all my expertise won't find anything incriminating, what are all the armed guards around the place for?"

"Maybe he's worried about industrial espionage?"

"Maybe," said Sullivan, putting down her cup and packing up her papers to leave for the night. In the process, she managed to knock over the dozen or so unanswered Christmas cards that she'd allowed to accumulate on her desk these past weeks, a reminder of how much the work on her samples had kept her from preparing for the rapidly approaching holidays. "Or perhaps it's because he's got something else to hide—something that can't be found by prowling around outside the building and using a geneticist's tool kit. In any case, I'm certainly going to be keeping my eye on Agrenomics."

"What's the matter, Mom?" asked Lisa, looking at her across the kitchen table with green eyes and auburn hair identical to her own.

"You've barely touched your dinner. And after I slaved at least six minutes in front of the microwave making it for you."

Kathleen Sullivan smiled. "Oh, it's just some trouble I had with the media today."

The teenager cocked her head and twisted her youthful features into a skeptical look. "Come on. You never worry about the media. In fact, you relish every dustup I've ever seen you in, and it's you who starts most of them." She dipped a buffalo wing into a glob of blue cheese. "What's really the matter?"

"No, seriously—"

"Mother, is this about Steve Patton?"

Sullivan leaned back in her chair and, feeling an odd mixture of sadness and pride, studied the slim young woman who, in growing up fast, had become so astute. Ever since her father had walked out on them seven years ago, Lisa had all too quickly stepped out of her childhood and developed a tough-mindedness that would serve her well in life. But that jump had cheated her of the innocent silly phase most of her girlfriends got to pass through in their early adolescence. For the millionth time Sullivan felt a familiar regret over what her own failures as a wife had cost her daughter. She gave a rueful smile and said, "Who made you so smart?"

"I've told you to dump the guy."

"Lisa, it's not like that. We're friends—"

Lisa stripped the wing with her teeth, got up, and retrieved a bottle of cola from the refrigerator. "If a man slept around on me, you'd say I should dump him."

"Lisa!"

"Have you even told him how you feel?"

"Not exactly, but—"

"My God, Mother, how could a woman who's so smart be so silly? And to think I've relied on you to advise me about my love life."

Sullivan started to laugh. "So I'm great at genetics, lousy with men. It's embarrassing enough that I don't need to be lectured about it by my know-it-all seventeen-year-old—"

"Oh, yeah, tell me which part I got wrong. Let's see: He's got other women, it's driving you crazy, and yet you grin and bear it because you both promised not to get involved beyond being pals who happen to have sex together."

She felt herself go red. "Lisa!"

"Are you not going to eat this?" said the teenager, helping herself to most of what remained on her mother's plate.

Sullivan burst into laughter. "Come here, you woman of the world. What I need is a hug."

Her daughter grinned, stepped around the table, and gave her a big squeeze. "You deserve the best from a man, Mommy. You taught me to expect that. Don't forget it about yourself."

Sullivan waited until eleven that evening before finally phoning Patton. *Lisa's right,* she told herself. *I can't continue like this. Time to have a talk with my sex pal, and admit I'm just not sophisticated enough for this type of arrangement. How could I have been so stupid to have ever thought it would be good for me?*

As she dialed his number, her mind drifted back to the night about twelve months ago when they'd become lovers. Her own latest relationship having just gone on the rocks—the fifth to have ended that way in as many years—Steve had invited her out to the Plaza Hotel for a benefit and dinner dance. "Can you take a piece of advice from a man fifteen years your senior?" he said in all seriousness as he waltzed her around the floor.

"Maybe."

"You know how to avoid going through a string of men who you can never really like or love because they aren't half as bright as you, Kathleen?"

"Tell me."

"Cut the loneliness by having sex with a friend who has smarts equal to yours, no strings attached. It'll keep you from getting mixed up with losers you'll only have to disentangle yourself from later."

"And who might this friend be?"

He'd suddenly pressed her to him, taking her breath away as their thighs glided against each other. The fierceness in his eyes as they locked on to hers said he wasn't kidding.

"Yes, Steven, I think I'd like that," she'd said, the idea appealing to her at the time in its simplicity.

It had been wonderful, for a while, until his other sexual adventures began to bother her. Even though he made no secret of what he did and repeatedly told her to pursue anyone else she wished, she found herself becoming more emotionally attached to him than either of them ever intended. Yet she felt increasingly reluctant to say anything about it, afraid that by doing so she'd make things between them impossible, especially their work, and her turmoil grew worse.

"Hello," he said, breaking her out of her reverie, his voice husky and his breathing audible through the receiver.

Her insides did a somersault. She knew from all the times they'd been in bed together what he sounded like when he was in the throes of making love. She forced a laugh. "Sorry, Steve. I guess I caught you at a bad time."

He gave a wicked chuckle. "Not at all. This is pretty exciting, Kathleen. Kind of a fantasy I had." His breathing got coarser.

"Good night, Steve," she said, fighting the impulse to demand to know who he had with him, and put down the receiver harder than she intended.

She got out of bed and started pacing the length of her small bedroom. She felt buffeted by feelings of jealousy and fury at him for having such a disruptive effect on her. Having to admit she couldn't really fault him for any of it was even more frustrating. After all, he'd provided exactly what he'd promised—sex with a friend and no strings attached.

"Damn!" she muttered. "Damn him to hell."

After a few dozen revolutions through the room, she determined to take Lisa's advice and "dump the guy."

4

The Eve of the Third Millennium
Rodez, France

The massive stone spire of the giant cathedral loomed over Pierre Gaston as he hustled by. It seemed to be floating on the mist, its stained-glass windows glowing with soft blues, reds, and greens that bled like watercolors into the surrounding gray. Yet he found no beauty in the sight. Instead, the weightiness of the structure oppressed him, and made him huddle even deeper into his coat than did the cold.

He knew that something more than weather and medieval monuments was the source of his morose mood. The real reason—that on this night of nights in a thousand years he hurried home from work to a solitary meal and a lonely vigil before the television as he always did—galled him to the point that his stomach burned. It would be even more wretched than usual, since he'd be watching the entire world attend a party to which he hadn't been invited. At the age of forty-two, unmarried, and labeled an ordinary talent by his *patron* at the lab where he'd worked for the last decade, he needed no such additional reminders about the mediocrity of his life.

He tried to ignore the people who brushed past him as he trudged up the narrow cobblestone street leading to his apartment. But their gay chatter, laughter, and shouts of greeting to each other echoed along the centuries-old stone walls, following after him until he couldn't help but imagine the galas that they were hurrying off to prepare for. Even the rattle of metal shutters being rolled down all over the quarter bothered him, since it served as notice that shopkeepers were closing early because they also had somewhere special to go. Through the windows of bistros and restaurants, the sight of the waiters inside shaking out white tablecloths, laying out place settings, and scurrying around in preparation for the festivities depressed him further.

He reached his building—a stained, plaster boxlike structure built in the fifties with no regard to the surrounding architecture. He slammed the heavy front door behind him, perversely intent on keeping even a hint of the celebratory sounds outside where they wouldn't penetrate the dingy hallway and its musty smells and thereby make his living quarters feel more unbearable. He lumbered up a set of steep stairs covered by the threadbare remnants of a once maroon rug, got out his key, and caught the scent of the perfume.

It lingered in the stale air at his door.

She's here! he thought. She must have let herself in with the key he'd given her.

Instantly he unlocked his apartment and stepped inside. "Ingrid?" he said softly. No answer, only the silence of his empty rooms. He snapped on a light. The drab forlorn furniture of his salon greeted him. A glance into his bedroom, kitchen, and bathroom completed his search. Nevertheless, his excitement persisted. She'd returned to Rodez, and that meant surely he'd see her. Yet he remained puzzled. She'd come to his apartment and left. Why hadn't she stayed as she had the other times? She must have known that when he recognized her perfume he'd realize she'd been here—he'd bought it for her the last time they'd been in Paris together. There had to be a note, a message, something to explain what was going on. Quickly he went through his apartment again, this time hunting for a scrap of paper.

Nothing.

He had another thought. He went over to his computer and clicked it on. When his screen lit up, he saw that it contained a new file. He tried to open it, but a beep sounded and instructions appeared, demanding a password. He typed *Ingrid*. The machine flashed him a happy face and then yielded what he wanted. Eagerly he read the document.

My Darling, it is far too dangerous that we meet here. I'm sure that I'm being followed. Bring what you have for me to "the place" and erase this message.

He raced down the steps two at a time and backtracked through the streets toward where he worked. In his excitement, even the surroundings affected him differently from before, because now he felt part of the festiveness since he, too, rushed to an encounter. And such a meeting it would be. The thought of her naked body and her special appetites shot him full of desire. He felt himself harden as he hurried his pace.

She controlled when they saw each other, where they went, and the sex—especially the sex. It had been that way since they'd first met at the conference in Paris where he'd been lecturing less than a year ago. Yet as little as he saw her, she'd become the one part of his life that made enduring the rest worthwhile. Never in his wildest dreams had he believed he'd ever have such a woman interested in him. His own reflection in the store windows cruelly summarized why. Overweight, not too tall, prematurely balding, he wasn't the sort of specimen women of any kind sought out, but especially not women like her. He could hardly avoid admitting to himself the real reason she took such an interest in him—the secrets he passed to her—but even then she made him feel proud to do it, that he was helping the world and serving a cause that she held sacred.

He recalled how she had seemed to single him out from all the other speakers that first time. Tall, long necked, her hair woven like a gold skein and piled atop her head, she'd appeared regal. "Can I buy you a drink?" she'd offered in English, her blue eyes boring into him as she claimed to be Norwegian and unable to speak French.

English had been just fine with him.

Over cocktails, her questions about his work had seemed endless and amazingly informed. That night when she took him to bed, he'd felt like a rock star with his own groupie.

Since then she'd come to him at intervals of her own choosing. He always took pains to have a "secret" ready for her. Her degree of pleasure with what he came up with invariably determined the degree of his pleasure afterward in bed, sometimes even whether he got there at all. But when he gave her something that particularly pleased her, she murmured how much she adored him during their subsequent passion. Those were the moments in which he could fool himself into believing her.

It had been especially good last time. He passed on a tidbit that, from all her questions, he knew would interest her, and the revelation ignited their lovemaking beyond his wildest dreams. It also took her demands to new heights. "Take what you made in the lab one step further, and give me a sample that is live," she ordered, gyrating over him while teasing his cock to new ecstasies. "I'll go public with it, and the revelation will so shock the world that government leaders will have no choice but to enforce better safeguards."

Secretly he'd scoffed at this grandiose proclamation, just as he had at all her other jingoistic pronouncements in the past. Whatever she'd been doing with the information he'd given her, her cause hadn't made a single headline with it. Not that he cared. His own cause—to have her whenever he could—remained his first priority.

"For that prize, I would award you with the biggest orgasm of your life," she'd continued, purring into his ear, and he readily agreed.

When he spotted his bus pulling away from its stop up ahead, the prospect of her fulfilling that promise tonight spurred him on to such an uncharacteristic burst of speed he overtook it in time to clamber aboard.

The plant housing his lab sat in an acre of floodlit lawns, shrubs, and trees located at the edge of town about a kilometer from where the public transit routes ended. The building itself was a single-story, windowless sprawling structure covered in beige aluminum siding and topped off by a roof bristling with vents. The grounds bordered a farmer's field at the back and looked out on an oversize iron gateway in the front. A modest sign attached to the bars read AGRITERRE INC, the sight of which always brought a cynical smile to Gaston's lips. The locals still believed the company developed fertilizer products to increase crop yields—a clever distortion of the truth that the managers of the place took great pains to preserve. Since the company's inception, they'd imposed a strict code of secrecy on the staff and enforced it with the threat of stiff fines.

Standing in the mist under the surveillance of an overhead video camera, he got out his pass card, slipped it into the automatic lock of the gate, and let himself through. Walking up the path leading to the main door, he felt the particles of moisture in the air cool against his face and found the sensation soothing. Inside, the lone security guard who'd drawn the bad luck to be working on this unique night in history wished him *bonne année*. Gaston returned the greeting, signed in, and went on to his office without explanation. The nature of his work had everyone used to his comings and goings at all hours.

He unlocked his desk and took out the computer disk that explained the method behind what he'd done. This copy was for Ingrid. Then he stepped into the lab and found the vial of the substance itself, which he'd secreted away in a specimen refrigerator amongst some other work handled only by him. The clear tube contained an opaque liquid that looked like little more than watery milk, yet he knew it could possibly change the world. For once, Ingrid's hyperbole might not be so off the mark, he thought. If this time she really did expose what he gave her to the media, its revelation would probably shock legislators into regulating genetic vectors just as she claimed, not that he cared.

And Agriterre Incorporated, he knew, would go berserk. Even when he'd first started passing information to Ingrid, he'd understood it was the sort of company that tried to send whistle-blowers to jail. In this incidence especially, if they traced the source of the leak back to him, the company lawyers would have a clear-cut case for charging him with theft. But recently he'd taken a special precaution that would give him the bargaining power he'd need to avoid prison if he ever got caught. Taiwan and Oahu. Those two words involved the part of the secret he hadn't revealed to anyone, not even Ingrid. And Agriterre, along with its parent company, Biofeed International, would agree to anything, he knew, to keep it that way. The thought of a letter he'd composed and left in the safekeeping of his notary—to be sent to Dr. Kathleen Sullivan in the event of his arrest—gave him comfort as he left the facility and headed for the place where he knew Ingrid would be waiting.

Construction of the Rodez cathedral began in the first part of the last millennium and had taken four centuries to complete. Nearly the size of Notre-Dame in Paris, it dominates to this day the town that has built up around its base over the centuries. Even viewed from a distance, the spired edifice appears enormous as it sits atop a gentle hill, the houses and shops with their tiny upright chimneys huddled around its skirts like reaching children.

Stepping inside the gloom of its interior, he found this grandeur to be haughty and arrogant, designed to make the supplicant feel cowed when looking up into the dim recesses and vaulted ceilings. He shivered as the cold dampness from above descended on him, until it clung like a clammy shroud, chilling him far more within this house of God than he'd felt without. What light he saw came from the hundreds of candles that flickered everywhere—on the altar, beside the confessionals, and in the dozens of side chapels where a few people huddled in prayer. The dark rows of pews were empty, as much as he could make them out, for they receded into the blackness at the back of the church. He walked along a side aisle toward this dark section, thinking that if Ingrid was hiding anywhere, it would probably be there. His steps echoed on the stone slabs which composed the floor, the sound blending with the hushed murmurs of prayer and an occasional muffled cough.

She'd always warned him that if she ever felt it unsafe to meet at his apartment, the cathedral would be where he'd find her. "It's the perfect place for a person to sit alone in the dark, or two people to huddle together and whisper, with no one thinking it odd," she'd once told him in all sincerity. He'd found it all rather melodramatic, yet he began to worry about what had set her off tonight. Not because he really believed that they were in any immediate danger— that would come once she went public—but because at other times when she'd been afraid of being followed, she'd cut short their time at his apartment, foregoing the sex. She better not pull that shit tonight, he thought, suddenly growing angry. He'd protested on some of the other evenings when she'd tried to leave early, and occasionally she'd relented, insisting they at least get away from his building. Then he'd had her in out-of-the-way places—back alleys, parks, anywhere there were shadows—and the furtiveness had seemed to excite her more. The memory of her at those times caused his loins to stir again.

He'd strolled nearly three-quarters of the way down the length of the church—a distance of over a hundred meters—when he passed a large alcove situated behind wrought-iron bars but with its gate ajar. A good-size area, it contained a large ancient confessional off in one corner, and at its center stood a table with two chairs. Here the light became particularly dim, and massive columns on either side of the recess obscured the sight lines to and from the rest of the church. The sign over a receptacle for offerings read CHAPEL OF RECONCILIATION.

Exactly the kind of place Ingrid would choose, he thought, pausing with his hand on the bars while wondering if he should check farther back still. But all he could see in those shadows was a collection of raised, ancient stone crypts, their covers supporting full-sized statues, presumably of the holy men whose remains lay within, and some scaffolding where renovations to a crumbling wall were under way.

He decided to look there anyway, thinking she might be hiding behind one of the tombs, when he caught the scent and froze. Though faint, it was definitely her perfume. TABOO, the label had read. Over the months since he'd given it to her, it had become an aphrodisiac to him, and already half aroused, he found that even such a dilute trace of it made him fully erect and ready for her in seconds.

Controlling his breathing, he remembered how once he'd caught a whiff of some other brand on her hips. He'd driven himself crazy, imagining other men giving her such gifts and plying her body. But he'd never dared ask about her other lovers. Shoving all such torments out of his head, he'd thought only, Tonight she is mine.

Yet, where was she?

He stepped briskly toward the above-ground graves, but immediately all hint of her aroma vanished. He returned to the chapel gate where he caught it again, yet the alcove remained empty. He looked around for any other place she might be concealing herself, seeing nothing.

He pulled open the gate and went inside. The traces this time filled his nostrils with an authority that made his heart quicken. They became even stronger as he approached the wooden confessional. Made of dark mahogany, it consisted of two side compartments and a much wider central chamber for the priest. The air intoxicated him now, as he reached to open the middle door.

Enough light spilled into the darkened interior that he could see her sitting sideways on a bench seat, naked, hugging her long legs to her breasts and smiling at him. "What took you so long, my love, and what do you have for me?" she whispered.

He stepped inside, pulling the door shut behind him. The side grates through which the priest would normally speak let in sufficient illumination that he could still see her eyes sparkle as she reached for him and made him bend toward her. "I asked what you had for me," she repeated into his ear.

He'd carried the vial in a bag, to keep it cool in the night air. He took it, along with the computer disk in his jacket pocket and tucked both items among the folds of her clothes, which she'd placed in a neat pile off to one side.

"What if a priest had come?" he asked her as she stood and started undoing his belt buckle.

"I would have heard his confession."

When his pants were around his feet, she turned her back to him and ground her hips into his groin. Spreading her legs, bending forward, and extending her arms to lean on the bench, she cooed, "This is how we'll do it here." Deftly arching her back, she reached a hand between her legs and glided him into her. Excitedly he grabbed her rear and started to thrust, but she shoved against him, until her hips had him pinned against the door. "You don't move," she commanded softly.

When he went still she began to pump him, slowly, expertly, and ever so silently. It was all he could do to control his breathing so as not to make any noise. Just as he felt about to climax, she'd stop her movements, wait, and then start again. She repeated the process several times until he thought he'd faint. "Lean forward, my love. You mustn't fall now," she quietly advised, as if she knew the dizzy state she'd aroused him to.

He shifted his weight, placing his hands above her on the back wall of the booth for support. She proceeded to grind him again, but this time with an urgency that told him she would finally let him come. As he surrendered to her control and she brought him ever closer to his release, he barely noticed the door behind him slowly open. The change in light ultimately caught his eye, yet even when he started to turn his head, he got barely a glimpse of the shadowy figures outside the confessional. *My God, the priests have found us,* he thought in the seconds before one of the intruders grabbed him from behind and snapped his neck with a vicious twist.

As she savored his final spasms, Ingrid smiled and murmured, "Your biggest yet, my love, exactly as I promised."

The Plaza Hotel, New York

"Happy New Year, Kathleen," Steve Patton said, raising his champagne glass as revelers all around them blew party horns, threw streamers, and showered the gilded ballroom with confetti.

"Really, Steve?"

"Of course."

"But that depends partially on you."

"What do you mean?"

"I can't continue the way we've been."

He froze, still holding his drink toward her.

"I'm just not able to compartmentalize sex the way you do," she continued. "That's not a criticism. It's simply that I don't have it in me to be one of your string of women. It messes me up."

He looked at her as if she were speaking a foreign tongue.

"You didn't do anything wrong, Steve," she added. "You are what you are, an elegant rascal and a wonderful lover. What you gave me this last year was exactly what I needed, in a raw sort of way, but now I must move on with my life. I guess I'm old-fashioned enough to require more from a man. Above all, I don't want to lose you as a friend, and it's vital we remain close colleagues, especially now, with so much important work to be done—"

He silenced her with a finger to her lips. "Kathleen, I'd welcome a chance to be the man who gives you more. I just thought you wanted room and no commitments. My affairs are dalliances, marvelous interludes between me and consenting women that harm no one, and I don't apologize for them. But never think what I have with you is so casual. You're my best friend, and this past year I've felt like the luckiest man alive." He took her hand. "Let's you and I move in together."

She pulled back. "Steve, you're kidding me."

"I had liaisons because they fit my lifestyle. On the road, traveling around the country, and living most of the year in hotel rooms. My work, I always figured, made it impossible to have anything with a woman. You changed all that, Kathleen."

"Steve, what are you saying?"

"Come back to my apartment and let me show you."

He made love to her that night with more intensity and passion than she'd ever known from him. His fierceness liberated her, igniting a shamelessness that she abandoned herself to as she sat astride him and brought them both to the limits of their pleasure, held them there, quivering on the edge, until their ecstasy ebbed enough that she could resume the rhythmic moves and repeat the deliciously slow ascent.

Then his phone rang. To her surprise he answered, yet motioned her to continue.

She hesitantly went on with her movements, suddenly feeling shy about being overheard.

"Hello," he said in that familiar husky voice, raising his hips and thrusting deeper into her, making her let out a moan in spite of her sudden self-consciousness. Grinning mischievously, he arched higher just as he said, "Why Mandy, Happy New Year to you, too." She felt him throbbing inside her, urgent and imploring.

At first she hesitated, then thought, What if Mandy is the one who was with him the other night? A delicious excitement flooded through her, releasing an impulse to let the woman know what it felt like to be listening at the other end of the phone, and she ground into Patton, withholding nothing, determined to take him to climax in earshot of her rival. This time it was his turn to moan. He let the receiver fall onto the bed, grabbed her buttocks, and they both came noisily together. She then collapsed onto his chest, giggling and thinking, Take that, Mandy, whoever you are.

An hour later as she rode home in a cab, she felt shaken by what she'd done and the feelings she'd experienced. On one level it had been fun, but on another, her electric response to his kinkiness disturbed her, and the prospect of where such games might lead left her uneasy. Though she probably meant more to Steve than she suspected, he was what he was, she told herself, a womanizer, perfect for a "marvelous interlude," but not much more. Despite his outrageous offer that they live together, she knew she could never expect better than being number one in his string, the way she had been tonight. And that could become a kind of control, especially when fueled by jealousy, she realized, thinking of his eagerness to play Mandy and her against each other. She'd no illusions that his being with the others, especially if she continued to care for him, would make her far unhappier than it already had and eventually consume her. Revulsed by the pall of such sexual masochism, she shuddered, watching the slick blackness of the millennium's first morning slide by outside the window, and renewed her determination to break off with him. Lisa's right. I deserve better.

When she got out of the cab at her apartment in the East Village, a cool drizzle tingled against her cheeks. It felt like a cleansing shower.

5

Steele's first days of convalescence didn't go too badly, for no other reason than the doctors and Martha had laid out his every move in a schedule. Between his twice-a-day walks with regular half-block increases, his carefully planned meals three times a day, and all his follow-up visits for tests and checkups he'd had little time to think, which was fine by him.

Except at night. Then he mostly sat in the living room, staring at the grand piano and nursing a tumbler of scotch. No need to worry about my breath in the morning, he told himself as he switched back from vodka.

"It doesn't say anything about continuing with alcohol on these sheets of instructions you brought home," Martha pointed out, scowling at him and shoving the papers in his face after he'd been home a few days.

"Two drinks a day, Martha. It's good for the heart. Been in all the medical journals for years," he declared, raising the amber fluid in a toast.

"Oh, really. Then you should have already had the healthiest heart in the land." Without waiting for an answer, she huffed out of the room and headed off to bed, muttering, "And did they mention the *size* of the glass by any chance?"

The piano had been Luana's. Whether playing professionally for choirs, teaching at schools, or giving private lessons, she'd possessed a boundless passion for music all her life, including a dream to some-day take a master's program for concert pianists. When diagnosed with inoperable cancer of the pancreas, prognosis six months, she immediately signed up to take the audition she'd so often postponed. "At least I'll know if I'm good enough," she explained, submerging herself in the hours of daily practice necessary to prepare her presentation piece—Mozart's Piano Concerto no. 20.

Steele had found the urgency of the playing nearly impossible to bear. Each note, exquisitely poignant to the point of pain, seemed to tick off how little time she had left. As the date of the competition approached, she became too weak to sit at the bench for long periods, and his despair for her deepened. She nevertheless persisted, resting between segments of the score and insisting that he make a tape of her playing. On her behalf he submitted the recording to the judges, along with a letter from her doctor attesting that, for medical reasons, she could not perform in person. A week later she received a telegram announcing that they'd accepted her, conditional on her being well enough to attend classes.

The flash of pride he'd witnessed in her gaunt eyes at that moment seemed as much for her spirit's triumph over the cancer, despite its destruction of her body, as for her musical victory. When he tried to tell her how much he loved her and that he felt in awe of her courage, she smiled.

"I'm proud of me, too, and that makes me feel sexy," she'd said. "Come here," and she pulled him weakly to her for what would turn out to be the last time they made love.

The day she'd died he shut and locked the keyboard cover. She wouldn't want him to, he knew, but the thought of hearing anyone else play the instrument she'd poured her soul into proved too much for him.

One night Martha asked, "Do you want me to sell it? It's morbid how you sit and look at it all the time."

"No!" he'd snapped.

She never raised the subject again.

"Returning to Daily Activity" was what doctors called the portion of the printed schedule that allowed him more and more leeway. In his case it left him knowing less and less what to do with himself. As a

result, he resorted to dropping by the hospital, hoping to chat with colleagues and get caught up on the institutional gossip with the staff of his own ER. At first they welcomed him with open arms.

"Thank God you're all right."

"We sure miss you!"

"But we'll scrape by until you're back."

When he started checking files, hovering over physicians' shoulders, and giving unwanted second opinions, he quickly became such a nuisance that eyeballs shot skyward at the mere sight of him.

"Dr. Steele, you're here again?"

"We're managing okay, really."

"Excuse me, Richard. Gotta run."

He ended up spending his afternoons strolling in Central Park instead, trying to find warmth in the thin sunshine of midwinter. Failing that, he added a detour to his excursions, dropping by a bar in the Plaza Hotel with an armload of newspapers for a drink. By week's end, the waiters considered him a regular and even knew his name.

At home, relations between him and Chet remained as strained as ever. It seemed the boy couldn't get out of the house fast enough as he headed off to school each morning. When Steele did get up sufficiently early to join him for breakfast, the teenager hurriedly gulped the remainder of his food in sullen silence, making it evident that he preferred his father's absence. Evenings proved no better. The boy routinely arranged to do his homework at a friend's house, and if father and son did encounter each other at supper, the meal became a repeat of breakfast, Chet staying at the table only as long as it took for him to wolf down Martha's excellent cooking.

"If it wasn't for his appetite and your culinary skills, I'd never see him at all," Steele lamented as he and Martha finished supper one evening after the boy had gone off as usual.

"I'll keep making the meals to get him here. Getting him to talk, you'll have to do on your own."

"And how do I accomplish that?"

"With more of what you said to him in ICU."

"He spoke with you about that?"

"Yeah. And he also wanted to know if I thought you meant it."

"Oh, my God!"

"I told him, 'Of course, he did,' but Chet needs to hear it from you."

An hour later Steele had already poured himself his drink and sunk into the overstuffed cushions on the sofa, settling in for his nightly brood, when the doorbell rang.

"I'll get it," Martha called out cheerfully. "I forgot to tell you. Your friend Greg Stanton called this afternoon and asked if it would be all right to drop in. I told him, 'Sure, come ahead.' That you'd be glad to see him."

Over the years he'd learned for certain that the woman never forgot anything. "Martha!" he exclaimed sharply. "You deliberately didn't mention it."

"Now, why would I do that?" she called over her shoulder, her voice filling with innocent surprise as she made her way to the door.

Because maybe you figured I wouldn't let anyone, not even an old buddy like Greg, interrupt my nightly feeling sorry for myself, thought Steele, growing surlier by the second.

The tall man who strode into the room wore an immaculate dark suit with a gray shirt and charcoal tie. He also looked fit and lean. Even with frizzy blond hair retreating to the sides of his bare scalp, he appeared younger than Steele, though the two were approximately the same age. My friend, as usual you have the appearance of a vain man, thought Steele, feeling particularly mean-spirited.

Steele had always found him a bit fanatical about looking good. When they'd first met in medical school, Greg had been an avid swimmer, not so much to keep in shape or to win races, but to have a six pack of muscles on his stomach when he took off his shirt. He became even more obsessed about training when he prematurely lost his hair. "Hey, possession of a flat tummy is the only way I can keep my youthful looks," he often joked.

"That and great sex," his wife, Cindy, usually chimed in.

He'd added the high-priced suits to his routine after he'd become dean.

Steele, getting to his feet, absently patted the beginnings of the paunch he'd acquired since leaving work and smoothed his rumpled jersey. "You're looking great and dressed to the nines, like always, Greg. Even seeing you makes me feel dissolute."

"Hi, Richard," his friend greeted warmly. "Is that why you stopped answering my messages? I promise to get fat, if it will do any good."

Steele winced at the barb. It jolted him into admitting he'd been deliberately thinking the worst of the guy, all part of his ongoing campaign to hold anyone who made him remember happier times when Luana was still alive at arm's length. Greg Stanton he'd worked particularly hard to avoid.

The man had tried more than anyone to be there for him when she died. That hadn't surprised Steele. As far back as when they were students together he'd been quick to offer moral support, his acerbic wit and love of excellence a perfect tonic against the discouragement all doctors in training fight off from time to time. Nor was it just as classmates they'd been close. After Steele's marriage to Luana, Greg and Cindy, both outgoing, quickly made her one of their friends, which led to the four of them spending joyous times together. Following the arrival of children on the scene, Greg's two daughters, several years younger than Chet, became like sisters to the boy, and he adored playing older brother to them. Devastated as they all were by Luana's death, Greg and Cindy rallied around Steele and Chet, doing their best to comfort them. But Steele, hell-bent on shutting out all memories of what he'd lost, declined their many efforts to be with him, first rebuffing their overtures with repeated pleas of being too busy—then not returning their calls at all. Eventually Cindy, then Greg, stopped phoning.

"Why don't you call *them*?" Martha had suggested exasperatedly.

Because they finally got the message to leave me alone, he'd thought to himself, immersed in one of his better wallows.

Yes, Greg Stanton was a vain man, but he'd also been the best buddy Steele ever had. "Sorry, Greg. I've been an ass," he replied, snapping himself out of such painful recollections. "I simply felt too embarrassed, still being so screwed up, especially after all you and Cindy did for me—"

"Hey, I didn't come over to help you feel guilty," he interrupted with a dismissive wave of his hand. "That you can do well enough on your own time. The fact is, I'm here in a professional capacity as your dean. I need a favor, for the faculty. I want you to take on a special assignment."

His abruptness threw Steele off guard. Having been expecting, and dreading, the man's sympathy, he found his phrase *special assignment* intriguing, doubly so since Greg, Dean of Medicine, spoke as his ultimate boss. All resentment at being ambushed in his own home quickly changed to curiosity. "Oh?" he replied. "Have a seat, and how about a drink?"

Greg nudged his brow up a notch, eyeing the oversized concoction in Steele's hand. "I'm not that thirsty, thanks," he said, and then perched on the edge of an easy chair, quickly coming to the point of his visit. "The UN is hosting an international conference about three and a half months from now, in early May, on the risks to human health of genetically modified food. I've been asked to designate a physician to accompany the American contingent. I'd like you for the job."

Steele's initial tingle of excitement vanished. "That stuff's all about plants for Christ's sake," he protested, dismayed that Greg had even approached him with the offer. "It's for horticulturists or botanists, not doctors!"

"It's about food, Richard! Food that we all eat, including our kids."

"So get a dietitian," he retorted, increasingly certain he caught a whiff of charity behind the proposal.

Leaning forward Greg nailed Steele with a hard blue stare. "Don't be so dismissive. The trouble with the delegation is that it's already top-heavy with plant experts, bench scientists, and food specialists." He paused, pursing his lips, as if unsure of what to say next. "I can't make any public pronouncements because I've no hard evidence," he continued, lowering his voice as if sharing a confidence, "but this stuff scares me. Hell, I think it should scare all physicians. Now, don't think that I expect you to simply take my word for it. Look up what's on the Internet about genetically modified organisms, and educate yourself. If by tomorrow you aren't as alarmed as I am, then I'll send someone else. One way or another, I'm going to have a top clinician at the conference, and you can rest assured that's why I came to you—not because you're sidelined or I took pity on your sorry ass."

Steele started, taken off guard by Greg's mind reading.

"Face it, Richard!" his friend went on, sounding impatient. "Despite the hole you've dug for yourself and your cutting off from everyone, there are some of us who still think you could be mighty useful to your profession. Now, if you'll excuse me, it's been a long day, and I've got to get home to Cindy and the girls." He got to his feet, and before Steele could utter a word, added, "By the way, if you can stand more bad news, they'd still really like to see you, and, of course, Chet. They feel you've abandoned them, and frankly, I'm tired of making excuses for you." Without waiting for a reply, he pivoted and strode out the door.

Steele sat staring at the piano for a long time, hardly touching his drink and feeling as if Greg had dumped a bucket of ice water on his head. "Guess I'm out of danger for being pitied," he muttered, finally getting up off the couch and heading for the den, where he and Chet shared a computer. Laying aside his scotch and pulling up a chair, he logged on to the Internet, entering *genetically modified organisms* into the search engine. The screen informed him that there were over five thousand entries on the topic. Better narrow it down, he thought, adding the proviso *danger to human health*. That gave him only half as many items to choose from.

He immediately saw that a lot of these were declarations from environmental groups involving catchy headlines and little science. *Frankenstein Foods, Deadly Digestions, The New Killer Tomatoes*—the Web page titles made him chuckle. Some had clever artwork, mimicking horror movies from the fifties. Others mocked the advertising of brand-name food products, showing such icons as a familiar but sickly cartoon lion offering some dubious green-looking cereal, the contents of the box reading like a chemistry set.

At the opposite end of the spectrum he found impossibly mundane articles documenting how plants, immunized with genes from such esoteric organisms as the cowpea chlorotic mottle virus, could pass the new genetic material on to any other microbe that happened to be living in their stems or leaves. Who cares, thought Steele, until he clicked on a link to *horizontal gene transfer*. The article that popped up drove home why so many scientists were focused on the process.

If we modify the genes of a plant or animal, there is abundant evidence that the altered genetic material will also pass to potential human viruses, bacteria, parasites, or insect tick vectors living on that host. There are also studies which suggest that ordinary animals ingesting such genetically altered plants might acquire these same man-made strands of DNA through the gut into their bloodstream. This is particularly worrisome, since it evokes a scenario where a so-called normal animal could introduce genetic vectors into any microorganisms residing in its gut or circulating throughout its body.

Steele immediately thought of animal species known to be reservoirs of human pathogens, such as cattle with TB, rodents with hantavirus, or deer carrying ticks loaded with the spirochete that causes Lyme disease. The idea of these lethal organisms having a DNA makeover gave him the creeps.

He scrolled further, skimming through the summaries of other scientific papers that supported these claims.

Ingested foreign DNA survives transiently in the gastrointestinal tract and enters the bloodstream; DNA ingested by mice reaches peripheral leukocytes, spleen, liver, and gonads via intestinal wall mucosa; we become what we eat.

Wait a minute, he thought. The implication here is that the DNA in what we ingest could end up as part of our own genetic structure. But if so, it's been happening since the dawn of time. Why the fuss now? Reflexively, he began critiquing the article the way he would his own medical journals. Then he read the author's real concern—how the vectors themselves could be changing an ancient phenomenon for the worse.

> Until now, evolution and time have screened the DNA we've been exposed to. Genetically altered foods, on the other hand, subject our systems to man-made strands of nucleic acids that have never existed in nature, that are designed to jump species barriers, and that may have totally unknown long-term effects. In fact, these artificial vectors, meant to overrule existing natural barriers to horizontal gene transfer, may be sidestepping a system of checks and balances that has regulated such "jumps" in our favor for millions of years.

Totally absorbed now, he started poring over more recent publications, growing ever more uneasy. He first read that a group of scientists in Norway fed laboratory rats potatoes that had been genetically modified to produce lectin, a substance intended to increase the plant's resistance to worms and insects. The rats lost weight, the lectin bound itself to their white cells, and their T-cell counts went up, a reaction suggesting some sort of immune response. The authors blamed it on the genetically modified food. Critics of the study claimed the rats might have lost weight and shown an immune response because they were malnourished, there having been no protein added to an exclusively starch diet. Both sides, however, suggested that further studies be done with better controls on all the variables before the product be released into the food chain.

What utterly flabbergasted Steele were the follow-up stories. The scientists who'd released the initial data lost their jobs, no one attempted to repeat the study, and the editor of the journal that had published the work became the target of heavy criticism by prominent spokespersons in the bioengineering industry. To her credit, she subsequently issued an eloquent rebuttal defending her decision "*to favor debate over the suppression of information.*"

Right on, thought Steele, cheering the beleaguered woman for sticking to her guns.

Continuing to punch up articles, he soon found himself veering more and more into the political landscape of the issue. A broad trend in North America quickly became clear to him—the voice of commerce and industry had seized control of the debate. *"There is no established proof that genetically modified foods are harmful to human health,"* he saw quoted over and over by various experts with economic interests in the business. *"So there is absolutely no justification for controls that might restrict our right to trade in the product."*

Just like the tobacco industry used to say, thought Steele.

Some scientists, clearly a minority voice in this corner of the globe, gave the obvious reply, *"There hasn't been time yet to see what the side effects may be,"* but few public figures seemed to pay heed. One suggestion he found particularly ingenious appeared on the *Environment Watch* Web page for public radio.

Prominent geneticist and media personality Dr. Kathleen Sullivan suggests using polymerase chain reaction techniques, or PCR, to check the plant life around any lab using genetic vectors, to see if any contamination of the local environment has occurred.

Sounds like a good idea to me, he agreed.

Next, flashing ahead through a series of newspaper articles, he learned that both the Republicans and Democrats favored the economic prospects of bioengineering—each side wanted to develop the technology at home as well as export it around the planet—and that hundreds of billions of dollars were at stake. He also saw, not surprisingly, that the two parties received hefty contributions from all the players in the industry, the biggest names coughing up equal amounts to each side of the political equation. Skimming further, he began to realize that one company's name dominated all the rest—Biofeed International.

Shoving back his chair and stretching the fatigue out of his back, he grabbed a pad and pencil to make notes as he thought over all that he'd read. He soon came to three conclusions. First, the United States appeared to be fighting tooth and nail to avoid tighter controls on the business of genetically modifying organisms and the commercialization of making genes jump the species barrier. Second, given the many examples he'd just seen of possible unintended consequences from the technology, the prospects for a significant mistake harmful to humans were staggering. Third, if a serious error ever did occur, there would be no undoing it or recalling the mistake, the way a company pulls a defective product or the Food and Drug Administration bans medication that turns out to have unexpected and dangerous side effects. Instead, the fault would be indelibly incorporated into the victim's genome. Nor would it end with him or her, if reproductive tissues—ova and spermatocytes—were involved, and if the host lived long enough to reproduce offspring.

"Holy shit!" Steele uttered under his breath, incredulous that such a potential catastrophe for humankind had been unfolding in his own country and that he could, along with most everyone else it seemed, be completely oblivious to it. "You weren't kidding, Greg. This stuff *is* scary."

He glanced at the time indicated on the corner of the computer screen and was surprised to see that it was nearly two A.M. Four hours had slipped by without his noticing. Even his drink sat untouched where he'd left it. He hadn't become so absorbed in anything since Luana died.

He picked up the brochure for the conference that Greg had left him. He immediately recognized the moderator's name, Dr. Kathleen Sullivan, from the *Environment Watch* page he'd read earlier. He also recalled having seen the woman's TV program a few years ago and being suitably impressed by her imaginative thinking. I'll look forward to talking with her, he thought, already having decided to attend. Only then did he notice the locale of the meeting— Hawaii.

He was about to switch off the computer when another title

caught his attention: *Identification of a Brazil-Nut Allergen in Transgenic Soybeans.*

The next time he looked up from his reading it was dawn.

"Dad?"

"Morning, Chet," Steele greeted across the top of a steaming mug of coffee. Rather than go to bed, he'd showered, dressed, and, after solving the idiosyncrasies of Martha's percolator, made enough brew to supply an ER shift. Seated at the kitchen table, waiting for his son to get up, he'd already sipped his way through a third of the pot.

The boy glanced at his watch and declared, "You're awake early." It sounded like an accusation.

Steele experienced the same giddy hesitation he often felt at the start of a resuscitation when, standing poised over the near dead patient, he sized up what had to be done and readied himself for the feat to come. Except in ER he had a practiced technique to call upon, and in that shining instant he could always replace doubt with a plan before plunging into action. Facing his son in an attempt to reanimate their moribund relationship, he had only his instincts to fall back on, and they were rusted with disuse. "Actually I've been up all night," he began. "Please sit down. I want to talk."

Chet immediately furrowed his young brow. "Why? What's the matter?" he demanded, continuing to stand.

Steele pursed his lips a few times, as if his mouth needed warming up to form the words he wanted to say. " 'What's the matter' is that I made you a promise in the hospital, and I've been slow to keep it. I want to apologize."

The teenager deepened his frown, but remained silent.

Oh, boy, thought Steele, wishing Martha would appear and coach him about how to do this. After all, wasn't it her idea? "If you'll let me, I really do want to be your daddy again."

Chet recoiled from his side of the table, twisting up his face as if he'd just bitten into a lemon. "Da-ad!" he protested, managing to give the word two syllables. He shifted his weight restlessly from one leg to the other.

"It's okay, son. I won't embarrass you anymore. Just know that I love you, and I'll try not to be such a jerk around here. If I am, give me a quick kick in the ass, will you?"

The strain in Chet's features slowly dissolved into a look of disbelief. "Have you spent all night thinking up this corny, sugar-coated crap? Jesus!"

Ouch, thought Steele, feeling his frustration mount. "Come on, sit down," he persisted, hoping to exert the same calming influence on his son that he could routinely cast over an entire ER in the worst of crises. "I admit I'm awkward at this. Maybe one reason it sounds so strange is that we haven't really talked in a long time—"

"And who's fault is that?" Chet snapped.

"Mine," replied Steele softly, his gaze never wavering from his son.

The admission seemed to leave the boy at a loss for words. He flushed and then swallowed repeatedly, as if something got stuck in his throat.

"Your mother could put feelings into words," continued Steele. "I suck at it, I admit. But that doesn't mean we can't try, even if we are hokey and clumsy at it. After all, you and I—we're the only family each of us has—"

"Don't you think I know all this!" Chet cried. "Jeeesus, you still treat me like a little kid. And it was Mom who made us a family—she knew how. You *never* will!" He angrily shouldered his schoolbag, grabbed a couple of yogurts from the refrigerator, and stomped out of the house.

"Jeeeesus!" muttered Steele, stretching out the profanity long enough to top his son by at least a syllable.

"You have it?" the man asked, the minute Morgan answered the phone.

"Yes, she delivered it safely last night, as soon as she got off the plane from Marseille."

"And what's the latest word on the police over there?"

"From what she reported, everything seems to be going our way. The authorities are treating it as if Pierre Gaston simply ran off. His landlady confirmed that he'd been seeing a rather glamorous-looking woman over the last year. You know the French—they are assuming that it's an affair of the heart and that he's in hiding somewhere to avoid an angry husband."

"What if they find the body?"

"That, I'm assured, is highly unlikely."

The caller thought this over in silence. "Still, it was an all too risky operation, in any case," he said after a moment. "We can't afford any more moves like that. Tell your 'messenger' to advise her boss."

"I'm not telling that woman anything. Some of her crew described to me how she actually offed Gaston. She may be a looker, but she enjoys what she does a little too much for my liking. Besides, she had a message for you."

"What's that?"

"Her boss is still impatient."

6

Five Weeks Later, Tuesday, February 29, 2000, 1:00 A.M.

Morgan felt his stomach lurch to the back of his throat as the helicopter tipped forward and plunged down into the darkness, throwing him against his harness. "Shit! I told you, no cowboy crap," he yelled into the microphone of his headset.

The man beside him replied by whipping the joystick left and slamming the craft through a turn that would have done a roller coaster proud. Just as abruptly, he pulled up, flashing a grin in the gloom of the cockpit and sending the maneuverable unlit craft skimming over the tops of what should be their target, a field of two-week-old feed corn. He flipped a switch, and a spotlight from under the fuselage illuminated sprouts barely inches high laid out in long tightly knit rows like braids, not fifteen feet beneath them. Hitting the release for the specially adapted spray tanks bolted to the underside of the fuselage, he lowered a pair of fourteen-foot nozzles that trailed under them like the legs of a giant insect, brushing the tops of the fledgling plants as they went. After peering repeatedly out his side window with his night goggles, he said through the headset radio, "I can't see anything visible streaming out behind us. It's like we're not dropping a load at all. What is this stuff?"

Morgan, busily swallowing to keep from throwing up, indicated he couldn't reply for the moment. Waiting for his stomach to settle, he studied his illicitly acquired map of Biofeed's massive farming operation along the Red River in southern Oklahoma and fretted that they might not be in the right place. The document clearly indicated the acreage where a new fast-growing feed corn had been planted, but he'd no idea if the yahoo beside him had followed the coordinates properly. Not having thought to provide himself with the same night-vision gear the pilot wore, he could see precious little outside the windows to help him get his bearings, especially since they'd timed the flight to occur in the maximum darkness with a minimum of moonlight.

When his stomach seemed calm enough that he could talk without gagging, he considered his words carefully. In planning tonight's operation, he'd decided to keep all the technical explanations as close to the truth as possible, to make sure the man at the stick understood enough detail not to take any disastrous shortcuts that would blow the whole mission. "They're microscopic gold particles shot out at extremely high velocity, designed to pierce the waxy surface of the plant's foliage and allow access of what comes next."

"Won't the farmworkers see the holes?"

"Not with the naked eye."

"And the part that comes next—the stuff in the tank car?"

"That's an industrial secret."

"Hey, I don't have to haul what I don't know."

Morgan pretended to mull over whether to entrust him with the information. "It's a new kind of insecticide and fertilizer," he lied, hoping he had just the right amount of reluctance in his voice. "That's all I can tell you, except that it's no more dangerous than the usual organic phosphates you deal with. Use the same precautions, and you'll be all right."

That seemed to satisfy him, for he returned his attention to the hoses below.

Morgan sat in silence, staring into the night, uncomfortably aware of how close they were to the ground as they skimmed along. While scouting the site last fall, he'd hung out in a lot of cafés asking farmers about which crop duster had the most experience and the least fear of flying low. The search brought him to Mike Butkis, the bald, tattooed middle-aged daredevil at the controls by his side.

"I've flown all terrains in every copter known to man, from gun ships in Vietnam to the little mosquitoes used by drug lords and munitions runners in the jungles of South America," he'd boasted at their first meeting.

Could be our man, Morgan had thought, buying him a beer. "We're testing new products for Biofeed International all across the southern states," he told the pilot by way of explaining what had to be done. "Except it's what scientists call a double blind trial. We have to apply the substances in secret to specified fields at night. That way evaluators trying to identify noticeable differences between treated and untreated crops at the end of the growing season won't know beforehand which is which, and will render an unbiased judgment."

Butkis hadn't seemed to care. "How much?" he drawled, downing his drink. Within minutes he agreed to a huge retainer that bought both his services and a promise that he'd keep his mouth shut.

Morgan continued to stare into the blackness ahead, gripping the armrests each time a tendril of mist hurtled at him out of the night. He felt no more at ease than when they first started, and kept expecting a building or tree to loom up in their path, despite knowing that Butkis's view was nearly clear as day. "Next time you get me a pair of those goggles as well," he ordered the pilot through the microphone. "It's nervewracking, not being able to see a goddamn thing."

"Oh, my God! A house!" shrieked Butkis, lurching them upward a few feet with a sharp jerk on the controls.

Morgan's heart did the bunny thump inside his chest, until he heard Butkis's cackling laugh in his headset and realized it had been a prank. "You shithead! That's not funny!" he screamed.

A few hours later they'd finished preparing the fields to be sprayed and landed by the isolated rail siding on which the tank car rested. Butkis, wearing the industrial gas mask and protective rubber clothing he usually donned when handling insecticides, attached the appropriate hoses and began pumping the contents of the railway car to the containers on the helicopter. Even though the machine could heft three hundred gallons at a time and spray up to thirty gallons a minute, Morgan had calculated it would still take ten nights before they covered all the acreage to be done here.

In his briefcase he carried the telephone numbers of the six pilots whom he'd recruited in addition to Butkis. They were standing by, waiting for his word on how tonight's first mission went before beginning identical operations elsewhere in the country. A half dozen fully loaded railcars like this one were already in position near Biofeed sites all over the southern United States, and every week Agrenomics International sent another on its way.

Minutes later he and Butkis were once more flying across the surface of the field they'd just left. "That's more like it," the pilot commented as he activated the spray while peering through the side windows. "This stuff I can see."

Morgan sat stark still. Until now he'd been preoccupied with the logistics of pulling off their scheme, the dangers of getting caught, or the physical risks to themselves from making a mistake with what they were using. But now that he was releasing the first of their vectors—putting it irretrievably into the food chain—he became drenched in a cold sweat at the enormity of what he'd set in motion.

Not that he felt he'd suddenly discovered a conscience or experienced late-found guilt. Surely he had enough greed in him and sufficient desire for payback to overcome that kind of handicap. No, he attributed this to what he presumed a first-time killer would feel seconds after the act, that in all eternity there'd be no taking back what he'd just done. Except in this case he'd unleashed the first genetic weapon of mass destruction ever used.

He tried to drive out any thought of what would be happening below, but his mind kept racing through a past briefing session where one of the "client's" surviving technicians had zealously explained it all too well. "The naked vectors carrying the viral genes, delivered in a spray of lipid particles to keep them intact, will soon penetrate the tiny holes that the previous bombardment had produced in the cell walls of the corn seedlings. By that time these cells will have mounted an injury response, which includes the release of ligases, enzymes specialized in cutting and pasting strands of the plant's DNA as part of its repair mechanism. Except in this case, the enzymes will also cut and paste genes from the invader.

"By morning fragments of the vectors and their special cargo will be inside the nuclei of cells in the plant, ready to enter their host's genetic machinery. Here they will be read, copied, and passed on to newly formed cells as the seedlings grow, thereby creating what we call a genetic mosaic. By mid-May this new crop, already altered to mature quickly, will have produced seed and be ready for harvest months ahead of the regular feed corn. According to our inside information, Biofeed intends to promote it commercially as a fast germinator suitable for a second planting in the late spring. Farmers will undoubtedly find the prospect of doubling their yield in a season attractive and put the seeds in the ground. No one will be aware that the majority of kernels are also carrying a deadly genetic message that they will pass to the next generation of plants. By the end of summer, when the second crop matures, it will become feed not just to farm animals, but to scavengers as well—rodents, birds, even insects. We're betting that in at least one of these creatures our passenger will find what it needs to survive, establishing itself in an American host where it will replicate—just as it once found a living haven in Africa, and, over two millennia ago, we think, in Athens. Then the dying will start, except this time, it will be in the heartland of America."

"And what is this American host where it will get a foothold?" he'd asked, skeptical that the entire spiel might be more of the boastful rhetoric these people kept resorting to.

"That knowledge is our most closely guarded secret—only a handful of our leaders know it—and this is the beauty of the plan. No one on the planet besides them, not even at your all-powerful CDC in Atlanta, has ever been able to discover what this history is—despite their testing a thousand animal candidates."

"And how have you succeeded where the CDC failed?"

"Read the history of the organism. Research with it is so deadly that only a dozen facilities in the world are equipped to handle it, and only then within strict limits because of the extreme hazards involved. As a result of this temerity, the most lethal organism on the face of the earth also remains the most mysterious—its pathogenicity poorly understood, the living reservoirs where it hides between attacks unknown, and its mechanism of entry into primates an unsolved puzzle. All of which suits our purposes."

"You still haven't explained how you identified the host."

"We had far more devoted workers—virologists and geneticists willing to pay the ultimate price, not only to acquire the secrets of this perfect killer, but to identify the portion of its genetic code that produces its lethal toxins and encrypt it into a highly infective vector. Besides that, they managed to fit the hidden genes with timers and triggers by using genetic regulators—promoters and transposons, they called them. In effect, code from the virus will only activate and be completely expressed when it ends up in the presence of an enzyme unique to its natural hosts, thereby assuring it won't inadvertently interfere with the growth of the feed corn. But as soon as it arrives in the gut of an animal it could thrive in—arthropod or vertebrate—it will turn on, penetrate that host's cells, start replicating, and pour out its poisons."

"It sounds like a lot of empty gobbledygook to me. How do I know you've done any of this?"

"Look," the technician had instructed, switching on a video monitor.

Morgan shuddered in the windy confines of the cockpit, trying to bury all memory of what he had seen next. But the grainy images replayed themselves in his head anyway, as vividly as when he'd first viewed them, except they'd since become so much a part of his nightmares that he recalled them the way he dreamed—in black and white. Intended to show the genius of what their hero geneticists had developed in that faraway place, before U.S. planes bombed them and their lab to hell, the tape documented the test trials those so-called scientists had conducted and filmed. Scenes flickered before his eyes of men, women, and children squatting to shit in their jail cells, their skin covered with dark blotches while blood streamed from their noses, mouths, and rectums. Some of them stared back at the camera with incredulous looks on their faces, as if to say they couldn't yet believe the misery that had befallen them. Others moaned and writhed on the ground, stealing furtive glances at the camera, their eyes dull, black, and imploring making it seem even in their final hours they clung to the hope that someone could release them from their torment. Still others seemed to have accepted their doom, lying motionless amid their filth, occasionally blinking and looking emptily into space. Their blank expressions hung off them as flaccid as loose skin.

For the most advanced cases only their labored breathing signaled they remained alive. Bewildered children stood beside their dying parents and screamed unheeded while stretching out their tiny arms in a futile plea to be comforted. One such child, a naked little boy smeared with dark streaks of his and his mother's mess, stopped prodding the unresponsive woman's chest and tottered toward the camera. As he wailed and reached his hands through the bars to be picked up, the man filming him coldly intoned, "The major abdominal organs— liver, spleen, and to some extent the kidneys—liquefy in a matter of days. . . ."

Butkis once more banked the craft through a hard turn and sent them skimming back toward the tank car for another load. Through a break in the clouds the moon made a brief appearance and cast its shimmering light over the wet young leaves they'd just sprayed, turning the entire field silver. "Pretty, isn't it?" the pilot commented, then threw back his head and sang, "Ohhhhh-klahoma, where we drug the corn to the sky . . ."

II

spring

7

Wednesday, May 3, 2000, 2:00 P.M.
The Outskirts of Kailua

The air was absolutely still, yet Kathleen Sullivan saw a white curtain in an upstairs window shift slightly as she approached the run-down, gray stucco farmhouse. The heat baked the treeless yard, and the parched ground under her feet felt hard as concrete. What few tufts of grass remained had long turned to yellow straw. There were no dogs—she'd stayed inside her car a full minute before opening the door, making sure none would bound out at her. Nevertheless, she remained wary, walking slowly while peering nervously beyond the house, where a ramshackle barn and midsize shed leaned toward each other like two piles of bleached driftwood.

Seeing nothing, she began to suspect he had no animals at all. Neither did she catch so much as a glimpse of machinery, such as a tractor or plow. *Perhaps he no longer works the land,* she thought, eyeing the few small fields that stretched from a rickety fence in back of the barn to the steep base of the Koolau Range less than a mile away. She did spot a relatively new red pickup truck parked under a dilapidated carport, the vehicle seeming completely at odds with the impoverished appearances of the place. Then an empty, rusted-out chicken coop built alongside the tumbledown fence came into her line of sight. It commanded her attention more than anything else.

Proceeding to a faded green front door, she stared in through the grimy windowpanes that bracketed it and knocked loudly, the force of her knuckles on the wood dislodging flecks of peeling varnish from its sunburnt surface.

Only silence came from the dark interior.

She stepped back and looked up in time to witness a hand release the curtain she'd seen move a few seconds ago. "Mr. Hacket?" she called out. "My name's Dr. Sullivan. The Department of Public Health suggested I talk with you. I'm studying the bird flu outbreak that happened here eighteen months ago."

Still nothing.

Damn! she thought, wondering if she shouldn't just march over to the area around the coop, grab her samples, and leave. She'd arrived for the conference a few days early specifically to gather such specimens and collect as much data as possible about the case. She'd even arranged the use of a genetics lab in the university where she could run a polymerase chain reaction analysis on anything she turned up, all in the hope of finding genetic vectors and demonstrating how they could cause a disease to jump the species barrier. She'd actually asked Azrhan, her chief technician, to accompany her from New York and help with the work, but he'd begged off. "My parents are visiting from Kuwait, and I couldn't leave them alone in New York," he'd explained, sounding miserable about missing the excitement of the meeting and whatever she might find.

Eighteen months ago, when word first broke that bird flu had jumped the species barrier in Oahu, she'd pushed the planning committee to settle on Hawaii as the conference site, it being only one of several places considered. "After all, it's a cogent argument that if such crossovers can happen by random accident without the aid of genetic vectors, then surely we must consider the possibility of such catastrophes occurring much more easily with their help. And what better way to drive home the dangers of horizontal gene transfers," she argued at that time, "than by involving the clinicians and scientists who so successfully contained the resulting infection. Having them tell the story in the very community where the deadly gene swap actually occured will make an abstract threat frighteningly real for every delegate present." She kept her intent to carry out tests at the site to herself, knowing the UN body would shy away from such controversy.

Shuffling footsteps from beyond the door brought her out of her reverie. She heard the lock turn, and the door opened a crack. A cool dampness flowed over her, accompanied by a musty odor of mold. "Mr. Hacket?"

The opening widened enough that she saw a stooped old man with a sharp thin face and deep-set eyes staring out at her. The initial aroma of the house's interior grew stronger, tinged with the sourness of unwashed skin, the smell of cigarette smoke, and a hint of stale urine. "What you want?" he demanded belligerently in a high voice that could almost be a woman's.

"Mr. Hacket, I'm studying the bird flu outbreak—"

"I don't want any more trouble about that. Damn neighbors won't even talk to me no more—sayin' I started it, and got all their hens slaughtered. You get outta here. I won't have you or anyone else stirrin' up that trouble again—"

"Mr. Hacket, I just want to take some soil and vegetation samples from around the coop where you kept the chickens—"

"What for?" His bushy gray brows arched like a pair of angry alley cats.

"Because we're suspicious something may have altered the virus to make it attack humans."

"What altered it?"

Oh, brother, she thought. How am I going to explain genetics to a hermit. "Well, it's complicated, but some companies are changing the gene structure of food crops, and the vectors they use—"

"You mean them Frankenfoods I been reading about. We don't have anything like them here."

Maybe he's not such a hermit after all. "What about coffee plants? Some experimental farms are growing genetically manipulated strains designed to be caffeine free. Any like that near you—?"

"No! Now, get off my land and don't come back. I got a shotgun for trespassers!" He slammed the door and locked it.

"Christ!" she muttered, eyeing the distance she'd have to run if she wanted to scoop up a vial of earth, then skeedadle. She really had counted on including the results in her presentation. But an old coot like that just might take a shot at her.

"Damn! Damn! Damn!" she said, abandoning the idea and turning to leave.

"Must be from the mainland," the old man muttered, peering out the window and noticing the woman's lack of tan as she walked back to her car. "Not bad lookin' either," he added, watching her ass move with each step as she went and enjoying the sight of her legs as her skirt slid up when she got into the driver's seat.

Making sure she pulled back out on the highway, he continued to mutter his thoughts out loud, as was his habit—the result of living alone for a lifetime. "Last thing I need is her pokin' around that virus business and bringin' old fights back down on me. But *they* may like it even less," he added, getting up and walking to the bureau drawer where he kept his important papers. "And if they're worried, it might just be worth more to them that I keep my mouth shut than before. Hell, maybe I can buy a boat to go with the pickup." With his left hand he held the card away from his eyes so he could read the phone number as he dialed.

"Goddamned bastards," he uttered while listening to the ring through the receiver. He'd always kicked himself that he didn't demand a bigger payoff from them for his silence. But they arrived on his doorstep even before the public health officials—as soon as the papers began reporting that a kid in the area died of bird flu. Ten grand they offered him, for damages to his flock, they called it, provided he kept his mouth shut about buying a batch of hens and a supply of feed corn from them the week before. He took the cash and insisted they throw in a truck he'd been wanting, all in exchange for a promise to keep his recent purchase from them secret. Then the authorities connected the dead boy to his coop and questioned him for days about his business transactions involving either the birds or their eggs. Scared that he'd end up in jail if they found out he'd initially withheld information, he continued to insist that he'd acquired no new hens recently, but the stress of the ordeal left him resentful, especially since he'd settled for so little money. "They'll pay big this time," he mumbled, still waiting for someone to answer.

"Biofeed International, Hawaiian office!" sang out the receptionist.

He gave the name of the man whom he'd dealt with.

"Mr. Bob Morgan no longer works for our company. Do you wish to speak with his replacement?"

"Yeah, I would."

But after a few minutes of talking with a very junior-sounding man and carefully alluding to the "arrangement" he'd made with Morgan over "damages" to his chickens, Hacket decided that the guy knew nothing of the previous deal. "Give me the operator again," he gruffly ordered.

"Our last forwarding address for Mr. Morgan was at a company called Agrenomics International near White Plains, New York," she cheerfully told him. "Let me give you their number."

After hanging up, he thought about the long-distance costs, then figured the call would be worth it. All he'd need from Bob Morgan was the name of someone at Biofeed who knew about their secret and who might be interested that a Dr. Kathleen Sullivan was now poking around his farm asking about bird flu. Of course, that person, whoever he or she turned out to be, had better be willing to cough up at least the price of a nice inboard cruiser for the information.

Monday, May 8, 7:15 P.M.

Steele hadn't seen anything like it since the street theater protests he'd witnessed during his student days at university. Outside the entrance to the Honolulu convention center actors dressed as giant monarch butterflies ran in circles and fluttered their wings, then flopped to the sidewalk, dying with an aplomb suited to a lepidopterous version of *Swan Lake*. Other thespians disguised as giant mutant corncobs handed out pamphlets demanding, DO YOU KNOW WHAT WAS IN

THE CEREAL YOU ATE AT BREAKFAST TODAY? A chorus line of spotted tomatoes oozing green slime from open sores danced and swirled throughout the crowd.

Passersby rushing home from work, most of them Hawaiian, treated it all as a fiesta, laughing and pointing at the various costumed characters. This prompted the quick intervention of zealots with loudspeakers who immediately rushed over and tried to squelch any such outbursts of fun by bellowing, "Stamp out toxic foods!" Shaking his head as he made his way through these humorless, in-your-face activists, Steele found their aggressive tactics completely alien to him and figured the only things they'd rid the earth of would be people's smiles.

Once inside, however, amid the crush of delegates around the registration desk, he sensed a more kindred excitement—one similar to what he'd known a quarter century ago at disarmament marches, antiwar demonstrations, and save-the-planet rallies. The hum of fax machines spitting out notices replaced the clatter of mimeograph copiers, the laptop had become the tool of choice for issuing global manifestos, and the incessant trill of cell phones gave the sounds of an aviary to the assembly—but the special electricity that fills the air when the world's brightest and best gather to lead the charge against a great wrong hadn't changed a bit. It remained as palpable to him now as it had been then.

The predominance of women confirmed something else which had stayed constant—it's mostly the female of the species who answers the call when mother earth is threatened. He smiled at the memory of joining one or two causes simply to chat up a pretty coed. That's how he met Luana—he'd seen her painting protest signs and picked up a brush to help out. He couldn't even remember what they were rushing to the rescue of. He was still grinning when it struck him that he'd been able to savor a memory of her without it ripping his guts out. Well, well, he thought, recognizing the first hint that he might be slipping the chains of his grief.

At the reception that evening he stood in the thick of the throng and watched as waiters in "Aloha dress"—Hawaiian sport shirts and creased trousers—wielded trays piled high with red shellfish, yellow peppers, and green avocado, each wrapped in white rice and black seaweed. Around him, he heard a language both familiar and strange. Terms like *retrovirus, ribosomes,* and *gene expression* belonged to his jargon, but they came to his ear woven in words like *transposons, plasmids,* and *promiscuous genes.* He'd no idea what the new terminology meant, so much so that he began to doubt if he'd be able to follow the proceedings. To make matters worse, he seemed to be the only physician at the party, and the big *MD* on his name tag became a beacon for the other delegates.

"Oh, you're a doctor."

"Right!"

"Do you have any concerns about the uptake rate of genetic material in the host recipient of edible, genetically engineered vaccines?"

"Edible what?"

"What's your position on the use of retroviral vectors?"

"Retroviral? You mean like AIDS?"

"Attenuated, of course."

"I should hope so."

Many such conversations later Steele spotted a woman at the other end of the room who seemed to be receiving similar attention. To his relief, he saw that she, too, sported an *MD* on her identity tag, it being just as visible through a crowd as his. He also took in her well-tanned skin and the fact that she wore a traditional Polynesian wrap with her hair done up in a braid reaching down to her waist.

Perhaps she lives here, he thought, continuing to stare while she smiled and gave lengthy responses to all the inquiries directed at her. In fact, she looks like she could teach *me* a few pointers on how to answer all the questions this bunch keeps asking. Glad to have a reason to introduce himself, he drifted toward her.

But before he got halfway there, the man who'd grilled him about edible vaccines waved him over to another ring of people. "Dr. Steele, there's someone you should meet who agrees with your stand against retroviral vectors—"

"My stand?"

"Dr. Steele is the medical authority for the conference," he persisted.

"Authority? Oh, no, not by a long shot. I'm afraid I'll have to observe and learn a great deal before being of much use."

"Nonsense, Doctor!" interjected one of the more senior men in the circle. "We've been crying for a real physician at these shindigs for years." He had gray curly hair, wire-rimmed glasses, and sported the clothing—dark blazer, pale blue shirt, tan pants—of someone about to step onto his yacht. He swept his arm around the room. "Everyone here is running around making doomsday claims for the health of the human race, and most have never had anything more than rats as their patients."

A ripple of laughter ran through the group.

"Well, it still seems a whole new world to me," Steele answered, chuckling along with the rest. "But thanks for the encouragement."

"You don't hesitate to let me know if I can be of any help," he replied, offering his card. "My name's Steve Patton, and I'm an over-the-hill environmentalist who never outgrew the sixties," he added with a grin. He then excused himself, turned, and strolled over to where a half dozen reporters were interviewing a pretty woman with short auburn-gold hair and the most remarkable green eyes. She and Patton greeted each other with a formal-looking peck on each other's cheeks, and the pair proceeded with the interview together.

That's Dr. Kathleen Sullivan, the geneticist, thought Steele, recognizing her from her television program. He'd have to speak with her later, to find out what panels she wanted him on. Excusing himself from those still around him and continuing to move toward the woman he'd set out to talk with in the first place, he glanced at Patton's card. PRESIDENT—THE BLUE PLANET SOCIETY, he read, recognizing one of the most high profile conservation groups in the United States. Slipping it into his pocket, he muttered, " 'Over-the-hill environmentalist,' my ass."

He stopped a polite distance behind her, waiting for the latest group of questioners to finish up. She stood near the edge of an open balcony, outlined against a fan of flaming orange, crimson, and fuschia streaks as the last of the sun dipped below the ocean. In the final flare of light, he saw the shape of her long legs and the swell of her hips illuminated beneath the thin material of her outfit. He looked away, embarrassed at being such an accidental voyeur, yet kept taking quick surreptitious glances in her direction. Purely to see if she's finished talking, he kept telling himself. Yet each time her silhouette remained as revealing as ever, until he slowly returned his gaze and held it on her, surprised to find himself interested.

A breeze stirred the folds of her dress, lifting it ever so slightly up around her body like a floating bell jar. While he watched she widened her stance, as if to better let the cool air run freely around her lower limbs. Ashamed of his sudden lasciviousness, he nevertheless let his eyes roam upward, surveying her thin waist and particularly noticing, the nape of her long elegant neck, where a few strands from her braid had slipped loose to nestle against her bronze skin. He could not see her face, only the line of her cheek, and in the afterglow of the sunset he made out a thin covering of down on its surface, delicate as an aura. The smell of her perfume completed his intoxication.

She finished speaking, excused herself from the last of her audience, and turned, only to catch him staring at her. "Hello," she said hesitantly, her expression puzzled.

He felt his face grow flushed. "Uh, hello. I'm Dr. Richard Steele from New York," he began, holding out his hand. "I was hoping you could give a fellow MD some help. You seem at ease with all the inquiries being put to you. I'm new to this business and am not doing nearly as well. Frankly, I'm beginning to feel stupid."

She studied him for a second, her arms crossed and head cocked to one side, long enough for him to immediately appreciate the delicate shape of her slender nose and full lips. Then she smiled, the corners of her mouth easily forming into laugh lines, but her eyes didn't join in the greeting. They remained dark and recessed, giving her gaze a sadness at odds with the rest of her expression. "Of course, I'll help you if I can," she said, extending her hand and uncovering her name tag. "I'm Dr. Sandra Arness, from Honolulu. I'm afraid that's why you've seen so many people buttonholing me. Mostly they want to know about good places to eat."

He chuckled. "Well that's a relief. Here I thought I was hopelessly unqualified compared to you. What kind of medicine do you practice?"

Her eyes darted away from him ever so slightly. "I'm a family physician," she said quickly, "but I'm on sabbatical right now. What about yourself?" The question came at him like a return serve.

"ER. Except I was sidelined with a heart attack over five months ago."

"Oh, I'm sorry. Will you be able to go back?"

"Hopefully. My new masters, the cardiologists, insist I wait until they're sure. But I've been fine."

She seemed at a loss for what to say next, twirling the long stem of her empty champagne glass between her fingers.

"Say, can I get you a refill?" he offered.

"Sure," she answered.

As they walked together toward the bar, he noticed that she wore no wedding ring.

Their drinks replenished, they found a table in a corner. Slipping into small talk, she evaded telling him much about herself, admitting in passing that she'd been divorced, vaguely citing "health problems" as the reason behind her sabbatical, and, when he inquired why she was at the conference, stating simply, "The topic interests me." Yet her questions about him were so probing and empathetic that before an hour passed he confided to her his difficulty in adapting to being a widower, his troubled relationship with Chet, and the emotional shakeup he'd experienced after nearly dying. "Are you sure you're not a psychiatrist?" he quipped nervously, instinctively pulling back after realizing how much of himself he'd poured out to her. "I haven't told anybody this stuff back home."

"I know a lot about loss, is all," she answered, "and I find you easy to listen to." She reached across the table and laid her hand softly on his forearm, her eyes as full of pain as two fresh bruises.

Steele returned her gaze and thought he read an invitation to become lost in those dark liquid pools. Should I suggest we go to my room? he thought, barely able to breathe. He reached to run his fingertips along the back of her wrist when he heard from a distance, "My goodness, leave it to the only two MDs in the place to find each other and start talking shop."

Sandra darted her hand away.

He turned to see Kathleen Sullivan descending on their cubbyhole with a big smile and outstretched arms.

"Hi, Dr. Steele, I know we haven't met yet," she greeted. "I'm Kathleen Sullivan. Welcome to Honolulu!" She turned to Sandra. "And you're Doctor—?" She squinted at the name tag, trying to make out the small letters in front of the big *MD*.

"Arness," volunteered the woman, smiling sweetly as she extended the same hand that had been touching his so invitingly seconds before.

Sullivan clasped it warmly. "I hope I'm not interrupting anything, but I must steal Dr. Steele from you for a minute—" She broke into a giggle. "I'm sorry, but I love making puns!" she exclaimed, continuing to laugh. "Lowest form of humor, they say, but then I'm the kind of gal that likes a low joke. The minute I saw his name on the list of participants, I knew I had to try it. But I do need to borrow him, Dr. Arness," she added, her expression suddenly turning serious and her voice apologetic, "just for a minute to brief him on tomorrow's schedule—"

"Of course, Dr. Sullivan. He's all yours. I was about to leave anyway." She got up from her chair. "Good evening to you both. I'll see you at the sessions tomorrow."

Steele jumped to his feet, but before he could think of anything to interject, Sandra nodded, turned, and walked toward the door.

"Good night, Dr. Arness," Sullivan called cheerfully after her, then took the chair where she'd been sitting. "Dr. Steele, I want you on the panel with me for the plenary session on the dangers of naked DNA. We'll be focusing on the case of bird influenza that jumped the species barrier here eighteen months ago, to illustrate the kind of event that these vectors can enhance. . . ."

As Steele retook his seat opposite her and listened, he watched Sandra Arness disappear out the door. Well, thanks a heap, Kathleen Sullivan, he thought sarcastically. You certainly managed to keep me safe from what might have been my own encounter with a little DNA tonight, naked or otherwise.

"How did this bird flu learn to kill humans?" demanded Dr. Julie Carr the next morning, standing beside a massive screen on which she'd projected a black-and-white electron micrograph of an influenza virus.

Nobody answered, everyone in the packed auditorium recognizing a rhetorical question when they heard one.

"The answer lies in these bristles," she continued, indicating with a laser pointer the spiked surface on the ovoid. "They're made of glycoproteins. Some are rich in hemagglutinin, a three-pronged molecule that recognizes and locks on to a specific receptor site at the cellular surface of its host, thereby determining which species the virus can and cannot invade. Others contain neuraminidase, a molecule able to cleave these bonds, setting the virus free to spread elsewhere if infection at a particular cell doesn't occur for some reason. Together they also form the molecular template against which a host mounts its immune response. Even slight variations in either of these two structures will allow the virus to evade antibodies acquired during the host's previous exposure to old strains, and will result in increased infectivity. Now this guy here should only have spikes which fit with the molecules of chicken mucosa. . . ."

She clicked to her next slide, again of an influenza virus, but with parts of its prickly projections colored brilliant green.

"What you're looking at is a color-modified computer image to show where these specific protein keys picked up the ELISA reagent for H5N1, the bird strain, on this particular influenza bug. But when I added ELISA for the H2N3, or human strain, I got this . . ."

An image of an influenza virus brightly spotted with a mosaic of both red and green areas flashed onto the screen.

". . . a virologist's worst nightmare—the true hybrid, its protein coat containing two sets of structural keys, giving it access to both bird and human cell membranes. It could only have acquired this dual identity through what we call a recombinant event—the exchange of genetic material between two organisms—in this case the incorporation of genes from the bird strain into the human influenza's own genetic code." She paused, took a sip of water, and then continued, "We figure it happened inside the boy's nostrils, where he already had human influenza incubating. He probably got droppings laden with bird flu on his hand when he held one of the sick hens, then rubbed his nose, and bingo, the two strains were side by side. Thankfully history suggests that recombination between H5N1 and H2N3 seems to be a rare event—the known cases of humans contracting H5N1 being limited to this one and an occurrence in Taiwan three years ago. I say thankfully, because the virulence of bird flu in humans on a large scale is unimaginable. We have no immunity to it—after all, the virus has been safely off in birds for millions of years. If the hybrid which occurred here had gotten a foothold and spread, we'd have been in the same situation as say, the original Hawaiians were when they first encountered measles carried by European explorers during the eighteenth century. Having never been exposed to this children's disease, well over twenty percent of the local population who got infected died. The fact we avoided a similar fate eighteen months ago had to be nothing short of a miracle, even with the prompt actions of the Public Health Department and our extraordinary luck that the boy lived in a relatively isolated area where he hadn't had much contact with other children. Thank you for your attention."

Dynamic speaker, thought Steele, adding to the enthusiastic applause that accompanied the petite virologist as she returned to her seat. She was three chairs down from Steele, part of the panel of a dozen experts Sullivan had assembled on stage.

"Thank you, Julie," said the geneticist, hopping up to the microphone. "As you've seen, Dr. Carr is a world innovator in devising imaginative staining techniques for electron microscopy. Back in New York, those blowups of hers would look right at home alongside a Salvador Dalí in the Museum of Modern Art." She paused, allow-ing a response of mild laughter to peter out. Then she grinned slyly and added, "You could get a lot more for them there, Julie, than what most of us get paid as scientists." That brought on a thunderous round of agreement.

"Right! On with the show. Now we've seen how a disease can jump the species barrier and what a catastrophe that can be. Thank-fully, as Dr. Carr pointed out—nature keeps the event rare. But would it remain an uncommon occurrence if genetic vectors accidentally be-came part of the scenario? My fear is that these man-made concoc-tions will make such events more and more likely—think of them as the equivalent of worms if you like, infectious DNA worms which might invade, break open, and insert themselves irrevocably into the strands of genes in other species, including, possibly, our own." She paused, surveying her absolutely rapt audience.

"Picture this," she continued. "Suppose a farmer has genetically modified crops in his fields. Broken bits of plant or seeds—all carry-ing the DNA of whatever genetic vector had mutated them—could easily get carried from the field to the area where the chickens roam. Let's also suppose the cells of that vegetation died, spilling their naked DNA, including that of the vectors, into the soil. Hens hunt and peck. If one already infected with H5N1, or bird flu, foraged around with its beak, it could stir up dust and inhale a dose of parti-cles containing that naked DNA into its respiratory tract—DNA that's turbocharged with gene regulators—the transposons, enhancers, and promoters which genetic engineers routinely slip into a vector to make it promiscuous and therefore more likely to get into the genes of its target organism."

Her choice of words produced a ripple of laughter.

"But being uncloaked naked DNA, this randy little bugger doesn't need a special 'key' to invade anything, unlike, as Dr. Carr demon-strated, ordinary viruses do. Instead it can directly penetrate whatever cell it comes in contact with, including those lining the chicken's res-piratory tract where the H5N1 bird flu has already taken up resi-dence. Once this vector penetrates these cells, it floats right alongside the RNA genes of the invading H5N1 virus, and the bird's own genetic machinery starts replicating both into copies of messenger RNA, the first step in expressing them genetically. The possible result is a bird flu strain of influenza turbocharged with strands of transposons, enhancers, and promotors from the vector. Place *this* little baby which is *really* ready to party alongside the human H2N3 variety, say in the nostrils of an infected farmworker, and who's to guarantee that all the natural barriers which have kept recombination between the two strains a rare event over millions of years won't suddenly be breached? In other words, if the DNA of the two strains do freely mingle, we'll once more end up with a hybrid influenza to which humankind has no immunity—one that's likely to be widespread this time."

A murmur of whispers weaved through the crowd, reminding Steele of the dry rustle a nest of snakes makes when they're disturbed under a blanket of leaves. He leaned over to a stone-faced Steve Patton sitting beside him and commented, "She's certainly got their attention."

"Yes, hasn't she," he replied politely, his expression growing worried as the audience became increasingly noisy. "Except sometimes it's not too wise, getting people so stirred up like this with speculation alone. I keep warning her that it's better to provoke the biotech industry only with what she can readily prove, for the sake of credibility on our side of the argument. But she's adamant about broadcasting the hypothetical dangers." He paused to catch his breath, having spoken in the rushed manner of a man who's kept what he has to say bottled up for too long. "Not that her concerns about lethal influenza strains aren't well founded or those hypotheses soundly based in science," he added, continuing to speak rapidly, "but they'll only get her in trouble because as of yet she's no hard evidence to substantiate them. Don't take me wrong, she's a great gal with brilliant instincts in the lab—her ability to project herself into the interior workings of a cell and grasp what's happening in there on a molecular level is uncanny—" He cut off his diatribe, glancing over to where Sullivan vainly kept requesting that the audience settle down, her eyebrows gathering together like ridges on a storm front. "Excuse me," he said, quickly getting out of his chair, "but I'm the next speaker, and I think she needs help."

Sounds like he's frustrated in dealing with her, Steele thought, watching him stride over, put a hand on her shoulder, and whisper something in her ear.

At first she seemed to accept his touch; then her neck stiffened. Turning, she walked to the other side of the podium, beyond his reach. Placing a covering hand over the microphone, she said something back to him through a fixed smile, her eyes becoming fierce and her lips pulling ever so slightly away from her teeth. From the barely concealed sparks, Steele figured there had to be more between them than a difference of opinion over tactics for their cause. Divorced maybe, he concluded, noticing how practiced she seemed at quietly giving the older man hell.

"Dr. Sullivan," interrupted a loud voice over the PA system accompanied by an ear-piercing screech of feedback. "Who do you think you are, using your position as chairperson to push such unscientific, unfounded crap onto the agenda of this assembly?" Everyone's attention immediately swung to the microphones in the aisles where people from the audience were lining up to have their say, and the room fell quiet.

The person who'd just spoken, a bald, middle-aged giant of a man, wouldn't have looked out of place in a pro-wrestling event. "My name is Sydney Aimes," he continued, his flush of anger suffusing even his gleaming scalp, "and I'm the chief negotiator of the U.S. trade delegation for this conference. I go on record here and now that this country's right to trade freely in genetically modified organisms will be determined by evidence-based science, not through unsubstantiated slander. In other words, watch what you say, lady, or in some states you could find yourself being cited for damages."

A collective gasp, followed by boos and hisses came from some parts of the crowd while applause broke out in the rest. Kathleen Sullivan's own jaw dropped so low she looked as if she'd just popped by for a dental exam.

Shaking his head, Patton took the microphone from her hand, gave her an *I told you so* glance, and signaled the audience to settle down. She pivoted away from him and strode back to join the panel, her face crimson and her eyes glowing a molten green. She took the only seat available, the one Patton had vacated.

Boy, she's doubly pissed with him now, thought Steele, feeling her seethe beside him, probably because he'd been right. Clearly she'd underestimated the impact of her disturbing scenario.

Patton waited for the audience to grow quiet again, introduced himself, then added, "For those of you who aren't aware, what Mr. Aimes referred to a second ago is the fact that legislators in some states have passed what we call *veggie libel laws*, intended to squash the kind of open discussion we're having here today." A smattering of laughter went through the room. "But don't worry. The wise politicians of Hawaii have resisted such madness, and here we can still speak freely." A few more chuckles erupted. "After all, while some would call a discussion among scientists about what could result from genetically modified organisms 'slander,' Dr. Sullivan and I call it responsible."

Again isolated boos and cheers broke out, but most of the assembly accepted his declaration with quiet.

He gestured to where Aimes stood waiting by the microphone and, looking straight at him, added, "It's precisely that type of discussion which leads to good investigative studies and the hard scientific evidence that you say you want, Sydney. That we all want. But as Dr. Sullivan repeatedly states in her publications and the Internet's *Environment Watch* page recently posted, accidental contamination of plant life by genetic vectors cannot be properly assessed without the investigators knowing what to test for and which primers to use—"

"Yes, yes, Steve, we've listened to all this hypothetical fear-mongering before," said Aimes, rolling his eyes at the ceiling to better telegraph his exasperation. "And as usual, you've nothing new! Move into the realm of *real* science and admit there's no proof that genetically modified foods are positively harmful to human health."

From the familiarity between the two men, Steele quickly sensed that they were engaged in their latest installment of a long-standing public quarrel. Such ongoing fights in his own world of medicine were legion, and he'd witnessed enough of them to know the signs— combatants well known to one other, each side's position rigidly staked out, and both parties shamefully willing to grandstand as they trotted out their same old arguments in any forum they could find. Posturing and speaking in emphatic declarations, not content, were the usual currency of such set tos.

"But we do have something new, Sydney," Patton declared, clicking a handheld controller wired to the podium and filling the screen behind him with a dozen brilliantly colored vertical lines. Aimes seemed caught by the unexpected diagram the way an animal can be mesmerized by the lights of an oncoming truck.

"The Blue Planet Society managed to find geneticists from various commercial laboratories situated in a variety of countries who shared our concerns about the risks of naked DNA," continued Patton. "They secretly provided us with samples of their vectors along with cuttings of plants, grasses, and trees from the grounds of their facilities."

Murmurs of excitement swept the room.

"Yes, ladies and gentlemen, I'm proud to present our findings, now that we have finally been able to carry out an accurate screening for the unintentional uptake of genetic contaminants." He directed his laser pointer to indicate the height of the bar graphs. "Each line represents the percentage of positive results in a single facility. As you can see, in every case we found the vectors to be present in high concentrations."

An explosion of voices erupted, and this time it was Aimes's turn to drop his jaw. "It's a bunch of lies," he recovered enough to say. "And how do we know you didn't plant the evidence?" Others joined in, hurtling similar accusations.

Patton ignored them all, continuing to flick slides of graphs up on the screen and proclaim their meaning, his voice rising like an evangelist's, overriding the chorus of denials and disbelief that greeted each revelation. "Here we show significant concentrations in leaves, but not roots, suggesting airborne contamination."

A new symphony of mutterings joined the fray.

"Oh, my God, no."

"This'll kill sales."

"I gotta call my broker."

Reporters lounging in the back of the room started drifting toward the stage, bathing everyone on it in the glare of floodlights as they turned on their video cameras.

"Yet on this slide, we can see where the high values in the roots and lesser amounts in the foliage indicate that naked DNA can be taken up from the soil as well."

Steele found himself intrigued by the flashes of information racing by up on the screen. It seemed he'd barely time to begin thinking through the impact of it all when he heard, "That's the last slide, folks, and now I'd like to call upon our health expert, Dr. Richard Steele, to share with us his medical impressions regarding any threats such contamination might pose to humans."

Steele started, flabbergasted to be singled out for an opinion so soon. He felt even more on the spot as the audience which had been so unruly during Patton's performance suddenly grew silent, and every lens in the room zoomed in to record his response. "Uh, thank you, Mr. Patton," he began, as one of the panel members slid a table-top microphone his way and switched it on for him. He stared at the red light in its base, desperately trying to collect his thoughts, then glanced sideways to Sullivan, hoping to get a clue from her about what to say.

"Stress the need to test the workers at the labs," she whispered helpfully, her face having returned to its normal color and her eyes coolly professional.

"Thanks," he murmured, pulling the live mouthpiece nearer to him. "Obviously these extraordinary findings warrant serious follow-up studies," he began, "ones that include human subjects, such as the people employed at the laboratories." He paused, sensing he was doing not badly, and added, "Perhaps a call for precautions in how these vectors are handled or disposed of would also be in order, until we can assess their impact."

Sounds of approval swelled throughout the room.

"Would you like to make that an official motion?" asked Patton.

"Of course," agreed Steele, thinking, Why not? In for an ounce, in for a pound.

"Wait a minute!" boomed Aimes's voice over the PA.

The ring of lights surrounding Steele turned back toward the floor microphones where the man once more hulked over a podium that was too short for him. "I'd like to ask Mr. Patton if any of his spies reported that the trees, plants, and grasses surrounding these workplaces were any the worse for wear."

"Pardon?" said the environmentalist.

"What kind of shape were the plants in, Steve. Dead? Dying? Turning purple with pink spots?"

Patton bristled. "Of course not," he snapped.

" 'Of course not' what? No pink spots, or no evidence of any harm to the plants at all?"

"Evidence of genetic damage takes years, generations to appear—"

"Oh, yeah, we're back to the 'It's too early to tell' argument you guys keep spouting. Let's see, trees can live three hundred years. Are you suggesting we shut down the bioengineering industry until then, just to be safe?"

"You know I didn't mean that—"

"Because what really matters is whether these bits of DNA do any injury to anyone or anything," Aimes continued. "And until you provide proof of that, you've no right to be mouthing off—"

"I'm calling for a vote on Dr. Steele's motion right now," Patton cut in, paying no attention to the furious protests and wild gesticulations coming from Aimes.

It passed, but barely, reflecting the breakdown between traders and scientists in the room.

Aimes came up to Steele once Sullivan adjourned the meeting and the media had moved elsewhere. "You fucking creep," he said.

"You just put a hundred-billion-a-year industry at risk. That's a lot of Americans who could lose their jobs, and most of them, when they see you on the news tonight, will now consider you their worst enemy."

"I think I was reasonable," Steele told him quietly. "You can't ignore health risks in any business."

"This issue is about trade, asshole, not medicine. So butt out!"

Sullivan, who'd been standing nearby, walked over after Aimes had stormed off and slipped her arm through Steele's. "I couldn't help but overhear. He's a jerk, but unfortunately the jerks have the upper hand on this matter, at least in this part of the planet." She started to stroll with him toward one of the conference hall's exits.

"You're kidding! How can they ignore those studies?"

"With the money and power that they've got behind them? Easily! Steve's right, even though he infuriated me the way he rubbed it in. Until I can get proof of direct damage to humans, idiots like Aimes will block us every step of the way—until there's finally a disaster that even he and his fat-assed cronies won't be able to sit on. By the way, you did well with the media today. You're going to be a bit of a star, at least for tonight, once the networks get hold of the feed. I can have my office in New York call your home if you like, to let anyone there know when they can see you on TV."

"No, that won't be necessary, thanks," he replied, figuring he'd call Chet and Martha himself. He wasn't going to pass up a chance to inform them that he'd done something worthwhile for a change, instead of being the usual jerk they'd had to put up with for almost two years now. As an afterthought to Sullivan's offer, he suddenly wondered if she'd just subtly probed his marital status.

"Can I buy you a drink, then?" she offered, the pitch of her voice slipping up a notch.

He had other plans. "I'm sorry, but I can't right now. Could I take a rain check?"

"Sure," she said, smiling up at him as she disengaged her arm.

At that moment Steve Patton came through the door up ahead and spotted them. His step hesitated ever so slightly, and the hint of a frown appeared on his face. In an instant it vanished, and he called out, "There you are," continuing toward them. "Jesus, Kathleen, don't get mad at me for saying this again, but your expounding that theory about genetic vectors and bird flu without proof is making us look like idiots. Aimes is out in the lobby talking up a storm with the press, claiming that by showing up here with nothing to offer but speculation, to quote the son of a bitch, 'The famous Kathleen Sullivan herself admits she can't produce a single shred of proof linking genetically modified foods with bird flu or any other human illness.' "

Steele thought he saw a hint of red appear in her cheeks, but it disappeared as fast as it came. She nevertheless slipped her arm back in his before quietly replying, "He's a crock."

Patton seemed taken aback, whether by her soft tone of voice or her apparent claim to another man's company, Steele couldn't tell. "Yes, of course, he is," the environmentalist curtly agreed after a few seconds, "but by discrediting you, he's also undermining our study. Already he's insisting we're blowing smoke over nonexistent risks with it as well. 'Making too big a deal about a few strands of naked DNA turning up in otherwise perfectly healthy plants,' was how he put it. Kathleen, I'm telling you, if his bottom line remains unassailed—'No evidence exists that any human has ever been harmed by genetically modified foods,' " he mimicked, this time catching Aimes's bombast perfectly, "and we don't deliver hard evidence to the contrary soon, I'm afraid he'll successfully block the UN from adopting any new regulations regarding vectors."

"But the vote," said Steele. "Our motion passed."

The two looked at him as if he were an idiot.

"Kathleen, I know you," Patton resumed. "Whenever you do go out on a limb with your speculations, you usually have a study or experiment in mind to prove or disprove your hypothesis. If you've got anything up your sleeve that could even possibly link vectors with the spread of bird flu to humans, now's the time to bring it out."

"I'll do what I can," she answered.

Once more he seemed staggered by the quietness of her reply.

"Yes, I'm sure you will," he said. "Well, if you'll excuse me." He nodded to them both, turned, and rushed back out the way he'd come in.

"You think you can get such proof?" Steele asked, intrigued by what he'd heard, but wanting to keep their conversation within the safe bounds of professional matters. He'd no intention of becoming a pawn in whatever existed between her and Patton.

"Possibly."

"But where?"

"Not far from here, actually." She disengaged her arm from his for a second time. "See you tomorrow," she added, and exited by the door leading to the street without looking back.

Through the glass he saw Patton waiting outside for her. The man tried to take her by the elbow, but she pulled away. His face reddened, and he went on talking with her, making imploring gestures with his hands the whole time. She gave him a withering look, then left him standing on the steps

Christ, thought Steele, watching her go, this whole day's been the scientific equivalent of the *Jerry Springer Show*.

8

In the grove of trees where she hid, the trade winds buffeted the palms high over her head, whipping them back and forth and filling the air with a continuous rushing sound loud as a passing train. Looking up, she thought of tall brooms trying to sweep stars off the belly of the night, then shifted her focus to the silver-tipped clouds racing in from the sea, their leaden bottoms scudding over the mountain ridge behind her. I'll have to keep up with their shadows, she decided, readying herself for a sprint into the open. Once more she surveyed the moonlit farmhouse in the distance, trying to spot signs of movement. Apart from the occasional flap of shingles lifting up from the roof and threatening to fly off, nothing stirred. Neither could she see a trace of light. If she hadn't known Hacket lived there, she would have thought the place abandoned. It had the gray, dried appearance of a thing sloughed off, like a husk some insect might shed and discard in the dirt. Crouching low, she stepped into a field of waist-high grass and started running toward it.

Half an hour ago, just before midnight, she'd parked her car a quarter-mile up the road, then crossed the fields to the back of Hacket's property where the foliage and trees provided better cover. But now, making a two-hundred-yard beeline to the fence where the chicken coop would be, she felt exposed. Trying to keep up with the pools of shadows racing her along the ground, she kept her eyes on the house, imagining Hacket standing in the blackness behind one of those windows and watching her while she approached. From the way the curtains hung listless, ghostly white sentinels at the sides of the frames, she figured the place must be shut tight against the wind. It'll be hotter than Hades in there, she thought, the night air still warm despite the breezes. Surely no one could sleep in that kind of heat. Hell, maybe he's not even at home.

The barn loomed large as she crossed the final hundred yards of the field, obscuring her view of the house beyond. Drawing closer, she heard it issue up loud creaks and groans, until it sounded like a massive wooden ship straining against the wind. No sooner did she reach the fence and was running along behind it than a loud bang, deafening as a gunshot, pulled her up short, sending her pulse racing. Ducking down, she peered through the slats, only to see a wide wooden door set in the side of the building swing open and repeatedly slam into the wall behind it.

Seeing no one, she got to her feet, scampered over the rickety barricade she'd been hiding behind, making it sway beneath her weight, and dropped to the ground in the farmyard.

Seconds later, on her knees in front of the coop, she hurriedly began to scoop bits of soil, tufts of grass, and clumps of weeds into her sample cases. If I could just find traces of genetic vectors in these, she thought as she worked, then at least I'll have shown them to be in the vicinity of the infected birds. Not a smoking gun, but the first link in a chain of circumstantial evidence.

Next she pulled up a handful of dried corn kernels. Probably left over from chicken feed, she figured, filing them away. Another loud *wham!* from the wooden door at her back set her heart pounding again. "Christ!" she muttered, steadying her nerve and regretting that her relationship with Steve had soured to the point that she balked at asking him to accompany her.

When she'd first stopped sleeping with him it had become difficult for them to do anything together. She thought he would be more sophisticated about it, but he initially couldn't seem to accept her decision, pressuring her to remain his lover until she no longer felt comfortable whenever he came around. The very thing she wanted to avoid, their friendship falling into tatters, seemed inevitable, until, a few weeks later, he began to pull himself together, eventually apologized, and slowly became his old debonair self. "Forgive a middle-aged man his foolishness, Kathleen," he said over a cup of coffee in the student's lounge of her building one afternoon. "Please put it down to the profound effect you had on an aging roué. And I can assure you I'm not so stupid as to let emotions fracture our working relationship. You were absolutely right—it's too important."

Their continuing collaboration, however, had proved difficult, particularly on the vector study. Too often their debates over legitimate scientific differences became so charged with emotion that neither one of them seemed capable of being objective in the other's presence. But in the end the bickering lessened, and they succeeded in seeing the project to completion, appearing to have taken the first difficult steps in putting their affair behind them. She'd even allowed herself to hope that, with time, they might possibly become an effective team again. That's why his *I-told-you-so* attitude had infuriated her today. It felt like a slap in the face after all their hard-fought efforts to remain colleagues, if not actual friends. What a mess, she thought, regretting ever having allowed him to seduce her in the first place.

Richard Steele, on the other hand, interested her. The night before, as she'd briefed him about the conference, his quick grasp of everything they discussed had impressed her immensely. "You're a quick study," she complimented him when they were through.

"You're a good teacher," he'd replied, shedding the overly serious expression he'd worn up to that point and surprising her with a sudden smile.

Wow! You should do that more often, she'd nearly blurted out, startled by how much more attractive he became with the change. "Why, thank you," she said instead.

They'd made professional small talk after that, about New York, university politics, and in particular the impact of her field on his practice of medicine, until he pleaded jet lag and excused himself. But by then she'd sized him up as a man who could match her own quick intellect stride for stride. Since her divorce five years ago she'd had affairs, yet each relationship had ultimately floundered upon a single shoal—the difficulty some male egos had in dealing with her being both intelligent and successful. Except for Steve Patton. Ironically, he'd always delighted in her intellect, seeming genuinely pleased whenever she beat him to the punch solving scientific problems, which was why she found their arrangement so refreshingly appealing at the beginning. Obviously with him, however, compatibility in "smarts," as he'd put it, did not a relationship make.

But Steele's prowess in that regard she nevertheless found attractive. Not that she wanted to do anything about it just now. She'd only offered to buy him a drink to learn more about him, in addition to asking for his help. But once he'd said that he had other plans, she felt too embarrassed to press him about a midnight skulk in a farmer's field.

Later she'd spotted him with Sandra Arness at the hotel bar and understood what those "plans" of his entailed. God, that woman's got haunted eyes, she observed at the time. Then she took a closer look at Steele and thought she caught a hint of a similar darkness in his gaze. Perhaps the man has a few ghosts of his own to contend with, she mused.

Resuming the business of grabbing more specimens, she admitted to feeling more than a twinge of jealousy watching the two of them. "Hell, why is it sad people always seem to seek each other out?" she muttered, expressing her frustration at being overlooked, even if only for a one-night stand that she probably wouldn't have agreed to anyway. Yanking extra hard at some larger weeds from an untrampled area near the end of the coop, she pulled them up along with a stunted corn stalk that had evidently grown from kernels in the feed. I'll label these later, she decided, wanting to get away from the place as quickly as possible, and stuffed them unceremoniously into her handbag. But she also needed samples of straw and feed from the relatively sheltered roosts inside the pen. These might contain dried bird droppings, and if she could demonstrate evidence of vectors in excrement, she'd have proven another necessary link in the chain of events she'd postulated—that these genetic carriers designed to promote mutations were actually present in the infected birds and could have been transmitted along with the virus to the child. Best of all, she knew, would be to find remnants of the bird flu virus itself in the excrement and analyze it for vectors, but that would be unlikely after all this time. Unfortunately the original viral specimens taken from the boy no longer existed. The CDC in Atlanta, once the scare of an outbreak was over, had disposed of the samples Dr. Carr had sent them.

Retrieving the latex gloves that she'd brought in her kit and pulling them on in case something infectious had survived, she found a dilapidated gate leading into the cage. When she slid it open, the rusty hinge protested with a shriek so loud that she feared Hacket might wake up. Nonsense, she reassured herself. Even if he were home and did hear anything, surely he'd put it down to the sound of the wind. Nevertheless, running swiftly to the corner of the barn, she peeked around it, looking up to see if a light had snapped on behind one of the windows.

At first they seemed as black and empty as before. Then, just as she was about to turn away, she saw the pale blurred contours of a face emerge from the darkness behind one of the smudged panes upstairs and stare right at her. Through the grime and in the half light, the features were impossible to make out, but the eyes appeared to be hollow shadows, like those of a death mask, and the entire visage seemed suspended in midair. In a flash, the floating apparition twisted sharply to one side and disappeared.

Oh, my God, she thought, and started to run back toward the coop. Throwing open the gate again, she raced inside, reached in to the partially sheltered roosts along the back, and grabbed a handful of old straw. Whether it had a good coating of dung she'd neither the time nor light to see. Cramming it into her purse with everything else, she fled the enclosure and headed for the fence. The moon overhead suddenly emerged from behind the clouds, and the field became bathed in silver, every foot of the two hundred yard trek as visible as day. The trail through the tall grass she'd left coming in formed a dark telltale path that would easily give her away should she follow it. Over the sound of the wind she heard a slam from the direction of the house, then someone shouting.

She couldn't even be sure it had been Hacket she'd seen, but his words—*"I got a shotgun for trespassers"*—echoed through her head. Could he be crazy enough to actually shoot at someone? If he did come after her, she'd never make it to the woods and cover before he got her in his sights. She turned, scanning the barn for a hiding place, and sprinted for the door still noisily bashing against its frame. Ducking inside she pulled it closed behind her and held it in place, until she realized he might notice it wasn't making noise anymore. She let it open a crack, enough to peer outside, intending to let it swing free again if Hacket hadn't appeared yet. To her dismay *two* figures ran into view, both wearing hoods and carrying handguns. They held the muzzles straight up, and at the ends of the barrels she could see the outlines of stubby round cylinders. Their weapons had silencers!

From the pit of her stomach to the back of her throat she felt as if a fist had clamped off her breathing. Her head started to reel, and she struggled to keep her knees from buckling. Yet a corner of her mind remained rational enough to ask, Why would Hacket have men here with silencers?

They spoke to each other in quick bursts of a language she didn't understand. She could make out that their hands were dark skinned, and thought at first they might be native Hawaiians speaking a Polynesian dialect. But the harshness of what they were saying didn't sound at all like the soft words she'd heard a smattering of on the island. The two men then passed from her line of sight, leaving her desperately wanting to know where they were.

Listening for their steps was useless, as the whistling and moaning of the wind through the airy, creaking barn made it impossible to hear anything that quiet. She had to find a place where she could see out. Ever so slowly she pulled the door shut again, attached its inside hook, then looked for a window or opening. She saw a shaft of moonlight coming through a smudged rectangle of glass to her right. After a few seconds her eyes adapted to the dark, and she realized she'd retreated into a small cubicle with no way out. She made her way through a mass of tools—shovels, picks, rakes—that littered the floor. After a few steps, she tripped on a tangle of coiled hoses, falling heavily and striking her kneecaps on an iron bar. She let out a yelp of pain, then waited to see if they'd heard her, listening to the wail of the wind through the rafters, unable to even breathe.

No one came running to the door.

Getting to her feet, she covered the rest of the distance to the window and got up on tiptoe to see out. Immediately she spotted one of the men silhouetted against the moon as he perched on the fence looking out over the field. She couldn't see the second pursuer. Thinking he might be just outside the door after all, she desperately sought a place to hide, darting her eyes to every shadowy nook and cranny.

She saw none.

The man on the fence gave a call, and she heard an answering shout from somewhere in the field.

Thank God, she thought, grateful for the momentary reprieve. But they'd check the barn once they realized she wasn't hiding in the grass. Time to bring in the cavalry, she decided.

She fumbled in her purse, got out her cellular, and dialed 911. "I'm at the farm of a man called Hacket just off the shore road north of Kailua," she whispered to the dispatcher, continuing to watch the man on the fence, "and I'm being stalked by two men. They both have guns with silencers!"

"Stay on the phone with me!" ordered the woman on the other end of the line. "We'll have the local police there in minutes. Are you able to hide?"

The figure on the fence turned in her direction and seemed to survey the back of the barn. He swung his far leg back over the top, dropped to the ground, and started toward the door she'd just hooked into place.

"Oh, my God, he's coming," she squeaked into the phone.

"Do you have a weapon?" demanded the officer.

"No!"

"Where are you hiding?"

"In a part of the barn. The door's hooked, but he'll easily break in and see me, and there's no other exit." She pressed herself against the wall at enough of an angle to keep him in view as he got closer.

"Does he already know you're there?"

"He suspects it. I can't talk anymore, or he'll hear."

"One more question. Does the door open out or in?"

"Out."

"Then listen to me, honey! Look for something heavy—a tool, a bar, even a length of wood. When you have it, get against the wall on the hinge side of the door, and be ready for a swing at him with whatever you've got, but not until you can see his head the instant he pokes it in for a look around—"

Sullivan snapped the phone closed, deposited it with her purse on the ground, and grabbed a pickax. She'd no sooner moved into position than the door rattled heavily as he tested the lock. There followed a flurry of thuds from his kicking at it with his boot, and the wall behind her shook so forcefully she had to brace against it with her feet not to be thrown forward.

He'll see me and shoot before I can clobber him, she kept thinking, her panic mounting with every blow. Or if I do manage to get him, the other one will surely kill me.

With a splintering sound one of the boards near the hook buckled inward. After a few more hits it gave way entirely, and a hand protruded through the opening. As it groped about, the slowly exploring fingers moved ever nearer to the hook in its attaching eyelet. Tightening her grip on the pickax while holding it horizontal, she took a batter's stance and swung as hard as she could. She struck a bit off center, but the point of the curved steel easily penetrated the flesh, plied through the bones, and buried itself in the wood underneath. The fingers instantly splayed open, and a screech of agony exploded from the other side of the barrier. While she watched, the impaled appendage curled and writhed around the metal shaft like a dying spider.

Knowing he could still use the gun with his free hand, she wasted no time flipping up the restraining hook and shoving hard on the door. His screaming trebled as the wind caught the broad surface and pushed it away from her, dragging him with it. In the foot of clearance between its lower edge and the ground she could see his feet slipping in the dirt as he strained to keep it from swinging out farther. He ultimately lost the struggle, unable to overpower the force of such a giant sail for long. It began to move faster on its hinges, and he backpedaled furiously in order to keep upright, but didn't go quickly enough. He ended up dangling on his pinioned limb and being pulled over the ground until he slammed against the barn wall. Roaring with pain, he dropped the gun at his feet, reached around, and flapped with his other arm trying to grasp the pickax.

Ignoring his howls and sobs, she stepped forward, scooped up the weapon, and scanned the field for his partner. She saw him racing toward her, but he was still a hundred yards away. Pivoting to her right she sprinted for the far corner of the barn. Rounding the turn, she heard what sounded like a wasp zing by her ear.

"Shit!" she yelled, accelerating in the direction of the house and the highway beyond, the wind buffeting her as she ran. Her breathing reduced to jagged gasps and her chest burning from lack of air, she knew she'd never outlast her pursuer over a long distance.

Desperate plans raced through her head. The house she estimated to be sixty yards away. She could take cover on its far side and keep him at bay with the gun until the police came, she told herself. But eyeing the unfamiliar object in her hand, she wasn't even sure she could fire it. There were various small buttons on the handle, one of them probably a safety lock, and she'd no time to figure out which of them did what.

Perhaps she could make it to the road and flag a passing car. It hadn't seemed that far on her previous visit. She threw a quick look over her shoulder and saw no sign of him yet. Maybe he'd stopped to help his friend instead of coming after her. She felt a tiny swell of hope.

Then she remembered Hacket and his shotgun. Would he be waiting for her up ahead at the house? In a flash she slowed her pace, warily peering at the curtained windows again. She saw no sign of him behind the silvery webs of lace, but figured that's where he'd be lurking. Get to the base of the walls, where he won't have a clear shot!

her instincts screamed, and she poured on the speed, expecting a bullet to tear through her at any second. But as she drove hard with her legs, the distance between her and the front of the place seemed to elongate, as if she were sprinting in a dream. She threw a quick glance behind, to see if death would come from there. Still no one. She nevertheless started to zigzag, hoping to spoil both their aims and every stride of the way she kept straining to hear the first hint of a siren. Nothing sounded above the wind but her own breathing.

It must only be a few minutes since I made the call, she kept trying to reassure herself, but it felt like an eternity. She cursed herself now for not remembering the exact address. What if the name Hacket's farm wasn't enough to let the police find her? They couldn't trace her cellular. They might not be on their way at all.

Hot bile surged to the roof of her mouth as the possibility slammed home and dashed whatever feeble hopes she'd had of escaping. Passing below the first of several ground-floor windows, she started to choke on the sour liquid, until the force of coughing made her stumble, and she nearly lost her footing. Once more she glanced behind her, and this time saw her pursuer fly into view from behind the corner of the barn. Flashes of light spit out chest high in the darkness between them, and the air about her head buzzed like an entire swarm of angry hornets.

Terror shredded whatever logic she still possessed. She saw her nearest cover—the open door of the main entrance a few yards to her left. Operating on raw instinct, she veered toward it and threw herself into the ominous dark hallway. She barely noticed the pain of abrading her knees and arms as she landed, having no thought other than to escape the figure behind her. Struggling to her feet, she ran blindly through the darkness, only to trip on a staircase and sprawl forward again, her breath exploding out of her lungs in a loud cry. In an instant she once more regained her feet and tore up the steps. At the top of the landing she ran through the nearest door she could find, closed it behind her, and listened.

She heard his footfalls as he entered the house.

She frantically cast her eyes around the moonlit room, looking for a place to hide, and saw Hacket sitting in a large sofa chair staring at her.

She stifled a scream, and was about to bolt back out in the corridor before he could grab her, when she saw how still he was.

Catching her breath, she tiptoed forward, not taking her eyes off him. His arms dangled by his sides, and in the closed air the sour odor of urine tinged with the slightly sweet stench of excrement cloyed in the back of her throat until it was all she could do not to gag. She brought herself to reach into the folds of skin under his collar and feel for a pulse, but at her touch his head lolled forward onto her hand like a rag doll's, a sickening crepitus like a bag of shaken bones coming from his neck.

The thudding of her pursuer racing up the staircase catapulted her out of shock and sent her diving down behind the oversize chair in which Hacket's body lay. As she crouched in its shadow listening to the gunman approach the room, she thought she also heard, faint like a wheeze on the wind, a distant siren. A second later the door flew open and he entered.

She couldn't see him from where she hid, but the absence of creaking floorboards told her he stood completely still. Clutching the gun, she listened to his heavy breathing and attempted to silence her own. Surely he'll hear the approaching police, she thought, and just leave.

But he didn't budge.

Please go, she prayed silently.

Still no reaction.

Christ, he must know the cops are coming. Why doesn't he run?

Abruptly he strode past the chair and over to the window. He stood looking through it with his back to her, his pistol in his right hand.

Oh, God, she thought, her eyes frozen on his silhouette against the dimness outside. She'd no idea if she lay in a dark enough shadow that he wouldn't see her when he turned around. At the very least she'd have to hide her face without him hearing her movements. With him standing not ten feet in front of her, the slightest rustle of her clothing would be enough to catch his attention. She decided instead to try and wound him.

Holding her breath, she slowly raised the gun, pointed the muzzle at the middle of his upper back, then moved it a half foot to the right, aiming at his shoulder. Exhaling softly, she squeezed the trigger.

It didn't move.

She nearly cried out in despair, but kept her nerve enough to slide her thumb around feeling for some of the buttons she'd seen on the side of the handle. Locating one that felt promising, she pressed it.

Nothing.

She squeezed the trigger again.

It remained locked in place.

Another attempt to find the release proved just as fruitless. Terrified that he was about to turn and see her, she noiselessly put the gun down beside her, then stealthily lowered her head until she could cradle it in her arms against the floor.

She waited, not risking even a peek at him, hearing nothing but the wind outside and the ever louder sirens. If you must kill me, she began to pray, make it a clean shot to my head.

9

Steele woke to the sounds of many sirens racing through the night and cutting out somewhere not too far away. When the last of them died, he lay listening to the roar of surf rolling onto rocks thirty feet below the balcony to the bedroom and the sibilant rustle of wind rustling through the palms. Occasionally the gusts would start the stiff long leaves waving up and down, sending them rattling across the open slats of the windows the way fingers play a washboard. With all the racket, it took him a few seconds to hear Sandra Arness crying softly at his side.

He turned toward her and saw in the moonlight the elegant shape of her naked back, hips, and legs that had so inflamed him the night before. Except now she trembled before his gaze, arousing only his sadness for her instead of desire.

Their lovemaking had been a disaster. They started fiercely enough, hungrily clinging to each other as he explored her body with his hands and mouth the way a man long marooned might attack the first food offered him. She responded in kind, urging him to caress her everywhere and helping him to find her special spots, rushing him from one to the other. But despite her willingness, she made no moans of pleasure, and her cries that he touch her here and there soon took on a desperate quality, as if nothing he tried worked. When he did enter her, he found her dry. He offered to withdraw for fear of hurting her, but she became even more frenzied to have him continue, straining frantically against him while uttering pleas that he pump her harder, until Steele's own desire flagged along with his stamina. Out of shape, upset by his inability to bring her to climax, and embarrassed by his own libido slipping away, he simply petered out on her.

"Do you want me to leave?" he'd asked, miserable to the core about his pathetic performance.

"No! Don't go," she'd insisted, pulling him to her.

"Perhaps we can try later?"

She hadn't replied—just lay there in his arms staring into the darkness.

He'd stroked her hair and her back until she fell asleep and rolled away from him. At the time he noticed in the bursts of moonlight between passing clouds that her bedroom looked as unlived in as the rest of her house—everything neat, nothing lying around, no books, records, or magazines to suggest a nest where she relaxed and let herself go. A lack of personal photographs added to the sterility of the place, though a series of unfaded rectangles on the walls made him wonder if she'd once hung something there that she no longer wanted to look at. The clinician in him suspected that the meticulously ordered setting probably reflected how she organized the rest of her life, overly structured, rigidly controlled, and stripped of any reminders from her past—in effect the same strategy he'd used—to keep the terrible desperation he'd witnessed tonight at bay. But the woman's as brittle as china, and sex had breached those carefully constructed defenses, unleashing God knows what misery, he diagnosed just before he fell asleep, regretting that he ever got involved.

The sight of her crying now only reinforced his previous clinical assessment of her. He attempted to keep the cold stare of his medical eye from continuing to rove through her pain, classifying and slotting her while they lay naked together, but he might as well have tried to stop breathing. A trained physician's mind can never truly let a possible pathology drop without giving it a thorough going-over first, even when an intimate is concerned. So the mental process went on despite his finding it obscene, until he began to look on her as a woman with an agitated state of mind who needed professional help, not the potential lover he'd gone to bed with. Feeling an irrevocable chasm open between them, he asked as gently as he could, "Sandra, what can I do?"

"Nothing," she whispered, keeping her back to him. "Nobody can do anything for me."

"Why? Tell me what's the matter. Surely you don't think my bungled attempt at sex tonight is any reflection on you—?"

"Richard, I'm not that superficial," she rebuked. "I'm talking about grief. When I met you, and heard you describe your struggle with it, and then saw that you wanted me, I thought maybe I could escape my own hell, just for a while, a night even. Obviously I can't. I don't think I ever will."

"Grief? I thought you said you were divorced. Your husband's dead?" His questioning began feeling to him like taking a patient's history.

She didn't answer immediately. "No. I lost a child," she finally said, her voice barely above a whisper. "My beautiful little Tommy, over a year and a half ago. He's the boy killed by that bird flu you've been discussing all day."

Steele felt the back of his mouth go dry.

"He'd barely turned three," she continued. "Every minute since has been an agony, everything I do meaningless. My only peace of mind lies in those few seconds when I first awake and haven't yet remembered that he's dead. I suspect I'm one of those people for whom all that will never change—who will never 'get over it.' I know what they're like. I've seen them in my practice. We're the living dead."

He floundered around for something to say, but she continued to talk.

"I went to this conference for the same reason a murder victim's loved ones attend the killer's execution. I thought it would help me find closure, my seeing the experts tell me why my son died, watching them demonstrate how they'd at least conquered his killer, exerted the dominion of my profession over that filthy disease!" Her tone suddenly became bitter and her shoulders shook with a new wave of crying. "It didn't help any," she sobbed. "Nothing can change how dreadfully I miss him. Nothing at all."

Steele couldn't utter a sound. A lifetime of consoling the living about the dead had taught him there were no words to comfort a parent over the loss of a child, though he'd always struggled to find them. "I'm so sorry, Sandra," he started to whisper, moving closer and reaching around to hold her to him. At once she stopped being a psychological entity to him and became a fellow parent, one who'd suffered an agony he prayed he would never have to face. "So very, very sorry," he repeated. Even with the heat, she felt cold as ice.

When he next awoke, she'd left the bed. "Sandra?" he called out. No answer.

He glanced at the luminous dial on his watch. It read 2:10. He'd been asleep for barely an hour. "Sandra?" he said again, louder this time, as he got out of bed. Then he saw her, standing naked on the low stone wall running around the edge of her balcony. "Sandra!" he screamed, and raced for the sliding glass door that separated them. She remained with her back to him, her legs slightly spread, just as she'd stood when he'd first seen her, but now her long black hair, no longer braided, streamed out behind her.

Throwing open the panel, he felt the full fury of the wind and heard an avalanche of water thud onto the coral beach below. "Sandra, for God's sake!" he pleaded as he started across the thirty feet separating them.

Her skin bathed in moonlight, she seemed white as marble and just as impenetrable. Whether she heard his approach above the noise of the waves, he never knew. Before he could grab her, she flexed her knees, arched into the air, and disappeared over the edge in a perfect dive.

"You were damn lucky he didn't spot you hiding behind that big easy chair," said the detective in charge.

"I know," replied Kathleen Sullivan, her voice barely audible.

The cop continued to scowl down at her, holding open the rear door of the patrol car in which she sat and looking not at all happy with the explanation she'd just given about why she'd been there in the first place.

Unable to think of anything useful to add, she pressed herself into the interior of the vehicle and tried to stop shaking. The difference between the gunman seeing her and what ultimately happened had been a passing cloud obscuring the moonlight during the seconds he had turned to run from the room. Finally she asked, "What were they doing here, and why did they kill Mr. Hacket?"

He sighed heavily. "It looks like you walked in on a particularly vicious home invasion. They were probably trying to rob him—people get killed for less than a hundred bucks these days—and old folks living alone are a prime target. Everybody around here knew him, including us. Rumor had it he'd come into some money lately, after he gave up farming well over a year ago and bought a snazzy new truck. Some of the local gossip went as far as to suggest he kept a small fortune hidden in this old place. I don't buy *that* story—it pretty much looks like he lived from hand to mouth, from what we can see inside. But I guess tales of a secret stash were enough to attract his killers. They certainly took him by surprise. He never even got to that shotgun of his—it stood cocked and ready in the front hallway. They were probably trying to frighten a nonexistent bundle out of him when you showed up at the party. So they broke his neck and came after you, to leave no witnesses."

She shuddered, remembering the ghostly head she saw snapped to one side in the window. "But they had silencers," she said, still trying to rein in her trembling. "If they had silencers, why didn't they shoot him?" In her state of shock she initially had no idea why that particular incongruity should matter to her. Except as a scientist, if something didn't make sense, however trivial, she reflexively saw it as a void that needed filling.

"Who knows?" replied the detective with an impatient wave of his hand. "Maybe the creeps liked wringing necks." He turned to watch a large black van marked HPD pull into the yard.

His callous remark made her shiver. "Officer, let me explain something to you," she said, getting his attention again. "I'm a woman in a profession where my whole life is predicated on a simple notion that if I find the *reason* things happen, I can control what happens. A person like me gets particularly rattled when the random luck of a passing cloud determines whether I live or die. So my way of coping with an event like this is to understand the how and why of it. Maybe then I can kid myself into thinking I could spot it coming, if there ever is a next time. Otherwise I'm liable to end up scared that I'll get jumped for no reason and with no warning every time I go out. So for my sake, please, humor me."

By the vehicle's interior light she saw his face squinch into a puzzled frown as he studied her. "I don't really know why they didn't shoot him," he said after a few seconds, his voice all at once hesitant. "It looks like they intended to torch the place afterwards—we found some cans of gasoline in one of the front rooms. Maybe they didn't want a bullet in his body, to try and make it look accidental. But it would never have worked. A coroner might attribute a broken neck to the guy falling a couple of stories as a burning house collapsed on him—charred remains wouldn't tell him much else—but no way could the arson squad miss a fire set with something as crude as gasoline." He straightened up and arched his back, stretching it with a grimace. "Hell, doped-up hotheads who kill these days—they often don't make sense. One thing you can be sure of," he added, giving her a dour smile while the troubled expression in his eyes deepened, "we'll be going after these two in a big way, whoever they are or wherever they're from. In paradise we don't take kindly to anyone importing this league of viciousness."

Parked haphazardly around them sat a half dozen police cars, their overhead lights making the night pulse red, white, and blue. He looked up as a second wave of vehicles, station wagons and RVs with media logos on their doors, began pulling into the yard. "You understand, you're not to talk about this case, even though the media are going to have a field day about you being here," he ordered, glowering at these latest arrivals.

She nodded.

A young officer ran up to them from the direction of the barn. "Here's her phone and purse, sir," he said. "We found it just where she said it would be, full of weeds. And the door there is exactly the way she described as well, broken boards and all. There's not a sign of the two killers though, but we traced bloodstains to the field in back. We've got lots to sample for DNA of the one she got in the hand, and the pickax should have the prints of the other guy who likely helped pull it out."

The chief detective's frown grew as he received the articles. "Have you put out an APB?"

"Already done, sir!" said the younger man. He stooped down to peer in the door and said, "Ma'am, my family and I, we always watch your program. I'm so glad you're all right."

She looked up at his youthful face and thought he didn't look much older than the boyfriends Lisa brought around these days. Wondering how long it would take to mold that eager expression into the hardened mask caked with fatigue and cynicism of his superior, she replied, "Thank you, Officer." When he left, she all at once wanted nothing more than to hear the sound of her daughter's voice.

"Could I have my things, please?" she asked the older detective. "Then I'd like to go. I've got to get my samples to the genetics lab at the university, and I'm due to fly home to New York at noon. If you want, I'll make myself available for any additional dispositions you'll need through the NYPD."

He hesitated, then handed her purse to her. "You know, I watch your program, too, Dr. Sullivan." His voice was all at once gentle and, to her astonishment, his weathered face shedded its weariness as he broke into a smile. "My oldest daughter's a real fan, and is in the biology undergraduate program here in Honolulu. She'd be thrilled if I could give her your autograph."

Sullivan scrawled her name on the back of an evidence envelope, marveling at how misleading the cop's gruff exterior had been. She'd barely finished when the radio in the front seat crackled, "All cars in the Kailua vicinity. We have a 911 call by a man reporting a suicide at 205 Kaliki Road. Please respond."

"Jesus Christ, that's just a few minutes from here," muttered the detective, reaching to grab the microphone from under the dashboard. "Must be the full moon," he said, clicking the TALK button to take the call.

Steele raced from Sandra's bedroom after calling 911 and peered over the edge of the balcony, desperately searching for a way to reach the ocean. A story below and fifty feet to his left, he saw steps leading down the cliffs from a small yard. Not bothering to dress, he ran inside, raced to the ground floor, and found another set of glass doors opening on what must have once been her son's play area. In seconds he reached the stone staircase he'd seen from above and started down it, desperately scanning the churning waters for any sign of Sandra. Each time the moon emerged he saw white surf curling around large black knuckles of coral amid open sections of frothing water. Maybe she landed in a deep tide pool, he prayed, but as he watched the thundering breakers and hissing foam of their aftermath, his hopes plummeted.

He reached a small cove and started scrambling over the rocks, slicing his palms and soles yet paying the cuts no mind. "Sandra!" he screamed, barely able to hear himself over the roar of the ocean. Occasionally a swell rose enough to engulf him, and he ended up clinging to spiny outcrops as the water surged back out to sea, threatening to suck him with it. At one moment he lost his grip and felt himself being swept away until an incoming breaker slammed him back toward shore. He managed to get his legs up to break the impact between himself and the jagged surfaces waiting for him there, then screamed as the entire length of his body scraped over their projections and into shallower water.

Scrambling to his feet, he found himself on a flat rise where the surf only occasionally reached. He peered into the maelstrom around him, vainly trying to catch sight of her, and had all but given up hope when he spotted what looked like a patch of seaweed caught in a tide pool. A breaking wave parted the black strands to reveal the white roundness of her face and breasts as she floated on her back, seeming to stare at the stars with sightless eyes.

In seconds he was down to her, cradling her neck in his arm and covering her cold lips with his in an attempt to blow into her lungs. But he'd no sooner begun when he felt his arm covered in some sort of sludge. At first he thought it had to be a kind of pollutant, perhaps from a sewer outlet. Then he realized that it had the consistency of toothpaste squeezed from the tube, and that strands of the stuff were streaming out the back of her skull.

He instantly retreated into the familiarity of technique, diligently providing her with two puffs of air followed by fifteen compressions on her chest—exactly as he'd always taught his residents in cases of a solitary rescuer—rather than face the reality that her lungs would never breathe again.

That's how the paramedics, the police, and the accompanying media found him—naked, methodically doing CPR on her corpse, and oozing blood head to toe from his abraded skin.

10

His story would normally have appealed only to the local appetites with a taste for the lurid. But because he'd been on the national networks the previous evening calling for the regulation of naked DNA, the media swarmed all over the tragedy. By noon local time he'd become the lead item on all the major evening news broadcasts back East. Images of him draped in a blanket, looking dazed, and still smeared in blood while being led to a police car began to fill television screens across four time zones as commentators read out seamy story leads.

"Yesterday's outspoken critic of naked DNA, Dr. Richard Steele, is himself found naked, early this morning, in a suicide's love nest."

"The naked truth! DNA expert now questioned in doctor's suicide."

"From triumph to tragedy: Credibility of advocate for regulating naked DNA ends up on the rocks. Details after a word from our sponsor."

No one bothered to mention that the cops released him later that same morning. Neither did the announcers show any qualms about smearing the concerns of an entire scientific community in their eagerness to get him. But that they reduced Sandra's death to little more than a titillating aside he found the most disgusting of all.

"Bastards!" he screamed, hurling his remote at the TV in his hotel room, then wincing with the effort. His many scrapes and cuts had been tended to in the ER of Honolulu General, but they still burned like hell.

The television survived his assault, only to show some media stud with blow-dried hair who proceeded to gleefully report what Kathleen Sullivan had been put through last night.

"My God," said Steele, having heard nothing about it. Aghast, he tried to phone her, only to be told that she'd already checked out and left for the airport. She may not even know what a circus I've made of things, he thought, wondering if she'd caught the bulletins about him before getting on her plane.

Next he called home and got Martha on the line. "I'm all right," he quickly reassured her. "The police let me go—"

"Just come home, Richard," she interjected. "Now! Chet needs you here. He's too ashamed to go to school in the morning."

Three hours later he got a standby seat. Before boarding he called Dr. Julie Carr and requested that she inform him when the memorial for Sandra would be.

"Of course," she replied without hesitation. "But what about you? Are you all right? It must have been awful for you."

The kindness in her voice nearly broke the tight hold he had on his emotions. "Oh, I'll be okay." To his own ears he didn't sound too convincing.

"Dr. Steele," she said, "this may be presumptuous, but you probably need to hear someone tell you that you didn't cause her death."

Nor did I prevent it! he nearly snapped back. "Thanks," he said instead. "I appreciate your saying it."

"Take care of yourself."

By dawn, New York time, he pulled up to his front door at Thirty-sixth and Lexington. Depositing his luggage in the entranceway as noiselessly as possible, he went directly to Chet's room, where he tiptoed over to the head of his son's bed and waited for him to waken. As he sat watching the boy sleep, the sun peeped through the blinds and spread across the youth's face. Hesitantly Steele reached out and stroked the dark unruly hair. Chet stirred in his sleep, then fell still, accepting the touch with a contented smile.

One Week Later

Morgan stared sullenly over the gray surface of New York's East River as it surged south toward the tip of Manhattan, the Statue of Liberty, and the ocean beyond. The color reminded him of the paint used on his garage floor—glossy and meant to disguise grease or oil, but never quite doing the job. Its rush to depart America made him entertain similar ideas of leaving the country.

He raised his eyes to where, on the Queens side opposite him, a giant *Coca-Cola* sign bade the water's flotsam adieu. The *C*s towered nearly as tall as the multitude of towers, grimy chimneys, and concrete silos that dominated the industrial stubble of that far shore. Behind him descended the continuous noise of traffic from the overhead Franklin D. Roosevelt Drive, the sounds blending with the cries of seagulls. Further back still, the buildings of New York City Hospital and the protean complex of the medical school, each edifice sporting an insignia that resembled a giant happy-face button, smiled down on him. Over it all fell a glistening drizzle, the droplets too fine to be seen yet substantial enough to make the air feel like a filmy gauze against his face.

"You tell our client that he damn well better not arrange another 'wrong place at the wrong time' type of accident for her anytime soon!" exploded the man standing beside him. "It would look too suspicious. As it is, with those idiots of his bungling everything the way they did—I mean, using guns with silencers during what's suppose to be a home invasion—give me a fucking break! We're just damn lucky that despite everything the Honolulu cops still interpreted the fiasco more or less the way we intended."

Morgan said nothing in reply, continuing to stare into the distance as the murk of evening clotted around them. In forty-nine more days, I'll be fixed for life and safely hiding out in a tropical paradise, he kept telling himself. But the business with Sullivan and the increasing prospects of getting caught had left him so rattled that the promise of unlimited wealth no longer steeled his nerve the way it used to. Nor did the chance to destroy the livelihood of those at Biofeed International who'd willingly profited by what he'd done and then spit him out when it went bad fire him up anymore. He'd even begun to fantasize about bolting, except he knew that their "client" would have him hunted down and killed. For the first time in his life, sleep no longer came without the help of pills, and all too often when he did nod off, he'd awaken a few hours later, his heart pounding and his breathing labored.

"Panic attacks," his doctor had decreed, handing him yet more capsules, red this time instead of canary yellow.

A gust of wind slapped him from behind, pulling him out of his reverie with a dash of cold rain to the back of his head and neck. He glanced sideways, studying the man who had recruited him to this madness with the lure of money and revenge as bait. He knew he better choose what he said to him with care, or he'd reveal the extent his appetite for seeing it through had weakened and get himself tagged a security risk. "But if she finds the vectors and goes public," he began, "someone at Biofeed may panic and decide to come clean. Then it'll be my name and the connection with Rodez that turns up. You know she has to die before we let any of that happen."

"I know, goddamnit! I know! But kill her now, and the police will rethink her 'close call' in Hawaii. Right off, they'll suspect that she might have been the target all along, after which it's not such a stretch to consider somebody didn't want her snooping around Hacket's farm looking for genetic vectors related to bird flu. Once they start marching their homicide investigation down *that* particular path of inquiry, panicky tongues at Biofeed will be even more likely to loosen, and for sure the cops will find the trail through Biofeed to you. I repeat, tell our 'client' to call off his dogs!"

Morgan's sensation of feeling trapped tightened its hold on him, juicing a squeeze of cold sweat from his already damp skin. "And how the hell am I going to persuade him to do that?" he snapped. "Don't you get it? His team won't quit. They're probably already here in New York, still intent on offing her."

"Get a message to the man. Remind him how little time there is to go. Tell him that it will take at least another three weeks for the lab workers in Hawaii to finish processing her specimens, perhaps longer. Even if they manage to uncover the vector, which is no sure thing given their inexperience, the discovery will be so unbelievable I'm predicting she'll doubt the result and won't dare release the findings without first confirming them at the lab here in New York. That could give us a few weeks more. We can stop her then, just before she finally links it all to Biofeed—"

"Too many ifs and maybes," Morgan cut in, allowing his long simmering resentment at being ordered around to creep into his tone. "He won't wait."

"But he must! By that time, whether the cops pass her death off as a good, old-fashioned random act of violence, New York style, will hardly matter. Because whatever they finally decide, it will take them a few weeks more to figure it out, and then it will be too late for them to stop us."

"That's playing it unbelievably tight."

"Kill her now, and you'll end up giving the cops a full seven weeks to find you. Do you prefer that?"

Morgan's stomach clamped into a knot. "Of course not!" he started to say, but the taste of bile tickled the back of his throat, and he had to swallow several times more before he could force it back down.

"Then we agree," the man continued, taking advantage of Morgan's difficulty speaking. "Except for God's sake convince him to let us handle her this time. The way his exotic imported help does things, they're liable to screw it up again."

"What if she figures it all out and goes public earlier than you expect," Morgan challenged as soon as he got his voice back, "before we can silence her?"

The man glared at him. "Don't worry. My position gives me sufficient access to her that I can keep tabs on her progress."

"We both know you can't guarantee that," Morgan countered, his defiance growing.

"The topic's closed, Bob! Understand?" His bellow sent a dozen seagulls that had gathered around them to look for a handout flapping skyward and screeching in protest. "Or would you like me to start dealing with our 'client' directly and inform him that you no longer have the enthusiasm you initially showed for our project?"

Morgan immediately fell silent, feeling more ensnared than ever. His skin grew even stickier against his shirt, and he caught a whiff of his own sweat—sour and stale as it wafted out of the collar of his coat.

"Good. Then let's consider that matter settled," declared the man, his voice all at once as nonchalant as if he'd just passed some minor motion at a routine business meeting. "How's our crop doing in the south?" he asked brightly.

Morgan couldn't change gears so easily. Still seething over their exchange, he sullenly answered, "According to my sources, it'll start being harvested, marketed, and replanted on schedule next week."

"And you've made our client understand that as a weapon, it will be a sleeper, not like what we're using for the initial strike. I don't want him tracking us down afterwards with complaints that he's getting impatient for results."

"He's been duly advised."

"Good!"

Another item on the agenda imperiously dispensed with, thought Morgan as silence once more congealed in the space between them.

"Now, there is someone you should take care of immediately," the man suddenly announced a few seconds later, "before he becomes a big problem."

The statement caught Morgan completely off guard. "Who?"

"That doctor, Richard Steele—the one who spoke so eloquently at the conference and was on TV, then made such an ass of himself."

"Him? I've already had him checked out. He's harmless. My security people tell me he mostly spends his afternoons in the park with the other old men."

"Don't underestimate him. As a physician, his medical knowledge could neutralize this whole part of our operation"—he gestured up at the FDR—"if he found it out in time. And a doctor doesn't rise to the top in ER without having brains or his share of nerve. Should Sullivan ever get him revved up enough that he teamed up with her, and the two of them were on our tail, we'd be in trouble. Now here's what I have in mind . . ."

The chatter of an approaching helicopter drowned the man out. No longer able to hear him, Morgan looked up and spotted the craft against a slate of black clouds that promised yet more showers. In seconds the stuttering roar amplified enough to hurt his ears as the machine drew closer, hovered above them, and then slowly descended to an asphalt tarmac off to their left that looked no bigger than a couple of tennis courts. Standing beside the surrounding chain-link fence, they were close enough to the accompanying blast of dusty air that they had to turn away, hunching their backs as it erupted around them. Morgan fished around in the pocket of his raincoat, its hem whipping about his legs, and brought out a disposable panoramic camera that he'd purchased from a souvenir shop on the way over. Looking very much like a tourist, he snapped a string of photos of the craft after it had settled onto the ground, making sure to include the familiar sight of the UN building in the background—as a landmark for his pilots.

"You're sure our three copters will fit on that wee bit of space?" his companion shouted through cupped hands into his right ear, making it throb even more.

As if in answer, a second machine appeared overhead, adding to the din while it, too, slowly lowered itself until it rocked to a stop beside the first. While the whine of the rotors died down, Morgan pointed to the yellow markings within the landing area indicating where there remained room for a third, then continued to snap pictures. He seemed to be capturing the passengers as they disembarked and entered the small trailer home that served as a heliport depot for the greatest city on earth. In reality he focused on the nearby pumps and fuel storage tanks. In another shot he raised the lens enough that he also got a good picture of the hospital. In yet another he swung around a little further south, capturing a wide angle view of the waterfront in that direction as well.

"And it's certain we'll have access to this facility at the precise time we need?" questioned his companion.

"Absolutely," Morgan replied, finishing off the roll of film and pocketing the camera. "None of the companies using this port can park here overnight, and local air traffic will be shut down a half hour prior to the start of the show. We've scheduled our arrival to refuel just in time to beat that deadline. Then we'll feign mechanical difficulty, to postpone taking off until it's time to start the attack."

The man turned to survey the expressway overhead. "And how much of *it* will be shut down this year?"

"Twenty-eight blocks—from Fourteenth to Forty-second." Looking up, he gestured with both arms wide open as if he were telling a fish story. "And because it's the millennium, they're also closing off a smaller section below the Brooklyn Bridge."

His companion continued to scan the edge of the elevated roadway in either direction, and Morgan, in spite of himself, began to picture what it would be like crammed with people. In his imagination he added a crowd along the river's edge and an even bigger throng of latecomers jamming the streets leading to the river. As for the number of onlookers that could pack themselves onto every available rooftop, he'd no idea, but the city had already issued an estimate that total attendance in this particular area would hit a new record, topping at least three hundred thousand.

"How will you deploy the craft?"

"One for the FDR. One for the walkways at the river's edge where we are now, and one for the side streets, including the rooftops, all the way back to Lexington. That third pilot will be paying particular attention to people on the hospital buildings." He paused, visualizing each of the dozen or so structures capped off with a teeming crown of revelers. Then he added, "With any luck we'll infect half their medical staff in a single pass, which will ultimately add to the confusion once victims start showing symptoms and come into ER. Of course, by then it'll be their own DNA that's making them ill, and they'll be beyond medical help." He hoped that his forced enthusiasm sounded convincing. In truth, the more he talked, the more filled with loathing he became.

"What height will you be spraying from?"

"At least a hundred feet, and it will feel gentle as a mist. Unlike what we shot into the corn plants, this vector, since it's designed to be inhaled or to simply settle on exposed skin, eyes, or lips, can be delivered from much higher up with a far wider dispersal. At least, that's what our lab simulations told us. And we figure the microscopic lipid particles we use to keep the invasive DNA intact will give the liquid a slightly greasy texture. At the end of a hot day, it might actually feel soothing to sunburned skin, inviting the targets to massage it into flesh that's already inflamed. In fact, to minimize panic and everyone's running away, we're going to phone in rumors to the media that a skin-care company is pulling a publicity stunt, releasing one of their after-sun products onto the crowd. Hopefully that'll maximize the numbers who we'll douse."

"And the infection rate?"

"According to our own animal trials, about forty percent of those exposed will succumb. That's a hundred and twenty thousand people."

"Oh, my God," the man whispered, as softly as if uttering an actual prayer. He stared up at the expressway, wearing a look of dismay, the way a person might appreciate a troubling work of art.

Watching him, Morgan wondered if up to that moment the man had seen their plan only as an academic exercise, much as he himself had until one night over a cornfield in Oklahoma. Had his companion's coming to the site and hearing the practical details finally driven home to him the full impact of what they were about to do? Now, maybe you'll start to sweat it the way I have, he hoped. If so, from here on in, you and I will at least be on the same footing as far as nerve is concerned, and that ought to put an end to your unilateral threats to report waning enthusiasm. But in his own mind's eye he continued to see the crowds as if they had already gathered in the freeway and along the river. They were all craning their necks and staring in his direction—compelled to see the monster who would fatally alter their genetic core.

"Now about this business of Richard Steele," continued the man at his side, breaking a silence that had seemed to go on forever.

Tuesday, May 23, 6:55 A.M.

It had been a summons, not an invitation.

"I'd like to see you for a breakfast meeting, Dr. Sullivan," Greg Stanton had told her over the phone last week. "How's Tuesday morning at seven?"

She shivered as she made her way through the darkened deserted hallways leading to his office, but not from cold. The Bunker, generations of medical students had labeled this place. It sat atop a twenty-story obelisk otherwise filled with labs and classrooms where these would-be doctors got their basic training in medical sciences before being set loose on patients in the hospital. From it emanated the decisions that regulated their daily existence, shaped their subsequent residency choices, and in some cases whether or not they even had a career in medicine.

But the latest batch of these healers-in-training wouldn't flock around their professors on the floors below and settle in for yet another day of their four-year journey until an hour later, at eight. And the administrators who kept the process running would stream into the carpeted offices she now hurried past no sooner than a half hour after that. A 7:00 A.M. appointment with the dean, she knew, usually meant that he wanted no one else around to hear the yelling or crying he expected from whatever nasty or particularly sensitive matter he intended to discuss.

"Good morning, Dr. Sullivan," greeted Greg Stanton after she'd knocked on his open door. He stepped out from behind his massive rosewood desk and crossed an expanse of taupe-colored broadloom to shake her hand. The smell of fresh coffee filled the air, and she spotted a sterling pot alongside a plate of croissants on a table nestled amongst a quartet of beige sofa chairs. The really brutal encounters, she'd learned from other victims of these early sessions, didn't include breakfast. So it must be simply a sensitive topic, she guessed, somewhat relieved.

"Morning, Greg, and please, it's Kathleen," she replied, determined to keep their encounter on a first-name basis. A veteran of unequal power relationships in the world of academic medicine, she always found that a touch of informality never hurt, and that sometimes it could tip the unlevel playing field a little to her advantage. As nice as Stanton had appeared to be in his previous dealings with her, the authority of his office over her work and professional standing remained absolute, and that left her instinctively wary of him.

"Of course. Kathleen it is, then," he replied, offering her a place to sit. "Coffee?"

She accepted the cup he poured for her, measuring his expression for any hint of unpleasantness to come, but his hard blue eyes and polite smile remained inscrutable. As usual he'd dressed to impress, sporting an impeccably tailored tan suit and aqua shirt, which suited his complexion. Around the faculty club a few wags would refer to him from time to time as "the model." When he caught her studying him, she quickly rallied, "You look wonderful, Greg. Obviously you don't let the pressures of this job interfere with your swimming," and settled back, signaling her readiness to hear what he had to say.

He took the chair opposite her, not bothering to take a coffee for himself. "I'll come right to the point," he began. "Since your meeting in Hawaii I've taken a lot of flak—mainly on account of your sensationalist speculation about genetically modified food being linked to that case of bird flu they had over there a year and a half ago."

She instantly tensed. "Now wait a minute. That meeting has nothing to do with you. I was named chairperson by the UN independent of my faculty appointment here—"

"I know, I know!" he cut in. "But the biotechnical industry doesn't make such fine distinctions. In short, a group of CEOs represented by that asshole Sydney Aimes have insisted on a retraction, or they threaten to withdraw their endowments to our school, which, I'm sure I don't have to tell you, are considerable."

"That's blackmail!" she sputtered, already bolt upright at the edge of her chair.

"Yes, and I'm mad as hell about it, too. But the University Board of Directors has tied my hands. Either you comply, or I'm to demand your resignation."

At first she couldn't speak, his blunt ultimatum so took her breath away. "You'd sell out academic freedom like that, Greg?" she finally squeaked. "I don't believe it!"

"Of course I wouldn't. And I'd support you to the hilt if you had a shred of proof to back your claims. But you haven't produced anything concrete, Kathleen. And you didn't help your credibility any, sneaking out to that farm in the middle of the night. The bloody press made you look like an amateur sleuth rather than a reputable scientist. Thank God at least you weren't hurt."

His rebukes made her cheeks burn. "Why? Would my getting killed have lost you even more endowment money?" She sprang to her feet, determined to walk out on him.

"That's a cheap shot, Dr. Sullivan!" he said, rising and stepping to bar her way. "You know I've always promoted you and your work, and I intend to continue doing so now. Frankly, I'm shocked you don't know me better than to think I'd bow to that kind of pressure." He ended his stern reproach with a carbon copy of the smile he'd first greeted her with and gestured for her to retake her seat. "Now sit down, and let's figure a way out of this mess. It so happens I share some of your fears about the vectors they're using to swap genes these days."

She paid attention only to his eyes. Their cool gaze told her nothing.

"Please, Kathleen," he added gently, as if the harshness of his outburst had never occurred, "give me a chance to help. Your cause is too important to lose you over something like this."

She hesitated, cooling her temper and calculating whether she should trust him. Again she considered her past experience with the man. Just as he claimed, he'd always been a supporter of her research and her presence in the medical school. But through her discoveries and publications, along with her high profile, she'd generated her own fair share of endowment money over the years as well. How much would he stand up for her now that she threatened to become a financial liability? She knew he'd certainly done his share of taking an ax to the place, but that was the norm in all medical schools during this age of cutbacks. Nevertheless, she'd listened to the expected grumblings about his ruthlessness from some of those whose programs he'd chopped. And if he'd ever stood up to the pressures of the buck and the board to take a moral stand, she'd certainly not heard about it. The fact that he dressed like a successful stockbroker didn't boost her confidence any that he would do so. "What do you have in mind?" she asked, remaining on her feet.

He gave his instant smile again, making her suspect he'd practiced it before a mirror. "Is there anything you can show me that will back your claims about genetic vectors being infectious to humans?" he demanded, his eyes flashing with eagerness. "Even if it's only a preliminary result, I could take what you have to the board and use it to argue your case. For instance, I inferred from the newspaper articles that you actually gathered some specimens on your escapade to that farm, before all hell broke out. Are you analyzing them?"

Her researcher's instinct not to divulge data prior to publication—honed from years of guarding against plagiarism amongst colleagues—prevented her from answering immediately. "Why, yes," she finally admitted, figuring Stanton didn't pose that kind of risk. In fact, not cooperating with him could prove more dangerous to her career than any copycat ever had. "They're being analyzed at Honolulu University. We ought to know in another three or four weeks whether we've got any rogue strands of DNA indicating the presence of a man-made vector, but I think a find there is a long shot."

He grimaced. "Would you be willing to give me a report immediately if you do get anything that even suggests you're on the right track? I'd keep it confidential, of course, but with something in hand, I'll be in a position to not only insist that this *is* an issue of academic freedom after all, but that . . . let's see . . . how shall I put this so it will sound good for the board?" He paused, making a show of searching the ceiling as if the right words might be hidden there. " . . . Your un-orthodox way of getting the samples in the first place is a credit to your scientific doggedness, not a symptom of your being . . ." Trailing off again, he stared straight at her, flashed her a grin both wicked and wide, and then added, "Shall we say, *flaky?*" He let loose a low chuckle that seemed to fill the room.

For the first time since she'd entered his domain, she saw his eyes give a spark of amusement to match the ever-ready pleasantry of his mouth, and she at last started to feel a bit more at ease. "Flaky?" she said, playfully cocking an entire side of her brow at him.

"Not that *I* think you are, of course," he quickly countered, the merriment still in his face. "It's the impression the media gave." Then his visage darkened. "Of course, Richard Steele's fiasco didn't help you any. If he hadn't gotten himself in such a scandal, the press probably would have handled your story with more respect. I apologize for foisting him on you. Obviously the man's judgment is still in the toilet."

The sudden criticism caught her off guard. "What do you mean?" she said, finding herself rising to Steele's defense. "His judgment at the conference seemed fine." Surprised at how protective of him she felt she added, "Hell, if one tenth of your profession caught on to the issues as fast as he did, we might finally have some medical organizations speaking out officially in support of our concerns, instead of the shameful silence that's been the norm so far. And what that poor woman did, along with his being with her, had nothing to do with poor judgment—" She abruptly checked herself, seeing a look of astonishment on Stanton's face at her outburst. "Sorry, it's just that he did a fine job with us, and the way they attacked him in the media seemed so unfair. I figure the last thing the poor guy needs is someone else badmouthing him." She paused. "What's his story, anyway, I mean besides his heart attack?" She tried to sound offhand.

"His wife died nearly two years ago, and he doesn't seem able to get over her death."

"Oh!" she exclaimed, somehow not having expected that answer. Divorce, maybe; that he'd become a workaholic and driven his family away, yes; but not that the woman in his life was dead. He seemed so close to her own age that the possibility he'd already suffered that kind of loss hadn't crossed her mind.

"I thought the conference and the issues would be the perfect opportunity for him to make himself useful again," Stanton continued. "Have you talked with him since you got back?" His voice sounded pained.

"No. He left a message on my machine, apologizing for causing so much embarrassment for everyone, but when I tried to reach him—a dozen times at least in the last week—to tell him he's got nothing to apologize for, he didn't take my calls. How is he?"

"Who knows? The man won't speak with me, either." He sighed, and studied her as if making a calculation in his head. "Are you interested in him, by any chance?"

"No!" she countered far too quickly, feeling her face redden. And what business is it of yours if I am, she very nearly added, but held her fire. She'd begun to sense more to Stanton than his being worried over a troublesome staff member. "Dr. Steele seemed a nice man, but sad," she continued, retreating into formality. "I felt sorry for him is all, and still do, even more so, now that you've explained what he's been struggling through. But why do you ask? Is he your friend?"

"He was. I don't know what we are now. To make matters worse, Aimes also seems determined to make an even bigger example of him."

"What do you mean?"

"He's demanded Richard be fired outright, and he's not offering him a way out the way he did to you."

"What? I can see Aimes coming after me, but why take such a hard line with Steele?"

"Because he can get away with it, for starters. The board is already furious at Richard for all the sordid headlines he generated. In practically every article or news item the reporters stressed his affiliation with the university and New York City Hospital, and that kind of negative publicity boils down to fewer endowments. For that reason alone, they're more than ready to carry out Aimes's demand."

"The creeps!"

"But Aimes's real motive, I suspect, is to provide a warning shot to any other high-profile medical authority who may be thinking of adding his or her voice to a call for controls on genetically modified foods. No offense, but while everyone has gotten used to environmentalists and geneticists raising a ruckus from all the fuss they've made in Europe, respected American physicians starting to sound the alarm—now that would be a whole new order of PR problem for Aimes's clients. People listen to doctors, especially homegrown ones. That's why Aimes wants him dismissed for his part in making 'unsubstantiated, unscientific slander.' So you see, poor Richard is in more trouble than you are, given the mood the board's in."

She felt aghast. "Can't you protect him?"

His posture seemed to crumple inside the snappy clothes. "Who knows?" He shrugged, looking defeated. "Even if I could save him from those jerks, which I don't know is possible anymore, I can't protect the man against himself."

"Pardon?"

"Before his heart attack, his staff found him increasingly difficult to work with. They only tolerated him because's he's such a brilliant clinician. But even if he's found medically fit, he can't go back to ER and continue to behave the way he has."

Her incredulity grew. "You mean he could actually lose his job even without Aimes's help?"

"Oh, God, I hope not, but it looks bad—" He stopped and drew himself erect. "I really can't discuss this with you," he coolly announced.

"Sorry, it's just that during the bit of time Dr. Steele and I talked, he gave me the impression—well, that his work seemed all he had."

Stanton now appeared uneasy, perhaps even embarrassed in front of her. "Do we have an understanding about your keeping me informed of your test results or not?" he asked, his take-charge tone back in full force.

"Of course," she answered politely.

"Good. But three to four weeks—that's a long time for me to stall the board. You can't hurry up those people in Hawaii any?"

"Afraid not. The testing procedure is long and complicated, and they have their regular work to do besides."

"Remember I don't need a finished study with every *i* dotted and *t* crossed. I suggest you check every few days, and whatever they find, however insignificant you might think it is, let me see it right away." He broke into another of his polished smiles. "I'll argue that it's promising."

She nodded and smiled back, extending her hand to say good-bye. He took it, but seemed distracted by something behind her. She turned and saw through his corner window a magnificent view of the East River, the molten colors of the rising sun advancing over its slick black surface like liquid fire. To the southwest were the World Trade Towers, already aflame in the early light.

"That's quite a sight," she commented appreciatively. "We have a view of the towers from my offices, but this is fantastic."

"Yes, I never tire of it," he told her, continuing to stare at the spectacle.

The wheels of the subway squealed like a half-slaughtered pig as Kathleen hurtled toward her stop, the noise adding to the headache she'd been nurturing since saying good-bye to Stanton. She'd been so upset over Steele's predicament that her own situation—the fact that she could lose her laboratory if she lost her appointment at the medical school and university—had only just started to sink in. Because while private funding from industrial contracts and media revenues paid part of the rent, the harsh reality remained: She'd never be able to fund the overall operation on her own.

She took the steps leading to the street in pairs and strode the three blocks to her offices overlooking Washington Square at a record pace. But the exertion, normally a remedy for whatever pain the tense muscles of her scalp and neck could muster, failed to help her today. As she passed the stone arch and cut through the treed park toward the science building, she rotated her shoulders trying to win some relief, also to no avail. Instead, whenever she jostled elbows with the many students on the stone paths who were rushing to classes, new spasms shot up and over her skull. Even her usual friendly wave to one of the cops who staffed the park's permanent police station—a silver trailer that some wag had once christened *the Doughnut*—left her grimacing.

Taking the elevator to the top floor, she arrived to find Azrhan Doumani standing at her desk, excitedly speaking French to someone on the phone.

The minute he saw her he broke off whatever he'd been saying, exclaiming, *"Excusez-moi, Monsieur, mais elle est ici,"* and handed her the receiver. "It's an Inspector Racine from the south of France," he said. "In a little town called Rodez they found the body of a man, a geneticist named Pierre Gaston, who's been murdered, and among his papers there's a letter addressed to you."

11

"Good morning, Dr. Sullivan. I take it your assistant explained who I am and why I'm calling." He had only the slightest trace of a French accent.

"Yes, but I never knew anyone of that name—Pierre Gaston, you said?"

"That's right. We found his body in an above-ground crypt at the Rodez cathedral. Workmen were doing renovations in the place, and about a week ago they accidentally shifted the stone cover while lifting the tomb with a winch. The stench immediately alerted them that something much riper than a mummified, centuries-old priest lay inside. We identified Gaston using dental records, and autopsy confirmed that whoever killed him had snapped his neck like a stick."

A ghostly face wrenched to one side in the darkness flashed through her mind. "Oh, my God!" she uttered in a whisper, her throat constricting.

"Pardon, Madame?"

"Nothing," she answered, quickly recovering her voice. "But I don't understand what it has to do with me."

"We're not sure, either, Madame, except that he left a letter with his notary to be forwarded to you 'in the event of his arrest.' It got turned over to us along with all his papers, including his will, after the discovery of his body."

"In the event of his arrest?"

"Yes, those were the exact written instructions. But we have no idea what he meant, nor can we find any indication he'd done

anything that he'd be in danger of being arrested for. I had hoped perhaps you could tell us what it's all about."

"I'm sorry, Inspector, but as I said, I never knew the man, at least
not that I can recall. I meet a lot of people at conferences whose
names I never remember."

"This man we think has been dead since New Year's Eve, so any
personal contact would have been before that. And he may only have
known you through your publications, *Docteur*." His accent drew the
title out and seemed to give greater homage to her profession than
she'd been in the habit of hearing on her side of the Atlantic. "When
we opened his computer files, both at his place of work and in his
apartment, we found that he had flagged many of your articles on the
Internet. According to his log, the site he visited most recently involved a feature on you by a group called *Environment Watch* just before Christmas. In it you called on biotechnical companies to
cooperate with testing for genetic vectors in plant life around their
laboratories. This interests us, because it also relates to the contents of
his letter. Shall I read aloud what he wrote to you?"

Her pulse quickened. "Please."

"The note itself is dated December twenty-third," said the
inspector.

Dear Dr. Sullivan,
    You're on the right track. Now I suggest you test around
our plant. There's a secret there related to well-known events
in Taiwan and Oahu that will shock you. Then get me out of
jail, and I'll show you something even deadlier.
    Merci!
    Pierre Gaston

By now she could barely contain her excitement. "Where did this
man work?" she demanded.

"At an agricultural research facility called Agriterre Incorporated.
But as I told you, when we first interviewed his superior there, a Dr.

Francois Dancereau, he assured us that nothing about Pierre Gaston's professional activities seemed amiss."

The name Francois Dancereau sounded vaguely familiar to her, but she didn't pause to dwell on it now. "And is this company involved in engineering crops using genetic vectors?"

"They claim only to be an 'agricultural research laboratory developing products which facilitate crop yields.'" He sounded as if he quoted the company's official line, but with a sarcasm that would have done a bistro waiter on the Champs-Élysées proud. "They refused to provide details, citing confidentiality agreements between themselves and the clients they work for. We didn't force the issue."

"But the letter—"

"We only just got court clearance to read it, well after our interviews with Dancereau and others at Agriterre, so at the time we had no grounds to consider that any of them had anything to hide or were connected to Pierre Gaston's death. Now it's entirely a different story, and we'll be going over the place with a microscope, but before we showed our hand, I wanted to hear if you could make anything of what he wrote. For instance, do you have any idea what he means when he says Taiwan and Oahu have something in common?"

Her imagination had already leaped into overdrive, making connections she hardly dared voice aloud even to herself. "I don't know," she said guardedly. "Let me mull it over awhile."

His answering silence suggested deep discontent with her reply.

"But I could do tests on samplings of plants from the grounds around that laboratory," she added, "looking for evidence of genetic vectors as he suggests. I'd explain to you how to take the cuttings, but you'd have to courier them to me immediately. I'd prefer to do the analysis in my own lab using my own team rather than come to you."

"*Magnifique,* Madame! I prayed you would offer us your services. I know you're a world-respected leader in this field—I took the liberty of looking you up on the Internet." He spoke so loudly she had to hold the phone away from her ear. "As you can understand, we're most anxious to find out this secret he's referring to, and obviously it has something to do with the genetic vectors you've been so vocal about. I'll have the specimens you require in New York by tomorrow afternoon."

His Gallic enthusiasm sparked her own scientific caution. "I have to warn you, without knowing the specific vectors involved, I'm liable to come up with negative results. Which makes me wonder, if your Pierre Gaston had really wanted me to find out what they were using, why all the cat-and-mouse stuff? Why didn't he just tell me outright, the way all the other scientists who responded to that article did?"

The line remained so quiet that for a moment she feared their connection had been severed. After a few seconds, she said, "Inspector Racine?"

"I am here, Madame, thinking over your very good question, and perhaps have even struck on an answer." She heard him suck in a breath, then exhale long and hard. He must be smoking a cigarette, she thought, instantly conjuring up her image of a French gendarme—based, she had to admit, on Claude Rains's performance in the movie *Casablanca*. "Despite the denials from the CEO at Agriterre that a crime has been committed against the company," he went on, "it's obvious that Gaston had done something which he knew could land him in prison. Maybe, when he wrote this letter, he only wanted to use the threat of you looking for whatever vectors are there, as leverage against whomever he feared could send him to jail. The promise to show you 'something even deadlier' he probably added as an additional hook, intending to snag your actual help in setting him free, in case his first plan failed to keep charges from being brought against him."

Maybe you're right, thought Sullivan, except he'd got his neck wrung instead.

The inner gloom of the downstairs bar at the Plaza seemed unusually crowded that afternoon, the noise level suited more to a waterfront tavern than a decorous watering hole for pampered guests of a luxury hotel. At four-thirty Steele shoved back from the darkened oak table that had become as familiar as his desk at the hospital, gathered up his pile of newspapers, and folded the wad of journalistic wisdom under his arm for the stroll home.

"Hey, Doc, you barely touched your drink again today," said the waiter, a burly stump of a man who also seemed out of place. He appeared more the type to sort out brawls and dispense draft by the tableful than serve up a champagne cocktail. "Why not just order a club soda? You still get the peanuts," he suggested. His lips and eyebrows, both thick as ropes, curved to bracket his puffy cheeks from above and below.

Steele took it as a smile. "I'll do that," he replied, and made his way through a maze of revelers getting a jump on happy hour.

Outside, a light drizzle felt cool on his forehead as he strode briskly along Fifth Avenue. Pulling his raincoat around him, he started passing the others in the crowd, weaving between their umbrellas by using a syncopated zigzag step that took all his concentration. The aroma of franks and pretzels carried far through the humid air, filling his nostrils and perking his appetite long before he reached the dozens of vendors' carts that populated the street corners ahead. He liked how their gay, candy-striped canopies punctuated the gloom in white and red contrast to the more sober, darker marquees of Saks, Gucci, or Wempe. He found himself using them as markers to measure his progress.

But within a few blocks the exhaust of the stop-and-surge traffic had burned the pleasant smells and tastes from the back of his throat, and it was the cumulative noise of horsepower, marching feet, and a thousand conversations, constant as an urban rapids, that filled his head. Tuning out the din, he turned his thoughts to the person who'd been most on his mind since his return.

Chet.

He'd managed to persuade him to return to school before the boy even got out of bed that very first morning. "Hey, there wasn't so much as a peep about me on the radio news in the taxi coming from the airport," he reassured his mortified son. "Nobody remembers that kind of smut for longer than it takes to move on to the next scandal anyway."

"I do!" came his surly reply.

"Any friend who's worth having won't ride you over it."

"No, but people who *aren't* my friends will. My name will be a joke."

"Chet, who cares about them? A good woman died, took her own life because she lost her son to a filthy disease and couldn't find any reason to go on living. Anybody gives you a hard time, remind them of that. What happened won't be a joke anymore."

"Gimme a break, Dad!" he snapped, glowering at him with a sullen hard stare. "I can't say that to a bunch of kids." But by seven-thirty he'd packed up his books and, his young jaw set with determination, left for his first class.

In subsequent conversations Steele found the answers increasingly hard to provide.

"Why did you go with that woman?" Chet had demanded over dinner that night.

"I liked her—especially talking with her. And she seemed to like me."

"Don't you think Mommy would be angry with you?"

"I think she'd be more angry if I kept moping around the way I have been and didn't get on with my life."

Chet gave a start and swallowed a few times, then said, "She still wouldn't approve of what you did in Hawaii."

"Chet, the only thing I think she'd disapprove of is my not being alert enough to stop that poor woman from taking her life. That's what I blame myself for. As for my being interested in the lady sexually, your mother would probably think, 'It's about time!' "

The boy's eyes nearly fell out onto his plate. Steele had never given him so frank a glimpse of his father before. The revelation that a parent, especially his own, could harbor such doubts and desires obviously came as a shock to the youth. For the rest of his meal he talked mainly with Martha and only about school, but occasionally, his normally smooth forehead corrugated like the brow of a perplexed puppy, he would sneak a glance at Dad. After that Steele trod lightly whenever they talked.

Just before Fiftieth Street he slowed his pace in front of St. Patrick's Cathedral while a funeral procession under a double row of umbrellas descended the massive gray steps. Like some black centipede, it deposited its cargo in a hearse waiting at the curb, and he picked his way through the stragglers, reaching the corner where, pivoting left, he began the three-block trek to Lexington. There were fewer pedestrians here, and as he picked up speed the exertion felt good.

Covering the distance in no time, he glanced at his watch and saw that he still had over an hour before Martha would have supper ready. Instead of turning south toward Thirty-sixth and home as usual, he continued in the direction of the East River, deciding to swing around to the hospital and pick up some insurance papers that his secretary had left in his office for him. Increasing his stride, he went on thinking about Chet.

After their encounter on his first night back, the boy had begun to hang around the table following mealtimes, at least long enough to keep Martha filled in about the happenings in his life. A school concert he'd be playing guitar at, how his preparations were going for final exams, that he didn't yet have a date for his end-of-year class party—Steele listened in on it all, grateful for at least having been granted the privilege of observer status. In the last few days, however, Chet had begun to direct some of the conversation toward him. They'd even had a brief discussion about renting a cottage somewhere on the ocean for a few weeks that summer, but left the plan comfortably vague for the moment.

"It's a start," Martha had said approvingly one evening after Chet had gone back upstairs.

Steele turned his thoughts to how he might best enter the hospital to avoid meeting anyone he knew. Since returning from Hawaii he'd stayed away from the place completely, having no stomach to endure the inevitable snickers and stares. By going to his office now, at the end of the day, he hoped to escape seeing anybody in the administrative wing of his department. He figured with a little luck he could evade everyone else if he went in through a back door and stuck to the staircases.

He especially didn't want to run into Greg Stanton. As good a friend as he'd been, Steele knew him to be a consummate politician whenever it came to his role as dean of medicine. "A particularly mean son of a bitch," he'd heard others put it when it came to anyone interfering with the flow of endowments to the faculty. And Steele could believe it. He'd heard the man rage on about "tenured parasites" often enough. Better let the dust settle awhile, he figured, having no doubts that his blast of bad publicity had already made Greg's life difficult with the money counters in the rest of the university. The decision about whether he'd resume his work as Chief of ER wasn't due for a month, and he hoped by then they'd all have moved on to new problems and that the embarrassment he'd caused would be less of an issue.

He also didn't want to encounter Kathleen Sullivan. Although he knew her visits to the hospital would normally be fewer than Stanton's, his secretary had advised him that she'd "dropped by a few times hoping to catch him in."

The thought of facing her filled him with embarrassment. What could he say, after giving her opponents, the Sydney Aimeses of the world, more ammunition to broadside her cause than they ever could have mustered on their own? Yet she seemed overly determined to speak with him. There were more messages from her on his machine again today, insisting he call her back. Except this time she'd tried to bait him, hinting at having "important new developments" she wanted to discuss with him. Yeah, right, he thought, figuring she must simply be trying to make him feel useful by keeping him in her loop. He found the idea that she would go out of her way to show him kindness annoying. "I won't be anybody's damn charity case!" he muttered while waiting for a red light to change at First Avenue. As he stood there fuming, he allowed that maybe when he got back to work, and had regained at least that status, he'd give her a call.

Getting the green arrow, he crossed the busy thoroughfare, turned south again, and passed in front of the United Nations Building. The crowds were fuller here, a mix of sightseers rushing through the front gates in an attempt to catch the last tour and delegates from every country in the world streaming out of the place, unable, it seemed, to vacate the building fast enough. Steele always enjoyed the snippets of conversation he could pick up here.

". . . don't know if he's CIA or the dumbest agriculture advisor they ever sent me . . ."

". . . of course, we're officially at war in counsel meetings, but declare peace in bed every night . . ."

". . . you protest the arms sale, I'll deny it ever took place, then we'll be done in time for the Rangers game. The Germans gave me their seats . . ."

At Forty-second he turned left, entering an end piece of the infamous street that couldn't be more desolate or at odds with its reputation for sex and glitter. Lined with nothing but windowless redbrick walls, a dozen shabby doorways, and the loading docks of a few rundown factories, it had little to attract anybody except for a fenced-in dog run halfway up the block. An abundance of weeds sprouting up between the cracks of the deserted sidewalk gave prolific testimony to how little human use it saw. Even the noise of the city didn't enter here. The traffic from midtown behind him and the FDR Drive up ahead sounded mute compared to the echo of his steps.

Following his New Yorker's instinct not to get caught alone in an isolated place, he made a beeline for the opening under the elevated driveway that gave access to the East River Esplanade Park. From there he could walk along the water's edge amongst joggers and bicyclists all the way down to Thirty-third and the hospital.

A few taxis passed him en route to the freeway, the windows rolled up and streaked with drizzle. A truck rattled after them, headed for the same destination. Then the street fell silent again as he hurried along. A few seconds later, a black van drove slowly by, its motor so quiet he didn't hear it until the vehicle drew abreast of him. He became instantly alert, wondering what the driver wanted, watching him pull to a stop in front of the dog run about fifty yards in front of him. Two men dressed in gray uniforms with peaked caps climbed out and released a pair of German shepherds big as timber wolves from the back of their vehicle. Steele instinctively slowed when he saw the animals weren't leashed. But one of the owners gave a curt command, and the two dogs eagerly ran through a double gate leading to the fenced-in area where they proceeded to romp about.

Must be security guards, he thought.

The man who'd issued the order proceeded to take off his jacket and throw it along with his cap back into the van. Pulling his shirt out of his waist band, he picked up what looked like a tool kit and ran off toward the park access half a block away.

Listening to the slap of the man's leather shoes against cement, Steele found it an odd outfit to go running in.

The companion entered the enclosure, where he proceeded to lounge on a bench with his back to the street, watching over the two animals as they lunged at each other in playful mock battle.

When Steele drew closer, the dogs broke off the workout they'd been giving each other and sat side by side in the middle of the pen, silently eyeing him, their large pink tongues flicking nervously over black lips. He found himself estimating the height of the fence and wondering if they could jump out. It had to be at least five feet, he figured, but it didn't take much imagination to picture those massive brutes easily clearing it in a single bound. Thank God they seemed obedient, he reassured himself, scurrying up the street while feeling their pitch-dark stare on his back every step of the way.

The passage under FDR Drive leading to the esplanade always reminded Steele of a giant dungeon. It stretched over eighty feet wide as well as long and had iron bars its full height on either end with no interior lighting. Completing the impression of a massive holding cell, the concrete ceiling arched across the entire space at little more than ten feet above the stone floor.

From a small iron gateway he peered into the dark interior before entering, paying special attention as usual to the shadowy corners where he figured someone could lurk unseen. Even though New York was a whole lot safer than it used to be, he felt this dimly lit place practically begged for trouble. It also stank. The clammy air reeked of urine and worse, making him revert to breathing through his mouth, a trick he used for dealing with similar aromas in ER. Otherwise the area seemed empty.

He glanced behind. Neither the dogs nor the man were paying him any heed. Chastising himself for feeling so skittish, he stepped inside, striding briskly through the gloom, making for the exit, and light, at the other end. He went the length of the passage in less than thirty seconds. But when he arrived at the far gate, he found it chained shut with a padlock.

"What the hell?" he muttered, the chamber amplifying his voice to a shout. The echo pulsed throughout the low cavern a few times before blending in with the hollow roar conducted through cement and steel from the steady traffic overhead. Puzzled, he started to turn back the way he'd come when a new sound insinuated itself into the general noise. He froze. Out of the darkness behind him rose a low sustained growl, its volume undulating ever louder, its echo adding to itself and swelling it further still. A second snarl joined in. Slowly turning his head he saw two pairs of eyes glinting over the flash of white fangs.

He didn't breathe, didn't even blink.

He strained his eyes as far around in their sockets as they'd go, trying to see if the owner had come with them.

No one.

They must have escaped the pen, he thought, expecting any instant to hear the man call them off.

Nothing.

The growling intensified.

Should I scream at them? he thought, panic flooding through him. Or will that trigger an attack?

Out the corner of his eye he saw one animal hunch down and take a step closer. The other followed, its jaws half open, its lips pulled back, the guttural sounds issuing from the back of its throat more savage than ever. He felt locked into their stares, paralyzed by the blood lust he saw burning in their molten pupils and reading in them a hunger as primeval as that of any jungle beast. An instant later he saw the haunches of the one closest to him ripple with movement.

Time to move.

"Help!" he screamed, leaping forward, grabbing the iron bars, and scrambling up them as fast as he could.

The first dog jumped and seized his left calf as he climbed the barrier. Shrieking with pain he kicked and shook the animal free. The other missed him entirely, springing a second too late and striking only where he'd been a moment earlier.

"Help! Help me!" he continued to roar, his voice reverberating loudly as its echo bounced around. He got himself horizontal on the bars, continuing to pull himself upward, hand over hand, leg over leg. But the drizzle had covered the metal with moisture. Before he could reach the top, his palms, already wet, lost their grip, and the soles of his shoes couldn't get traction. He started to slip.

The dog that had missed on the first leap gathered its legs into a crouch and launched itself straight up, grabbing a mouthful of raincoat. It hung on and, weighing at least a hundred pounds, dragged Steele down further. The second one joined in, and the two of them dangled below him by their teeth, spinning like canine trapezists.

"Let go, damn you!" Steele screamed as he clung there, his arms shaking with the strain of the added weight and his feet running in place against the bars. One by one the buttons started to pop off his coat, letting it burst open a little at a time, but the material held, and each lurching drop of the animals tugged him down a few inches more.

In seconds his lower limbs were higher than his shoulders. He felt the blood pouring from his wound begin to run up his leg, having already soaked his shoe, and the dark stain on his trousers spread toward his groin. He increased his screaming and cursing, not caring what he said as long as someone heard him. But when he glanced outside he couldn't see a soul.

One of the dogs dropped off, only to leap up again, this time snapping at his head. Jerking his neck forward he only just evaded the massive jaws, feeling their teeth graze his scalp and hearing them click shut inches behind his ears. Fear drove him to pull his upper body higher despite the weight of the other creature still hanging off him. With yet another leap, the first one rejoined the second, once more latching on to cloth and pulling him down again with the added load.

Steele knew he couldn't hang on much longer. He'd have to shed the coat. Getting a tighter grip with his left hand, he let go with his right, grabbed the lapels, and tried to shake the garment free of his shoulder. But the dampness glued it to him, and as he struggled, he steadily lost his hold on the bar. Reaching below him he pounded on the head of the dog in easiest reach with his fist. It gave a snarl, let go of the coat and, twisting in midair to bite at his wrist, fell to the ground. The second beast made a similar try for him and missed. Free of their weight, he scrambled the rest of the way to the top of the bars. There wasn't enough space to slip through, but he had room to hook his legs and arms over the railing and give himself a secure perch.

Below him, the animals twirled, snarled, and leaped, writhing with gnashing teeth at the height of each jump, yet they never quite reached him. Enraged, they started barking, making such a din that Steele felt certain someone would soon hear the ruckus. But outside the drizzle had graduated to rain, and as he scanned the walkway, so tantalizingly close, it remained empty. He turned his attention back toward the other end of the passageway where he could see Forty-second Street through the bars. His fear giving way to anger, he hollered, "Hey, you with the dogs! Get them the fuck off me."

Only the echo of his shout replied.

"Goddamn it, are you crazy! Call them off!"

Still no response.

He saw cars drive by on the other side of the bars and shouted some more, but their windows were closed against the rain.

He tried to get a look at his leg. The bleeding hadn't let up any, completely soaking the left side of his pants, and the pain felt worse by the minute. Again clinging to the bars with one hand, he managed to pull up the cuff far enough to expose where the dog had taken a chunk out of him. By the bit of daylight that streamed in from outside he saw a long U-shaped mash of serrated flesh and strands of torn muscle awash in dark red blood. Mostly venous, he thought, reaching to apply pressure to the wound using the material of his trousers as a pad. Such a basic violation of sterile technique made him cringe almost as much as the pain. I'm going to need a truckload of antibiotics, he lamented, knowing his chances of infection were now certain. But as the porous cloth sucked up the hemorrhage on the surface, he realized he had an even more immediate problem.

A bright jet of scarlet the diameter of a pencil spurted up from deep within the gash. "Shit!" he exclaimed out loud. Without hesitation, he reached into the wound with his fingers. The burning instantly trebled, and he screamed through clenched teeth, swallowing heavily to fight back the sudden waves of nausea that ripped through him. Still he continued to probe, following the warm stream by feel toward its source, keeping track of the anatomy as he pushed between the slippery bellies of the gastrocnemius muscles and crying out in agony as he sent them recoiling into spasms with his touch. But catching his breath, he went deeper, ticking off yet more landmarks as he slid through them—veins, ligaments, even a nerve that announced itself with a shot of electricity into his foot when he inadvertently trapped it against underlying bone. His breathing started to come in hot gasps, sweat broke out over his entire body, and his head swirled to the point he thought he'd pass out. Yet he stayed focused on the pulsing flow against his fingertips until it guided him to the pumping vessel at the site of the hemorrhage. Bracing for what he knew would hurt, he clamped down hard with his thumb, pinning the slithery torn artery to the back of his tibia at the exact place of the tear. Emitting his loudest shriek yet, he had to fight once more against throwing up as volley after volley of searing pain erupted in his leg and the fangs below him continued to snap the air around his head like a pair of demonic castanets.

He rolled his eyes back toward Forty-second Street. "Help me!

I'm bleeding like hell," he called out, his voice no longer possessing much strength.

The dogs continued to churn in fury beneath him. The sounds of the traffic went on unabated. The rain, coming down ever harder, seemed deafening.

"For God's sake, help me," he repeated, fast losing all hope that anyone would hear him. His thoughts became a jumble of flashes. How ludicrous that he would die being eaten by dogs! That it would happen in New York City seemed doubly absurd. That he wouldn't see Chet again hit him like a body blow, and his determination to survive surged.

But as his strength drained, his resolve to hang on soon seemed a fleeting, doomed impulse, and thoughts of escape became a pathetic fantasy. He found himself confronting the one last decision there remained in his power to make—how he would die. Better to slip into shock first, he coldly reasoned, in order to be as near unconscious as possible when I finally fall to the dogs. Except he felt so woozy and drained of strength from pain that he'd no idea how much longer he could cling to the fence. To have any hope of hanging on for the time it would take to bleed himself into some degree of anesthesia, he'd have to release the pressure on his leg soon.

Once more the thought of Chet abandoned to grief flashed through his head. No! Damn it, I can't take that way out, not while there's the slightest chance.

He looked desperately over to the esplanade. It remained empty. He peered through the gloom toward Forty-second Street again.

The movement in the darkness occurred so slowly that at first he thought his eyes were playing tricks on him. Seconds later a match flared in a shadowy corner near the entrance, illuminating a thin, pockmarked face under the peak of a security guard's cap. Jesus Christ, thought Steele in horrified disbelief, the creep must have been standing there, watching all along! This wasn't an accident.

An instant later the flame vanished, leaving him staring at the glowing tip of the man's cigarette. Before he could recover enough to say anything, there came a shout from the walkway behind him.

"Hey, mister! Do you need some help?"

He craned his neck around and saw a woman bedecked in rain gear holding back a pair of waterlogged spaniels straining at their leashes to get into the fray.

"Yes! Call 911 for the police! There's a maniac here who set his dogs on me. And an ambulance, too. They cut an artery!"

He saw her delve into one of her pockets and whip out a cell phone.

From the shadow where the man stood came a shrill whistle. As if a switch had turned off their rage, the dogs instantly spun about and bounded toward him as he rushed out the gate. Seconds later the black van squealed through a U-turn and disappeared back up Forty-second Street.

12

know I can't prove any of it, Greg. It's just that the similarities in the two deaths—both men having their necks snapped—and an H5N1, or bird flu, outbreak being the only thing Oahu and Taiwan have in common . . . well, it's got me spooked."

"You really believe a geneticist in France and that farmer in Oahu were killed to cover up something about the bird flu? Come on, Kathleen. This morning I asked that you get me hard scientific evidence. Instead you show up back here tonight with conspiracy theories."

She stiffened. His attitude had been increasingly skeptical since she first opened her mouth. She began to think it had been a mistake coming here to talk with him. After her last class they'd run into each other just as he'd been leaving for the day. On impulse she blurted out that there'd already been a new development since their morning meeting. He graciously insisted on hearing about it right away, and invited her to the faculty club for drinks. In the decorous setting of overstuffed, floral-printed sofa chairs, vases of fresh-cut spring flowers, and recessed lighting, he'd listened to her story, then proceeded to downplay what she'd told him.

"I don't believe anything yet," she countered. "I'm just saying that there's an alarming possibility suggesting itself here." She took a sip of her beer and wiped the foam off her lip onto the back of her hand.

Stanton left his white wine untouched on the table. "And I'm saying you're speculating again. Christ! It's exactly what I warned you not to do."

"Look, I've always ridiculed the extremists in the environmentalist movement who concoct conspiracy theories about what the biotech industry is capable of doing to cover up its mistakes. But this is different, and it's personal."

"I don't get what you mean."

"Because, Greg, if that old man getting killed in Kailua has anything to do with a bird flu outbreak that happened eighteen months ago, then isn't it obvious by the timing that they weren't just worried about him?"

"You're not suggesting what I think you are?"

"You're damn right I am. It couldn't just be a coincidence that they killed him within days of my going out there and demanding soil samples to test for genetic vectors. I've got to consider that they wanted to kill me as well."

"Oh, my God, Kathleen, that's absolute paranoia! If the board gets wind of you going around spouting stuff like that, no way can I help you keep your position on staff. Please, drop it now, before you do your career more damage than I can repair."

"Really, Dr. Stanton, I am not paranoid," she shot back, giving free rein to her Irish temper. His sitting there in his deluxe suit, all pampered and comfortable while dismissing her fears, left her wanting to douse him with his wine. "There's a solid logic to back up the idea of those men with silencers being hitmen and me as their intended target."

"Dr. Sullivan, I really don't want to get into this—"

"You'll be hearing me out, Greg Stanton!" she interrupted. "And then you can dismiss me as nuts or let Aimes and his cronies have their way with my career—whatever you want."

He opened his mouth as if to reply, eyed her expression as her fury grew, and seemed to change his mind.

"Every detail fits," she continued. "Their keeping him cooped up in that sweltering house with all the windows closed, so I wouldn't hear any noises he made that might tip me off; their waiting to kill him until I arrived, in order for our times of death to be similar; the fact that they avoided using a gun on him, yet were willing to put a bullet in me and then were going to burn the place in a clumsy attempt at arson—it's all consistent with their setting a scene. One intended to make the police think that robbers were attempting to make the first death look like an accident, and that they then shot me only because I blundered onto the scene."

"Now why would they go to all that trouble?" While his tone retreated into a cold civility, his eyes said she was nuts.

"Because the killers couldn't make it obvious they wanted me dead without also making it pretty clear they were trying to stop me from running tests on the samples."

Stanton wearily shook his head and leaned forward to rest his elbows on the table. "Have you told these ideas of yours to anyone else, Kathleen?" he asked, cupping his face in the palms of his hands and massaging his temples with his fingertips.

"Why, yes, I discussed it with a few close colleagues. Why?"

Stanton peered up at her and sighed, sliding his fingertips to the corners of his eyes where he continued to work them in small circles. "Who?"

"Uh, Dr. Doumani, my chief technician . . . uh . . . Steve Patton of course—he and I have been working together on this subject for years, so we routinely exchange information."

She didn't add how precarious their professional association had become recently. To his credit, though, Steve's response to her story had been enthusiastic. "Now you're getting somewhere," her former lover had told her. "Let me know if I can help."

"And I tried to run it by Dr. Steele," she continued to tell Stanton, "to see what he thought, since he's up to speed on the issues and has a fresh point of view—"

"And what did Richard make of your ideas?"

"I don't know. I left a message on his answering machine earlier, but he didn't get back to me yet. He may still be avoiding my calls."

"I see. And you've spoken to nobody else?"

"No. Why?"

"Because I'm still going to try and protect you from Aimes and the board, Kathleen. So don't blab a word of this to any more people than you already have, understand, and stick to getting hard scientific evidence as we planned. Now, when are the specimens arriving from France?"

"Tomorrow afternoon."

"And how long do you think it will take before you finish running tests on them?"

"With my team working full out on it, about three weeks."

"As I explained this morning, that's a long time to stall with nothing but hot air. Just as we agreed for the Hawaiian data, you'll have to give me anything that turns up right away."

"Absolutely."

"That's settled then." He leaned back and finally took a sip of his wine. "You know what?" he asked, a genuine smile recruiting his eyes as it spread across his face. "If any of that data of yours shows a link between bird flu and genetically modified food, we could be looking at Pulitzer money. Hell, maybe even a Nobel Prize." He toasted her with his glass, placed it back on the table, still virtually full, and placed his hands on the armrests of his chair, ready to push off. "Now, if you'll excuse me, I've got to get home to my wife and daughters."

When he arrived through the door by ambulance, instead of behaving as a patient, he started ticking off what his staff and residents did to him like an auditor. IVs were running within seconds. Cardiac and blood pressure monitors had his vitals pegged before they even asked him his insurance number or mother's maiden name. Then a nurse gave him a shot of midazolam, and he stopped caring.

He floated between vaguely interested and asleep as the residents poked about in his wound. "Stirred, not shaken," he quipped when one of them returned with a syringeful of antibiotics and mixed it in with the contents of his IV bag. He then listened in on their conversations about the artery having a longitudinal tear, and the caliber of the stream being a reflection of the length of the rip, not the size of the vessel involved.

"Just tie the damn thing off!" Steele heard himself growl from far away.

"All in all, Richard, it's not too bad," the chief of vascular surgery told him when he arrived dressed in a tuxedo, obviously having deserted some society function in order to come in. It was the kind of professional courtesy a doctor would usually extend to a colleague. "We'll be able to do the repair under local."

He drifted in and out after that, wriggling his toes when they asked, listening as the senior resident who'd "done one" talked the junior who hadn't through the repair, and watching the shreds of skin and muscle he wouldn't need anymore pile up in the kidney basin they'd wedged between his thighs. At one point he could hear so much snipping and cutting down there that he loudly accused them of trying to take off his "whole friggin' leg!" A second hit of midazolam returned him to the state where he didn't mind if they did.

"This is quite a file we're getting on you, Dr. Steele," joked the head nurse afterward as she anchored the dressings to his calf. "Two visits in six months."

"Right." He smiled wanly, embarrassed at the ruckus he'd caused. He detested being on the wrong side of the white coats among his staff and residents. To make matters worse, he'd had to lie facedown as they'd all worked on him. At the scene of his greatest triumphs, where he'd held command over matters of life and death, he was reduced to worrying whether his backside hung out the back flaps of his hospital gown.

"Where do you want this?" the nurse asked, her eyebrow doing a suggestive jackknife as she stood over him drawing up a syringeful of tetanus toxoid for his booster shot.

He demurely offered her a bare shoulder.

"But that's no fun," she pouted, and then drove the needle deep into his nearest cheek.

He then asked for a phone, so he could call Martha and Chet. They must be worried sick about him.

———

"Oh, I'm sure he's just run into one of his cronies at the hospital and lost track of the time," Martha McDonald reassured as she passed yet another cup of tea to her visitor. "I'd call him on his cell phone, but he's stopped wearing the damn thing lately."

"That's fine, I don't mind waiting," replied Kathleen Sullivan, feeling increasingly embarrassed at being there at all. She'd come on an impulse, determined to see the man and telling herself that even if he didn't want to talk with her he had to be warned about the threat to his job.

After saying good night to Stanton, she'd swung by her apartment, showered, and slipped into a pale green blouse with a matching skirt. She added a pair of small emerald earrings that she hardly ever wore, took a few swipes with a brush at her short, ever-practical hair, and headed toward the door. "I won't be long, Lisa," she called over her shoulder.

The skinnier, younger copy of herself looked up from watching television. "Oooh, Mom's got a date," she teased.

"And what makes you think that, smart aleck? I'm off to a business meeting is all."

"Then how come you put on *the emeralds*, Mommy dear?"

Sullivan gave her daughter a wry grin. "You are an imp!"

"And you're beautiful, Mom. Have a good time."

She'd felt like a nervous schoolgirl when she rang his doorbell and asked to see him. The housekeeper had stared so unbelievingly at her that at first she thought it must be the wrong house.

"Please, come in," the woman had finally said. "I'm sorry to have acted so surprised, except he hardly has any visitors," she added, and led her into the room where they now sat. That had been an hour ago, and they'd been making small talk ever since. As they chatted, Sullivan had a chance to survey the surroundings. A grand piano, the top down and keyboard closed, dominated everything. The rest of the furniture looked tasteful yet comfortable, luxurious plants grew in every nook, and the walls were painted a warm yellow. It must be wonderfully sunny in here during the day, she thought. But what really got her attention were all the photographs.

She'd gotten up to take a closer look at a cluster of them while Martha prepared tea in the kitchen. In each she saw a smiling, dark-haired woman with thick wavy hair and wonderful warm eyes. A lot of the shots had caught her during candid domestic moments—waving a spatula at a barbecue grill like a female d'Artagnan; ducking a splash at a poolside; laughing while holding up a small boy who had thick, unruly black curls and brown eyes identical to hers. Others, especially the ones where the child appeared much younger, captured her during more posed moments, but nothing had tamed her magnificent smile. It's the look of a woman who knows she's loved, thought Sullivan.

Steele appeared in some of the frames, but most of the time he seemed to have been the photographer. Where he'd taken lone photos of just the boy, they were the same sort of first-time milestones she herself had captured on film with Lisa—the child proudly riding a bike, his holding up a fish in triumph, or the little fellow scoring a goal in a soccer game.

Minutes later when the older version of that child had come downstairs to say hello in person—"I like your programs on TV," he told her shyly—she estimated it had been about two years since any new images of all that youthful happiness had been added to the walls.

"Are you sure I can't get you something to eat, Dr. Sullivan?" Martha inquired for what must have been the sixth time.

"No, I'm fine, thank you," Sullivan insisted yet again, just as from somewhere in the house came the sound of a phone ringing. Martha excused herself to answer it.

Within minutes all three of them were in Sullivan's car, racing the short distance to the hospital. "Imagine that man," grumbled Martha. "Attacked by dogs, then insisting we don't make a fuss and telling us not to come in!"

Sullivan discreetly remained in the waiting room of the Emergency Department while the other two ran through a set of swinging doors that read NO ADMITTANCE. As she loitered among all the walking wounded and watched the ambulance stretchers stream in, she felt the sense of awe that always overtook her whenever she passed by an ER. The sheer brutality of the trauma and illness she witnessed here seemed so far removed from her own molecular take on life. Yet it struck her that this gallery of human agony gave as true a glimpse of Richard Steele's world as the photos back in his living room. What special courage he must have, she marveled, to treat such extremes in suffering day after day. And at one time, it seemed, he'd possessed the strength to remain sufficiently unhardened by the carnage that he could still love the extraordinary woman whose ghost now looks down from the walls of his living room.

Five minutes later Martha returned, acting as if she'd never been anxious at all. "Ah, it's nothing. Imagine dragging us down here for that little scratch." Smiling at a very relieved looking Chet and giving him a hug, she glanced at her watch and added, "On a school night as well. Come on, young man, you and I are heading home." To Sullivan she whispered, "Dr. Steele's got to lie around here for a while the nurse told me, to make sure the anesthetic's worn off." She gave a chuckle. "Apparently it's his own rules, and he's fit to be tied."

"I'll drive you home," Sullivan quickly offered.

"Not at all. You go in there and tell him what you've been so patiently waiting to say. He's got nothing better to do but to listen, and besides, if you don't get him now . . ." She leaned in as if about to impart a terrible secret. "He doesn't return his phone calls, you know."

With a wink and a parting grin, she hustled out the door. Chet, following behind her, called out over his shoulder, "Good night, Dr. Sullivan."

"Good night, Chet," she said, remarking again how much the boy's eyes resembled his mother's. Except for one difference. While hers had the look of someone well loved who knew it, the boy had an uncertain gaze, the kind that suggested he didn't know for sure.

Steele flushed with embarrassment as soon as she entered his curtained cubicle. He lay on a stretcher, the head of it elevated almost straight up, and his hospital gown drawn tightly around him. She couldn't tell for sure, but it seemed he'd lost a few pounds since Honolulu. "Dr. Sullivan," he greeted her gruffly. "Thank you for bringing my family over, though I have to say I'm surprised to see you here."

"I do apologize for barging in on you like this, but it's important we talk, and Martha said it would be okay."

"Martha said—"

"Yes, she's such a dear woman. She obviously dotes on you. And let me add what a fine young man Chet is. He must make you proud."

"Why, yes, he does. But—"

"And please, call me Kathleen. May I sit down?" she added, pulling up a folding chair and plopping herself in it before he could answer. "Martha said you were all right?"

"Yes, I am."

"What happened, anyway? The hospital told us only that a pair of German shepherds attacked you. Had they escaped?"

"Look, Dr. Sullivan—"

"Kathleen, remember."

"Yes, of course, Kathleen. I wanted to say if it's about the mess I made of things in Honolulu that you want to discuss, I'm deeply sorry for all the trouble I caused you—"

"No, Richard," she said sternly, "you definitely don't have anything to apologize for to me. It's the media that should say they're sorry. They behaved atrociously in how they treated you. And they wrote barely a word about poor Dr. Arness. That in particular turned my stomach!"

Steele looked startled, as if he'd expected another reaction out of her altogether.

Poor man, she thought. He's probably been beating himself up for not picking up on Arness's being suicidal. "And you aren't to blame for her death, Richard, you hear me!" she added, looking him straight in the eye.

His jaw loosened a little on its hinge. Even the tightness around his mouth slowly disappeared. "Thank you, Kathleen," he replied. "It helps to be told that."

Seeing how her reassurance had made his expression soften so, the last thing she felt like doing was to hit him with the real reason behind her visit. "Tell me about the dogs," she repeated, wanting to postpone as long as possible the unpleasantness of warning him that his career hung by a thread. Perhaps she should wait until tomorrow after all.

His jaw tightened again. "Some maniac set them on me."

"What!"

"You heard me. The guy just stood there smoking a cigarette while his beasts tried to rip me to shreds. He only called them off when a passerby saw me and phoned 911. He's got to be a psychopath."

"Oh, my God! Was he trying to rob you?"

"He was trying to kill me, period. He never said a word about money. No 'Give me your wallet!' or 'Hand over your cash!' I presume the other guy with him was in on it, too."

"Other guy?"

"Yeah. There were initially two of them. His partner went ahead to lock a gate so I'd be trapped."

The fact that there were two attackers made her come up with a ridiculous idea. She tried to pass it off, but the thought persisted. I'll humor it, and then maybe it'll go away, she told herself. "What language did they speak?"

"They never said a word."

"What did they look like?"

"The usual 'adult, male Caucasians of medium height' you so often hear described," he said, a lopsided grin on his face. "But these two both wore pretty recognizable outfits, and the smoker had a big distinctive feature."

"Oh, Caucasian," she replied, absently feeling a tightness release from somewhere deep inside her as a crazy notion that they might have been the same pair who'd attacked her scuttled back into the nether region of nightmares where it belonged.

"Yeah, they were dressed as security guards, and one had an incredibly bad set of acne scars, what we call in medicine a real 'pizza face.' "

She felt her throat tighten.

"With a mug like that there may actually be a chance the cops will find him. . . ."

His voice faded away as she heard a ringing in her ears. It can't be, she kept telling herself. Can't goddamn be!

". . . they better, or that creep will end up murdering someone . . ."

I won't have it! No more conspiracy theories! Yet the possibility paid her no heed. It persisted in her head swirling through her thoughts until she felt dizzy with it.

". . . Kathleen? Kathleen, what's the matter? Are you all right?"

The sound of his voice cut through her inner tumult. "Yes," she quickly reassured him. "I'm okay." She only then realized that he'd sat up and grabbed her wrist with his fingers on her pulse.

"You went so pale that I thought you were about to have a vasovagal episode. Here, put your head down."

"No, I'm fine—"

"Put your head down!"

She obeyed. "What's a vasovagal episode?" she asked from between her knees.

"A faint."

"I don't faint!"

"Good. But you better stay in that position a bit, until your pulse picks up, or you will."

"Are you always this bossy?"

She heard him chuckle. "Around here we call it 'taking charge.' "

"This is embarrassing."

"It'll only be embarrassing if you don't do as you're told and end up clunking your head on the floor."

They spent a minute more arguing; then abruptly he declared, "Your heart rate's fine now. You can sit up again." But he continued to bend over her and keep his fingers on her pulse.

"Well, it's about time—"

The sight that greeted her as she raised her head made her stop in midsentence. Springing to her aid, he'd loosened the ties of his hospital gown, leaving his rear end hanging out the back in full view. She started to giggle.

"What?" Steele asked, truly puzzled.

Her giggle became a laugh—a loud, wonderful redemptive laugh. It fleetingly overrode her shock at hearing his would-be killer's description. Not even her incredulity that the attacker could be the same pock-faced security guard she'd seen at Agrenomics stopped her from giving into it. For a second, the dread, anger, and fear she'd been carrying washed away.

"What's the matter?" he repeated, still not getting it.

In response she guffawed so hard she couldn't speak.

Wearing a puzzled look, he began to chuckle, clearly having no clue as to why.

Tears running down her face, she marveled at how wonderfully infectious laughter could be, especially after what must have been a long drought for him with none whatsoever. That the noise coming out of his mouth sounded like a dry cough made his responding at all seem even more a miracle.

"What?" he managed to ask yet again.

This time she pointed at what she found so hysterical. When he turned to look, the shocked expression on his face sent her over the top, and she broke into gales of full force, unable-to-get-her-breath shrieks.

He made a grab at the open flaps. His face seemed to strain against the grip of sadness that had encased it for so long, then fought its way into as glorious a smile as she'd yet seen on the man, and his feeble chortle erupted to life.

"Hey, keep it quiet in there!" called one of the nurses.

They tried as best they could to stifle their howls, but no sooner did one settle down than the other let out a half-smothered snort, and they'd start again.

"God, that felt good," she managed to gasp during one of their tenuous intervals.

"Better than a thousand psychiatrists," puffed Steele.

It all ended abruptly when a massive, ebony-colored hand parted the curtains and admitted the rest of the man it belonged to. "Which one of you clowns is the attempted murder victim?" he thundered, flashing a badge and identity card that identified him as Detective Roosevelt McKnight, Homicide, NYPD.

Any afterglow from their zany moment together soon vanished as she listened to Steele describe the attack on him. When Detective Mc-Knight asked if he had any reason to suspect why someone might want him dead and he replied, "No," she studied the floor in grim silence, thinking of a pockmarked face illuminated by a match.

"What's bothering you, Kathleen?" Steele asked.

She looked up to see both men staring at her. "Nothing," she answered much too quickly.

"Bullshit!" said Steele.

"Richard, it's too crazy to mention. Even crazier than the idea I ran by Stanton today, and he hit the roof—"

"Stanton?" he interrupted. "What's he got to do with this?"

"He doesn't. It's just that I told him something that struck me as a weird set of coincidences, and he went ballistic. He's already having enough trouble with the board over the flap my speculation in Honolulu caused—"

"Excuse me!" broke in McKnight, the polite words sounding as blunt as if he'd hollered *Shut up!* When he had their attention he said, "Dr. Sullivan, why don't you start at the beginning, and tell what you have to say in a way that an old flatfoot like me can keep up, okay?" It was an order, not a suggestion.

"Well, I really don't know if it has a beginning, there are so many parts—"

"Start!" he commanded, pen and notepad at the ready.

She first told him about her visit to Agrenomics before Christmas and the guard with severe acne scars who'd nearly discovered her. When she related her misadventure in Hawaii, pointing out how the timing of the so-called home invasion might suggest that she'd been a target, the attentive silence from the two men stood in stark contrast to the derision she'd gotten from Stanton. The story of Pierre Gaston's murder, especially his letter to her mentioning the only two areas on the planet where there'd been an H5N1, or bird flu out-break, brought Steele bolt upright in his bed. The fact that the French geneticist had had his neck snapped just like Hacket's left McKnight with his pen poised in midair, his forehead furrowed and fertile with worry. Maybe my notions aren't so crazy after all, she be-gan to think by the time she finished.

"So what master plan links all these isolated incidents together?" McKnight demanded, his voice sounding weary.

"Why, I suppose it could be people in the biotechnical industry trying to keep some catastrophic mistake they've made from becom-ing public."

"And who might these people be? Do you have names?"

"Of course not. I only just learned—"

"And what's the 'catastrophic mistake' they're trying to keep secret?"

"Presumably it's the sort of thing I've been warning about all along, but related to the bird flu outbreaks. I've never been one to ascribe sin-ister plots to multinational companies, but in this case I can't help won-der to what lengths they'd go to cover something like that up."

"When you were at Agrenomics yourself, did you see or find any evidence that this particular company might be guilty of having caused the sorts of things you've been warning about?"

"Well, no. In fact they came up with a perfectly clean set of test results. But that in itself I found suspicious."

"How?"

She flushed. "It sounds silly, but the possibility that they alone had put in the kind of protective filters I've been calling for made me wonder if they already knew vectors of naked DNA could escape into the environment."

He issued a king-size sigh, leaned back in the chair he'd comman-deered from the nursing station, and pocketed his notes. "So? You should have been reassured. They were being good corporate citizens."

"Or they were using something they didn't want detected by test-ing techniques such as mine."

"It's all quite a story, Dr. Sullivan," he said, giving his giant knuckles a crack and his back a stretch as he got up to leave. "Unfortunately it's got nothing to do with the jurisdiction of the NYPD—except the part about the 'pizza-face.' "

"Wait a minute," interjected Steele. "You don't think we should consider the rest of what she's told us? How can you dismiss—?"

"Doc, we're sure as hell going to make this wacko who attacked you a priority. Hell, setting dogs on people—I haven't seen that since I was a kid in Alabama over forty years ago. I'd like you to spend some time with one of our police artists tomorrow, as well as look at some mug shots. Once we have a likeness, if Dr. Sullivan identifies it as the same man she saw at this Agrenomics place, we'll subpoena them to give us the name of the security firm they use. As for all that other stuff she said, it sounds way out of my league. If she ever does get any real proof, maybe she can interest the FBI, or Interpol. In the meantime, I advise you both to be very careful."

She wanted to scream at the big detective, not only for his apparent offhanded dismissal of her suspicions, but also for behaving as if she weren't even in the room. But out of respect for being on Steele's turf in his ER, she struggled mightily to hold her tongue.

"That's it?" Steele demanded. "Be careful?"

McKnight pulled on a rumpled, beige raincoat that resembled a stained tarpaulin more than a piece of clothing. "Let me explain something to you, Doc. You're lucky you pulled me. I'm the New Age, sensitive type of cop the NYPD is trying to cultivate. As for most of the other guys at the precinct, well, let's just say they aren't as open-minded as me. If they heard Dr. Sullivan's story, you know what they'd say? 'Gee, we've got a Frenchman who basically writes *I've got a secret about Taiwan and Oahu,*' then gets his neck wrung, probably for running around with some guy's wife. Six months later we get a farmer in Oahu who has *his* neck snapped by a couple of pukes who were robbing the place. But because Oahu and Taiwan both had a case of this bird flu, we've got a conspiracy? I don't think so!' "

"Now you be holdin' on there, Detective McKnight!" she exploded, jumping to her feet and unleashing both her fury and her Irish at the man. "You won't be dismissing me so easily."

He looked down his nose at her, the pose seeming to come easily to him. Given his height, she figured he probably got a lot of practice at it. "Don't take me wrong, Dr. Sullivan," he said, "I'm a big fan of yours, and I sincerely do think you should be careful. But unless you get some hard evidence to back up all your theories, you'll receive the same kind of razz that I just gave you, and worse, from any police force in the world."

Knowing he spoke the truth—and resenting it—she fumed in silence for a few seconds, getting a crick in her neck from glaring up at him. Until a bit of mischief popped into her head. "You asked for a name. Then I've got a straightforward suspect for you—someone who I heard with my own ears warn Dr. Steele that he'd just made a whole lot of enemies."

"Oh? Who?"

The deliciousness of what she was about to do played at the corners of her mouth, but she managed not to smile. "I think you should question a man named Sydney Aimes."

"Do you think I'm paranoid?" Sullivan asked after the detective had left.

"I wish I did," Steele replied glumly.

She retook her seat beside his bed. "Does that mean you agree some kind of cover-up could be going on, that there could be a connection between it all, including the attack on you?"

"I don't know. It sounds pretty far-fetched. . . ." He let his voice trail off, thinking for a moment. "But all those coincidences—they're hard to dismiss, and as a doctor, I've got a real aversion to writing off any set of events as isolated incidents connected only by chance." Words from a well-thumbed textbook rang in his head:

Better to assume there's a solitary pathological process behind whatever disparate symptoms and signs the physician observes, not postulate that there are several unrelated diseases active at the same time.

But he also recalled the words of his other great teacher. "Don't look at the rest of life so simplistically," Luana had always reminded him whenever he became too immersed in his clinical way of thinking. He found himself wondering what she'd have made of the story.

"I'm afraid there's more bad news," said Sullivan.

He waited for her to continue, but a heavy silence settled between them. He found himself studying her and thinking a more confident, self-possessed woman he couldn't imagine. Her physical appearance—an unpretentious, simple hairdo, no makeup, at least as far as he could tell, and a subdued pastel green outfit—suggested a lady who felt comfortable with herself. Even the stones she wore in her earlobes were understated compared to the sparkle in her emerald-colored eyes. "Well?" he said encouragingly, after watching her swallow once or twice and make a few false starts. For a person like her to be so reluctant to speak, there must be something very wrong.

"Greg Stanton called me into his office this morning—one of his seven A.M. specials."

"Oh, dear. With or without breakfast?"

She grinned. "With."

"Whew," he teased.

"The trouble is, I think you may be down for one without."

"What!"

"You and I have a shared problem. It seems Sydney Aimes is out to discredit me and make an example of you."

Over the next few minutes she saw his expression harden as he listened to what the board had in mind for them. By the time she finished, he looked poleaxed. For a few seconds he said nothing, and she heard only the sounds of ER around them—the beeping of monitors, the murmur of conversations between patients and staff, the retching of someone throwing up.

"Christ, I knew they wouldn't be happy, but I never dreamed I'd lose my job," he said, his voice far away. She found the bitterness in his eyes hard to look at. "And Greg is willing to let it happen?" he demanded through clenched teeth.

"Not exactly. He's going to hold them off for as long as he can," she replied.

"And what good will that do?"

"It'll give me time to find out whatever secrets lie in the samples I'll be getting from France tomorrow. Maybe then we'll know what we're up against." She couldn't tell by his rigid expression whether he'd taken any comfort from her plan. In fact, he seemed so stunned by the prospect of losing his job, she found herself wondering if he even realized that both of them might still be targets and at risk of losing their lives.

"How can I be of help?" he asked after a few seconds, his voice as far off as if it came from the other side of a wall.

As she eyed his partially naked chest and the rest of him under that flimsy gown, a fantasy of possibilities tripped to mind. In good Irish wake fashion, the prospect of death had always ignited in her a rebellious passion to celebrate pleasures of the flesh. Instead, she replied, "Nothing for the moment. Just keep that fine mind of yours warm for me. I suspect we'll need it, once I start getting data, to put all the pieces together. As I told Greg Stanton, because you're an outsider to my field, you'll have the advantage of a fresh way of looking at things. But you'll need to brush up on your basics in molecular biology. I'm going to send you over some books—they're real doorstoppers, so I'll flag the sections I want you to read." She then said good night, gave him a reassuring pat on the hand, and walked out of the cubicle.

A few minutes later an orderly taught him the fine art of using crutches. Despite his having ordered thousands of patients onto them over the years, he found that he sucked at it.

1 3

Mother of God," Sullivan muttered once she unpacked the samples Racine had taken from the grounds of Agriterre Incorporated. They'd arrived from France in a large Styrofoam cooler by late afternoon the next day, just as he'd promised. Except when she'd laid them out in front of her, they covered the entire length of a twenty-foot workbench.

He'd followed her instructions precisely, providing her with individual packets of soil, roots, and, depending on the type of vegetation at a particular spot, blades of grass or stems and leaves. And they were all taken at varying intervals along or distances from the side of the building, also as she'd requested. But unlike her own clandestine visit to Agrenomics, his official unrestricted access to Agriterre had proffered over twelve hundred individual specimens to be tested.

"We'll start with the ones from closest to the building," Sullivan declared, speaking over her shoulder to Azrhan Doumani and the four technicians whom he'd selected to work on the project with them. "Any vectors present will consistently be found in the highest concentration there. The rest we'll have to store for the moment. I'm afraid we're facing a late night, so if anyone's expecting you, better call home."

They quickly sorted out who would do what, and began the routine that by now had become familiar. Some emptied small amounts of each sample into mortar vessels, giving them all a shot of liquid nitrogen. The white vapors flowed over their gloved hands as they proceeded to grind the frozen material with a pestle until it became a fine mash. Others subjected the subsequent powders to the chemical wash and spin in a centrifuge that separated out the chromosomes from the rest of the debris, leaving them floating on the surface like sludge on a bath. Doumani and Sullivan took on the task on siphoning off these supernatants and giving their DNA contents the cut-and-paste treatment with an arsenal of restriction enzymes, ones designed to fragment the entire range of DNA vectors that had shown up in the worldwide study, not just those specific to the cauliflower mosaic virus. It meant additional work, since they would now be testing each specimen nearly a dozen times.

Within an hour they were plating the first fifty of these solutions onto thin strips of electrophoretic gels, readying them for the journey through a special electrical field that would spread out the subsequent bits of DNA strands according to size and molecular weight, a process that would take until morning. And they'd only dealt with five sets of cuttings out of the entire shipment.

"Eleven hundred and ninety-five to go," she cracked to Doumani, flashing him a big grin as she switched on the electrophoresis equipment, a freestanding machine only slightly bigger than a photocopier that would hopefully unravel Pierre Gaston's secret.

Her assistant simply gave her a wan smile and went on preparing a gel for the next specimen.

Odd, she thought, I'd have expected him to be as pumped up with excitement as I am. "Are you all right, Azrhan?"

"Of course, Dr. Sullivan, just tired is all," he answered quickly, evading her gaze.

She didn't believe him. He'd been acting distracted by something ever since her return from Honolulu, and "just tired is all" didn't half explain the extent that puffy crescents of loose skin had been building under his eyes lately. She'd already spoken to him once about it—a few days ago when he'd botched a key step while helping one of her doctorate students with a research project. But she'd only received some vague explanation about his having family problems, along with multiple apologies and assurances it wouldn't happen again. Better not, she thought, what with the load they had ahead of them. But the fatigued look of him left her worried.

Into the night they worked, repeating the steps for each packet. By eleven-thirty they'd exhausted their capacity to do electrophoresis, having filled their other five machines, and had barely made a dint in what remained to be done. "Do you think we could beg, borrow, or steal some more of these units?" Sullivan asked Doumani, tapping the beige surface of the one nearest her. "It's obvious we'll be doing little else than separating out DNA over the next few weeks."

"I'll phone around to other labs," he replied, looking at his watch and yawning, "as soon as they're open."

"Then everyone else home for a sleep," she ordered the technicians. "From now on we'll work in shifts to optimize the use of the equipment we do have. I'm afraid I'll need two of you back here in seven hours when the results from the first batch should be ready; evenings we'll make from four till midnight. Work it out amongst yourselves about who does what. Azrhan, I think one of us should be here at all times to supervise and keep an eye on the equipment that's running, so we'll each pull a twelve-hour duty. Do you want days or nights?"

"Days would be better, because of my fiancée—"

"Fine!" she cut in, not exactly thrilled with leaving him alone, whatever shift he chose.

Once they'd all left the lab she returned to her office and unfolded the bed concealed in the couch. She wanted to be awake at seven, unwilling to leave those all-important first results for Azrhan to check on his own, not in the state of mind he seemed to be in. She'd also have to brief her regular staff when they arrived about what regular projects they would suspend in order to make room for the Rodez work. But as exhausted as she felt, she couldn't sleep. Rain peppered the tall glass panes that stretched above where she lay, and over the city lightning branched into molten roots as if trying to sink itself into the nearby buildings. Booms of encouragement followed each attempt, and during the intervals, every sound in the big old building, from the clanking of pipes to the thumps and bumps of what she couldn't identify, further assured she wouldn't sleep. Instead she tossed and turned, thinking about the bizarre note Pierre Gaston had left for her, and whenever she closed her eyes, the ghostly image of Hacket's face staring at her seconds before he'd had his neck snapped hovered in the darkness.

Did the samples in the next room hold a secret about the bird flu outbreak in Taiwan and Oahu? And did that secret relate to the man who had tried to murder Richard Steele? From a lineup of computer-generated likenesses showing acne-scarred men, she'd picked the composite of the man whose face she'd seen at Agrenomics without the slightest hesitation. Detective McKnight seemed to take her a little more seriously after that.

Restless, she kept getting up to check the electrophoresis equipment in the lab, impatient for the results despite knowing that nothing could hurry the fully automated process. The half dozen machines simply sat there, silent but for an occasional soft click, their operating lights and digital timers glowing red and green in the dark. The fact she couldn't see anything external to mark their internal progress only heightened her frustration.

Finally, as dawn penciled a gray line across the horizon, she drifted off, and dreamed of being chased through fields of tall grass by hooded men in black who kept shouting at her in a harsh and alien language.

Over the next few days and nights they settled into the second stage of their monotonous task—harvesting suspected vectors from the pink areas of electrophoretic gels, giving them a wash with GENE CLEAN, then using the appropriate primers to link up with and replicate the specific excerpts of these fragments by which they could be identified. This step, which took but an hour in the PCR machine, often generated so many distinct pieces of DNA that it took a few days' worth of electrophoresis to sort them all out.

But identify them they did, and the more data they gathered, the more depressed Sullivan became. Everything they discovered simply replicated the findings of the world study as far as the vectors were concerned. Over and over they kept turning up DNA sequences from the same dozen or so carriers, the cauliflower mosaic virus being the most frequent. Also prevalent were a variety of commonly used transposons, promoters, and enhancers meant to help integrate, replicate, and express whatever gene the vector carried once it arrived in its new host. It all seemed so ordinary she kept wondering, What could it be that Pierre Gaston had intended me to unmask?

They worked into the Memorial Day weekend, still appearing to get nowhere. The only bright spot in the tedium occurred when Richard Steele dropped over, albeit on crutches. He'd done the reading she'd given him, but wanted more. She offered him unlimited use of her on-site library, and felt pleased when, the following week, he started coming in regularly at the end of each day, soon only with the help of a cane, to talk over anything he hadn't understood.

"Your passion for genetics is infectious," he said during one of their sessions together. "You must be a great teacher."

"It's the power of the gene that's the fascination," she told him without hesitation, delighted by his compliment and eager to share her enthusiasm for the work she loved. "I don't see how anyone can look on DNA and not experience the same awe that, say, Einstein and Bohr felt for the atom. Certainly the potential to manipulate that power for good or evil is just as great."

An hour later McKnight phoned and quickly put an end to their pleasant interlude by delivering more discouraging news. "Agrenomics, it turns out, hires its own security guards individually," said the detective. "They claimed to have fired the man with the acne weeks ago—Fred Smith is the name on his employee record. 'Bad attitude,' they gave as the reason. They'd originally hired him, they said, because he offered the services of his trained watchdogs as part of the deal, yet everyone else felt too scared of the animals to have them around. The personnel office gave us where he lived, and guess what? The guy moved leaving no forwarding address. In fact, apart from a driver's license and birth certificate, there's no record of the man. 'Fred Smith' is probably an alias."

"What about Sydney Aimes?" she asked.

"I thought he'd blow a gasket, he got so mad when I paid him a visit in his offices. As soon as I mentioned that his comment to Dr. Steele could be taken as a threat, he summoned a half dozen lawyers into the room. After that, he wouldn't tell me the way to the can without whispering with them for five minutes. But apart from infuriating the guy, I got nothing."

By the end of the second week she'd grown convinced that whatever Pierre Gaston had wanted her to find that was *even deadlier*, it didn't have anything to do with the makeup of vectors, which is what they'd been testing for all this time. It must be one of the genetic packages that they transport, she reasoned, referring to the gene or genes intended for a leap across the species barrier and insertion into a new organism.

If that was the case, she might as well try and find a particular grain of sand on a beach as guess which primers would fingerprint it for her. The possibilities of what it could be were that endless. And genetic mapping, the only process that can sequence the nucleic acids of a completely unknown strand of DNA, was out of the question. It involved costly, highly specialized equipment found at such a limited number of research centers and constantly in such high demand she'd not get access to one anytime soon, if ever. After all, she was on a fishing expedition, chasing she knew not what, the only evidence that it even existed being a five-month-old message from a dead man. Hardly the stuff to put on an application for a turn with a sequencer. Besides, even if she did have the means to map a gene, which sample would she start with? She didn't know which vectors among the thousands they'd isolated contained the thing she was after.

She nevertheless dug out the gels showing the fragments of cauliflower mosaic virus and the other carrier microbes they'd already replicated and separated out into "fingerprint" patterns. Slipping them one by one through her microscope, she saw near the bottom of each a horizontal smudge of DNA. These were the intact chromosomes of the carrier along which the primers had lined up to set off the replication process. More lengthy, and therefore heavier than their parts, the strands had hardly budged during their exposure to the electrical field. Buried within them, she knew, would also be the genes that the vector had been assigned to carry. "The DNA I want is in there," she muttered. "There must be a way to tease it out." Yet as she stared through the microscope at this line on a gel, it taunted her, like a horizon she would never reach.

She sat struggling with the problem, scarcely noticing that most of her staff and Doumani had gone home. Getting nowhere, she eventually took another tack. Maybe Inspector Racine can help me, she thought. If he raided Agriterre and put the place under a microscope as he'd planned, he'll likely have already seized their records. And if I can get a look at their scientific files, perhaps I'll learn from them what sorts of genes they were transposing. At the same time I can ask him if he's any more leads on who killed Pierre Gaston. After all, knowing that might shed some light on who attacked me in Hawaii, or the identity of the man who tried to kill Steele.

Would it be too late to call him now? Glancing at her watch she saw 7:15. Given the time difference, that made it 1:15 A.M. in France. She whipped off her request by e-mail instead.

Logging off the Internet, she went back to scrutinizing the gels they'd run so far. Twenty minutes later she remembered a promise to call Greg Stanton at seven o'clock. "Damn!" she muttered, reaching for the phone. Ever since their meeting ten days ago, he'd continued to insist on regular updates. Yet each time they spoke about the Rodez samples she seemed to raise more questions than provide answers, and she hadn't much better news for him regarding the specimens taken from Hacket's farm.

As she dialed, she flipped open the notes she'd scribbled during her many conversations with the Honolulu lab. The samples they'd analyzed so far had contained no evidence of DNA vectors whatsoever, and the last time she spoke with them, they informed her that their own research had started cutting into the electrophoresis time they could spare her.

"What specimens do you still have to check?" she'd asked the technician in charge, barely able to conceal her frustration at the slow pace.

"A few large weeds, a corn plant, some individual kernels, and of course there's the bird droppings. We sent a sample of them over to Julie Carr, for viral cultures as you requested, to see if there were any remnants of the H5N1, or bird flu microorganisms, but those results also came back negative. I guess eighteen months is a long time to have expected the virus to remain intact. But Julie suggested that while we're checking the droppings for vectors, why not include a primer for traces of H5N1 RNA? A bit might have survived, and would provide just as good evidence of the virus having been present in the bird's gut as a positive culture. She's already sent off a request that the CDC in Atlanta forward us the restriction enzymes and primers we'll need."

"Sounds good," Sullivan had replied, trying to sound cheerful while strangling the receiver in the face of even more delays.

A robotic voice from the automated switchboard for the medical school pulled her from her morose thoughts. Navigating the options it offered, she finally punched in the right numbers to get the infuriatingly bossy recording—a male voice this year—to shut up and connect her with Stanton's extension. To her surprise, she found the man still waiting for her call.

Twenty-four hours later she got Racine's reply.

My Dear Dr. Sullivan,

What an excellent idea it is that you should inspect their files. Unfortunately, while our initial strike caught the people at Agriterre completely off guard, enabling us to get the samples to you unhindered by any red tape, the company's lawyers have now marshaled their forces, preventing us further access to the facility. In short, we are engaged in the kind of bureaucratic paper war for which we French are famous.

With any luck however, our courts shall soon order their CEO to release all company documents, at which time, I shall forward them to you immediately.

As to our investigation into Gaston's murder, I'm afraid there, too, we haven't made much progress. We already knew from our initial enquiry into his disappearance that on the afternoon before he vanished, a woman visited his apartment— a woman who, according to his landlady, "Had been there several times in the preceding six months and was 'far too beautiful for a toad of a man like him.' " We still have not found out this visitor's identity, let alone where she is or if she had anything to do with his death.

We do know that the night Gaston disappeared, New Year's Eve, he returned to the Agriterre building, went to his laboratory, and left again. No one knows why, and the CEO, Dr. Francois Dancereau, remains adamant that nothing is missing from the premises.

In the meantime, I can only say that I share your frustration. May I assure you that your efforts in our behalf are greatly appreciated, and I remain humbly at your service.

Sincerely,

Inspector Georges Racine

He could call himself whatever he wanted, but she knew e-mail from Claude Rains when she saw it. As she read his words on her computer screen she could practically smell his Gauloises and see him gesturing with it, the smoke curling up from its tip. Except unlike his character in *Casablanca*, he hadn't rounded up "the usual suspects" yet. Disappointed, she started to log off, then wondered again why the name Dr. Francois Dancereau sounded vaguely familiar. Perhaps he'd presented a paper at some conference she'd attended or published an article she'd read. Instead of shutting down, she clicked onto the Medline page—the most complete listing of publications in the health science field—and typed in the man's name.

No matches found.

Oh, well, worth a try, she thought, and got back to her latest batch of gels.

Monday, June 5, 9:00 P.M.

"Relax! She's skirting around the truth like a moth around a flame, but so far she doesn't get it," he reassured Morgan over the phone. "And according to her latest e-mail from that police inspector in Rodez a few days ago, he's not making any progress, either."

"You haven't had a homicide detective at your door."

"He wasn't there for you. Besides, that was well over a week ago, and he hasn't been back. Obviously he can't find any link between that idiot guard and Agrenomics beyond what your personnel people told him."

"When do we take care of Sullivan and Steele?" Morgan persisted, sounding increasingly frustrated. "The cops may not have found a connection, but those two won't stop until they do—now that we've made them both suspicious as hell about the place, thanks to you and your bright ideas about using our own people!"

"Soon," he told him softly, and hung up, choosing to ignore the criticism. Leaning back in his chair, he stared out his window and savored the view as the setting sun once more ignited the Twin Towers. "Soon," he repeated, "we will have taken care of everything, including you, my frightened little friend."

Tuesday, June 6, 5:50 A.M.

She heard his voice far away, yet he seemed to be yelling, speaking in the same harsh language used by the hooded pursuers.

She flew awake, at first confused as to where she lay. She stared about her, the thin first light of dawn only dimly illuminating the office. In seconds she remembered—her sofa bed, sleeping over at the lab—and settled back on her pillow, her heart still pounding.

She must have had another nightmare, she thought, feeling cold and pulling her blanket around her. The dampness in the place had gotten so bad with all the rain that everyone complained of feeling perpetually chilly, and none of the doors would open or close properly. The fact that they routinely lowered the heat in May whether the weather warranted it or not didn't help matters.

As she lay there shivering, hoping to warm up enough to get a few more hours of sleep, she didn't pay it any attention at first, it sounded so faint. Even when she did, her mind initially dismissed it as a distant radio. Until an instant later a sudden increase in its volume made her realize the guttural sounds of her dream were coming from somewhere down the hallway outside her door.

A chill ran through the length of her body that had nothing to do with the temperature. Instantly she sat bolt upright, her heart sprinting to triple digits in a second flat. While she listened the sounds continued in brief spurts, then broke off. Occasionally there were repeated yells followed by silence. As far as she could tell, only a single male voice spoke. A telephone conversation?

Even though she couldn't make out the words, the rapid staccato cadence and irregular explosive rhythms of the person's speech definitely mimicked those of the voices that now haunted her dreams. It can't be one of them, she tried to tell herself, her throat growing tight. She sprang out of bed, tiptoed on bare feet over to her desk, and reached for the phone, intending to call 911. She had her hand on the receiver when she thought, The extension light! If I pick up, it will flash on his end and warn him that I'm here.

She spun around, thinking she could use her cell phone instead, but in the gray light couldn't spot where she'd left it. Keeping an ear tuned to the distant conversation while figuring he wouldn't be coming for her as long as he kept talking, she quickly checked beneath the couch where she'd been sleeping.

Nothing.

Riffling through the pile of clothing she'd discarded before going to bed produced the same result. Thrusting her hand into the pockets of her lab coat where it hung in the closet . . . she couldn't find it anywhere.

I must have left it on the workbench, she thought, her insides lurching into a knot.

She pulled on her dress and slipped into her shoes, planning on being able to run if she had to. Careful not to let the crepe soles squeak on the linoleum floor, she went up to her door. Slowly opening it, she immediately could tell from how much louder the voice got that it came from one of the rooms nearby. The sudden amplification enabled her to better hear the words themselves—foreign and harsh, yet terrifyingly familiar—erasing any doubts she had about the language being the same as the killers'.

Peeking down the hallway, she saw where a thin wedge of light slashed the darkness in front of Azrhan's office. His door stood partially open, and a shadow from within moved back and forth across the frosted glass. The conversation sounded even angrier now—the person breaking it off in midbreath as if he'd been interrupted, then cutting off the brief silences with a furious tirade that she would have guessed to be profanity in any language.

Is it only Azrhan? she thought, confusion adding to her panic and leaving her barely able to breathe. She'd heard him speak Arabic before, but this sounded altogether different. Could his voice be so distorted by the strange dialect and rage that she could hardly recognize it?

To reach the room where she'd left her cell phone, she had to pass that door. It also stood between her and the exit to the outside corridor where the elevators were. Despite her fear, she stepped into the dark passage and crept forward. But as she got closer to the sliver of light, she began to wonder even more if it wasn't him. After all, I heard no one breaking in, so whoever it is must have had keys, she reasoned. Shouldn't I try and take a peek first before calling the police and avoid bringing them for nothing? After all, if it is him, he has a perfect right to use his office any time, day or night, or to speak any language he wants. Yet the prospect of his speaking that particular language, despite her best effort not to think the worst, sent darker implications nibbling like parasites on the edge of her thoughts.

She'd gotten nearly abreast of the door when she heard a particularly vehement string of gibberish and the receiver slam down.

Uh-oh, she thought, frozen in midstep. As she watched, the shadow within grew darker on the glazed window.

He's coming out! her mind screamed, and she instinctively backed up, ducking into her office again. She swung the door closed behind her, but it jammed before she could shut it enough to snap the lock. Applying more pressure, she pushed so hard it lurched into place with a bang.

Not daring to breathe, she stood there listening. At first she heard nothing. Then tentative footsteps approached along the hallway. "Dr. Sullivan, are you awake?" came Azrhan's voice.

14

I didn't mean to disturb you." His voice sounded strained, and at
least a half octave too high.

"Why are you here in the middle of the night?"

"It's a long story," he said, jigging his leg nervously and looking
miserable as he took a sip of tea.

"Get on with it," she commanded, making him wince. She'd not
let him say a word while she'd boiled the water, prepared the pot to
steep, and folded up the sofa bed. The familiarity of the routine
helped her to get a rein on the pounding in her chest. Only when
they were seated on opposite sides of her desk, cups in hand, did she
permit him to try and explain.

"Okay," he began, his body visibly slumping, as if he were surren-
dering to a wrestling hold. "As I told you, I've been having family
problems. My parents in particular. While doing my postgraduate
work I met an American girl. We live together. When my parents
came to visit, they were appalled—about her being an American,
about us living in sin, about it being pretty obvious that I don't intend to return to Kuwait. You see, my parents are devout Muslims,
and they can't accept any of it. Worse, I have a younger brother—he's
twenty—who wants to follow in my footsteps and live in America.
My father blames me for that as well."

"What language were you speaking tonight?"

"Farsi. My family is originally from Iran. After the fall of the
Shah, we escaped to Kuwait, and are citizens of that country now.

While we all learned the local Arab dialect of our new country—I was a little kid, so it came naturally after a while—my father insisted that we continue to speak our native language at home. Now, we revert to it when we're alone, especially to argue, which is all the time these days."

"Do any other nationalities speak it?"

"There's a dialect in Afghanistan that's very similar. Otherwise, it's unique. Why?" he asked, his voice all at once a half octave higher and sounding a little too innocent.

"Because I told you about the attack on me when I got back from Honolulu, including a few phrases I remembered of the strange language I'd heard. Did you realize that I'd been describing Farsi, yet say nothing?"

He didn't answer. Wouldn't even look at her.

"You did know!"

"Yes," he admitted, looking miserable.

"Then why didn't you tell me?"

He remained silent.

"Azrhan, either you come clean with me, or I'll have your resignation. Now, why the hell didn't you say that you recognized what language I heard?"

His head jerked up, his eyes black with anger. "All right, I'll tell you. Do you have any idea what it's like, Dr. Sullivan, being an Arab in this country? Even a 'good Arab' like me—a superbright, overachieving, hardworking one—is far too often looked at askance while walking in the street, asked by police to pull the car over, and targeted for special scrutiny whenever it comes to airport security."

"Azrhan! I never measure you other than by your ability—"

"I know you don't. Under your tent, I've received nothing but equal opportunity. I'm talking about out there." He gestured to the window.

"But I'm not responsible—"

"I don't advertise I'm Iranian, okay! Not to any American. If I must declare my original nationality, I say Persian. Why? Because even though it's been over twenty years since the hostage crisis, the images of that outrage are burned indelibly into the American psyche. I say Iran, and that's what an American thinks of. Something happens in your eyes, whoever you are, or however intellectually open and liberal you happen to be—as if an inner lid comes down, and you see me differently from then on. If I say I'm from Kuwait, I'm everybody's pal, because you all feel so good about having liberated us, and you sure as hell know we're not the enemy over there."

He snapped his gaze away and glowered into the bottom of his teacup. The outburst had left him breathing heavily, but as she watched, the rise and fall of his chest slowed.

"I can't stand seeing that lid come down, Dr. Sullivan," he continued after a few seconds, speaking softly now, his initial anger having vanished, "especially when it happens in people who are important to me. It's like a curtain descending on the relationship, and somehow we're never the same together again. I didn't let on I knew the language, because I knew you would ask me how I knew it, and either I'd have to lie, or you'd learn my real nationality. I couldn't bear the thought of seeing that lid descend on my relationship with you."

"Azrhan, look me in the eye, right now!" she ordered.

Raising his head, he reluctantly did as she asked.

"What do you see?"

He didn't reply, but held his gaze steady on her.

"Well?" she said impatiently.

He gave a tentative smile. "I see you're pissed off as hell at me."

"Any 'lids'?"

"No," he said with a nervous laugh.

"And if you don't be wantin' to ever see the likes of 'lids' in these baby greens of mine, don't you ever be lyin' to me again, understand?"

"Yes, ma'am!" he answered, his face breaking into another smile.

"But why did you come here to use the phone in the first place?"

The smile vanished. "Time zones," he answered quickly. "Middle of the night here is when it's best to reach my father there. Knowing he and I would probably have another fight, I didn't want to disturb my fiancée by using the phone at our apartment."

She watched his eyes again. They shifted ever so slightly, then held on her.

"Okay, then let's get ready for the morning staff," she said quietly.

After he left her office, she felt uneasy about the encounter. Everything he'd said had a ring of truth to it, and Lord knows she wanted to believe him. But it particularly bothered her how she could have worked so closely with him and never have picked up on the resentment he felt so profoundly. Had she been racist by default, not clueing in to how he saw things because she preferred not to do so? Or was she ignorant of his anger because he'd chosen to conceal it from her in order to keep their working relationship easy? That would be understandable, noble of him, even. But could he also have kept so much of himself hidden from her for more sinister reasons?

Fueled by her fatigue, driven by her desperate need to discover who might want her dead, and at a total loss over how to unlock whatever answers lay in those unknown fragments of DNA, she allowed her own hidden lids to come down, and she thought the unthinkable of him. Could he be part of what was going on in Rodez and Maui? Had their professional congeniality been a carefully acted sham from the beginning? Had he, in fact, gotten himself placed with her to keep an eye on what she did? Like released pus, paranoia poured out of her mind unchecked, until even his not accompanying her to Honolulu started to look suspicious. Was his refusal because he'd been in contact with those men and knew they were going to try to kill her? She suddenly felt sick for ever having asked the question.

No! Damn it! I won't let myself think that way.

But she had thought "that way." And it changed how she looked at him. Ashamed, she found herself avoiding his eye. When she did inadvertently catch his gaze, she saw a dark impermeable sadness that nearly broke her heart.

Damn! she cursed silently, loathing herself. Damn! Damn! Damn!

Friday, June 9, 11:46 A.M.

He rolled the car to a stop on the shoulder of the road under a solitary oak tree. It cast a giant shadow speckled with winks of light from a noonday sun in a high, unbroken blue sky. From Steele to the next hill stretched a mile of asphalt between two fields of young corn, the new sprouts barely two feet high. Approximately half a mile away he could see the Agrenomics facility. The oasis of treed lawns surrounding the long, low building and the deserted railway spur curving away from the rear of the grounds toward the west looked exactly as Kathleen had described it for him. But her brief mention of the massive greenhouses behind hadn't prepared him for the actual size of the monstrous glass and metal structures. Each of the six could have housed one and a half football fields, and using his rusty memory of the conversion from square yards he figured the area under glass to be about seven acres in all. A tall chain-link fence topped with curls of wire ran around it, the occasional flash from the coiled strands suggesting they were laced with razors.

It's like a prison, just as Kathleen said, Steele thought.

What intrigued him even more: the entire complex looked practically deserted. The parking lot held fewer than a half dozen cars, and apart from a solitary security guard at the front gate, he saw no one, not on the grounds or around the greenhouses. He paid particular attention to the latter, scanning the place with the binoculars he'd brought along, but couldn't discern any movement behind its highly reflective panels.

Settling back, he lowered his windows and felt a warm breeze flow over him. Outside the passenger door a bee droned intermittently, making its rounds through the purple lupines and early phlox that grew wild in the ditch. Mingling with the pinging noises of his car as it cooled, the leaves above, dangling from the branches like quivering, silken emeralds, filled the air with a soothing rustle.

He'd driven up that morning hoping some of the staff would be willing to talk with him about the pizza-faced man who'd once worked with them—at least more than they had when, two weeks earlier, McKnight had asked the questions. Timing the visit to arrive at lunch hour, he figured he could follow some of the workers to a local eatery where they'd be off company property and might feel more inclined to speak up, especially if he bought them a few beers. "For openers, I'll show them my leg wound, and attest that they'd been right all along to feel uneasy about Fred Smith with his beasts," he'd explained to Sullivan when they first discussed his coming here. "One thing I've learned in ER about getting information out of people is that when it comes to casual acquaintances—distant neighbors, people who work together, that kind of thing—nothing gets tongues wagging more than people having their worst suspicions about some-one confirmed."

She'd clucked at his cynical take on human nature, then railed at how he shouldn't have to be doing the police's job in any case. "It's despicable how they refused to press the issue that someone at Agrenomics might have set the pizza-faced man onto you," she de-clared, brimming with indignantion. "No?"

"That's how I read it," he'd assured her.

"So why don't the police see things the way we do?"

"Because we haven't the slightest idea who in the place would go after me, or why. Because nothing links them with Rodez or Hawaii. Because the only evidence you can show that Agrenomics is behaving suspiciously is how they came out pristine clean in your tests. Is it any wonder McKnight won't act?"

Those eyes of hers had flared so luminously at him that for a sec-ond he feared he'd been far too blunt. But the blaze died, and a few seconds later, she mumbled, "I guess you're right."

"So it's time we learned everything we can about the place. While I'm talking to people there about Pizza Face, I'll try and poke a stick beneath that squeaky clean surface and stir up the bottom a little. There's got to be somebody who's willing to tell us what's going on."

But no one obliged. Even though Steele had driven by an inviting-looking roadside café and bar not five miles back, an hour passed and not a soul came out of the laboratory premises to go eat. "Must all be a lunch bucket crowd," he muttered, wondering what he should do next. The idea of sneaking up on the place seemed fruitless, the area being so open. Besides, what good would it do him? As much as he'd like to see inside, scaling the fences around the greenhouses looked impossible, and the solitary guard would certainly spot him if he tried to gain access to the main building. Maybe I can intercept people when they go home? he wondered, glancing at his watch. But that wouldn't be for another three and a half hours.

He found himself looking at the railway spur again. Retrieving his binoculars he brought it into focus, and followed its roadbed through the fields with his eye. Trees and shrubs lined it most of the way, and it passed close in front of the greenhouses. I might get a glimpse inside them from there, he reasoned, and if I approach using the tracks, I don't think anyone would spot me.

His left leg hurt as he walked the ties between the rails, yet he made good progress. It had been seventeen days since the attack on him, and a week since he removed his own stitches. His only difficulty occurred when he pushed off with the ball of his foot and worked his calf muscles. Despite the tears and missing strands, the filaments were mending, but the scarring foreshortened their range of movement.

The sun blasted the stone ballast with the full heat of the afternoon, and the dark treated wood beneath his feet released such a pungent perfume of creosote that it radiated all the way to the back of his nose to tickle his throat. His exertion left him breathing with his mouth open, and he unbuttoned his shirt, letting it trail out behind him while the breeze evaporated his sweat and cooled his torso. He took some pride in having lost the paunch he'd been developing over the winter; cutting back on drinking and keeping busy had started to take effect for the better. Around him the cicadas buzzed, their sound mingling with the continuous whisper of the bushes and young trees lining the tracks. The noise, he hoped, would cover the occasional crunch of his footsteps.

He'd driven a little under a mile past the front entrance of

Agrenomics before he parked once more on the side of the road. Slipping his binoculars around his neck, Steele walked several hundred yards through a field to reach the spur. From that point, atop a little hillock, he could see where the line joined the main track about another mile further west. Several miles beyond that, there seemed to be a railyard where strings of freight cars sat on dozens of sidings. Using his binoculars, he made out a small diesel engine poking its way through the various switches and tracks, coupling onto a string of boxcars, then shunting them farther down the line. He could also make out a man wearing jeans and a hard hat who dangled off a ladder at the end of the rear car, waving instructions to whoever sat at the throttle in the engine's cab. Around them stretched endless green fields of month-old spring crops made lush by all the rain they'd had. A sleepier scene he couldn't imagine.

Maybe I should visit those men when I'm through here, he thought, continuing to trudge along toward Agrenomics and eyeing the shiny tracks that indicated regular use. Perhaps I'll learn what they haul out of the place and where it goes.

The greenhouses loomed ahead on his left. As he drew closer, he kept an eye on the back end of the lab building through the foliage on his right. To his relief he saw that it had no windows.

Staying low, he veered toward the near corner of the razor wire fence and ducked behind a complex of massive pipes and flexible hoses. Satisfying himself that he remained out of sight, he took a closer look at what he'd hidden in. It seemed to be a device for pumping something into railway cars, and he could make out a similar structure located on the main grounds near the wall where the spur ended. His curiosity about what they shipped grew.

He proceeded to stride briskly along the length of fence leading farther into the fields. It stretched about three hundred yards, and he kept a sharp eye out for security cameras, planning to mimic somebody out bird-watching if he saw a sign of surveillance. Even when he failed to spot any peering lenses, he put on a show of periodically gazing into the sky through his binoculars, just in case.

Finally he reached the far end of the barricade, where he stepped around the corner while still keeping an eye out for overhead video equipment. He knelt to massage his calf, the uneven ground and his fast pace having aggravated it, then surreptitiously tried scraping away enough dirt to slip under the bottom strands of the chain links. His fingers hit a strip of concrete just under the soil. "Christ!" he muttered, realizing that the only way through would be with a pair of wire cutters. He next attempted to see into the nearest greenhouse, but while its peaked roof had clear glass, the panes on the sides had enough of a reflective surface that they prevented the identification of much of what was inside. All he could make out were tables of endless troughs containing scattered stalks of something that looked about six feet high, but the rest seemed to have been already harvested.

Disappointed, he turned and started back the way he'd come. He got halfway along the fence toward the tracks when all at once he thought he heard voices.

"Shit!" he said, glancing around him ready to do some fast talking.

But he saw no one.

Yet the voices continued, muffled so he couldn't make out the words, the way a conversation sounds when the people speaking are in the next room. It must be coming from inside one of the greenhouses, he thought, straining to see any sign of movement behind the glass of the one nearest him. But all he saw were silhouettes similar to those same scraggy stalks that he'd seen minutes earlier.

The voices continued. Someone even laughed.

"What the hell?" he muttered, looking around and feeling the bewilderment of a rational man who's suddenly beginning to consider he may actually be encountering a ghost. *Either that, or I got more sun than I realized,* he thought, determined to figure it out.

The voices still continued. Not so much behind, beside, or in front of him, as from below.

He studied the ground beneath his feet. It seemed like ordinary dirt. He scuffed it with the toe of his shoe. More ordinary dirt. He then swept his eyes to right and left, and spotted a rectangular metal cover coated with dust just inside the fence by where he stood. Kneeling down, he heard the voices grow louder. They were definitely coming from wherever that cover led.

Five Hours Later

The trilling of her cellular phone seemed to go on forever. Trying to rouse herself, she fumbled around on the floor in the direction of the sound and, upon opening her eyes, couldn't remember for a few seconds why she'd been asleep in her office. Retrieving the receiver, she glanced at her watch. "Bloody hell!" she muttered, seeing 7:50 P.M. and all at once recalling what she'd intended to do. "Only a half-hour snooze, and I'll be as right as rain" she promised her technicians two hours ago, unable to keep her eyes open. The night shifts were wreaking havoc with her sleep despite afternoon naps at home and Lisa's tiptoeing around after school so as not to disturb her. "I want to get at the latest batch of gels," she added, "so be sure to wake me." They obviously hadn't.

"Kathleen? It's Dr. Julie Carr. Sorry to disturb you, but have I got news! It's stranger than anything you could imagine."

"Julie, from Hawaii?" she answered, struggling to sit up. Outside her window to the west of the Twin Towers she saw a slash of orange across a dark horizon marking the end of the day.

"That's right," the virologist replied. "It's not even two here yet, and we just finished running confirmation studies on what we found in your samples from Hacket's farm."

"Really?" she answered, still a little groggy. "But why are you involved? And only a few weeks ago the chief technician told me my stuff had gotten bumped—"

"That was before the mistake, and it changed everything. Let me start at the beginning."

"Mistake?"

"First of all, we found evidence of genetic vectors in the kernels of corn farmer Hacket had been using to feed the chickens," said Julie, barging ahead. "The carrier portions were mostly made of cauliflower mosaic virus, but we picked out a few other types employing all the primers you and Patton included in your world study."

"My God! So I was right—"

"We also found small fragments of bird flu H5N1 DNA in the hen droppings, this time using the restriction enzymes and primers for the virus that I got from the CDC in Atlanta."

Sullivan's brain snapped to full alert. "So we've got a case for my theory—the vectors and the H5N1 virus *were* in close proximity inside the chickens' GI tract. Julie, that's enough to publish. It gives my theory that the vectors made the H5N1 jump the species barrier much more credibility. Sydney Aimes, eat your heart out!" The flush of vindication sent her spirits soaring despite the grim prognosis that her discovery might hold for humankind. It was a macabre kind of ecstasy, she knew, a glow of accomplishment peculiar to doctors and scientists when they unearth a suspected truth even when the news is bad, but she relished it just the same.

"Hold it, gal. You ain't heard nothing yet. I haven't explained what happened after the mistake."

"What mistake?"

"As you know, the people in the lab here were processing your stuff whenever they had time, and that meant the most junior personnel often ended up doing the work. A technician confused the primers, and added the one intended to demonstrate H5N1, the bird flu virus in the hen droppings, to the PCR machine while it was processing kernels of corn for vectors containing CaMV."

"She what?"

"I know, it sounds silly, but that's what happened."

"So? She should simply have thrown the subsequent mix away and repeated the PCR—"

"That's just it. She didn't realize she'd made the error, and another technician ran the resulting fragments of DNA through an electrophoresis gel."

"Wait a minute. What fragments of DNA? There shouldn't have been any replication of any DNA if she used the wrong primer."

"But there were fragments. Big long chains of them—all of it H5N1 DNA. That's where our bird flu came from."

"Pardon?"

"The H5N1 was in the corn, Kathleen! Brought there by a CaMV vector. Someone modified the corn with DNA from bird flu."

"You've got to be kidding!"

"I couldn't believe it, either."

"But how did it get there? I can't even imagine any way that someone could insert H5N1 into corn by accident."

"They didn't."

"Huh?"

"Like you, I couldn't conceive of how this had occurred. But when I looked at all these fragments of H5N1 and compared them to gels of the virus that the CDC sent me, I noticed that they didn't add up to an intact specimen. At first I thought pieces might have been missing because of natural deterioration, but as the results from more kernels came in, I saw that the same fragments of DNA were absent each time. And when I gave these strands a proper viral coat and placed them in a culture media, they didn't replicate. That's when I realized what we were dealing with."

"I still don't get it."

"Sure you do. Someone systematically removed those pieces of the DNA that let the virus replicate, Kathleen. They attenuated it, the same way we remove part of a virus to prevent replication when we want to make a regular vaccine, and still leave it intact enough that the surface proteins will stimulate an antibody reaction in the recipient. Except in this case, they made the modification on the level of the DNA itself."

"Are you saying what I think you are?"

"The corn's a genetic vaccine, Kathleen. A poorly made, highly dangerous genetic vaccine. Those birds on Kailua didn't test positive for H5N1 surface protein and antibodies because they were sick. They tested positive because, unknown to us, they'd all been vaccinated against the infection through their feed. They'd incorporated the attenuated DNA into their own genes, manufactured their own supply of the virus's protein coat, and mounted an immune response to it. If we'd done a lot of confirmatory procedures on the birds, we would maybe have picked up on it, but we had a dead kid on our hands and rushed to judgment. What can I say? Those chickens were still bloody dangerous—pooping out a vaccine loaded with long strands of near-intact H5N1 virus, all turbocharged with enhancers, promoters, and transposons. It's no wonder a recombinant event between it and human influenza occurred, once little Tommy Arness inoculated his nose with the stuff. Hell, if we hadn't killed the birds off, anyone else with the flu who handled them might also have incubated the hybrid, and we would have had a real epidemic on our hands."

"My God!" Sullivan murmured.

"The shit's really hit the fan over here," Julie continued. "We've informed the Department of Public Health, they've notified the police, and since we all know that there's only one outfit on the island sophisticated enough to be dealing in genetic vaccines, Biofeed has already received an official visit from the law. The subsequent denials that they've ever traded in that kind of product are flying out of the CEO's office so loud you can likely hear them even in New York. Not surprisingly, a wall of company lawyers has formed around their records department, but the cops declared all documents in the place relevant to a possible case of negligent homicide—the death of the Arness boy—and word is they'll access them by morning. Those same detectives are also reevaluating the murder at the Hacket farm and the attack on you in the context of someone trying to keep the cause of the child's death from being found out. But I suppose you had your suspicions about that all along."

"More so recently," Sullivan replied, her mind already racing too far ahead to bother explaining about Rodez, Agrenomics, and Pizza Face. "Julie, can you courier me the restriction enzymes and primers for H5N1 you used?"

"Of course. Why?"

"Let's just say that I may soon come up with a surprise of my own."

After hanging up, she could barely contain her excitement. She especially wanted to tell Greg Stanton, at last having specific evidence that tied bird flu to the murders in Rodez and Oahu. When she reached him at home, she could hear the sounds of a party in the background. He nevertheless listened patiently, and when she finished, he said, "Well done, but I'll need Dr. Carr's reports in writing—to address the board about them. And when will you be running the tests for bird flu on the Rodez specimens?"

"I won't receive the reagents until Monday morning when the courier gets them here. Expect the first results by midnight."

"Great. And what are you going to do in the meantime?"

"I'll be in the lab, trying to finish the current tests and preparing the samples we'll need once those primers arrive."

"Just don't go making any preliminary announcements," he ordered, and rang off.

Despite his warning, she thought, why not call Sydney Aimes and let *him* in on the good news? Picturing the spectacle of the man at the conference, his bald head and thick neck tumescent with rage, she began to imagine his reaction with relish. The big prick will look like an erection on legs.

But her sense of triumph over him quickly died. From the dark recesses where instinct and inarticulate fears lurked ever ready to infest her dreams, there escaped a remarkably lucid warning. As clearly as if someone had uttered a whisper inside her ear, she heard: He's also going to become exceedingly more dangerous.

Better let Stanton handle him, she decided.

Instead she dialed Steve Patton's number. Telling him tonight's news would not only be a refreshing change from having nothing new to say for the last few weeks, it would give them something to focus on. These days their relationship seemed to have once more recovered to a stage where they could discuss work without being too awkward about it, and she wanted to nurture that progress. That's why she promised herself to be very discreet as she savored the sweet taste of payback for his "I told you so" attitude in Honolulu.

His phone rang a few times longer than it usually took him to pick up, and when he did, she recognized a telltale throatiness that once would have been enough to send her into a fit of despair. But now, even as she caught his barely concealed breathlessness and an occasional grunt in the background, she actually experienced a sense of relief from knowing he was with another woman. Somehow it made her feel off the hook. For a second she even toyed with the idea of hanging up without saying a word and calling him tomorrow, when he said, "Kathleen?" and all the noise of having sex ceased immediately.

His Caller ID–unit had given her away. What the hell, she thought, I might as well fill him in on Julie's discovery now.

Once she'd finished her account and explained what she had in mind for the Rodez samples, he said, "So your speculation turned out close to the mark after all. Congratulations, and please accept my apologies for criticizing you about it at the time."

His magnanimous response pleased her. To her surprise, he then stayed on the line, seeming in no hurry to get back to his guest. Rather he started asking questions about the implications of genetic vaccines, what she thought their presence in Oahu might mean, and how they could be connected to Rodez, or Taiwan even.

She also noticed his voice quickly returning to its normal, nonaroused pitch. What must your bedmate think? she had the impulse to tease, but she behaved, glad to be out of the man's private life. Focusing instead on answering his inquiries, she soon grew impatient, finding him slow on the uptake as she kept having to go over things two or three times. I guess I've gotten used to teaching the likes of Richard Steele, she thought. Not everyone can be as sharp and quick to the point as he is.

Poor Steve, she mused when he finally let her off the line. I guess I'm really free of you. The realization left her feeling a mixture of sadness and relief, and she found it strange how ordinary he now seemed.

Next she called Azrhan, to warn him that they'd have to clear the decks of all routine work on Monday.

"That's fine, Dr. Sullivan. Do you need me this weekend, to help get ready?" His tone remained impeccably neutral, the way it had since their confrontation four days ago.

"Thanks, Azrhan, I could definitely use you tomorrow." Her own reply smooth as glass, she rang off wondering if their relationship would ever be the same again.

Dialing Steele's cellular number she found herself looking forward to his reaction, anticipating that his excitement over Julie Carr's discovery would match her own.

"I'm sorry, but the person you have called is not available. Please leave a message," intoned a computer.

"Damn!" she exclaimed out loud, then realized that she'd recorded her disappointment at not reaching him. "Sorry, Richard. I'm such a foul mouth. Please give me a call. I've got big news."

She also felt a twinge of worry. He'd told her that he'd be driving up to Agrenomics today, in hope of getting some of the staff to talk with him. "I'll spend a lunch hour with them. What could happen besides a little indigestion from eating at some greasy spoon?" she'd recalled him saying. An uneasy gnawing set itself up in her own stomach as she imagined him asking the wrong questions to the wrong person.

She called his house.

"Oh, it's you, Dr. Sullivan," greeted Martha, her tone disappointed as if she'd been hoping to hear from someone else.

"Is Richard back yet?"

"He phoned me this afternoon, saying not to worry, but that something had come up and he wouldn't be home until very late. I thought it might be him calling now. Shall I have him phone you?"

"Yes, please, as soon as he gets in. Let him know I'll be up all night in the lab."

"Is it something serious?" she asked.

"No, not at all."

The woman's answering silence said she didn't feel reassured. "That man! Telling me not to worry," she grumbled after a few seconds.

"I'm sure he's okay, Martha."

An exasperated sigh came over the line. "Let's both pray he is. And thanks, Dr. Sullivan. I'll say you called."

Now, what the hell have you gotten yourself into, Richard? she fretted after hanging up. Absently looking out her window, she saw the sunset had narrowed to a thin line of fire, its northernmost point piercing a swell of purple and black thunderheads like a flaming lance hurled into their core. White lightning flickered out from around its point of impact as if it had set off a celestial short circuit, and columns of cumulus, their outer billows rendered in silver, gray, and gold hues, resembled bubbles of liquid lead at the mouth of a forge.

If you're still out there, she thought, I hope you've at least found shelter from the storm.

15

He hadn't prepared for rain.

The drops streamed down his face and got in his eyes, making it nearly impossible to see as he knelt in the darkness trying to cut through the fence with wire cutters. The wire proved to be much thicker than he'd thought, and he kept losing his grip on the handles as he strained to make each snip. He also couldn't stop shivering. Despite his exertions, the combined effect of the wind and wet clothing compounded his loss of body heat.

"Shit!" he said, the cutters once more slipping from his grasp. He felt more miserable by the second.

It had seemed such a good idea in the afternoon when he returned to his car determined to find out what lay below that metal cover. He drove over to the railyard as he'd planned, but on the way spotted a general store that catered to farmers. There he bought heavy-duty wire cutters, a crowbar, and a flashlight, the clerk eyeing him suspiciously as he checked the items through. While topping up his gas tank at a nearby service station, he also purchased a disposable camera with a flash. Picking up wet-weather gear had never crossed his mind at the time, not with the sky a magnificent blue spotted by little more than a few puffy, nonthreatening clouds.

Nor had he thought he should be in any hurry to get back to the greenhouses. Nightfall would be best, he figured. He might get away with wandering around the perimeter of the place behaving like a bird-watcher in broad daylight, but snipping his way in required the cover of darkness.

At the railway yard he posed as a train buff with his camera as a prop and struck up a conversation with the yardmen. He even popped a few photos of the rusting diesel switcher as it rumbled to and fro to complete the illusion, and before long turned the conversation to a topic he figured they'd bite at. "So, who uses railcars to ship stuff these days? I hear branch lines are dying out."

A wiry, gray-haired man who wore an engineer's cap shoved well back on a wizened forehead had glared at him from eye sockets as deep as a pair of wrinkled leather pouches. "Are you a reporter?" he demanded.

"No, I'm a doctor. I just like trains."

"It's those reporters that are always predictin' the end of the railroads," he declared sullenly.

Steele commiserated, and added the consolation that at least one new company seemed to have given them business, gesturing with his thumb in the general direction of Agrenomics.

One of the younger men let out a snort of derision. "Not anymore. We hauled our last shipment out of there a week ago. And even then it wasn't much of a contract this time, since we didn't send it very far. Plugged it into a local freight headed for Queens."

"They used to ship more?" Steele prodded.

"Oh, yeah. Once a week pretty well all winter," continued the youth, "and those cars we hooked into transcontinental freights, heading south or southwest. I remember because we always had to fill out waybills labeling them as hazardous products."

"Really? What kind of stuff would an outfit like them ship that would be dangerous?"

"Maybe he's one of them environmentalists," interrupted the old man, glaring at him again. "Don't tell him nuthin'."

"Oh, put a plug in it, Dusty," said the youth, giving Steele a wink. "Or you'll make the doc here think there's something to hide."

The old man scowled at his junior but kept quiet.

The youth leaned toward Steele. "Dusty's been suspicious of outsiders coming around ever since steam gave way to diesel. He figures all change is for the worse, and that people asking questions is the surest way to stir it up."

"So what does Agrenomics ship?" Steele pressed, trying to sound innocently curious.

The young man shrugged. "What farmers always use—products to make their crops yield more—except this time it's that genetically modified stuff that's been in all the papers lately. It don't bother me none. I figure those guys over there know what they're doing, and they're super careful, telling us to classify it in the same category as pesticides as far as handling instructions go, just to be safe. In other words, it's nothing you'd want to take a bath in, but probably no worse than a lot of the other toxic shit we haul."

A half hour later Steele had pulled into the parking lot of the roadside restaurant he saw earlier near Agrenomics. After ordering a beer for himself, the only person he managed to show his scar to and talk about Pizza Face with turned out to be the barman. "I never saw a guy who looked like that," he said, studying the composite drawing that Steele had handed him. "But I don't much see anybody come in from there anymore."

"Really?" said Steele, sounding incredulous and looking around at the neon and Western decor of the place. "But why?" he demanded, as if people who wouldn't hang out in such a fine saloon must be crazy.

"Layoffs!" the barkeep growled, imbuing the word with the rich contempt he obviously felt it deserved. He stood about six foot two, wore a blue denim shirt with cutoff sleeves, and had a motorcycle tattooed over a Confederate flag on one of his considerable biceps. His name tag read TEX; his accent said Brooklyn. "They started handing them out two weeks ago all of a suddenlike with no warning. Everybody's been told it's just a summer schedule, but nobody believes that. One of the women in their finance office says that despite all the hoopla when the place first opened, they never really got the volume of business she'd been led to expect. Hell, why should I be surprised? Half the biotech stocks I own tanked last March and still haven't recovered." If there'd been a spittoon in the place, Steele felt the man would have used it to put a period on the end of this bit of insight.

"Do they still use security guards?" Steele asked. "Maybe one of them can tell me more about the guy who set his dogs on me."

"They mostly work at night, and never come in here anyway. They seem to have kept their jobs a bit longer than the others, at least until last week. I go by the place on my way home at night, and see their vans parked in the lot. Since Friday though, it looks as if even they've been cut back. There's only been one vehicle left in front."

Steele returned to his car, where he used his cellular to call home and warn Martha that he'd be late. Then he drove back to where a country road crossed the rail line leading to Agrenomics and parked. So they're shutting down, he mused, sifting through everything else he'd heard in the course of the afternoon. And I suppose it could be because they're broke. What the rail men said about shipments falling off certainly jibed with the bookkeeper's lament about there being no new business. But the timing of the layoffs intrigued him.

He opened the door, got out, and stretched his legs. All around him blue fingers of dusk extended into the golden swirl of insects lingering over the fields. A pair of birds darted between the streaks of dark and light, the flash of their wings catching his attention and the occasional chirp of their evening song breaking the silence. Folding his arms and leaning back against the car, he watched the creatures dive and swoop for a few seconds, still ruminating about Agrenomics.

The attack on him had occurred seventeen days ago. McKnight had showed up here asking questions a few days later. They'd started issuing the pink slips right on the heels of that visit. Coincidence again? Maybe. "But not bloody likely," he muttered. Because if they were involved, McKnight would have rattled the hell out of them. Because even though I'd survived, they'd have felt secure that nobody, let alone Kathleen Sullivan, could subsequently link Pizza Face with them. Then a homicide detective arrives asking about a security guard with acne scars in connection with an attempt on my life.

His heart quickened. That's why they're clearing everyone out so fast. They don't want anyone around in case the cops come back and somebody lets something slip. He pushed away from the car and started to pace, certain that he'd just seen through Agrenomics's attempt to cover their tracks. Not an admission of guilt, he knew, but behavior suggesting that they had something to hide.

About that moment he noticed the rounded brow of a black cloud begin to peer at him over the horizon. But flushed with a sense that he'd somehow gained a step on whoever wanted him dead and might gain yet another if he found out what lay beneath the greenhouses, he'd refused even to consider putting off his planned sortie on account of a possible storm. Especially one that doesn't look like it will amount to much, he told himself at the time.

The rain continued pelting him as he struggled to sever yet another stubborn link of wire. Goes to show what I know about weather, he thought, blinking fiercely and trying to squeeze yet more runoff from his eyes.

The floodlight nearest him stood more than a hundred feet away, just inside the perimeter, leaving virtually no illumination where he worked. Yet he didn't want to risk using his flashlight, still convinced that simply because he hadn't seen any sign of surveillance didn't mean it wasn't there. He knew that the digital cameras they'd installed at the hospital could work in almost no light; and one of the technicians had showed how their computerized zoom could zero in on a face half a mile away.

Above him the lightning cracked and seared the air, each discharge so close on top of the other that the thunder seemed continuous. His forearms began to quiver with each use of the cutters, his strength sapped by the force it took to cut the steel strands. He started wondering if a bolt from on high might strike the fence and put him out of his misery when the blades suddenly bit through a particularly recalcitrant link. The handles snapped shut, his knuckles rammed together, and he gave a howl of pain that most certainly would have alerted any guards patrolling the main building had it been a clear and silent night. Massaging his fingers as the pain receded, he all at once considered the storm a blessing.

He renewed his attack on the fence, and within twenty minutes had finished snipping out the side and the top of a two-foot square, enough to fold back an opening he could squeeze under. Grabbing his crowbar and flashlight, he crawled through, his body sliding easily over the wet mud. Timing his use of the flashlight to the lightning, he found the metal cover in short order. Taking the crowbar in both hands, he slipped the tip of its curved end under the rectangle's edge and pried upward with all his might.

At first nothing budged. He gave another heave, and slowly it gave. Purchasing better leverage, he managed to slide the heavy slab a few inches off the opening.

No light came from the space below. Immediately he leaned over the dark slit and risked shining a beam from his flashlight into it.

Stairs. Heading perpendicular from the fence. But leading down to what?

Fearing he may already have set off some alarm by breaking the opening's seal, he figured he had very little time. See what I can and get out, he told himself, starting to count seconds in his head.

Wrestling the cover to one side, he gave himself enough room to get in and, again using his torch, descended about a dozen steps. He found himself in a low corridor still leading in a direction that would take him under the greenhouse; then twenty feet farther he came to a larger passageway at a ninety-degree angle to the one he was in. It, too, had no lights, but using his beam, he saw to the right that it ran as far as he could see. To the left he could make out a door where it ended about a hundred and fifty yards away. But not just any door. It looked like a hatch, the kind he'd expect to see on a submarine. And in the upper half he could see what appeared to be a window.

His count reached fifteen. He figured the distance from the main building gave him less than sixty seconds more before the guards arrived. He started to sprint toward the door, determined to at least get a peek at what lay on the other side.

16

"One steamboat, two steamboats, three steamboats . . ."

Resetting the clock in his head, he ticked off the seconds the same way he kept track of time while pumping a heart in ER. Racing at three strides a *steamboat*, he got twenty yards when his left calf muscles shot into spasm and snapped his tendons taut with the force of a rack.

"Shit!" he cried, stumbling forward and feeling as if someone had kicked him from behind. Staying on his feet, he continued to run but with a limp, and when his count reached fifteen, he'd barely covered half the distance. *I won't beat the guards at this rate,* he thought, not if they're already on the way.

As he hobbled along he looked for another passage leading off to the left hoping there might be a quicker way out for him. He saw none. In fact, there were no other exits or corridors leading anywhere. *Strange,* he thought, such a long tunnel with nothing but a solitary door at its end. As if they wanted as much distance as possible between what went on behind it and the main building. His curiosity soared, the count reached twenty-five, and his wet soles squeaked noisily as they slipped on the linoleum.

Overhead he spotted a tiny light glowing red as an ember in the darkness. Directing his flashlight toward it he illuminated a camera pointing straight at him. *Well, if the guards didn't know they had an intruder before, they do now.* He quickened his pace, the rock-hard contraction in his bad leg tightening with every step, and his breathing growing ragged.

Drawing close to the door he focused his erratically weaving beam of light on the handle and caught sight of a number pad. He knew similar locks in the hospital took a four-digit code to open and quickly resigned himself that there'd be no getting in without the combination. He pulled from his pocket the camera he'd bought that afternoon.

There still weren't any sounds of approaching guards in the corridor behind him. Maybe they're coming up to where I cut the fence from the outside, he thought. I'm trapped if they do. What then? A bullet in the head . . . or would they call the police and charge me with breaking and entering? A felony conviction would leave him without a license to practice medicine. If it weren't for Chet, he lamented, he'd rather the bullet.

At forty *steamboats* he reached the door. The thick window appeared to be made of Plexiglas and it distorted his light as he played it around the interior of the room inside. He made out lockers, benches, and a cart stacked with what seemed like surgeons' greens along with boxes of disposable latex gloves. It looked like the changing room of an OR.

He moved his light toward the back and saw windows on either side of another hatchlike door. Again glare made it difficult to see, but through them he spotted workbenches, ventilation hoods, racks of specimen tubes, and even an ovenlike incubator—all identical to the equipment found in any hospital bacteriology or virology lab. But when he shot his beam through the window of the second door and saw a space bristling with nozzles with a third airtight hatch beyond it, he knew this to be nothing like any ordinary hospital facility he'd ever seen.

Swinging the beam farther to the right he gave a start, seeing in the circle of light what resembled a row of human skins hanging limply against the wall. He quickly recognized that they were a dozen silver-gray outfits, each with gloves, boots, and a visored helmet attached in an ensemble. A black corrugated tube trailed out the back of the headgear like a dreadlock and led to a utility belt in the suit's waistband, suggesting a separate air supply. Three other such outfits hung nearby, these crimson and equipped with cylinders on much bulkier belt packs. Dangling from the ceiling overtop of everything were coils of small orange hoses with metal tips, the kind used to put compressed air in tires.

Sweeping his torch back to the foreground he saw an area of shelves stacked with what looked like binders, books, and videos. On an adjacent table rested a VCR and TV.

A door slammed against the wall in the distance. Voices and running footsteps followed. He spun around to see a faraway rectangle filled with light and small shadowy figures. Above them fluorescent lamps flickered to life, and the harsh white illumination marched toward him section by section.

He turned back to the window, raised his camera, and panned, snapping a string of flash photos the instant before darkness disappeared at his end of the corridor.

Then he ran for the exit, directly toward the men who were coming at him. He counted six shapes, but couldn't make out if they were carrying guns. They ordered him to stop, their shouts sounding hollow echoing along the closed space. He pulled his jacket up over the top of his head and kept his face down as he scooted under the camera, the way he'd seen mobsters do when they got nabbed in front of TV reporters. If I do get away, he thought, it had better be without leaving them picture ID.

Peering up through his eyebrows, he estimated the half dozen guards hurtling in his direction were twice the distance from the opening for the stairs as he was. They were also closing the ratio fast. His heart pumping as hard as his thighs, he tried to run faster. What would my cardiologist say if he could see me? he wondered.

The side hallway now looked fifty yards away, the men a hundred and fifty. He couldn't make out their features, but at this distance he'd no trouble hearing the menace in their words.

"Stop, you bastard!"

"Halt now, or we'll shoot!"

"You're a dead man, fuck-face!"

He saw one of them start to pull a gun from a holster.

Shit!

He poured on more speed, ignoring the throbbing in his leg and keeping his eye on the man with the weapon. He can't risk firing a shot and puncturing the sealed door behind me, Steele reasoned, relieved to see him keep the muzzle pointed at the ceiling. But once we're up top, I'll be an open target for sure.

A final spurt halved his distance to the stairs while they still seemed a hundred yards away. Rounding the corner he had barely a fifty-yard lead. He bounded up the stairs and pulled himself out the hatch in seconds. Grabbing his crowbar he sprinted to the opening in the fence and dived through it sliding facedown in the mud. Taking no more than a second to hook the flap into place with one of the cut links, he made for the darkness of the adjacent field.

The storm hadn't abated any, the rain hitting his face like a blast from a cold shower as his feet slithered in the soaked earth. Lightning bathed everything in white so continuously that he knew if he continued upright they'd see him easily. He dropped to all fours where he'd be hidden between the rows of corn and scurried on his hands and knees for what he guessed to be another hundred yards, then risked a glance over his shoulder into the dimly lit compound. His pursuers, their flashlights bobbing in the darkness, ran from greenhouse to greenhouse, still inside the fence. They hadn't found where he'd cut his way through yet.

Heading diagonally toward the railway line, he scampered crablike on his hands and feet traveling a few hundred yards more past a line of trees before he stood erect and ran full out. He found the tracks in a rare interval of darkness, pitching headfirst down a low embankment, landing on his nose, and skidding across the gravel to the ties. Stopping an inch before cracking his head against the rail, he muttered, "Where's the goddamned lightning when I need it?"

Fifteen minutes later he climbed in his car, wheeled it back toward the highway, and roared away from Agrenomics. He'd have to find another route back to New York. No way would he risk driving by their front gate.

"They're using moon suits, Kathleen, and the place has got an airlock with what looks like decontamination showers. I saw a level-four virology facility once during an ER conference at the CDC. It's where they deal with the most hazardous microbes in the world, such as Ebola and Lassa. I swear this could be a smaller version of it." He'd reached her on his cellular while filling up with gas and getting directions for New York. "Somehow I've got to get back in, especially to look at the documents and videos they've got stored there." He didn't add *If I'm not in jail*, but he thought it.

"Wait until you hear my news, Richard," she replied, and proceeded to tell him all about her conversation with Julie Carr.

"My God," said Steele when he'd heard her out.

"I even think the vaccine may be what Taiwan and Oahu had in common and the vectors for it are probably what Pierre Gaston wanted me to look for in the Rodez samples."

"Why would it be in Taiwan?"

"Because exploiting a natural outbreak of bird flu there by unloading a half-assed vaccine on unsuspecting farmers in order to make a quick buck is exactly the way some biotechnical companies would operate. Except in this case they did something particularly harebrained. Criminal, even."

"Knowingly criminal? You mean they knew they were risking a recombinant event from the outset?"

"No, about that they were probably as blindly ignorant as the rest of the world. What they deliberately ignored was that the use of any bird flu vaccine in an active endemic area should have been contraindicated, the same way giving a flu shot to humans who already have the flu is contraindicated because it would make them sicker. Farmers scattering the feed around a flock where some of the birds were already infected would only fuel the outbreak."

"My God! But how can you prove that's what Agriterre did?"

"Once I get the primers I need from Julie, I'll show they made the stuff. It'll be up to Inspector Racine to track down where they marketed it."

"So that's what the attempts to kill you and me have been all about? To cover up a faulty vaccine for chickens?"

"To cover up the fact it killed Tommy Arness, and probably the child who died in Taiwan. Any good lawyer there could at least argue the vaccine certainly made the outbreak worse. That's two counts of negligent homicide and a potential class-action suit for damages from Taiwanese farmers if the story came to light. You don't think trying to escape jail and massive lawsuits would be motive enough for murder?"

He didn't know what to answer. Her logic sounded plausible, sort of. If she were talking about just Biofeed in Hawaii and a few people trying to avoid prison, maybe he could see them killing Hacket and trying to kill her to keep the truth about Tommy Arness's death secret. But the scale and international sweep of what they were up against here—Agriterre in France, the murder of a French geneticist, the killers in Hawaii running around with silencers and speaking a language native to Iran or Afghanistan, and finally the attack on himself in New York—it all seemed such a massive web. Too big to be only about a careless attempt to immunize a bunch of hens. Besides, when companies of this size make mistakes, even lethal ones, they usually hired lawyers, not killers.

"Frankly, Kathleen, a lot doesn't fit," he said, and proceeded to tell her why. When he finished, silence reigned on the line, interrupted by spurts of static as a few flashes lit up the distant sky. Wandering away from his car to find an area where the reception would be better, he felt his wet and muddied clothes stick to him like paste, but at least it had stopped raining. "Kathleen?"

"I'm here. Just thinking over what you said."

"There's something else I can't make sense of. What's Agrenomics's interest in all this? They weren't even in operation until a year after Tommy Arness got infected."

She hesitated a few seconds. "I don't know. Maybe the person or persons responsible for that vaccine came on staff at Agrenomics in the meantime. Possibly they're even doing similar work with bird flu in the lab you saw, intending to market it again, and don't want the real story about how dangerous it is to get out."

"You don't need all the expense of a level-four facility to handle the usual strains of influenza virus, including H5N1. Masks, gloves, gowns, and vented hoods would suffice—basically the same level of precautions I've seen you take against the spread of genetic vectors in your own lab."

"It does sound like overkill," she admitted.

"Whatever they're making at Agrenomics, I think we have to assume they laid out all the money it would take to build what I saw because they actually need a level-four viral facility."

As he waited through another earful of thoughtful silence from her, he started to shiver. Soaked to the skin with nothing to change into he felt cold to the bone.

"So what do you think they're doing?" she asked.

He grimaced to keep his teeth from chattering. "I've no idea. You know the field. What would a geneticist be up to with those kinds of pathogens?"

"Whoa! You're scaring me, Richard."

"What are the possibilities?"

"None that are sane. There's always talk among research geneticists about trying to attenuate one of the really infectious monsters, like the AIDS virus, and using it as an even more aggressive carrier than the ones we have now to transport genes. But even that's not a level-four pathogen. The thought of a commercial outfit like Agrenomics playing with the organisms you mentioned? It gives me the creeps. . . ." She trailed off, her breath ending in the quick uneven gasps of a shudder. "Hell, only a lunatic would even think of that kind of thing."

Wondering if she intended the epithet to include him, he said, "So what do we try now?"

"I think the first thing you should do is come over here to the lab and comfort a lady who you've frightened all to hell."

His own breathing coasted to a full stop.

"I can hear you shivering, Richard. You must be soaked. From here it looked like a hell of a storm up your way."

He said nothing.

"We've got a place to shower, and our hot plate always has a pot brewing. There are no robes, but we've lots of lab greens and white coats you can slip into while we dry your clothes. Then we can discuss strategy. After what you just suggested, we need to do some fast thinking. How about it? But before you come, call Martha and put her out of her misery with a word that you're okay. I talked with her earlier, and she sounded worried sick."

He sensed full well what she offered here. To his own surprise, he found he wanted to accept. As little as a few weeks ago he might have backpedaled and said, "Thanks, Kathleen, but I better get home. I'm tired as hell, and for sure I'll think a lot clearer in the morning." Instead he took a few seconds to work out in his head what to reply, so as to still leave her room to back down, in case she felt as ambiguous as he did. "Are you sure? It's past ten-thirty, and it will take me another hour and a half to get back to New York." No sooner were the words out than his courage failed him, and the prospect of saying yes to the full extent of her invitation so intimidated him that he teetered on the brink of retreat.

As if reading his ambivalence, she added, "I'd like you to come to me, Richard, if you want to."

Again neither of them said a word. But unlike his silence, growing heavy with unsaid doubts and indecision, her quiet remained electric, quivering, and filled with unspoken offerings. Before he could collect his wits enough to say anything, he heard a soft click of the receiver as she hung up.

God, how could I have been so blatantly obvious, she thought, riding the elevator to the ground floor.

Frankly, when he hadn't shown by half past twelve, she'd given up on his coming at all and felt embarrassed for having issued the invitation. When he phoned from his car ten minutes ago to say he'd just pulled up in front of her building, she felt her face grow flushed. "I'll be right down," she managed to squeak, thinking she could pretend her invite had been for nothing more than what she'd said—a coffee, a chance to throw around ideas about Agrenomics, and a change of clothing. "Yeah, sure," she muttered, "take off your wets and step into my shower—I always offer men who get caught in the rain a midnight cleanup. Doesn't mean a thing. How could you possibly get the idea I was suggesting a quickie under the nozzle?"

The minute she saw him through the glass door, she burst out giggling. He was caked with mud from head to toe and appeared completely miserable. My God, he really does need a hosing down, she thought, sliding her access card through the security system and pushing open the door. Reaching to take him by the hand she laughed and said, "Look at you."

Back in her lab she first made him get under the steaming jets of water with his clothes still on. "Hand them out to me when the big dirt's off," she shouted over the sound of the faucet. "There's a launderette a few floors below that the students use. I'll go down and toss them in while you finish giving yourself a scrub. There's towels, a set of lab overalls, and a large white coat on one of the benches for you. Meet you back in my office."

"Yes, ma'am," he said, and reached from behind the curtain, giving her a dripping wad of what he'd been wearing.

She went back out in the hallway and walked over to the elevator entrance, only to find the car they'd rode up in back at the ground floor. Must be somebody else in the building, she thought, taking the stairs instead, the laundry being only three flights away. With ten stories of labs housing the projects of a thousand graduate students, one of them burning the midnight oil hardly seemed unusual.

A few quarters bought her a box of soap; for a few more she got the wash and spin cycle that went with it. Making a mental note of the time she should come back to put everything in the dryer, she returned upstairs. He'd already found the coffee and laid out two cups on her desk, both black. He seemed relaxed, lounging on her couch in bare feet. The lab outfit she'd left him didn't include socks.

"I don't know how you like to doctor it," he said, getting up and offering her the mug nearest him.

"Thanks. Neat's fine," she said, slipping into her usual chair and clasping the steaming drink between both hands. "You look a lot better." All at once feeling playful, she eyed him with a grin and added, "Of course it wasn't hard to improve on the state you were in."

He smiled back at her, but the corners of his eyes remained pinched looking, as if they'd gotten stiff from not being squeezed into laugh lines often enough. Traces of where the skin had once crinkled in merriment seemed to be still there, though, like markings on faded parchment.

She became determined to bring them out. "Maybe the improvement in you is totally thanks to this magnificent wardrobe I provided. The shoeless image especially suits you, Dr. Steele, makes you look casual, more like Robinson Crusoe on a beach instead of the very serious chief of ER you usually go around as."

His smile widened, and his face slid into pleasant warm contours as if it had wanted to be in that shape all along. "Why thank you, ma'am. That's high praise coming from the world-famous Dr. Kathleen Sullivan." Still on his feet, he all at once did a little pirouette, making as if to model what he wore. "I agree the naked-foot style sure beats the naked butt line I demonstrated in ER a few weeks ago."

She abruptly laughed into her coffee, spraying it across her desk. "Oh, please Richard, don't get me started again."

But start they did. She pointed at his rear end, he made a pretense of trying to cover it up, and soon they were doubled over, nearly choking as their sides ached and tears streamed down their faces. She once again felt lifted by their laughter, propelled higher and higher until the howls of glee reached a peak, then released them both, leaving her sated and spent, as though she'd just made love.

He stood bent over her desk supporting himself with his outstretched arms trying to catch his breath. She leaned forward in her chair, looking up at him. Their eyes locked, he slowly lowered his head, and they kissed softly. "Thank you, Kathleen," he murmured.

She reached up and touched his face. "For what?"

"Making me laugh. I used to think I never would."

They kissed again. It started even softer than the first, then went deeper, and longer. Her breath and heart quickened as she strained forward, sliding her hands around to the back of his neck and entwining her fingers in his hair. He gently pulled her to her feet and kissed her more fiercely, the desk still between them. She sidestepped it and walked into his arms, pressing against him. Through the flimsy material of his lab clothing she felt him hard and ready for her.

She melted inside and ground her pelvis into his, matching his growing frenzy while he continued to kiss her, his lips passing to the line of her jaw and along her neck. She heard herself give deep-throated moans and clung even harder to him. "Do you have something?"

"No," he answered, opening her buttons and caressing the tops of her breasts. "Do you?"

"Yes," she whispered, breathless as he slipped her blouse open and found her nipples with his mouth, teasing them with flicks of his tongue and gentle sucks.

She began to undress him, easily disposing of the loose-fitting lab wear, dropping it from his hips and sliding it off his shoulders until he stood naked before her.

He had a lean physique that felt muscular to her touch as she delicately trailed her fingertips down along his stomach and circled his loins with them, savoring the shuddering cry her strokes drew from deep within his throat.

"Shall we open the bed," she suggested, undoing the rest of her blouse, then her skirt, and letting them fall at her feet.

"I'm too old for the floor," he said, slipping his hands beneath her underpants to carress her buttocks and pull her to him. Arching backward, she guided his mouth once more to her nipples where he continued to suck and nibble them, sending waves of electricity into her groin.

That's when the fire alarm went off.

———

The cutting stench of gasoline filled their nostrils and choked their lungs as they raced down the stairs, each carrying a stack of boxes filled with the Rodez specimens to be tested for bird flu. Both were dressed in long lab coats buttoned to the collar, and nothing else. There hadn't been time.

"I smelled it when I went to the vending machine," explained the student who'd pulled the alarm and was descending the steps with them. A few other men and women from the floors below were also heading for the exits laden with boxes.

"Where the hell's it coming from?" puffed Sullivan.

"The elevator shaft," someone shouted from behind her.

Minutes later they were all on the pavement, everyone milling around and looking up at the darkened windows of the just-vacated building. In the distance were the sounds of approaching sirens, while around her she heard snippets of numerous attempts to explain how gasoline could have gotten into the elevator shaft.

None of them were convincing.

The street seemed otherwise deserted. A few vehicles stood parked at the far curb, most dilapidated enough that the owners probably figured any self-respecting car thief wouldn't glance twice at them. Beyond them stretched Washington Square, its flower beds, playgrounds, and lawns bathed in the glare of sodium lamps. Its treed pathways were as empty as the sidewalks around its perimeter.

The rough pavement pressing into her bare feet, the cool night air percolating under her lab coat, and the students' stares all reminded her that she and Steele weren't exactly fully clothed. "Do you think it'll be rainin' on us some more?" she said, figuring the weather would be as good a diversion as any for a group of acne-faced young men who seemed unable to take their eyes off her.

They quickly averted their gaze to the heavens.

"No, ma'am, don't think so."

"Not at all, Dr. Sullivan."

"Lucky for us."

She found herself enjoying the effect her near-naked state had on the youthful trio. "Of course, it could start again soon."

"Absolutely, ma'am."

"I agree, Dr. Sullivan."

"Me, too."

Steele had just slipped her a merry wink, when over his shoulder she spotted a slick black van parked half a block away. It's a coincidence, she told herself.

An orange dot glowed in the darkness behind the windshield.

Someone waiting for someone, is all, she insisted. Nothing to do with us.

By this time Steele had turned to see what had caught her attention. At that second the vehicle's motor started, its lights came on, and it slowly began to advance, coming toward them with the solemnity of a hearse.

"Oh, fuck," she heard him groan.

"This way," she cried, sprinting across the street with her load of samples and heading into the park.

He followed on her heels, yelling, "This way? Are you sure?"

"Yes. To the Doughnut."

"The what?"

"Run!"

The roar of a motor followed by the screech of tires behind them underlined the urgency. Throwing a quick look over her shoulder, she saw the van roll to a halt and six men jump out, all dressed in security guard uniforms.

She kept running.

Steele must have seen them as well. There were no more questions from him, only the sound of his huffing.

The police post stood at the other end of the park, a line in the sand against the night gangs that occupied the basketball courts and roamed the blocks farther west. She figured the officers on duty would already be making their way toward the science building in response to the alarm. She scanned the paths ahead for a sign of them, but saw nothing. "Help, police!" she screamed.

Steele quickly followed her example, braying, "They're trying to kill us!"

The tread of their pursuers scuffed loudly on the gravel and seemed to be gaining. But instead of frightening her, their drawing closer made her think, Maybe we can capture one of the thugs. Off to her left she finally caught sight of two uniformed officers, their guns drawn, running toward them. She pivoted, heading directly at them and yelling her head off.

A volley of curses and the scraping of shoes skidding on the loose stones exploded at her back.

"Shit!"

"Cops!"

"Let's get out of here!"

She and Steele put on a final burst, forging ahead like runners crossing a finish line while the patrolmen surged past them going the other way. Back in the street a half dozen fire trucks roared up in front of the science building with their sirens wailing, blocking the black van. Their attackers scattered every which way, but one of the policemen barked a clipped order into his lapel radio, bringing a quartet of blue-and-white patrol cars screaming up to the four sides of the park. Bullhorns appeared, orders to surrender ripped through the night, and soon the police had all six fugitives facedown, cuffed, and subdued.

Sullivan stood bent over, hands on her knees as she caught her breath, Steele doubled up beside her. Between gasps he asked, "Are you all right?"

She managed to nod.

Only after a young officer walked over and started to chuckle at them did they realize that a few strategic buttons had come undone during the chase.

He pushed his cap to the back of his head, grinned, and said, "So what were you two doing? A science experiment?"

17

Get me Racine," she ordered, still looking into the microscope. "He's expecting my call."

She flipped on the overhead screen and gave her staff a peek at what she saw in the Rodez samples. The H5N1 primers had separated out fragments of the attenuated vaccine like notes on a scale.

Voices of congratulation erupted.

"Well done!"

"Bravo!"

"Wow!"

Azrhan stepped over to the phone and started dialing, looking more sullen than at any time since their run-in six days ago. After Friday's attack, the tension between them had grown unbearable. As much as she'd tried to think differently, her former suspicions about him kept resurfacing. He sensed this, she knew, the hurt and anger in his eyes worse to look at than before. She ended up despising herself, especially since she hadn't a shred of proof against the man, but they remained increasingly on edge with each other.

"Beautiful job, Kathleen," said Steele at her back.

She resisted her urge to lean into him, continuing to feel shy with everyone around. They'd hardly found a moment alone together since the fire alarm had gone off three nights ago. The ongoing police presence in the lab along with the comings and goings of technicians who were working throughout the weekend made short work of their privacy.

Lisa had also moved in, for safety's sake. Sullivan didn't want her alone at their apartment in case more men in guards' uniforms showed up there. "Cool, Mom," said the teenager, inspecting the image of her mother's work and giving her a big hug.

"Thanks, sweetie." Sullivan savored the moment of her daughter's affection, wondering if she should say anything to her yet about Richard. Not that there was much to tell. Over the last few days there'd barely been the opportunity for a few stolen kisses in out-of-the-way corners.

"You're not sorry about what you've started?" she'd asked him during one of those feverish yet brief encounters.

"I'm only sorry we can't finish it," he whispered, trembling as his lips brushed her neck and his hands slipped under her lab clothes to resume their aquaintance with her breasts.

"You will, Richard," she breathed into his ear, feeling herself grow moist for him now. "You will."

"Inspector Racine's on the phone, Dr. Sullivan," said Azrhan, vanquishing her reverie.

When she finished describing the test results and explained what she needed from him, the French detective exhaled noisily into the line. "Do not worry, Dr. Sullivan. Our mutual project will go swiftly and well. In discovering the secret of Pierre Gaston you have provided a motive for his murder, and the freeze on the records at Agriterre will be thawed as soon as I can awaken a judge. Then we'll seize them. Any paper links to Biofeed or Agrenomics I'll forward to the appropriate police departments in your country myself, thereby bypassing the beast of red tape and bureaucracy that is the unfortunate passion of my nation."

"You're sure you can do all that quickly enough? When I warned the detective working on the case here and the one who's in charge in Honolulu that we might have new evidence for them, they both stressed the need to move fast, before documents start to disappear."

"*Mais, certainement,* Madame. You have my word it will be done within forty-eight hours."

She imagined him waving her concerns into the air with a *grand geste* of his hand, leaving a trail of smoke from yet another smoldering Gauloises perched between his fingers. But her foreboding that all their efforts could collapse under a morass of jurisdictional wrangling continued to mount.

Tuesday, June 13, 9:00 A.M.

"You've got to be kidding!"

"Sorry, Dr. Sullivan," said McKnight, looking very sheepish. "But my superiors, bless their pointy little heads, pulled my men and lifted your protection as of this morning. They figure there's no longer any point for anyone to murder you or come after the samples since you've already uncovered their secret."

"I didn't know killers were so rational."

"No, only the accountants who allot the funds for special details. According to them, your chances of violent death are now back down to those of the average New Yorker. That you deal with on your own budget."

"And what do you think?"

"Frankly? This case has more loose ends than my mother-in-law's knitting."

"There's no connection between those men you arrested and Agrenomics?"

"None. These guys weren't among the guards who worked there. At least there's no record of it, and no one admits knowing them."

"What are the chances of them talking?"

"Not good. There's usually two reasons people don't squeal—good hush money and fear. They seem to have plenty of both. They've certainly bought top-dollar legal help, but I also can't remember when I've seen punks so scared. It's as if just getting caught meant a death sentence."

"They won't even admit who hired them?"

"Nope. And when I ask what happened to Pizza Face, they blanch, go all sweaty, and claim not to know him."

"Did they explain why they dumped gasoline into the elevator shaft?"

"They didn't have to. We found a device to set it on fire—a set of crossed wires they'd fed down there and rigged to a timer scavenged from a coffeemaker. They'd plugged the whole thing into a wall socket and set it to start 'perking' at one-thirty A.M. The spark from the short ignites the gas, the oil along the length of the shaft sends it up like a Roman candle, and if the flames don't spread to the floors, the smoke flushes you out. That's what they were waiting for in the van."

He got up to leave. "I reread the reports of your and Steele's statements from Friday night. I know you both claimed to have no idea who's responsible, but the timing of the attack sure suggests someone knew what you had planned for Monday. Off the record, is there anyone with access to that information who you've entertained suspicions about?"

"No," she said, taking a half beat too long in answering and thinking of Azrhan despite her best effort not to do either. "A lot of people could know," she added, "including someone at Julie Carr's lab."

He studied her, his level stare making her squirm. "One other thing," he added. "Agrenomics reported a man broke into their premises, also on Friday night. It came across my desk because the local police knew I have an interest in the place. You wouldn't be able to tell me anything about it, would you?"

"No, not at all. Why would—?"

"Good, because I wouldn't want to arrest some very prominent citizens for breaking and entering."

"But you can't think that I—"

"The only way we can get into Agrenomics legally is if Racine links it to the vaccine. Is that understood?"

"Of course, yet surely—"

"Good! Because a couple of mavericks going in illegally and giving some hotshot attorney the excuse he needs to declare whatever's in there as inadmissible evidence is the last thing we need. Got it?"

But they have a secret lab designed to hold God knows what! she very nearly blurted out. She nevertheless held her tongue. Completely unused to making such tactical retreats into silence, her frustration grew, and her face did a smoldering burn.

Over the next few hours her staff members, including Azrhan, quickly got back to their usual routine, their Rodez work officially over.

But she had trouble concentrating. Every time the phone rang, she kept expecting it might be news from France. Neither could she stop thinking that Pierre Gaston had hinted at there being a second secret to be found at Agriterre. After lunch she got out the slides again, studying them into the late afternoon. Driven by the feeling that she'd missed something, she only managed to go through a fraction of the specimens—and in the end found nothing new.

As six o'clock approached, the prospect of resuming a normal home life with Lisa and sleeping regular hours boosted her spirits. The possibility of meeting Richard for some private time together she found even more enticing. "Why not drop over later tonight," she suggested, calling him before leaving the lab. She'd assumed his eagerness to get together remained as keen as her own. Just thinking about where they had left off made her nipples tingle, leaving her once more warm and wet for him. "I'll open a bottle of champagne, to celebrate getting out of jail."

He paused before answering, a matter of seconds, but long enough to warn her that he felt hesitant.

"I'm sorry, Kathleen, but Chet's playing guitar at a school concert tonight, and I promised him that I'd attend."

"And you must go," she said, hoping his reluctance had only to do with that. "I'll wait up for you, if you'd like."

"What about Lisa?"

"World War Three wouldn't wake her. So do I pop the bubbly?"

More silence.

"Or you and I could just check into a hotel for a few hours, and order room service," she suggested, only half kidding.

His returning laugh sounded strained.

She began to suspect his reticence had to do with more than an unwillingness to bed her while Lisa slept in the next room. "Richard, what's the matter? You'll have me thinking I only appeal to you when there're cops, firemen, and a hundred lab techs running all over the place making it impossible to fool around."

He again chuckled, but not to the extent she'd hoped. "No, believe me, you're as desirable as ever. I'd be there in an instant if it simply involved me. But this is Chet's night. You know I've only just started to get close to him again. In a crazy way, I'm afraid the reason he's starting to trust me is that he believes he and Martha are all I've got. There's no job right now to pull me away from him, and there's no one else around for me to lose that might send me over the edge again. So he's beginning to feel secure. I don't know how he'd take me going off in the middle of the night to meet you if he found out, and I don't want to begin lying to him."

She felt stunned. "That sounds like you've decided there's a problem between us extending beyond tonight."

"I'd be lying to you if I said no."

The quiet between them opened like a chasm.

"So what do you want, Richard?"

"Time. Enough to let him get more used to the idea that I'm not going to let him down again, no matter what."

Her desire turned cold and ran out of her like slime. "And how long will it take you to get over your own fears?"

"Pardon?"

"You heard me."

"But this is about Chet being afraid—"

"No, it's about you running from me. The only thing it has to do with Chet is that you're using him as an excuse."

"That's not fair."

"It's you who isn't being fair, Richard. Yes, Chet has to learn to trust you again, but it won't happen with you trying to wall your life off so there's nobody else to compete with your affection for him. Who the hell in their right mind would want that feeble kind of caring? I know I wouldn't. I'd feel the only reason I had a place in your heart at all is because it's otherwise unoccupied. Chet deserves better than that. You want him to feel secure? Love him enough that he knows he's your biggest priority even with a world of people clamoring for a piece of you. Assuming, of course, you haven't already driven everyone away who might be interested."

He didn't answer, issuing a long sigh instead. At the sound she envisioned him deflating like a stuck balloon and she knew what she'd said had hit home. Yet all at once she felt too hurt, rejected, and above all angry to care whether he realized what he'd done or not.

"I'm a man dragging a lot of baggage," he finally acknowledged, his voice steeped in what sounded a little too close to self-pity for her liking. "You don't need all my crap in your life."

"Damn you, Richard Steele, I certainly don't need you feelin' sorry for yourself. You're scared, pure and simple. There's a cure for that these days. It's called backbone. As to what else I do or don't require, it'll be me and me alone that'll do the decidin', one way or t'other!" She slammed the phone down.

By Wednesday evening Racine hit pay dirt.

"As you suspected, Dr. Sullivan, the files at Agriterre pointed to both Taiwan and Oahu," he told her, his voice triumphant even after traveling a horizontal journey of about three thousand miles. "In 1997, Dr. Francois Dancereau, the CEO, planned to take advantage of a bird flu outbreak in Asia and ordered the production of an oral vaccine against the virus. Pierre Gaston, the late geneticist, obliged. A tidy profit of sixteen million francs resulted, and ultimately the first boat shipment of the altered meal corn headed across the ocean, ordered by the Taiwan branch of Biofeed International, Agriterre's parent company. Six months later, however, Dancereau starts receiving correspondence from Agrifood executives in Taiwan saying that all the local farmers claim the feed is making the bird flu outbreak worse. Dancereau writes back, admitting it's possible, and suggests they pawn off the unused feed as regular corn in some area of the world where there is no problem with bird flu. Within two weeks he'd resold the lot to the Biofeed office in Hawaii."

"Did Dancereau or anyone else ever clue in to the fact that the vaccine could be dangerous to humans? That it had a role in the Taiwanese child getting bird flu?"

"According to their records, no one ever even considered the possibility. The prevailing attitude seemed to be that since they were just dealing with poultry, they didn't have to be careful."

The arrogance took her breath away. "Who is Francois Dancereau, anyway? His name sounds familiar."

"He's one of the virologists responsible for the AIDS-tainted blood scandal in our country during the mid-eighties—the kind of man you Americans call 'a real sweetheart.' He escaped prosecution only by informing on his colleagues. According to some internal memoranda we found, Agriterre put him in charge of its genetic engineering program precisely because they figured his willingness to cut corners would maximize profit."

The stark photo images of an air lock, decontamination showers, and moon suits that Steele had shown her a few days earlier flashed to mind. They remained rife with their own insinuations about what crazy manipulations someone willing to "cut corners" might be attempting closer to home. After hanging up, she shivered, once more trying to keep her imaginings in check but without much success.

As to thoughts of Steele himself and the rift between them, they persisted tenacious as a toothache and just as intrusive on her concentration. Boy, I sure can pick them, can't I, she lamented, furious that once more she'd let a man get hold of her peace of mind.

By Friday, a Detective Billy Ho of the Honolulu police department had the upper echelons of Biofeed, Hawaii, diving for cover.

"Racine's stuff made them the official prime suspect in the Hacket murder and the attempt on you," he told her over the phone, "so we were into their offices like a bad smell. Everybody there claims they don't know who okayed the purchase of the mutated corn, and they sure deny they ever participated in a cover-up. But one thing we found of interest is the bill of sale for a brand-new pickup truck in October 1999. The vehicle's serial number is the same as Hacket's."

He assured her that they wouldn't quit until they got at the truth. But it could take weeks before they finished questioning everybody and even longer to go through all the records.

By Monday the story had made front-page news in both France and the United States.

Vaccin Génétique Mortel screamed the Paris papers.

Lethal Genetic Vaccine Linked To Bird Flu announced the New York journals.

Biofeed: Negligent Homicide? questioned the Honolulu press.

But so far no police in either country had found a single piece of correspondence, trace of e-mail, or record of a telephone call showing a link to Agrenomics.

"I can't touch them," McKnight told her, shaking his head sadly.

Tuesday, June 20, 7:00 A.M.
The Dean's Office

"But we've got to get back in there, Greg," said Steele, gathering up his photos.

"I don't even want to know you've already been. Jesus, Richard, what you've done, that's breaking and entering."

"Christ, for two years now you've been telling me to get up off my ass and become involved in life again. Hell, you're also the one who gave me the I'm-scared-for-my-kids speech. Well now I'm scared for all our kids."

"Your job's hanging by a thread as it is, my friend, and Aimes has gone berserk with all the recent headlines. Because Dr. Sullivan here has seemingly slipped beyond his grasp by vindicating herself to the board, he more than ever wants to make an example out of someone, and for the moment, you're still the lucky guy."

"Why?" interjected Sullivan. "Destroying Dr. Steele's career isn't going to make the vaccine story go away." She spoke his name with a cold formality, and out of the corner of her eye saw him wince. Eat your heart out, bucko, she thought, still hurting from his rejection.

"It's called damage control," said Stanton. "If Richard gets a very public shellacking for 'unfounded speculation,' everyone else will be very careful to limit what they say about the issue, sticking only to proven dangers, namely the vaccine in question, and won't generalize their criticisms beyond the two specific companies involved. That way, Aimes figures, he can confine the damage to Biofeed and Agriterre, thereby protecting all his other clients from getting tarred by the same brush."

"Aimes told you this?" she asked.

"Of course not. But any fool can see that's what he's up to." Stanton pointed directly at Steele. "So don't even think of going after Agrenomics without hard evidence of wrongdoing, Richard, if you have the slightest interest in getting your old job back."

"You don't think these pictures I just showed you are proof that they're doing something dangerous?" Steele challenged, leaning forward in his chair.

Stanton gave a derisive snort. "You can't tell for certain that there's anything illegal going on from these snaps. How do you know they're not just being more careful with genetic vectors than even Dr. Sullivan advocates as necessary?"

Her eyes shot toward the heavens.

Steele groaned.

"Give me a friggin' break, Greg!" she said.

"Kathleen, you've got to understand something. You're off the hook with Aimes for the moment, and your stock is back up at the university, but hey, don't push it. You start saying things without proof again, and Aimes will be back on you with all his considerable financial clout in an instant. Make no mistake, you're still the worst enemy of all the companies he represents, and they'll be gunning for you."

She started back from him. "Does *gunning* include firebombs and hired thugs in black vans?"

"What?" His face skewered into a frown, and he seemed to need a few beats to understand what she meant. "Aimes is an asshole, but you can't seriously think he'd resort to those kinds of tactics. Why that's precisely the kind of careless talk that'll give him the excuse he needs to slap you with a slander charge—"

"Speaking of careless talk, Greg," she interrupted, "did you tell anyone about Julie Carr's finding the vaccine after we spoke on Friday night?"

His cheeks flushed scarlet. "Kathleen! Of course I didn't. How dare you even suggest that I'd be so careless with confidential material—?"

"How dare I? I dare because I don't like nearly being killed or having my lab burnt down."

"Now wait a minute—"

"Can you hear yourself, Greg? All you seem concerned about, now that my name can once more bring in the endowment money it always has, is that I stay a good little girl and keep my 'stock' up."

"Dr. Sullivan! I protest . . ."

"Don't you get it? I couldn't give a leprechaun's ass about how many contributors I lure in. Finding out what the sons of bitches who are after Richard and me are up to is my priority. I don't care who I offend in the process, whether it's Agrenomics, Sydney Aimes, or you!"

"But you've solved that mystery. Those men were trying to keep you from finding out about the vaccine. Let the police track down who's responsible, whether they're at Agrenomics or anywhere else."

She looked at him in amazement. Against the windows behind him a thick mist the color of watery milk lapped at the panes, obscuring even the nearest buildings. The sight of it made her feel slightly nauseated, reminding her of a chalky medicine her mother used to give her as a child.

"Either you are incredibly stupid, Greg Stanton, or you must think I am," she told him. "Is keeping me in line your latest way to make sure the biotech industry doesn't threaten to pull any more of their funding? And in the meantime, the medical school profits from both of us."

Before he could reply, she got to her feet, turned on her heel, and strode out the door.

Christ, I need a coffee, she thought, stepping off the elevator in the foyer. She reached the street and jaywalked toward an espresso outlet opposite the undergraduate building. Down at ground level the mist had thinned to a cool gray emulsion that actually felt soothing to her face. But it did little to temper her anger at Stanton for his trying to get her to back off. The nerve of the man, blatantly playing both sides of the street like that, all because a thug like Aimes can coordinate his clients into using their money as blackmail!

She arrived at the café, ordered a coffee, and took a table where she'd see Steele when he came out. As the cream she added hit the steaming surface of her cup, raising it to the brim and sending white tendrils coiling into the dark fluid, she wondered just how much farther the good dean might go to secure his precious endowments. She stirred the marbled swirl of black and brown, nudging the notion a little further. For instance, if Aimes and his clients were up to a little corporate blackmail, why wouldn't they be willing to engage in a bit of bribery as well. Hell, maybe that's what Stanton's dog and pony show just now was all about. Those sons of bitches might actually have offered to increase their funding as long as he made me behave, and the good dean might have accepted.

No, that's nuts. Surely he wouldn't be that sleazy, she told herself, adding a third spoonful of sugar to what had become café au lait. But still furious at him and unable to stop thinking the worst of his tactics, she wondered if his insistence about regular updates on every single detail of her work had been a way of keeping tabs on her. "Son of a bitch," she muttered, mulling the possibility over while taking sips of the syrupy liquid. Her empty stomach seized on the hot drink with a hungry abandon, sending out growling noises so loud she feared the people at the next table would hear. Within minutes the warm buzz of caffeine and glucose began suffusing her brain, but in-

stead of alleviating her foul mood, all that fuel kicked out a hypothesis darker than anything she'd surmised so far.

What if he's keeping track of my progress not just in a general
way, but to stop me before I get too close to whatever I'm not sup-
posed to find? After all, I'd just told him that I'd be testing for the vaccine vectors, and a few hours later those goons arrived. Her breathing
slowed. Could he have deliberately brought the attackers down on the
lab, or knowingly fed the information to whoever did? Was there an
endowment so large it could have enticed him to go that far?

Try as she might, she couldn't totally dismiss the idea, and in the
fertile ground of her uncertainty, the suspicion took hold. "We're idiots," she muttered, the realization creeping over her that she and
Steele may have just confided their knowledge of the secret pathogen
lab to the wrong man.

Feeling increasingly rattled, she glanced at her watch. Come on,
Richard, what's taking so long? We've got to talk.

And not only about what happened upstairs. Apart from a few
terse exchanges of information, they hadn't spoken together since
their fight a week ago. She'd come today determined to corner him
after the meeting and to clear the air, at least to the point where they
could work together without it being so tense between them. If talking will do any good, she thought. He may be as smart as me intellectually, but when it comes to personal insight, he seems about as
perceptive as a tree stump.

A quarter of an hour later she finally saw Steele exit the building. "What kept you?" she asked, after running across the street to
meet him.

"He was telling me what an asshole I was."

"That took fifteen minutes?"

"It was a let-me-count-the-ways kind of thing."

At least Stanton got that part right, she thought, and started to
suggest Steele join her back at the coffee shop, when her cellular rang.

"Kathleen!" said Steve Patton as soon as she answered. "How'd
your meeting with the dean go?"

"Don't ask."

"That bad? Well, this will perk you up. Drop everything you're doing, and get over to my office."

"What?" She instantly felt wary. He'd been calling her practically every day, offering moral support and listening patiently while she vented her frustration about being unable to find any leads that officially implicated Agrenomics. She'd actually appreciated the shoulder to cry on, but always at the edge of her mind lurked the worry that he might take it in his head to try and get back together with her. His presumptive summons had her backstepping like a drum majorette in reverse. "Look, Steve, I appreciate the offer, but I can't right now—"

"I won't tell you anything over the phone, except to say I've not only found a way to get you into Agrenomics, but you'll have unfettered access to that secret lab as well. Bring Steele along if he's still with you." And he hung up.

18

A retired watchman working weekends at Agrenomics?" said Kathleen. "Isn't that a little convenient, Steve?"

"Convenient?" He gestured skyward with a sweep of his arm that would have brought the house down in Carnegie Hall. "Hell, it's like manna from heaven. He came to us out of the blue, Kathleen, and offered his services. As long as I've been in this business, it never ceases to amaze me how often someone will have a crisis of conscience, step forward, and hand you what's needed. Why, six months ago, who'd have predicted all those scientists would have come up with the worldwide vector studies from their own places of work, all in response to a suggestion you made in an article on the Internet. But they did." As he spoke, Patton strode back and forth in front of a massive set of floor-to-ceiling windows occupying three sides of the room. It offered a panoramic view from south Manhattan of just about every important landmark in New York, starting with the Hudson River and TriBeCa in the foreground.

Steele knew it was as prestigious an address as could be gotten in the city these days. Looking around at the tasteful interiors—mahogany paneling, plush carpets on hardwood floors, and all the magnificent antique furniture—he wondered how many trees had died to furnish the eighteenth-floor offices. He also noticed that without exception, Patton's numerous assistants and secretaries were all female, attractive, and young. For "an over-the-hill environmentalist who never outgrew the sixties," he'd done all right for the Blue Planet Society, as well as himself.

Steele made yet abother observation, this one not without satisfaction. It was how guarded Kathleen seemed toward the man. She certainly didn't share his flamboyant enthusiasm. "I still think it's a little too pat," she said. "How do we know he's not linked up with Pizza Face or those thugs that descended on my lab?"

"You're absolutely right to suspect a trap, given all that's happened. Except we checked this guy out. He got to us through his niece who does volunteer work for one of our chapters. He's a local out of White Plains who got bored in his early retirement and took the weekend job with Agrenomics when they first opened. His niece, of course, was always onto him about the dangers of GMOs, so he started to read. All the recent headlines about the vaccine pushed him to come forward."

"It all could be a front," she said. "He still could be in cahoots with those others."

"There was no evidence of it when our people looked into his background and questioned the man. He was quite forthright about having seen the guy with the acne scars about the place, but said he never had anything to do with him. Remember, he's a watchman, not part of that armed guard group they've got out there during the nighttime. This guy wanders the halls and checks that no one left a tap running or a beaker boiling. He doesn't even carry a gun."

"I still don't like it—"

"What's the plan?" interrupted Steele. "And specifically, how does he intend to get me into the underground lab?"

Patton looked over at him and stopped pacing, a slightly surprised expression on his face as if he'd forgotten Steele was in the room. The light from outside reflected off the surface of his wire-rimmed glasses, making them appear like huge round eyes. Taken with his gray curls, the environmentalist's appearance resembled some kind of tufted owl. "You'll go?" he said.

Steele nodded.

A broad smile broke out where there should have been a beak. "Why, that's excellent, Richard."

Kathleen said nothing.

"Well, 'the plan' is to take advantage of the upcoming Fourth of July weekend," he began, remaining at a standstill in front of his window. "As you both know, Agrenomics, for whatever reasons, has cut back its operations. During the week, there's only a skeleton staff at best, but because the Fourth is a Tuesday this year, and Monday is also a holiday, even those few who are there want to take advantage of the four-day weekend. So when the regular watchmen and guards said they wanted that time off, too, our man 'volunteered' to work extra shifts, supposedly in exchange for them giving him a break next Thanksgiving. As a result, he's managed to make himself sole guardian of the place during the late afternoon and evening of the big day itself, July fourth."

"How do I get in?"

"The same way you did before."

Steele showed his surprise.

"The watchman can't override the cameras at the main entrance," explained Patton. "But he can shut down the ones that cover the back of the property. Apparently it's a low-light digital system with really delicate sensors, and they're constantly having to turn it off during lightning storms or they risk blowing the electronics. Once you're in the corridor, there's no problem. The video cameras along it aren't hooked to any alarms, and he'll provide us with the codes to open the hatch doors for the labs. When you're finished, exit the way you came in. He'll simply record over any tapes that captured your visit. They routinely reuse them anyway, as long as there are no incidents."

"Sounds simple enough."

"There are conditions, Richard. For the protection of the watchman, the Blue Planet Society, and everyone else involved, including yourselves, security must be absolute. You don't tell anyone, not even your family, about what you're doing. We all agree the timing of the attack on Kathleen's lab suggests a leak somewhere, either intentionally or by carelessness. If you get caught, Richard, we already know what their hired help is capable of, and we could all pay the price.

Even if they only played hardball through the legal route this time, it would be handcuffs and court, plus ruined careers, for every one of us. So secrecy is paramount."

"Of course."

"That includes your making up a cover story to account for being away on that day."

"No problem."

"And one final order. Don't, either of you, under any circumstances do anything to put Agrenomics back on the defensive over the next thirteen days. They probably think they've lucked out, since none of the Rodez stuff has touched them, and we want them unguarded, at least until we get into that lab."

"How long will I have inside? It may take some time to go through all those records I saw."

"Maximum, about six hours. You'll go in around five P.M. and must get out by eleven. That's well within his shift. Of course, you may not require anywhere near that long."

Steele, having no more questions, settled back in his chair. The prospect of getting a look at those documents excited him. In fact the whole mission had him energized and feeling the way he did whenever he walked through the doors of ER. That instant of coming on duty never failed to transform him, charging up his sense of purpose, making him a match for the life-and-death struggles he knew he'd wage during the hours ahead. The work then became like a state of grace for him, as, God forgive him, he found in a pit of human suffering the only place where he could know his worth with complete certainty.

But he hadn't savored the heady elixir for over six months. His sense of being useful badly battered, the July fourth rendezvous suited him just fine.

Patton started to beam, obviously delighted with Steele's response. The environmentalist then turned his gaze on Kathleen. "Just think, by the Fourth, we could all know what those sons of bitches are up to. You're not tempted?"

She gave a sigh so rich in high-octane exasperation that Steele flinched, though he wasn't its intended recipient. Wow, he thought, she may think I'm a jerk, but Patton's even more in her bad books. I wonder what his crime was?

"I'll go with Dr. Steele," she replied. "If we find anything, he'll need me to sort out the genetics of it, but next time you want to set up a plan, Steven, if it includes me, I'm the first person you contact before you start, understood?"

"Hey, sorry. It's just you were so busy with the cops and the Rodez tests, yet getting nowhere with Agrenomics, I figured you'd be thrilled if I helped out on that front. If you want, we can call the whole thing off."

Steele jerked forward in his chair, ready to protest, when Kathleen said, "No. Although it's against my better judgment, we might as well go ahead. If your man is playing it straight, it may be the quickest way to wrap this up, one way or the other, and that appeals to me. But I also have conditions. I want no hesitation about your calling in the cops if we holler for help or are as much as a minute overdue in getting out of there, you hear me, Steven? Better us all in cuffs, including you, than Richard and I dead."

The owl got very sincere looking. "Of course, Kathleen. You know your safety goes above anything with me."

Steele just liked the fact that she seemed to be calling him Richard again.

She studied Patton a few seconds, as if looking for flaws in his veneer. "Okay then," she said, seeming satisfied. "If we're finished now, I've got to get back to my lab. We'll have to work out the details at another time."

Patton started to stride again. "Don't you love her, Steele? All business, and yet so beautiful. Plus I knew I could count on her. It's always the sign of a thoroughbred. Show her the race, and she can't resist to run with all her heart."

She visibly stiffened.

Good, thought Steele. Not that he had any hope Patton's missteps with her would improve his own chances any. Apart from her resuming the use of his first name, her manner toward him remained pretty much as cool as ever, mainly infuriatingly polite to the point of indifference. It just helped him to know that he wasn't the only man in the room with an emotional IQ in single digits.

"What a great day for the environmentalists," Patton said, continuing to crow.

A look of distaste began to spread across Kathleen's face.

Keep it up, thought Steele, smiling encouragement to Patton.

"Hey, I just had an idea," the man went on. "If by any chance you do finish early on the Fourth, why don't you join me back here to see the fireworks? I mean, look at the view." He turned his back to them and made another of his grand arm gestures, this time as if he were personally unveiling the most famous cityscape in the world for the first time. "We can discuss what you've learned, plot strategy, and drink Champagne while watching the spectacle. It'll be a great sight from up this high. They're doing a special production for the millennium, you know. Imagine all that red, white, and blue going off, and us able to see it illuminate practically every important landmark in New York!"

Steele had to agree it would be spectacular. Normally he, Chet, Martha, and Luana before she died, watched from the hospital roof. "Sorry," he said, "but if we do get back in time for the show, I'll be joining my family. It's a tradition we keep."

"How about you, Kathleen? I'll invite a bunch of government muckety-mucks to join us. You'll be able to tell them the dirt you've dug up firsthand. The party will go on for a while, so you could come as late as you like."

"I've got family plans, too," echoed Kathleen, and quietly headed for the door.

Steele mumbled his good-byes and followed her out.

III

summer

19

In total darkness they stood at the edge of the long corridor, listening.
The air felt cool and clammy on Steele's face compared to the hot
mugginess they'd left outside, and the absolute lack of sound in the
place pressed in on him like a weight. He reached out in the blackness to reassure himself that the walls were keeping their distance.

"Which way?" whispered Kathleen from slightly behind him.

He took a step forward and snapped on the headlamp that she'd
insisted he use, directing the beam toward the lab. The distant door-
way seemed like a miniature suspended in the pale blue circle of light.
"Why do I feel like a white rabbit?" he heard her mutter.

In minutes they were punching in the four-digit code supplied to
Patton by the watchman. A soft buzz sounded from the interior of
the room. He grabbed the central wheel, rotated it counterclockwise
until the lock released, and pulled. The hatch opened with a sucking
sound.

Steele remembered from his Atlanta tour that they kept the lab at
a negative pressure relative to the outside, to prevent the escape of
contaminated air. They stepped through the opening, pulled the door
shut behind them, and heard a loud click as the locking mechanism
automatically reset itself, sealing them in. Glancing out the window
into the blackness of the corridor they'd just left, he imagined unseen
figures creeping up on them as they worked. We're sitting ducks in
here, he thought with a shudder. Trying to smother his fear, he

turned and, using his light, probed the darkness around him. The room seemed unchanged, until he pointed the beam over to where he'd seen the bookcases bearing stacks of documents.

They were empty.

"Shit!" he said, not any louder than a normal speaking voice, but in that absolute quiet, he might as well have screamed.

Sullivan jumped at the sound and issued a startled shriek.

"All their papers are gone," he added, paying her no attention. Sweeping the light a few feet to the right, he revealed an empty table. "And the videotapes as well. Even the VCR."

"Don't scare me like that."

"Sorry, but without those records, what the hell can we learn here?"

"First of all, let's make it easier to see." Snapping on her own headlamp, she located a row of switches on the wall, flipped them up, and flooded the area with a harsh white glare. Eyeing the air lock and the row of moon suits, she issued an appreciative whistle. "Quite the place."

"We better put these on," said Steele, indicating the surgical gloves and OR outfits on the cart parked by the door.

"Over our clothes?"

" 'Fraid not. The saying in Atlanta was 'scrubs only, and everything else that God didn't give you stays out here, except for socks.' "

Stripping beside her, his nerves on edge about being in the building, Steele also felt flustered by her nakedness. It reminded him of how stupid he'd been and the chance he'd blown with her. Not just for sex—though that figured prominently in his list of missed opportunities. But his seeing her in the flesh made her seem especially vulnerable to whatever lay ahead, yet here she was, gamely gearing up to face it with him. The sight forced him to admit what he otherwise might have denied forever. This magnificent, spirited woman could be his match—friend and soul mate as well as lover. And that's why he'd backed off. He found the thought of anyone ever again mattering that much to him terrifying.

She seemed completely unaware of his emotional tumult, making the change of clothing so quickly and clinically he might as well not even have been in the room. Probably she's already written me off, he thought, pulling on a pair of latex gloves. Closed the chapter and moved on, saying good riddance to an emotional coward.

They finished tucking in their sleeves and cuffs in silence, then walked over to the far windows, where they stood peering into the still-darkened lab on the other side. Under a big control panel of what seemed to be pressure gauges, Steele found a second set of light switches. Snapping them on, he watched as dozens of ceiling panels flickered to life and illuminated an area the size of an airplane hangar.

Kathleen let out another whistle.

"Holy shit!" he said. "I had no idea it was so big!"

In the foreground were the workbenches and isolation hoods he'd managed to see the other evening. Behind them were rows and rows of large cages, most empty, but some contained large animals curled up in them. One raised a sleepy head.

"They're monkeys," said Kathleen.

Occupying the back half of the room were over a dozen huge vats with pipes and wires attached to them. Steele estimated each to be about twelve feet across. "What the hell are those?" he asked. "They look like something from a brewery."

"You're not far wrong, except instead of beer, they're mass-producing genes, or a product from them," she said.

"How's that?"

"Do you know the way they manufacture human insulin?"

Steele felt embarrassed. "Actually, I never thought of it. I just draw it up out of a vial and inject it into patients."

The corners of her eyes wrinkled as she smiled. "I never yet met a doctor who did, so don't feel bad. It's in vats like that."

"How?"

"They first isolate the gene responsible for the production of insulin from human islets of Langerhans cells in the pancreas—" She stopped herself with a laugh.

God, I could get to like that sound, he thought as feelings he'd kept locked up for over two years tentatively crawled out of hiding.

"Sorry," she said, "I obviously don't have to tell you that part. Anyway, they use PCR technology to replicate massive amounts of that gene. In the past they added it all to a soup of *E. coli* bacteria, not the pathogenic strains that make people ill, but pampered lab bugs that couldn't survive sixty seconds in the outside world on their own. These days they use yeast cells to do the work. In either case, the insulin genes are made to infect these organisms, the microbe's own genetic machinery then reads the genes, and their mitochondria start producing human insulin—everything happening, as I said, in exactly those sorts of containers."

"So they could be making massive amounts of DNA, RNA, entire genes, or whatever the genes themselves are meant to produce. In other words, virtually anything. Except I don't think it's insulin."

"You've got it."

"Damn! Without those records, we'll never figure out what they're up to—"

She cut him off with a nudge in the ribs, and pointed to a counter far off to one side in the sealed lab. There he saw stacks of binders, a VCR, and rows of videotapes.

Yes! he thought, suddenly elated. They were going to get somewhere after all.

"But why would they put all that stuff in there?" she said. "That's a contaminated room. They'll never be able to take them out again."

"They must have moved them in for safer keeping. What better way to keep it under wraps? Nobody's likely to casually stroll inside and have a look at it. In any case, I'm going in for a peek." He walked over and lifted down one of the silvery outfits, surprised at how light and flimsy the material felt.

"Whoa! You told me you took a tour at the CDC, not a course in how to work one of those suits, or an air lock."

"But I watched *them* do it. See one, do one, teach one, as we say to the residents. Besides, the watchman gave Patton the codes for all the doors as in here. He obviously meant for us to have access if we needed it. How hard can it be?" He sat down on one of the benches and began to pull on the outfit like a one-piece ski suit.

She wandered over to the three made of red material. "What are these ones for?"

"I don't know. I've never seen the likes of them. They don't seem to be made for any attachments." He finished pulling on the leg part of the outfit and hiking the waist into place. "But I know the principle of these. Not only do they provide a separate breathing system for the wearer through those hoses hanging from the ceiling, but the incoming air keeps the interior of the suit at a positive pressure relative to the lab itself. This assures that any molecular exchange, bugs included, flows out from me into the lab." Slipping his arms in the sleeves and his head in the helmet, he immediately felt claustrophobic, an acrid odor of rubber, plastic, and stale sweat filling his nostrils. Fighting the impulse to gag, with her help he joined a zipper from the right shoulder to his left hip. Then they closed an overlying zip lock to complete the process. Sealed in, his breathing sounding in his ears and fogging the face plate, he felt far too warm. It's like being in a goddamn sandwich bag, he thought.

Turning to the counters behind him, he started pulling out drawers. "Do you see what looks like duct tape anywhere?" he yelled, to make himself heard through the Plexiglas. "Back in Atlanta they reinforced the joins between the gloves and boots with it."

"Duct tape?"

"Well, that's what it looked like. I presume it was some special stuff."

"Richard, this is nuts. God knows what they've been playing with in there, and you're using duct tape?"

"Here it is," he said, pulling out several wide rolls of the gray adhesive. He tore off a strip and wrapped it around one of his ankles. "Want to help me with the wrists?"

"Damn it, Richard, listen to me!"

"Kathleen, I'm not stopping when we're this close."

"But—"

A loud tearing noise cut her short as he peeled off another two-foot strip. Handing it to her, he winked and said, "Hey! And if you did persuade me not to go, don't pretend you wouldn't be heading inside yourself and having a peek at whatever's in those vats as soon as my back's turned."

She glared at him a few seconds, then began to wrap his wrists without comment. But the little crinkles reappeared at the corner of her eyes again, indicating that not only was she on the verge of giving him another of her wonderful smiles, but that he'd nailed her intentions cold.

He reached up and grabbed one of the dangling air hoses by its nozzle. "Do you see an insert for this on the belt somewhere?" His raised voice sounded deafening to his own ears.

"Let me check. Yeah, I think it's here. No, that's for this big tube from the helmet."

He could barely hear her. The suit must have a two-way radio hook up somewhere, he thought. As he felt her probing around his waistband and attempting to connect the various attachments, he glanced around inside his helmet and saw a small black disc on a thin wire at the lower margin of the visor. A microphone?

Behind him he heard a snap; then a hiss as cool air flooded around his head. The relief made him recall something else from his tour in Atlanta. A person couldn't go five minutes in these suits without that air supply before he or she would start feeling pretty uncomfortable from a lack of oxygen and too much carbon dioxide.

Together they managed to get the radio working, finding not only the switch on his head gear to activate it, but locating a sound system console on one of the desks and adjusting it to a frequency that piped his voice over speakers into the room.

"So I guess I'm ready," he said, standing at the air lock. His transmitted voice crackled in stereophonic competition against his own, the effect making him edgy.

"I hope so," she said, her brow creasing and concern filling her deep green eyes. All evidence of her previous smiles vanished.

He punched in the code and stood back as the door unlocked. Turning its wheel and pulling, he once more heard the *whoosh* of air as it rushed by him, this time into the chamber, the sound coming through his earphones like someone doing a Bronx cheer in his ears.

He unhooked his tethering hose, shutting off the cool flow he'd been enjoying inside his suit, and stepped into the air lock. Tugging the heavy hatch closed and securing it, he stood in total silence except for the sound of his own breathing. He found the isolation more final and oppressive in here as he looked about and wondered what he had to do next. Immediately he saw a red locking wheel in the center of the door leading into the lab, but didn't know if he should turn it right away or wait a few minutes in case he was at the mercy of some automated process controlling exits and entrances. His visor started to fog again, and the steel walls of the compact cube blurred, until he began to imagine they were closing in on him. Then he spotted yet another air hose suspended over his head, pulled it down, and reconnected to an air supply. The cool rush around his head and through his suit felt like a plunge into a mountain lake. "Talk to me, Kathleen," he said with a nervous laugh.

"Why, what's the matter? Are you okay?"

"Just need some company. It's spookily quiet in here."

Feeling increasingly trapped and wanting a way out, he grabbed the red wheel with both hands and tried to twist it counterclockwise. The sound of his breathing, already amplified through the speakers, became a prolonged grunt as he strained, but he couldn't budge it.

"Just take it easy, Richard," Kathleen said, her voice soothing even after the transmitter got through mangling it. "The pressure gauges out here seem to be doing their thing. Shouldn't be long now."

As if to prove her right, the wheel suddenly gave and the door unsealed. He pushed it open, disconnected his air hose, and stepped into the lab. No sooner had he swung the hatch shut again than the chamber's overhead shower nozzles sprang to life, giving the interior a good wash. He'd get the same thorough cleaning on his way out—Lysol, according to Atlanta, being the disinfectant of choice.

Looking around the large drab room didn't help his mood any, the walls, floor, and ceiling all a different shade of gray. The dreariness of the place chilled his bones.

He found the nearest air hose and connected it to his belt.

Instantly the cool flow of air resumed, but the rushing sound made him feel even more cut off. He turned back toward the window where Sullivan stood watching anxiously. Her lips were moving, yet he couldn't hear her. He pointed toward his ear and shook his head, indicating they'd lost communication. "Am I coming through?" he said.

She nodded eagerly, and again said something that didn't transmit.

"It must be a frequency problem," he said, finding the lack of her voice made him feel more enclosed and alone than all the sealed doors he'd just come through. He eyed the number pad at the airlock, resisting the impulse to step up and immediately punch in the code to get back out again. Instead he signaled to her with a thumbs-up sign that he felt okay and concentrated on slowing his breathing to normal.

His nerves settled as best as he could manage, he walked over to the benches where the rows of cages were located, disconnecting one hose and snapping into another as he went. His approach produced no response from the animals. Even the one that had raised its head paid him no heed. As he got closer he saw that the containers were completely enclosed in clear plastic, each connected to small pipes and hoses. "I see a couple of dozen primates of various kinds, and just about as many empty cages," he reported to Sullivan. "Every one of the animals seems to have an enclosed environment with its own air supply." He bent down to get a closer look at one of the monkeys. He didn't know anything about the normal simian breathing rate, but he could tell from the way its small chest heaved each time it attempted to take in air that the creature was in severe respiratory distress. When it blinked at him, its eyes dry and sunken, the sight reminded him of the hollow look a child gets from dehydration. He noted the food and water dispensers at the side of the cage seemed untouched.

The animal in the neighboring cage, a small dark-furred creature with a white face, appeared to be in equally bad shape, except from out of its black nostrils and parched lips issued a fine bloody froth. The animals beside it, on the other hand, seemed fine. In the first dozen cages Steele found this pattern to repeat itself—roughly half the creatures gravely ill, the other half apparently normal, the bloody froth at the nose and mouth common to most of the sick ones. Could this be bird flu? he wondered, his throat going dry as his imagination freewheeled in a spiraling rush to judgment. But the doctor in him urged caution. Any number of severe respiratory infections could result in a leaky lung with blood-filled foam flowing from an airway. The phenomenon even had an acronym—ARDS, short for adult respiratory distress syndrome. So slow down, Steele, he admonished himself. This may not be an H5N1 infection at all.

But it sure as hell looked like it.

He leaned in for another peek at an apparently healthy spider monkey when suddenly a spray the color of milk discharged from the nozzle in its cage. Like a mist, it floated down onto the animal's face and body, causing it to rub its eyes, lick its lips, and wipe it into its fur. The substance seemed greasy, matting the hair and leaving the strands shiny. Other than that it didn't appear to bother the creature any. Twenty seconds later came a small click, the vapor vanished, and the monkey continued to groom itself, apparently unconcerned.

Uneasy and more puzzled than ever, Steele moved onto the next group of cages, where he stopped in his tracks. All these animals were near death, but clearly from a different cause. Vomit the color of used coffee grounds spewed from their mouths, and diarrhea dark as tar spilled out their rectums. From their noses and gums streamed frank blood. They lay helpless in their own waste, the cage floors coated black with excrement and streaked in red.

Revulsion played at the pit of his stomach as he recoiled from the sight, while his mind reflexively tried to reason what could possibly be happening to them. The pitch-black of the diarrhea told him that at least some of the hemorrhage involved the stomach, the hydrochloric acid of its gastric juices characteristically turning the iron of hemoglobin black. Fresh blood from the nose and gums, on the other hand, suggested a coagulation problem as well. But these were probably all secondary signs. The profuse vomiting and diarrhea would indicate that the primary site of the illness would be a GI source, but what? He again noted that, not surprisingly, none of these animals had touched their food either, but in this case the feed corn lay scattered about in the mess. One of the poor creatures started to urinate where it lay. The stream arched weakly into the air, its color red, indicating the kidneys or bladder also were hemorrhaging. More diagnostic possibilities raced through his head, some of them among the worst nightmares known to medicine.

He found himself creeping backward, wanting to look away, yet his eyes stayed riveted on the dying animals. He felt as if he were looking into a vacuum where logic and reason had been sucked away, and there descended on him a terrible premonition that he stood in the presence of science turned evil. Because unless Agrenomics had suddenly entered the field of medical research and sought a cure for whatever hideous diseases they'd unleashed in these cages, no sane person would do this. Despite his protective wear, he grew colder, as if in that gray crypt of no sound or color, heat, too, like morality, could not exist.

His head whirling, he set off for the pile of documents and stacks of videotapes, desperately wanting answers, yet dreading what he'd find there. On the way he caught sight of a stainless steel table about three feet long with buckled straps at its four corners. It stood directly under a ventilation hood, had a shallow depression, and in its center he saw a drain with a bucket placed beneath it.

They're doing autopsies on the monkeys, he thought, coming to an abrupt halt. Here might be his best chance to find out what had gone on. Just as the ancients had examined entrails to find great truths, modern medicine still has no better way to provide a definitive diagnosis than by opening up a cadaver and scrutinizing its organs, albeit with modern equipment. The principle should apply equally well to sick monkeys.

He quickly began searching for the usual fruits of the postmortem—containers of pickled hearts, lungs, livers, and the like, along with slices of the tissues mounted and stained on glass slides. But among the racks of specimen bottles, preservatives, and test reagents lining the nearby cupboards he found nothing. Nor did the shelves under the gleaming counters yield anything but baskets of blood tubes, swabs, and culture media. He pulled open a few more drawers, only to find an array of scalpels, tissue spreaders, and bone cutters—the tools of the dissecting trade—arranged like a fan of playing cards and ready for the next case. Okay, he thought, looking around him, after all the slicing and dicing, where did they put the results?

Three counters away stood a row of microscopes. He walked over and impatiently continued to pull out drawers, until he finally spotted part of what he wanted—an assortment of familiar-looking flat containers, the slotted trays used worldwide to store microscope slides.

Someone had labeled the containers MIST TRIALS: RNA VECTOR 2, and subdivided everything as SUBJECT 1, SUBJECT 2, SUBJECT 3, all the way to SUBJECT 200.

"Oh, my God," he said aloud, all at once realizing what might be in the spray he'd witnessed. Then he remembered that Kathleen could hear him. In his frazzled state of mind, he'd forgotten to keep talking to her. "Sorry!" he said, spinning around and looking to the windows. She still stood there watching him, but was already dressed in full protective gear and wrapping tape around her wrists. She obviously intended to join him. "Wait a minute! This place is a house of horrors, and you need to be sealed up tight. Do you need help with your suit or the tape?"

She shook her head.

"You're sure? They're playing with at least two organisms in here, both of them deadly. One may be the bird flu hybrid, and I think they're conveying it with a genetic vector."

Her hands went still, frozen in the act of fixing a length of tape between one of her latex gloves and the suit. Not even the distance between them or the barrier of the window and her Plexiglas visor could keep him from seeing the look of horror that sprang to her eyes.

He watched her for a few seconds, giving her time to digest what he'd said, then added, "You'll be able to tell better when you see for yourself. Are you coming?"

She slowly nodded and moved toward the air lock.

He turned back to the counter, put the first slide of SUBJECT 1 into the nearest microscope, and, switching on the viewing screen, brought the image into focus.

What he saw took his breath away. He instantly recognized the pink lacy fabric of lung tissue without difficulty, there being little difference between man and primates. Except in this case the cells of the air sacs where oxygenation takes place, the alveoli, lay in tatters, awash in red blood corpuscles and ripped open as if exploded from within. More important, the carnage resembled exactly what he'd seen on the slides of Tommy Arness's lung at the conference in Honolulu. He started to quickly run through the other preparations, and saw virtually the same image in more than half the specimens.

"Can you hear me now, Richard?" interrupted Kathleen, her voice through the speaker sounding an inch from his ear and so startling him that he nearly slid off his stool. "I think I dialed in the right channels this time."

He spun around and saw that she was already through the air lock and attaching herself to an air hose.

Five minutes later they stood before the documents they'd come to see in the first place. Steele stole an uneasy glance in her direction, concerned about how pale she'd become since he'd shown her the horrors in the cages. A sheen of perspiration covered her face, and the underlying muscles had grown so taut that her skin looked stretched and bloodless over her cheekbones.

"Where do we start?" she asked, her voice as shaken as she looked.

He spotted a pile of beige folders bearing the label CORN TRIALS: RNA VECTOR 1. "I'll take these," he said, and started to flip through them.

She took a brief glance at a similar pile marked MIST TRIALS: VECTOR 2, but after a few seconds discarded them, saying, "These are more your turf." She started sorting through the videos instead.

He quickly realized that what he had were the clinical records of the monkeys with the hemorrhagic intestinal disorder. Organized exactly like a patient's chart, they held progress notes, vital signs, and laboratory reports. Skimming through each section dossier after dossier, he learned that the disease started with one or two days of vomiting and diarrhea accompanied by a low-grade fever. By days five and six, massive upper and lower GI hemorrhages were prevalent, along with bleeding from the gums and teeth, high fevers, and low blood pressure. Biochemistry results at that stage revealed massive liver failure, coagulation abnormalities, immunosuppression with falling white cells, and the beginning of renal failure. Death invariably occurred by seven to fourteen days, and mortality ran around ninety percent. Each grim fact narrowed down the diagnoses for him, until he arrived at the one organism on earth that could cause such destruction.

Ebola virus.

His throat so dry he didn't think he could speak and his head swamped with more questions than he had answers, he looked over at Kathleen to see that she'd settled on a solitary cassette. The others lay scattered in front of her, sporting computer-generated labels of either CORN TRIALS or MIST TRIALS, but the one she held in her hand looked more used than the rest and had a faded handwritten sticker on it.

When she saw him watching her, she turned the box so he could read it for himself. *Human Trials: Vector 1: Afghanistan.* Without a word, she inserted it into the VCR and pressed PLAY.

20

At first he thought the harsh grainy pictures had been filmed in black-and-white, until he saw the red blood. Otherwise the dark bruises, vomitus, and excrement against naked skin had no color.

The camera panned along a row of cells, peering in at emaciated, unclothed men who were shivering, from cold or fear he couldn't tell. Some retreated from the glare of the light, others sat blinking dumbly at the lens. Others still were doubled over, vomiting blood or crouched in the dirt, diarrhea flowing from them like water, sometimes black, sometimes crimson. In the background were male voices speaking what sounded like some form of Arabic.

"It's Farsi," she said in a tremulous whisper.

The camera zoomed up close, and the narrator pointed out in accented English the clinical features of each man—the chills, the dehydration, the hemorrhages from every orifice. Sometimes he'd bark out a string of guttural orders to the victims until they stood and adopted the position best suited to display a particular aspect of their grotesque condition to the camera. On other occasions he held up a chart documenting the victim's high-spiraling fever. But in every case he'd focus his camera on the patient's food supply, to make a point of identifying it as an uncooked mash made from corn.

Steele clutched the table to steady himself when the next cells came into view. The victims here were children, all in similar condition to the adults. They submissively cowered and whimpered as the camera probed their various clinical features. Some started to cry outright and tremble when ordered to stand and show themselves. When those who were too weak didn't respond, their tormentors released a fury of brutal screams until, wailing and shaking with terror, even these little ones struggled to comply, often unable to do little more than raise their upper bodies on quivering thin arms.

"These are the orphans of those already dead," said the narrator. "Next we look at the effect of the organism on entire families—"

Steele shut off the machine, unable to take any more.

"Mother of God," said Kathleen, starting to cry.

Steele slipped an arm around her shoulders, feeling her sobbing even through the bulky suits. She began to rock, the way children do to comfort themselves, while he had to keep swallowing hard in order not to vomit. "Let's get out of here," he said, bringing himself to the verge of retching just by opening his mouth to speak.

"But I haven't checked what's in those vats—"

"Fuck the vats, Kathleen! They're making genetic weapons here. That's Ebola they gave those poor people. Somehow they've figured a way to transmit it through corn. There's nothing more to know. We leave now, then bring down every cop, state trooper, and FBI agent within a hundred miles on these creeps. Let's move."

"Right," she said, "just give me a second," and made a beeline for the large containers. "You know why it's corn they used?"

Her voice had a strained falsetto to it that jangled like a warning bell. Patients in ER who sounded that way were often about to snap.

"Kathleen, we've got to get out of here—"

"Because it's the whorehouse of genetics. Takes all comers of genes, replicates them, expresses them, and passes them on to its progeny. Ebola, bird flu, it could handle them all."

He caught up with her, took her by the elbow, and steered her back toward the air lock.

"Now, if people boiled the corn," she continued, her pitch rising further still, "that might denature the Ebola, but bake it like a cornmeal—hell genetic vectors are put together at those temperatures—both RNA and DNA would survive just fine. Of course, even more effective would be if it got eaten uncooked, like feed corn."

He found her sudden chattiness to be another bad sign. She also looked paler than before, though he wouldn't have figured that possible. "Right," he said, and sped up the pace. They were halfway to the exit.

"Richard, what's the usual vector for Ebola?"

"Nobody knows." Ten more strides.

"Maybe they wanted the vector to get it, and pass it on to humans that way."

"Could be," said Steele, stepping up to the number plate and entering the code to open the door.

Nothing happened.

"What the hell?" He entered it again.

Still nothing.

The pupils of Kathleen's eyes dilated in alarm. "You're sure you've got the code right?"

"Yes." He tried it a third time.

Nothing again.

"Oh, God!" moaned Kathleen.

Steele stayed silent, but felt himself break out in a sweat from head to toe.

"So what now, Richard?" She sounded very frightened.

"I don't know. See any sign of an override switch or control panel anywhere?"

They scanned the walls, but to no avail.

"There's got to be another way out, some kind of emergency exit, in case of fire, no?" Her voice betrayed desperation more than hope.

"I don't think these people are the kind to worry about building codes. Where's your cellular?"

"In the antechamber, along with everything else God didn't give me, remember?"

He spotted a metal lab stool against one of the counters and started to walk over to it. "Maybe we can smash these windows with something like this, get to your phone, and call for help—"

Her scream interrupted him.

He spun around, and through the windows saw the door of the main entrance already open. Six swarthy men dressed in security uniforms stepped inside, one after the other. Two of them carried guns with silencers. Over the speakers in his helmet came orders the guards uttered to each other in the same tongue he'd heard on the video.

"A goddamn trap!" Kathleen muttered, her words strained through clenched teeth.

The heavy stool already in his hands, Steele immediately hefted it over his shoulder and heaved it at the window. "Help me break the glass before they get in their suits. It might scare them off!"

The projectile hit the clear surface and bounced off as though he'd thrown it against brick. Plexiglas, he remembered, and knew he'd never smash through. The men on the other side, initially startled by the sound, finished changing into OR clothing, then walked over to the moon suits and began to put them on.

Kathleen picked up another stool and climbed up on one of the counters with it, as if she intended to clobber anyone who came near her. Steele thought of another weapon. He ran over to the autopsy table, pulled open one of the drawers filled with dissecting tools, and grabbed some scalpels. Racing back to the area in front of the air lock, he handed some up to Kathleen. "Hold them like this," he said, gripping a pair in his fist so the blades stuck out each end, then did the same in his other hand. "I'll greet them at the door. If I can cut the suit of the first one into the lab, it ought to make the others think twice about coming through."

She gave him a wan smile of encouragement, but looked terrified.

One of the guards noticed what he was doing. The man smirked and walked over to the control panel where all the pressure gauges were. Steele watched him reach up and turn something, then felt his air supply shut down.

"Bastards!" he heard Kathleen mutter.

His mask immediately started to fog over from his breath again, and he saw a similar opaque film appear inside hers. Soon they wouldn't be able to see at all. "Get back to back!" he ordered.

As she jumped down from the counter and moved into position behind him, the same man strode over to the radio console and turned off their speakers.

Alone with the sounds of his breathing again, Steele fought to keep from panicking. Though his visor continued to steam up, he could still make out his and Sullivan's reflection in the window, the two of them weaving and flashing their blades. It made him think of an eight-limbed creature in Chet's video games, one that always brandishes its stingers before an enemy the way a scorpion does its tail. The man who'd rendered them virtually mute, deaf, and nearly blind stood watching, his smirk fading into a look of concern as the steel glinted under the overhead lights.

At least we'll go down fighting, thought Steele.

In minutes he could see only white shapes through a blurry haze. It took so much yelling to communicate that he stayed silent, conserving air, but he felt her back pressed to his as they waited. It already had gotten difficult to breathe, the closed-in heat of his own body suffocating him as much as the lack of oxygen or the mounting carbon dioxide levels.

More seconds ticked by. He began to feel light-headed and knew neither of them would last much longer. He tried listening for any sounds that might signal the suited men were on their way in, but could only hear the maddening noise of his increasingly jagged respirations. When he tried holding his breath in brief intervals, hoping that way he'd pick up some sound of their approach, the absolute silence so overwhelmed him it filled his ears like dirt and made him feel they'd buried him alive.

Another minute passed and his head began to swim. As he sank to his knees, a black figure lunged at him from the right without warning. "They're here!" he screamed, swiping at the form with a sideways swing of his blade. He felt solid contact and instinctively pressed the point of the scalpel in, completing a sweeping crosscut the way a surgeon opens an abdomen with a single stroke. Not even the suits could mask the shrieks of pain that followed.

He lurched to his feet and lashed out at a second attacker on his left. But a savage pull on his air hose from behind and a forward kick to the calves of his legs slammed him backward onto the floor knocking the wind out of him. Immediately someone stomped on his wrists, forcing him to drop his weapons. Before he could even breathe again, they yanked off his helmet and slammed his head against the floor. A starburst of light exploded behind his eyes, but he didn't lose consciousness. He could still see the white points dancing in his head when he felt the muscles in his chest give a reflex heave and fill his lungs with whatever the air in that room contained.

"You bastards," he heard Kathleen scream from nearby and knew that they'd taken her helmet off as well.

Two men dragged him over to the vats where they tied him up with masking tape below a big overhead nozzle that he hadn't noticed before. Seconds later they dumped her beside him, hands and feet also bound despite her valiant writhing and kicking.

"Ya' cowardly creeps," she bellowed. "Gutless is what ya' are! Gutless . . ."

As she raved at them, they ignored her and turned to their wounded comrade. Blood flowed from a diagonal cut across the chest of the man's protective suit. Two of the men attending him struggled to tape it up, their gloves quickly turning red as they worked. The remaining three went over to the dangling hoses and gestured into the antechamber that they wanted the pressure turned back on. A shadowy form on the other side of the window moved to comply.

Watching all this, Steele desperately cast around for a way he and Kathleen might still survive, and only vaguely realized that a seventh person must have joined their attackers. But his thinking disintegrated into little more than a flurry of partial thoughts from which he could barely stitch together anything coherent. Ebola's not airborne, he told himself. Only bird flu is. And the infected monkeys themselves are isolated.

The air lock hissed as the latest arrival, having donned a moon suit, stepped into the lab.

Steele again ignored the newcomer, continuing to concentrate on whether the air he and Kathleen were breathing would necessarily kill them. Only the technicians working with the animals might spread the vectors into the lab itself, he thought. But no one's been here all weekend. So if we're breathing bird flu right now, maybe it's a limited exposure and won't be fatal, especially if we can get our helmets back on. Maybe if I promise these creeps we won't struggle . . .

But before he could beg for their lives, a white spray cascaded down onto their heads from the nozzle above them, covering their faces and hair.

Caught by surprise, he tried to squeeze his eyes shut and clamp his mouth closed in time to keep the mist away from his mucous membranes, but he reacted too late. He could already feel its slipperiness on the inside of his lips, and though it had no taste, the oily texture of the liquid on his tongue made him want to gag. Neither could he detect an odor while breathing through his nose, but could tell that he'd begun to inhale the greasy droplets by the slimy sensation accumulating at the back of his throat whenever he swallowed.

Kathleen had once described what now permeated their eyes, lips, and skin as genetic worms. Yet the bland liquid basically felt no more noxious than if they were deluging him with soapy bathwater. Somehow that innocuousness made its invasion of their bodies seem all the more insidious.

Her screams were suddenly cut off with a sickening thud. His eyes sprang open. "No!" he roared, instantly twisting around and straining toward where she lay. But he found himself looking from behind at the man who'd just smashed her head into the floor. Crouched over her, he lifted it again by its short auburn-gold hair. The way it lolled lifeless under his hand must have convinced him that a second blow would be redundant. He simply let go, and it fell with a soft *klunk*. Then he turned, bringing his face into view.

Steele felt his stomach pitch forward until he thought it would turn inside out. "My God!" he said, barely above a whisper.

The sight before him made no sense. The spray must have scrambled his vision. He shook his head to try and clear away what had to be a hallucination. But when he looked again, his mind still felt as if it had catapulted into a blender. Because from behind the visor, an owl-like stare continued to blink back at him. Then Steve Patton reached over, lifted his head by the hair, and smashed it backward. Steele saw a flash more brilliant than the first, followed by blackness. Like dark blood it spilled through his brain.

21

Azrhan Doumani's pulse quickened as he looked into his microscope. For the last two weeks he'd been thinking like a terrorist. Specifically he'd been trying to imagine how he would advise someone like Saddam Hussein about a way to use bird flu, or H5N1, as a weapon. Not that he intended to. What got him obsessing on the subject was a spate of recent newspaper articles about New York's problem with the West Nile virus, a pathogen originating in Uganda and previously unknown to the United States until last year. At that time it had infected sixty-nine people in the metropolitan region, killing seven of them, and because the pathogen is transmitted from birds to humans by mosquitoes, the outbreak had set off a controversial program of spraying with insecticides. The discovery of an infected chicken in Queens last week had led to calls for a resumption of spraying, but what interested Azrhan were recent reports that the Iraqi dictator himself had once boasted of having developed a strain of West Nile virus that he would unleash on the United States as a weapon. Nobody believed that he'd actually caused this current problem, including Azrhan, but it got him wondering what this type of fanatic might try and do with bird flu.

Azrhan had been coming into the lab after hours to search through the Rodez slides and electrophoretic gels, trying to find if they held some trace of anything that could be Pierre Gaston's second secret, the "something even more deadly" hinted at in the letter to Dr. Sullivan.

This, he'd been doing almost every night since the attack on the laboratory had so poisoned his relationship with his mentor.

For as much as those suspicions hurt, the recent articles about terrorism had forced him to consider the possibility that the hooded men with silencers speaking Farsi suggested a far darker dimension to this business than he or anyone else had ever considered. And after watching her go over segment after segment of the Rodez material to no avail, he figured if he could uncover that second secret when she couldn't, it would be the first step toward regaining her trust. Because her friendship mattered so much to him, he'd pursue any dark avenue, no matter how disquieting, and endure any amount of work.

And at four A.M. he'd found something. A solitary electrophoretic gel on which the parts of an H5N1 bird flu vector had been spread out also contained a small extra smudge of debris at the bottom of the strip that wasn't on the other slides. According to the records the sample came from a blade of grass outside a single vent in the Rodez building.

He'd admitted the possibility existed that such an isolated find of extra genetic material could simply be the result of contamination. But since they'd found the bird flu genes in a similar anomaly, he couldn't possibly not test it.

And because he'd been thinking like a bioterrorist, he knew exactly what primers he'd use to unlock its secret. Because what would have interested a terrorist had to be the infectivity of the hybrid strain. But they wouldn't want to rely on a spontaneous recombinant event to produce it, as had happened in Taiwan and Hawaii with the help of genetic vectors. They'd want to make and use the hybrid itself. For what could be *even deadlier* than a genetic vector carrying an already combined, fully viable hybrid strain of human and bird influenza. Theoretically, it could have the killing power of the Spanish flu epidemic.

Fourteen hours ago, as the sun came up, he'd treated the smudge with primers for both bird flu, H5N1, and human influenza, H2N3. "By the dawn's early light," he sang as he worked before bedding down on a cot to get some sleep.

This evening his hand trembled as he focused his microscope on the resulting electrophoretic gel.

A pattern of horizontal streaks representing both strains greeted his eyes. He had the hybrid.

He grabbed the phone and punched in the number for Sullivan's cellular.

"I'm sorry. The person you have dialed is not available. Please leave a message at the beep."

He immediately tried her private number at home.

"She's not here, Dr. Doumani," said Lisa. "Left early this afternoon to work on something in the lab with Dr. Steele."

"I beg your pardon?"

"That's what she told me."

"But I'm at the lab. She's not here."

"Oh, gee! I'm sorry. Maybe they stepped out?"

"No, Lisa, I've been here all last night and today. This is very urgent. Do you have any idea where else she could be?"

"Did you try her cell phone?"

"She's turned it off."

"Um, well, you say it's really urgent?"

He sensed something in her question, as if she might have a way of reaching her mother after all. "It's a matter of life and death, Lisa, I promise you."

"Oh, gee, I don't know what to suggest. The only other thing my mother said was that she'd try to be back this evening in time for the fireworks, but couldn't promise anything."

It sounds like she's already enjoying another kind of fireworks, he thought, suspecting that he'd blown the woman's alibi for a tryst with Steele. There were rumors flying around the building that the night the attack occurred the two had left the lab in a state of undress. "Lisa, you're sure you can't reach her?"

"I told you, I can't." Her voice had started to waver.

Should I press harder? he was wondering when she added, "Is she in some kind of danger? What's happened to her—?" Her voice cracked before she could finish.

Damn! Now I've frightened her, he thought. I should have known to be more careful. The kid must be a nervous wreck what with two attempts on her mother's life already. "No, Lisa, she's not in danger at all. It's just that I discovered something she's been looking for."

"But you said it was 'life and death.' "

"Sorry. I got carried away. It's just some new genes that I found. I guess you know from your mom how that kind of stuff always is life and death to us geneticists. But still give her the message to phone me right away. She'll want to know."

He hung up, wondering who else he should call about this. Racine in France must be told immediately that a genetic weapon might be at the heart of why Gaston was murdered, not an industrial cover-up as he suspects. The Honolulu police also had to be alerted. His thoughts racing, he decided that the quickest way to deal with it all would be to call McKnight and let him handle it. He fished the detective's card out of his pocket. "Better cops talk to cops," he muttered, dialing the number. "No one's going to believe such a wild tale from an Iranian immigrant anyway."

"The party you have reached is not available right now . . ."

6:57 P.M.

Lisa Sullivan paced nervously by the phone, uncertain about what to do. She'd been trying to reach her mother every five minutes for the last half hour, but repeatedly got only a recording. Why haven't you checked your messages? she fretted, absently chewing her nails as was her longtime habit. When she passed in front of a mirror and caught herself in the act, she whipped her hand down to her side.

She usually loved the intrigue of playing backup to her mom's crazy exploits. Today she felt scared and kept thinking of when they'd said good-bye.

"By eleven P.M., if I haven't called you, phone Detective Mc-Knight and tell him where Dr. Steele and I really are," her mother had instructed on her way out the door that afternoon.

Dr. Steele had looked surprised, and said, "I thought Patton was going to do that."

"The man's become too attached to that lavish lifestyle of his. I don't think he's as ready to go to jail for a good cause as he used to be. We can't rely on someone who might dither about bringing in the police."

Her mother had then turned to her with a final instruction. "If anyone asks for me, I'm at my lab with Dr. Steele. And there's two people in particular, should they phone, with whom I want you to be very wary of what you say. One is Greg Stanton—"

"The dean?"

Even Dr. Steele had looked astonished at that.

"Yes."

"Why?"

"I have my reasons, Lisa. Just be warned."

"And who's the other?"

On hearing Azrhan Doumani's name, Lisa had felt even more appalled. "Surely you can't be serious, Mother."

"I told you, I have my reasons."

So what did his calling now and insisting to know her mother's whereabouts mean? Most of all, could his learning that her mother had seen fit to lie about her destination somehow tip him off that she'd decided to sneak into Agrenomics? She didn't see how, but the possibility worried her, especially after how insistent her mother had been that he not be told. *I've got to tell her what's happened,* she kept saying to herself.

Another pass before the mirror caught her chewing at her fingertips again. Instead of stopping this time, she simply changed her route, striding back and forth where she could continue to nibble and avoid being dogged by her reflection.

"Call, damn it," she muttered. "Get your messages and call me."

She first became aware of the pain flickering in the core of her skull. Then it seared through her scalp, across the back of her eyes, and down her neck. An instant later the muscles in her arms and legs knotted into spasms from having been restrained so long in one position, but in her semi-awake state she could just sense that they hurt, not understand why.

Only when her eyes shot open and she saw Steele lying motionless beside her did she remember everything that had happened. It rushed through her head with brutal clarity, especially the final seconds—trying to protect herself against the mist, feeling someone yank her up by the hair, seeing Steve Patton hovering over her in a confused blur—the sight of him turning her world upside down the instant before he exploded it into a blaze of white.

Disbelief, horror, confusion—her reactions coursed through her in a single convulsion. He'd tried to kill them! Probably already had with the spray. But it couldn't be him. Why would he even be a part of what they'd found here?

Her thinking grew more chaotic by the second, crisscrossing over past events, one instant denying what had happened, the next desperate to find not just answers, but some clue, some giveaway she could pinpoint and say, there, I see now what I missed that should have warned he could do this to me. The alternative, that he'd hidden such evil from her so well there'd been no warnings also raced to the forefront of her thoughts. This possibility she shrank from most of all, for it struck directly at the heart of her ability to know or trust anyone.

But as memories ripped through her head, appalling realizations flew at her like shrapnel.

His pressure for results in Honolulu had sent her back to Hacket's farm for more samples, and into the trap. . . .

All his questions the night she'd learned about the vaccine—he'd been probing her to see how close she'd gotten to figuring out the rest, before he set his goons on her. . . .

His instructions that they lie low and take no action against Agrenomics had effectively sidelined her and Steele for the last two weeks, leaving the place free to pursue what they did here. . . .

His deliberate deceit and the depth of his treachery set her head spinning as everything she ever knew about the man tore itself inside out. She still couldn't fathom his greater purpose, but became so suffused with rage over his monstrous personal betrayal that the anger congealed her mind into a venomous state of cold logic.

Before I die, I'll destroy him for this—she pledged, her entire body quivering—and, God help me, stop whatever he's set in motion. But what is it he's up to? And why has he chosen to kill Steele and me today, the Fourth of July?

Her thinking of the holiday by its formal name invoked the obvious answer. What better occasion to launch a terrorist attack? A surge of nausea welled up in her throat and held her on the verge of vomiting for what seemed like minutes, until her stomach finally yielded the remains of lunch. The release didn't help much, making her feel only slightly better from the neck down, but there was no way to purge the mad chaos in her head.

"Richard?" she managed to say, swallowing hard every few seconds to keep her stomach from starting to heave again. "Richard, are you all right? You've got to wake up. This is the night they're going to deploy the genetic weapons we just saw. I'm sure of it."

He made no reply.

"Richard, listen. Remember all the heightened security prior to New Year's Eve because of the new millennium? The authorities thwarted several bombing attempts back then. I think this bunch is going for a rematch, trying to humiliate the U.S. on the Fourth of July. It's why Patton wants us out of the way now."

Still no answer.

God, how badly hurt is he? Her fear shooting ever skyward, she squirmed near enough to place her head on his chest and satisfied herself that he at least was still breathing. In the process a few links of a chain that they'd padlocked tightly around her waist clanked against the floor. Straining to sit up, she followed it with her eyes and saw where it anchored her to one of the big vats. Steel seemed to be secured in the same way. "Mother of God," she muttered, flopping back, her skin clammy and her heart pounding so hard she thought it would bruise itself against her ribs.

There'd be no breaking free until Lisa called in the cops. But that wouldn't be until past eleven, well after the night's festivities were over. Whatever these creeps had planned, they'd surely take advantage of all the crowds watching the fireworks and release the vectors where they'd do the most damage.

A clock on the wall read 7:10. She shuddered, imagining the hundreds of thousands of spectators who'd already be cramming the length of FDR Drive. Jesus, the attack could start any time now.

How would they carry it out?

For one thing, they'd need sprays for the bird flu. Handheld canisters carried through the throngs could do the job. But it would be a suicide attack unless the people laying down the mist wore protective gear. Helicopters would certainly be better. As for the way they intended to deploy the Ebola, she couldn't imagine.

Again she racked her brains for why Steve Patton would be involved in such madness. Had he gone insane? Or been mad to begin with? Incongruously, making love with him flashed to mind, and she started to retch once more.

Frightened of choking, she managed to pull herself halfway through a sit-up, then looked about her, attempting to spot anything she might use to help them get free of the chains. Some of the greasy fluid from the mist had congealed into droplets on the tips of her lashes, framing everything she saw with tiny prisms of light. A memory of being with Lisa in a snowstorm, the flakes falling on their eyes and delighting them both with the same glistening effect cut through her like a knife.

How long will I have to prepare her for my death? she wondered. A day? Hours? Fighting back tears, she saw nothing nearby, not even a sharp edge against which she could sever the tape tying her wrists and ankles. The rest of the immense laboratory appeared deserted and was absolutely quiet except for the steady soft noise of Steele's rising and falling respirations, when from behind her she heard, "Surprised, aren't you, Kathleen?"

She screamed, jerked her head up and saw Patton ten feet away, leaning against a counter with his arms crossed. He still had on his moon suit and his voice had come through the speakers inside the helmet now hanging off her shoulders. He also seemed to have no face, the reflection from his visor hiding the lower half of his features while his round glasses, catching the light as they had in his office two weeks ago, made it impossible to see his eyes. She shrank away from him, as much as her chains would allow.

Chet stood on the front steps of his house watching the crowds stream toward the river. "Let's go, Martha," he called back over his shoulder.

"Patience, patience, my boy," said the housekeeper, picking up their picnic basket and taking an umbrella out of the front closet, just in case. Even though the forecasters hadn't predicted rain, it had been a steamy, cloud-covered day, and her rheumatism was acting up. "That roof isn't going anywhere."

"Yeah, but I want to get a good seat near the edge."

She stepped out onto the front stoop to join him, pulling the front door shut behind her. "We won't be going too close to any edge."

Chet grinned at her. They had the same conversation every year, even when his mother was alive, and he usually won out, on condition he let his father keep a restraining arm around him.

Martha worried that the man wouldn't make it back before the show started. He hadn't sounded too hopeful about it when he left this afternoon. Not that she believed for one minute that nonsense he told her and Chet about having to work well into the night at Dr. Sullivan's lab. "Today of all days," she muttered, convinced the two had decided to check into a hotel somewhere. She would have approved heartily at any other time, but after seeing the disappointment in Chet's eyes, she took Steele aside and said, "Just when you're getting somewhere with the boy, you let him down like that."

He'd simply grimaced and said, "It can't be helped."

Chet stepped into the flow of people, and she followed. The sultry air seemed electric, humming with the voices, laughter, and footsteps of not just the hundreds marching down their street, but the hundreds of thousands making their way through blocks and blocks of streets to the north and south of them. Over the city hung an ocher haze, and no breeze stirred the many Stars and Stripes draped from balconies or mounted on rooftops for the occasion.

She kept an eye on him as he pushed ahead of her, his tousled dark hair easy to pick out in the crowd. He's much taller this year, she thought, treading after him. The observation brought on a whiff of melancholy—a sense of years passing her by, of Chet growing up, of how little time there remained in his boyhood for Steele to bind the wounds that still existed between father and son. She tried to shrug it off, focusing instead on the gaiety around her—the hot dog vendors, the balloons, the people dressed as clowns. Shortly she caught up to where he'd paused to watch a juggler on stilts dressed as Uncle Sam. The delight in her young charge's eyes made her relax.

Ten minutes later they'd reached the hospital and were riding the elevator to the roof. Some of the other celebrants in the car, mostly doctors, nurses, and orderlies, recognized them.

"Hi, Chet."

"Boy, have you grown."

"What are you feeding him, Martha?"

As soon as the doors opened, he raced to the corner that was their usual spot and leaned over the waist-high wall, giving Martha the creeps.

She came up behind him, and, with her hand firmly planted on his shoulder, they surveyed the familiar view together.

Half a dozen barges were moored along the middle of the East River, each bristling with thousands of tubes from which tens of thousands of fireworks would be launched. Below them the FDR already seemed packed to capacity for a mile in either direction, but people continued to swarm up the access ramps. The quay along the river's edge also seethed with people, their brightly decorated short sleeves, T-shirts, and in some cases bathing suits turning them into a swaying mosaic of colors while calypso music from overhead speakers orchestrated the sinewy movements with a chorus of "Hot! Hot! Hot!"

Chet turned his head and said something to her, but she didn't catch what it was. The roaring chatter of a huge helicopter passing overhead drowned out his voice.

"Why, Steve?" she asked.

For a few seconds he said nothing, filling the room with a quiet so icy and stifling that she physically felt encased in it. Then he sighed, long and hard, signaling the full extent of his exasperation with her. "To think I lay awake at night, worrying that you'd land a motive for this whole business on my doorstep. Yet here you see everything all laid out"—he abruptly swept his arm in an arch that included half the laboratory, the sudden movement making her jump—"and you still don't get what I intend to do, or why?" Shaking his head, he turned to a large cardboard box behind him, lifted out a sheaf of papers, and started to sort them on the counter.

His indifference cowed her no less than a raised fist. It also sparked defiance. "Oh, I *get* what you've done easily enough. It's called betrayal—of me, the Blue Planet Society, and judging from the goons running around whom you've recruited from places not exactly friendly to Americans, your country. Everything you ever professed to care for, and I want to know why!"

He spun about and covered the distance between them in three strides. Leaning over he grabbed the front of her moon suit and pulled her head to within an inch of his visor. "I've betrayed what I cared for?" His voice came through her speakers taut as a piano wire and so high-pitched it squeaked as if he was writing his words with fingernails on a blackboard. "Oh, no, Kathleen. This is my finest hour, my crowning achievement. Had I not acted as I have—*that* would have betrayed my life's work. No way could I let all our warnings continue to fall on deaf ears while companies like Biofeed went on adding mutated DNA to the food chain of men, women, and children—"

"Spare me the speech Steve, I know the spiel! Been singin' it myself for years, remember?"

He froze, still holding her in his fists.

Up this close she could easily make out his eyes behind the glasses. They loomed over her wide with astonishment, as if the sight of her in his grip had suddenly surprised him. Slowly he laid her back on the floor, and she watched his pupils wane from glossy to a dull black, his lids settling around them like leathery buttonholes. He stood up, walked stiffly to the counter, and leaned forward, placing his palms on its surface. "And nobody pays attention to you, Kathleen," he said, his voice barely above a whisper, "even to someone so eloquent as your-self. You're quoted far and wide, but what good's it done? My favorite line you penned over a decade ago: 'The power of manipulating DNA is equal to the power of splitting the atom in terms of potential impact on human life. Dr. Kathleen Sullivan, Rio de Janeiro Earth Summit, 1992'—and still, today, no one listens. Instead we have more morons than ever rushing to defend their unfettered right to genetically modify food in the name of free trade and big bucks. So it's time for a lesson they can't ignore."

Hunched over with his head down, he radiated so much tension that despite his bulky outfit she sensed his muscles strung to the springing point, the way one animal can feel another is about to pounce. Except in his case she felt a man whose rage both held him together and threatened to blow him apart.

He also appears to want me to appreciate his genius, she thought, coldly seeing an opportunity to make him talk. If I can keep him de-fending what he's done, he might just let slip a valuable detail or two, like where he'll be hiding after tonight so I can send the cops over to nail his sorry ass. Or better still, I could learn something that would let us blunt the impact of the attacks. She glanced uneasily over to the monkey cages. "What sort of lesson do you have in mind?" she asked, trying to sound as submissive as possible.

His posture shifted slightly, as if he had relaxed.

A control freak always does, she thought, once he's back in charge.

But he said nothing, simply glanced at the wall clock and quickly resumed sorting whatever papers he had.

Maybe it's better I provoke him again, push him into another outburst. "I mean, excuse me, but did I miss something here? You're actually talking about killing people with genetic weapons in order to teach them the dangers of genetically modified food. I mean, give me a break! That sounds like the 'I burnt the village to save it' crap we used to hear out of Vietnam."

"Some will die, I admit," he said, waving his hand in the air as if trying to brush away a pesky fly. "But no one will ever be lax about the food chain again. It'll be like immunizing the country against its indifference, and we'll save millions of lives—"

"And how many millions of dollars will you get for helping that gang of terrorists?"

He answered without interrupting his work. "Using them for their infinite cash and special resources was a necessary trade-off. They get their terror, but I assure it demonstrates to America the errors of its ways." He took another quick glance at the clock. "That's why I'm making certain that when they find this lab, everyone will have everything they need to figure out what happened—records, specimens, even the bodies of you and Steele to do autopsies on."

She flinched, not just at what he had in store for them, but also at the indifference in his voice. She'd heard lab technicians refer to their rats with more feeling. "And while we're being dissected, I suppose you'll be safely off somewhere, hiding with your millions." She continued to steer the conversation exactly where she wanted it to go.

"Quite the contrary. That's why you have to die, so no one will ever suspect my role in engineering what is about to unfold. Because I plan to hang around, you see, decrying the tragedy, making sure everyone gets it, and playing the vindicated environmentalist. I'll have instant credibility, a new wealth of endorsements, and power up the wazoo, not to mention the world hanging on my every pronouncement."

And in about four hours I'll see you hauled off to a jail cell, asshole, she wanted to scream, where you can make pronouncements from here to kingdom come for all I care. Instead she said, "Oh, really?"

At her side, Steele began to moan and loll his head back and forth.

"Hell, I plan to do even more than that, Kathleen," replied Patton. "Setting up the Sullivan Memorial Fund in your memory will be a big priority and bring in a ton of cash, purely for good environmental causes, of course. And I'll further shape public opinion against the likes of Biofeed International, suggesting that accidents with their genetic vectors, such as the ones that caused the bird flu cases in Taiwan and Oahu, may have been what inspired these terrorists to replicate the process as a genetic weapon." He made another of his grand gestures, this time toward the animal cages used for the mist trials. "That's exactly how I got the idea of using a hybrid strain of influenza, by the way. When it occurred in nature through the help of a vector, I figured our own version would create mayhem. In any case, by the time I'm finished filling people's heads with these kinds of associations, the industry will be finished. You can at least take that satisfaction to your grave."

"What's the point of the Ebola?" she asked, going for the gold.

Silence again. But not like before. He was listening for something.

All at once she heard it. The thudding from the rotors of a large helicopter came through the walls and grew louder by the second.

"My ride's here," he said, and walked toward the air chamber. "You'll have to excuse me. I'm hosting a fireworks party in an hour and a half, in case I need an alibi. Who better to be with than the movers and shakers of New York?" Then he laughed, the speakers turning it into a tinny sound as if it came from a metallic mouth. "Too bad I don't have time to explain more, Kathleen. You'd have loved hearing about the genetics used in the Ebola." He stepped into the chamber, reached to pull the door closed, then paused, his hand still in midair. "Oh, I nearly forgot to tell you something. It always amused me how you used to employ Lisa as backup to your more risqué field trips. Just in case you violated my orders and told her what you were up to today, those 'goons' as you put it will be visiting her soon, to make sure she doesn't call the police, ever."

22

Morgan watched the garbage stir beneath the rotors of the helicopter as Butkis gently took the craft up. They rose a hundred feet
above the littered field, scattering dust and sending newspapers wafting
through the air like urban tumbleweed. Over them hovered a second
craft, its tanks already loaded. Below sprawled an industrial park with
acres of factories three and four stories high, all interwoven with rusted
rail lines and more weed-infested lots. It being the holiday, not a soul
was around, but Butkis stayed high enough to avoid attention.

As they drifted sideways, a third craft swiftly descended, landing
beside the parked railcar, and the pilot got out to connect up the
hoses. Morgan tried to show no reaction when he saw some of the
milky liquid pour out the end of the nozzle and spill onto the ground
during the procedure.

Morgan had never seen a man facing execution, but he imagined
it felt as he did now. Events seemed to propel him forward at obscene
speed, and being strapped into the seat left him claustrophobic. He'd
set his escape route, wired the money they'd deposited in his offshore
accounts to other offshore accounts, and packed his bags ready to
leave tonight. But he felt certain the attack looming within the hour
would start the countdown to his own destruction as surely as the
spray would for all those it touched. Because not only might their
client take it in his head to wipe out all witnesses, the way Patton had

been eyeing him lately, making comments about "lost nerve," and worrying about remaining anonymous, Morgan had begun to watch out for himself as well.

Some moments his fear of dying smothered him. At others, it seemed almost irrelevant whether either of them got him or not. Waiting for the bullet, however long it took, would make him a dead man walking for the rest of his life anyway.

The third helicopter finished taking on its load and rose off the ground. All three craft then ascended to a thousand feet. From up here, through the powdery gray dusk, Morgan saw the line of barges midriver and a mass of colored dots lining the FDR along the Manhattan side. Other helicopters were in the air, most ablaze with media markings—the no-fly zone didn't go into effect for another few minutes.

Butkis leaned his control stick forward, the craft tilted, and they slowly started toward the heliport, the other two pilots following, like glittering dragonflies in a chain.

Steele's skull hurt. And the room spun mercilessly every time he turned his head. He found it an improvement from when he'd first opened his eyes. The slightest movement then had made him throw up. Now he could manage the nausea, though it never completely abated, and he'd run out of spit from swallowing so hard.

"There, Kathleen!" he said, freeing her upper limbs. Twenty minutes earlier he'd managed to maneuver himself so that his hands were aligned with her wrists. It took him that long to remove the tape. But once her hands were released she quickly went to work on his.

Glancing at the wall clock, she said, "Oh, God."

He knew what she was thinking. It read eight-thirty, and Patton's goons could have already reached Lisa.

As they both struggled to undo their legs, he couldn't think of anything to say that would reassure her, nor could he get his own mind off Martha and Chet. They're already at their usual spots on the hospital roof, he thought.

Then came their chains. Several loops of them wound around their waists and the other ends were similarly attached to the heavy steel legs of the nearest vat. The locks holding them seemed indestructible, but the links themselves weren't heavy grade—Steele figured they'd been used to secure the monkeys—but neither he nor Sullivan could break them with their hands.

Steele took a running lunge against the restraint, hoping the full weight of his body would budge something, only to be yanked backward as if he'd been tackled. Kathleen did the same, the result being identical. After a few more tries they both gave up, realizing they'd snap their own ribs before anything else gave.

But they quickly discovered that their tethers allowed them to walk about ten feet in either direction. "We can try and pry one of the links apart where it's attached to the vat leg," said Steele, starting to prowl around and opening one drawer after the other, "if I can only find the equivalent of a crowbar."

Kathleen strained at the end of her leash to see the papers that Patton had been so preoccupied with. "Look at this. He's laid out bills of lading for where they shipped the corn seed. And here are some for the tank cars."

Steele came to her side, and the two of them leaned out like mastheads in order to see. "Why would he want everybody to know where the stuff went? To increase the terror?"

"It'll sure do that in these areas—there's a dozen states involved. But when he was talking to me he kept going on about how he wanted everyone 'to get it right.' I guess this is his way of making sure the public learns exactly what happened. 'A lesson they can't ignore,' as he put it." Stretching out her arm, she managed to retrieve a thick sheaf of papers that looked different from the others and began leafing through it.

Steele resumed his hunt for a crowbar.

"Mother of God!" she said. "This one explains their whole Ebola program."

"What?"

"Including where they sprayed corn with an Ebola vector. Dates, the lot numbers, and which farms—all owned by Biofeed."

"But why—?"

"Listen to this," she said, and proceeded to read aloud. " 'The vector carrying Ebola is in both regular and feed corn varieties that are already growing at various farms throughout the south. Some of the seed for those crops we grew upstairs, implanting the Ebola vector in young sprouts. Random testing of the resulting kernels showed Ebola genes on board, and when we germinated them, the entire vector carried forward into the next generation.' "

"My God," said Steele.

She flipped to another page. "And here's more. 'We harvested enough seed to ship several railcar loads to the Oklahoma-Texas border for spring planting. The progeny of that batch is already back in the ground, producing a hundred times the original crop, the Ebola still along for the ride. As for the rest, we inserted the vectors using a spray technique on young corn plants already in the field. Theoretically this method should work as well, but we didn't risk getting samples and testing them. So we won't know until an actual case of Ebola occurs in an area where the progeny of these crops are planted if we were successful.' "

"Could that work?" Steele interrupted.

She silently skimmed the next few sheets before answering. "According to how they described what was done, I'm afraid so—Jesus Christ, wait until you hear this." She pulled out a single sheet and read, " 'We've incorporated genetic timers into the vector that will turn it on only after the virus's natural host ingests it. The Ebola virus will then be brought back to life, so to speak, made to replicate and function.' " She looked up at him. "Do you understand genetic triggers— how some genes will turn other genes on and off only in the presence of a specific enzyme?"

"Go on," he said, having a pretty good idea what she meant.

She turned back to the paper. " 'The virus survives, not harming the organism that carries it, yet ready to infect any human who comes in contact with it via the host.' "

"They've identified the carrier?"

She scanned the rest of the page. "Yes, but they don't say what it is. It claims here that 'only a handful of their scientists working in Afghanistan knew the secret, and most of them were killed during a U.S. bombing raid on their lab in late 1998.' " She broke off from her reading. "Hey, I remember that. It was in all the papers. The CIA claimed they found something suspicious in a soil sample that made them think the place was making biological weapons."

Steele recalled reading about the controversy as well. The Afghanistan government had claimed the building housed a company involved in the manufacture of agricultural products.

Kathleen continued to read. "Those scientists, it says, were convinced an equivalent to that host lives in North America." She turned to him. "Isn't that a bit of a stretch?"

Steele sighed. "I'm afraid not. In the last twelve months an arenavirus similar to Lassa fever has killed two people in southern California. Its only host used to be a rat found exclusively in Africa. Obviously the bug has latched on to an American rodent that suits it just fine. And until last year, West Nile virus maintained itself by transmission between birds and mosquitoes unique to Uganda plus a few other surrounding countries. But it's now doing very well amongst the birds and mosquitoes of Central Park, Queens, and probably most of New York state. So why shouldn't Ebola find an equivalent host in the good old U.S.A.? Probably the only reason it hasn't so far is that none of its victims live long enough to bring it here."

Her face, already strained and resembling a fragile porcelain mask, went whiter still. "You can't be serious."

He tried to soften the blow. "There may be an upside. Transmission from the host to humans, in Africa at least, is a relatively infrequent event, occurring once or twice every few years. Most of the deaths occur from subsequent human to human spread. So even if these creeps have done what he claims and the virus does find a U.S. host, the outbreaks themselves might be limited." He didn't add that the geographical isolation of victims in Africa had always been key to containing the disease. Rural America would provide a much more populated breeding ground. And the thought of cases breaking out in an urban center staggered his imagination.

She fell silent and grimly flipped through the rest of the papers. When she reached the last sheet, she seemed to stop breathing.

"What's the matter?" said Steele.

She handed him what she'd seen.

Taking it, he read,

The vectors are also designed to turn on if any primate, man included, ingests the corn. When it's in the form of ground meal used for baked goods, the Ebola RNA survives the temperatures of baking. When it's eaten whole from the cob, even after boiling, the fleshy coat of the kernels provides sufficient protection to the added gene. As a result, a significant number still reach the gut intact, which is where they encounter the "trigger" enzymes that activate them. In other words, we believe we have devised a pathway for Ebola to reach humans directly, bypassing the host, and therefore increasing the rate of infection.

Steele swallowed a few times, unable to speak.

"You know another reason he's spelled out what he's done in such detail?" she said, her voice tremulous. She stared off into space.

He shook his head.

"It will force authorities to attempt a recall and it'll be a logistical nightmare. Just tracking down all the farmers who used the seed and knowing which fields it's in will be hard enough. To know if it's spread to adjacent crops or where accidental spillage has grown will prove impossible." She paused, tears welling in her eyes and emitted a half-stifled sob. "In other words, it's his in-your-face demonstration that genetic mistakes can't be undone, and the Ebola will be out there forever." She grabbed the paper from his hand and threw it back on the counter. "Excuse me, but I can't deal with this right now. All I can think about is Lisa, and that I've got to get out of here in time to warn . . ." Her voice trailed off as she started to cry. "Those sons of bitches will kill her!"

"Don't think that!" he said, moving to put his arms around her. He could barely keep his own panic about Chet and Martha in check, yet knew that the only chance he and Sullivan had of escaping and saving anybody, however remote, depended on their not going to pieces.

She pushed him off and started to whip open a row of cupboards that he'd already gone through. Her features crumpled in on themselves and her eyes were pleading as she said, "Just get me out of here!"

Her agony made him feel helpless, and he moved to the next counter trying not to think the worst—that they'd never break free in time. But as his search proved futile he started to consider how he could best hide a message to reveal that Steve Patton had done this to them. Maybe I could swallow it, he reasoned, so it'll be found in my stomach on autopsy. But would the writing hold up to gastric acids?

Their work was interrupted by a faint thudding coming through the walls again.

"Christ, they're back," she said, glancing at the wall clock.

It read a quarter to nine.

Despite knowing he was out of time, Steele continued to rummage for something, anything, that would break the chains. "If we can get free, then hide, we can ambush whoever comes looking for us," he said to Kathleen, "and force them to give us the proper exit code."

She eyed a stool that was a good ten feet out of their reach. "We could use the leg of that," she said, pulling her arms out of her moon suit and freeing the upper half of her body. Then she slipped her top off, pulling it over her head. "Come on Richard, you, too. Give me your clothes."

In less than a minute, stark naked except for their socks, they'd strung the two moon suits and OR clothing into a nine-foot lasso, the legs of the scrubs tied into a loop.

Steele threw the first cast.

It flopped to the side of the target.

"Let me try," said Kathleen.

Her attempt lobbed onto the stool, but slid off without catching.

She made a second try.

Same result.

Steele kept watch on the warning light over the outer exit.

A third throw managed to catch the lip of the round seat. She pulled slowly, tipping the stool in their direction. They both held their breath, and she pulled a little more.

The loop slipped off, the stool teetered away from them and crashed to the floor.

Steele saw the warning light over the outer door start to flash.

"Duck!" he said, dropping behind the counter.

Kathleen crouched down beside him.

They waited.

"Maybe we can still jump them," Steele whispered.

They began to hear voices transmitted from the outer chamber through the speaker system.

"Any sign of them?" said a man.

"Not that I can see," said another.

"Then where the hell are they?" cried a young woman.

"What the hell?" said Kathleen, standing bolt upright.

Steele joined her, and saw the astonished faces of Azrhan, Lisa, and Detective Roosevelt McKnight looking in the window.

9:28 P.M.
East River Heliport

Thirteen minutes behind schedule, silver sprays of molten flowers burst across the night sky in the opening volley, all to the accompaniment of John Philip Sousa's "Stars and Stripes Forever."

"Be kind to your web-footed friends," Butkis sang along, following the tune of the famous march as it blared from the PA system lining the FDR. "For a duck may be somebody's mooother—"

"Can it, for Christ's sake," said Morgan. "It's fucking time to go. They started thirteen minutes late." He gripped the side of his seat to stop his hands from shaking.

The manager of the heliport lay in the trailer office, his head oozing blood and what looked like gray toothpaste. Though seeming to have bought Butkis's story of mechanical failure, he'd insisted that the other pilots take off and vacate the no-fly zone before the deadline. When they refused, he went inside, threatening to call the police. "Leave this to me," said Morgan, following him in with a wrench. "I'll simply knock him out and tie him up." The first blow interrupted the man's dialing 911, but only dropped him to his knees, leaving him still clutching the receiver. To Morgan's horror, the man moved his thumb to press the final 1. The next blow made a wet cracking sound.

The pilot looked at him sideways and said, "Hey, man, chill out. Your face is the color of chalk." Still humming, he snapped on the microphone in his headset. "Let's go, gentlemen," he said, accelerating the rotor until the craft lifted slowly off the tarmac. Rising past the blaring speakers, he took his position a hundred feet above the FDR, his companions flanking him over the quay to his left and the rooftops on his right.

Directly below, Morgan saw a tapestry of faces looking upward, some right at him, their expressions a mélange of puzzled frowns and friendly smiles. Children were everywhere, their grins flashing in the glow of the sodium lamps spaced along the freeway. A few of the older ones waved. He broke into a cold sweat, unable to bear their gazes.

Butkis leaned forward, his hand hovering over the switch that activated the nozzle.

Morgan felt his mouth go dry, and for a giddy instant he thought of reaching out and snatching the pilot's hand away, as if in this last second he could not only recall what they were about to release, but the fate that awaited him.

Outside the cockpit, shimmering spheres of blue puffed into blazing streaks of red, each with the speed of an exploding star.

He shut his eyes against the flash of light, only to see the faces from below emerge in his mind like a mob of dark apparitions. "Christ," he muttered, and ended up staring into the distance to banish the phantom gallery, finding it as unendurable to look upon as the real one. A canopy of golden showers seemed to cover all of New York.

His impulse vanished, carrying with it any illusion that by stopping Butkis he could somehow save himself. He'd already crossed too many other lines of no return, beginning on a moonlit night in Oklahoma, and just now, a hundred feet below in a stifling little room.

The pilot flicked the toggle up and crept ahead, trailing a white mist behind his machine that floated down toward the crowd as delicately as lace.

Morgan's gaze followed its descent. The frowns below were replaced by expressions of surprise, anger, and shock as the mist settled onto people's faces and arms. Some wiped their foreheads with their palms and rubbed the greasy substance between their hands while examining it. A few went as far as taking a whiff of it off their fingertips. Others tried to wipe it out of their eyes and off their lips.

He could spot the ones who had heard the ruse about it being a skin care product. One young man dressed in only a bathing suit beckoned them toward him, then held up his arms making as if to shower in it, rubbing it over his shoulders, under his arms, and into his scalp. Others around him followed suit, many signaling thumbs up, presumably because they found the sensation pleasant on such a hot night. Those who objected responded with angry gestures, waving them to get out of there and giving them the finger.

"Remember, gentlemen," said Butkis into the microphone, "keep our forward speed at fifteen knots, and we spend no more than four minutes, tops, over the target."

Glancing to either side, Morgan saw that the other two helicopters had begun their runs as well.

The seconds crawled by, the slow speed giving him the impression they were standing still. The straps holding him to his seat seemed to impede his breathing, making him feel even more trapped.

And beneath him, like an endless human carpet, his victims continued to roll by, every one of them, it seemed, staring at him.

"Wow!"

"Beautiful, Steve!"

"Look at that!"

Geysers of pink and violet spiraled up from a collection of barges on the Hudson River, mesmerizing those gathered in his office. But Patton himself kept stealing glances in the direction of the East River where his own show was under way. Not that he could see any of it, yet the fireworks under which it would be unfolding were visible across the horizon, and he couldn't take his eyes off them.

"Yes, it's wonderful, isn't it?" he said, trying not to sound impolite. Half the people he'd invited hadn't showed up, and most of them had added insult to his injury by sending replacements who were clearly from their B list. A deputy assistant to the assistant director of state parks, a low-level Democrat from Albany, even a public works manager from the mayor's office, for Christ's sake—any low-rung freeloader who could be barely considered "green" they'd fobbed off on him.

He grabbed another glass of champagne from the tray of a passing waiter and downed half of it in a gulp. Within twenty-four hours, he thought, the symptoms will start to hit, and the first diagnoses of bird flu will be made. In forty-eight hours I'll insist the police declare Sullivan and Steele as officially missing, then suggest they search Agrenomics, it being a matter of record that she suspected someone there had set up two previous attempts on her life. Once the cops discover the lab, I'll step to the fore, offer to interpret what's happened, and be the most sought-after man in New York. And all these little pikers can suck my ass.

More eruptions of golden fire spewed into the night, their reflections playing along the full height of the World Trade towers located a few blocks to the east.

"Great!"

"What a way to party, Steve."

"Any more of those little quiche tarts?"

Yeah, right!

The faces of new victims kept scrolling into view.

"God, can't you go faster?" said Morgan, fidgeting noticeably in his straps. "I can't stand this."

"Hey, Bob," said Butkis, "this is the speed you told me to keep."

Morgan started to pluck at the release on his safety belt. "I've got to loosen this. It's so tight I can't breathe!"

"Relax and enjoy the show. The cops will take at least five minutes to realize something's happening and get their own copters over here. By then we'll have scooted back to Queens." Plumes of purple and white sparks arched overhead. "I mean, it's like doing an air gig on Broadway!"

Morgan tried to slow his respirations.

Butkis broke into song again. "There's no business like show business . . ."

The helicopter on their right was approaching the hospital, and Morgan glanced ahead to the roof, expecting to see it crammed with people.

It looked empty, except for three figures standing on the corner nearest him, two of them, it seemed, dressed entirely in red.

Surprised, he stared through the intervening darkness, trying to make the threesome out in better detail, until he suddenly realized they were all in moon suits, the two red ones exactly like the self-powered units they kept on hand at Agrenomics.

A freezing sensation crept along the inside of his skull, and he thought the unthinkable. Could Sullivan and Steele have escaped? Had they warned everyone at the hospital off the roof?

"Shit!" shrieked Butkis.

Morgan snapped his eyes straight ahead and saw a wall of lights approaching fast.

"Scatter! It's the cops," Butkis screeched into the microphone, revving the motor and slinging the craft upward. Except they'd blanketed him from above and behind as well. "Through the fireworks," he yelled, and rolled out over the water, streaking straight toward the barges, climbing as he went.

Balls big as planets exploded red, white, and blue in front of them.

"Yahoo!" whooped the pilot as he tore through the barrage. He got halfway to the other side when the craft on his left exploded in flames.

Morgan started to scream.

Butkis looked down and saw a sparkling cluster of rockets streaming right at them. "Oh, fuck—!"

A direct hit to the fuel tanks blasted them both into oblivion.

From his vantage point on the roof, Steele watched the debris fall into the water and the crowd in front of the hospital react in horror. Further along the freeway people didn't respond at all, the flame and noise probably seeming part of the show. Less easy to miss were all the police helicopters overhead hugging the shore as they stayed well away from the line of fire.

Stanton leaned over the wall and pointed out to Kathleen the uniformed patrolmen starting to cordon off the half-mile stretch where the attackers had managed to spray before being routed. "Right after you called me from Agrenomics," he said, "I contacted 911 and the director of the emergency response team. They're going to handle this the same way they would a mass exposure to radioactivity—everyone stripped and decontaminated, their clothing bagged for disposal, even the water used to hose them down contained. Then we basically Lysol the FDR . . ."

Most of the spectators continued to watch the ongoing fireworks, unaware that they were about to be quarantined, though a few at the periphery of the crowd began to point and take notice of the massive police presence and the arrival of school buses by the hundreds behind them.

". . . Of course it's going to be on a massive scale. We're looking at wherever we can house huge numbers—Madison Square Garden, Yankee Stadium, Shea—and it'll be a civil liberties nightmare in a few minutes trying to keep a hundred and fifty thousand people—"

"Offer them hope," said Steele.

"Hope? There is no hope for the ones who get sick. That's what's going to be so damn tough. Everybody's going to try and run—"

"Tamiflu," said Steele, cutting him off.

Kathleen made a face. "Tami-what?"

Stanton looked thunderstruck. "My God!"

"The idea came to me on the ride back here."

"Richard, you may be right. That's ingenious. Why didn't I think of it?"

Steele grinned. "Because you're stuck up in that ivory tower of yours."

"What the hell is Tamiflu?" Kathleen asked.

"We can start by raiding every pharmacy in the city," Steele continued as if he hadn't heard her. "Timing's critical of course. I doubt we have the usual thirty-six-hour window, what with the vectors directly invading the cells, and we'll need to find practically every dose in America plus ship it here by tomorrow to have enough—"

"I'll get on it right away," said Greg. "And the drug company itself is sure to have supplies—"

"Will one of you answer me?" interrupted Kathleen. "I said, 'What the hell is Tamiflu?' It sounds like a Debbie-Reynolds-gets-a-cold flick."

Both men stared at her.

Steele then chuckled, and said, "No, but it might give us a happy ending, just like her movies."

"So what is it?"

"A neuraminidase inhibitor."

"Called oseltamivir phosphate," added Greg.

Steele raised his eyebrows at him. "Hey, I'm impressed, buddy."

"Hey, yourself. I still read and keep up, you know, so no more ivory-tower cracks—"

"If you two don't start speakin' to me, and in English, I'll be throwin' the two of you off this buildin'—"

"Okay, okay," said Steele, with a laugh. "Remember Julie Carr showed us those electron micrographs of influenza and all its bristles? She told us then that those structures contain neuraminidase, a molecule able to cleave the bond between the virus and a cell, setting the organism free to go off and find other cells in the body to infect. Tamiflu, given early enough, blocks that setting-free action. The flu bug can't replicate and spread beyond the first cells infected as it usually does, so its damage is limited."

"But will it work on the hybrid? Especially a hybrid delivered within a genetic vector."

"That's the million-dollar question," said Stanton. "It won't stop the vectors from entering cells and the initial replication of the virus. But it may block the spread of these organisms to other cells. The trouble is, even in ordinary flu, some strains have a slight variation in their neuraminidase, making it less susceptible to the drug's blocking action. Whether this hybrid is one of those, we'll only know when we try." He slipped his arm around her shoulders and gave her a hug. "But it at least gives everyone, you two included, a fighting chance." He looked over at Steele. "And now that it seems I've got my best friend back insulting me the way he always used to, I sure don't intend to lose him to some damned bug."

One of the police helicopters overhead broke out of the pack and moved to hover above the hospital helipad where the air ambulances usually landed. Within seconds of touching down, the door slid open and McKnight appeared. "Can I invite Drs. Sullivan and Steele to join me?" he called out. "You two won't want to miss what happens next."

The display was building to its climax when the head waiter took Patton by the elbow and said, "There appear to be some more guests at the door, sir."

The environmentalist brightened, thinking that they might be some of the people he actually had wanted to come. "Oh, well invite them in. Better late than never, I always say." He stood in the middle of the room, where he would be best framed by the view, his preferred spot for greeting people who visited his domain. He began to feel better. The mission must be complete by now, he thought. He'd had a few uneasy seconds a few minutes ago when he saw a dirty orange smudge in the direction of the East River impose itself on all the glitter. But no one else around him seemed to have even noticed, and he attributed it to one of the rockets misfiring.

At first he could only see the shadows of everyone crowding through the entranceway, the lights in the office complex dimmed to enhance the vista outside. My, there's a lot of them, he thought, pleased to see so many had accepted his invitation after all. He extended his hand and smiled, but stayed put, intending that the newcomers would walk to him.

The first two figures started forward, and the color red emerged from the darkness as strident as blood. Then he saw how bulky their forms were, and he shrank back, unable to believe his eyes. A cascade of gold streaming up into the night behind him and bathing everything in its light cast its reflection in the visors of the moon suits.

Sullivan reached out and grabbed him by the lapels of his tuxedo, pulling him to her until his nose bumped on her faceplate. Patton's tall tapered glass of champagne slipped from his fingers, its sparkling contents splashing on his shoes like miniature liquid fireworks and leaving a wet spot on the carpet. "You're busted, Steve," she screamed at him through the Plexiglas. "And know what? There're a lot of people who will want you to get the death penalty for this. In particular, you better start praying nobody dies of Ebola in one of those southern states you messed with."

A new stain appeared at his feet. As McKnight stepped up to put the cuffs on him, it continued to spread and spread.

epilogue

The New York Herald, *Monday, July 24, 2000*

The death toll from the July Fourth attack on New York now stands at 423, two more infants having died last night as a result of the bird flu. These unfortunate children had been in intensive care for the last sixteen days. "As grim as these numbers are, they could have been much, much worse," said Dr. Greg Stanton, Dean of the New York City Medical School. "Thanks to the early warning by Dr. Kathleen Sullivan and Dr. Richard Steele, we were able to intervene quickly enough to thwart the bulk of the infections. As it turned out, thanks to a new class of drugs called neuraminidase inhibitors, many of the 75,000 people actually exposed to the spray had no symptoms at all, and the majority had only a mild case of the flu. Of the 10 percent who were seriously ill, almost 7,000 have recovered completely. Of course, these numbers are little consolation to the families whose loved ones perished. As is often the case, it was the most frail who succumbed, the very old and, tragically, the very young."

Almost all those who were quarantined are now released. When asked if the risk from the bird flu was over, Dr. Stanton replied, "We won't really know that for many months, and the highest risk of it reoccurring will be when the influenza season arrives next fall. Ironically, the technicians who perfected the delivery of this hideous weapon may have inadvertently helped us. They left behind a dozen monkeys who survived their exposure and now contain antibodies to the hybrid. Using sera from these animals, our researchers are fast-tracking a possible vaccine to prevent the disease which may be ready for mass distribution in about six months. In the meantime, if anyone experiences coldlike symptoms, I suggest they see their doctor immediately."

The New York Herald, *Wednesday, July 26, 2000*

Police continue to piece together how the Independence Day attack was mounted. Testimony from members of the Blue Planet Society reveals that Steve Patton used his worldwide environmentalist network as unwitting accomplices in his scheme. Members of the organization in Asia have testified that in 1997 during the bird flu outbreak in Taiwan they advised him about a genetic vaccine being used against the virus that in some areas seemed to be making things worse. At the time they were surprised when he appeared to ignore the information, but when the vaccine was withdrawn by Biofeed International, they let the matter drop. Members of the European environmental community, however, recall Patton showing a sudden interest in the radical fringes of the so-called green movement around that time, especially those factions that had resorted to violent action in the past. Police now believe it was through such extremist groups that he made contact with the terrorists in Afghanistan who subsequently supplied him with the money, resources, and manpower he used to mount the assault, including the construction of the Agrenomics laboratory north of White Plains, New

York. Neither the police, the FBI, nor spokespersons for the CIA will comment on the likely identity of these men and women or their organization, but it is believed that they are still at large.

In other developments, Honolulu Police have heard testimony and found records at the Oahu offices of Biofeed International which shed light on another participant in the conspiracy, Mr. Robert Morgan. Documents revealed that the man was an employee at the company in 1998 and had instigated the resale of a faulty genetic vaccine against bird flu to local farmers under the guise of it being ordinary feed corn. When the virus jumped the species barrier and infected a young child in the area, just as it had a year earlier in Taiwan, Morgan was promptly dismissed as part of an immediate cover-up carried out by company officials.

Police are also questioning a former Biofeed employee who has come forward to state that shortly after the infected child died and news of the case was broadcast around the world, a man claiming to represent the Blue Planet Society approached her. "He asked very pointed questions about feed corn containing a genetic vaccine for bird flu and if any had been marketed in the area by the Biofeed company. Being an active environmentalist myself, I did a bit of clandestine investigating for him, sneaking into computer files, and found bills of sale regarding recalled feed corn from Taiwan bearing Bob Morgan's signature. Though vaccines weren't specifically mentioned, I knew Morgan had been abruptly fired recently under suspicious circumstances. So I passed copies of the records to this guy from the Blue Planet Society and suggested he track down Morgan to learn what he had to say about the feed corn. I didn't hear anything further, so figured nothing had come of it. When I saw all the headlines about the July Fourth attack, there were photos of the man I had dealt with, Steve Patton himself."

The New York Herald, *Sunday Edition, July 30, 2000*

Authorities still have no definitive plan on how to deal with acres and acres of corn contaminated with the RNA of Ebola virus throughout the South and Midwest. "This is no hoax," declared one official. "Ground-up meal from these plants has been fed to laboratory monkeys, and every animal tested so far fell ill with the disease, 90 percent of them dying within 10 days."

Initial plans to burn the affected crops were put on hold as agricultural specialists consulted with European scientists who'd participated in "burn offs" of soya crops last year after they had been unintentionally infiltrated by genetically modified strains of the plant. "Our worry is that fragments of the corn stalks may escape being incinerated and end up carried for miles by the smoke." No one can say for sure if such a spread of debris would be dangerous, and experts on both sides of the Atlantic continue to study the matter.

But time is of concern. While humans can be prevented from eating the isolated produce, it's impossible to keep small animals and insects out of the affected areas. If one of these invaders turns out to be the unknown host for Ebola virus, then the organism will have a permanent foothold in America.

Another expert who insisted on remaining anonymous says that even the measures taken to prevent humans from unintentionally ingesting the contaminated product aren't foolproof. There are rumors that while most of the first crop already harvested was marketed for replanting as feed corn, several shipments inexplicably ended up being sold to the food giant's own flour mills, which in turn supply the corporation's retail division, the well-known Biofeed Grocery Chain. Officials for the company refused to comment further, but

confirmed that a nationwide recall of all their cornmeal products is in effect. So far no confirmed cases of Ebola have been
reported, but emergency rooms across the land are being
overwhelmed as anyone who experiences even the slightest
stomach upset from any cause is now running to see a doctor.
The drain on medical resources is preventing many hospitals
from dealing with their usual caseloads.

"While there is no treatment for the disease, early imple-
mentation of supportive measures, such as rehydration with
intravenous solutions, can increase the chances of survival,"
said a spokesperson for the CDC in Atlanta. "We are also
working on an experimental vaccine against the deadly virus
which looks promising with primates. Unfortunately, much
work still needs to be done in refining it, and human trials
are years away."

On the economic front, repercussions in the agriculture
sector show no signs of letting up. Prices for meat and poultry from the North have soared as Americans continue to
boycott produce from the South for fear the animals and
birds have accidentally been given the mutated feed, despite
assurances from state officials that they have successfully
tracked down and isolated all the crops that had been tam-
pered with . . .

Steele grimaced and threw down the newspapers, then leaned back in
his beach chair. Looking out at the sparkling ocean, he heard Kathleen Sullivan stir as she drowsed at his side, then felt her take his hand
and give it a reassuring squeeze.

"Try and relax, Richard," she said. "It's not our fight for the
moment."

He entwined his fingers with hers, and swept the shoreline with
his eyes until he spotted Chet and Lisa frolicking with Boogie boards
in the surf. At least I've been able to put my own little world back together, he thought.

They were spending the rest of the summer north of Portsmouth, Maine, having rented a beach house there after they got out of quarantine. Greg Stanton had insisted they needed the time off, and for a parting gift handed Steele a formal clearance to resume his duties as chief of emergency at New York City Hospital in September. Martha, once she had them properly installed, gently insisted on taking a well-earned cruise to Europe, leaving the two of them and the children to play house alone. As for his worries about Chet, it took Lisa about ten minutes to win him over, and the two had been practically inseparable ever since. She sometimes even included him when one of her many boyfriends came to visit and invited her for a drive or to the movies in a nearby town. "You're my birth control, in case they get any wrong ideas," she said at dinner one night, making his youthful face blush.

Chet picked himself up from where a big wave had deposited him on the sand, glanced across the blond dunes to where Steele and Kathleen sat, and gave them a big grin before charging back through the ruffled water. In that instant, as the sunlight bounced off the glittering surface and danced across his son's face, Steele could have sworn he saw a pair of familiar dark eyes flashing their approval.

acknowledgments

Many people generously shared their expertise and patiently played "What If" with me as I worked out the hypothetical scenarios that appear in this story.

To Angela Ryan, geneticist and passionate advocate for the ethical use of science, I say thank you for bringing the intricacy of the gene vividly alive in a way I never learned in medical school. In particular, her concerns regarding the all-powerful genetic vectors currently used to jump naked DNA from one species to another set my imagination spinning.

To epidemiologist Dr. DeWolfe Miller, who responded so wholeheartedly to my request that he play devil's advocate and challenge my story outline to rid it of any blatantly bad science, I say thank you for helping me make as plausible as possible the leap from documented fact to theoretical hazards.

To Dr. Lee Thompson, who placed his years of experience with level-four virology facilities (where he's worked with the deadliest organisms on the planet) at my disposal, my thanks for his detailed explanation of their inner workings and his "walking" me through what it's like to suit up and enter such a place. The compression of some of the details in order to move the story along is due to my own literary license and is not any lack of accuracy on his part.

Thank you to Magda Bruce, who paved the way for my becoming an observer at the January 2000 United Nations Conference on genetically modified food held in Montreal, thereby providing an opportunity to hear and meet with experts in biodiversity from all over the planet.

acknowledgments

I once again extend a heartfelt thank you to my longtime friends Dr. Jennifer Frank and Dr. Brian Connolly for their double-checking the medical detail and thereby keeping me lucid on that front; to my proofreaders Connie, Betty, Johanna, Joan, Jim, and Tamara, for their eagle eyes and ever-helpful editorial comments; to my agent, Denise Marcil, for unwavering support and for her constantly raising the bar; and to my marvelous editor, Joe Blades, who keeps the journey on track.

I'd also be seriously remiss if I didn't express gratitude to my partners in practice, Ivan and Michael, along with colleagues Judy and David, for taking care of patients and affording me time to write, and to Dr. Julie St. Cyr at my own hospital for showing me the particulars of electrophoresis.

And last but still crucial, a big thank you to Betty and Nathalie for organizing everything.

references

The following works were invaluable in the preparation of this story.

Too Early May Be Too Late and *An Orphan in Science: Environmental Risks of Genetically Engineered Vaccines*, both by Terje Traavik (Norway: Directorate for Nature Management, 1999), provided commentaries on the research into gene technology and genetically modified organisms of the last decade (including some abstracts of the articles Richard Steele came across on the Internet).

Molecular Biology of the Cell, Third Ed. by Alberts, B. et al. (New York: Garland, 1994); *Virus Ground Zero* by Ed Regis (New York: Pocket Books, 1996); and *Principles of Molecular Virology,* Snd Ed. by Alan J. Cann (San Diego, Calif.: Academic Press, 1997) were all useful reference texts.

Periodicals that proved helpful included the following:

Nordlee, J. A. et al. (1996). Identification of a Brazil-nut allergen in transgenic soybeans. *New England Journal of Medicine* 14: 688–728.

Schubert, R. et al. (1994). Ingested foreign (phage M13) DNA survives transiently in the gastrointestinal tract and enters the bloodstream of mice. *Mol. Gen. Genet.* 242: 495–504.

Schubert, R. et al. (1997). Foreign DNA (M13) ingested by mice reaches peripheral leukocytes, spleen, and liver via intestinal wall mucosa and can be covalently linked to mouse DNA. *Proc. Natl. Acad. Sci. USA* 94: 961–966.

Syvanen, M. (1987). Cross-species gene transfer: A major factor in evolution? *Trends Genet.* 28: 237–261.

———. (1987). Molecular clocks and evolutionary relationships: Possible distortion due to horizontal gene flow? *J. Mol. Evol* 26: 16–23.

———. (1994). Horizontal gene transfer: Evidence and possible consequences. *Annu. Rev. Genet.* 28:237–261.

A series of articles in the October 16, 1999 issue of *Lancet* under the general heading "Genetically Modified Foods: The Scientific Debate Now Begins" (pp. 1314, 1315, 1353, 1354) gave a framework to the back-and-forth arguments encountered by Steele on both sides of the controversy. Proceedings at the United Nations Conference on Biodiversity held in Montreal in January 2000, which stimulated some of the ideas expressed in this novel involved reports and the various position papers submitted by delegates from Europe, Africa, and Asia who advocated a precautionary principle to regulate the commercialization of gene technology and genetically modified organisms; and the protests against this principle by the so-called Miami group of countries (United States, Canada, Brazil, Australia, and New Zealand). Facts regarding polymerase chain reactions came from the Web site of the Department of Biochemistry at the University of Arizona.